AFTER I LEFT YOU

Alison Mercer

LIBRARIES NI
WITHDRAWN FROM STOCK

BLACK SWAN

TRANSWORLD PUBLISHERS
61–63 Uxbridge Road, London W5 5SA
A Random House Group Company
www.transworldbooks.co.uk

AFTER I LEFT YOU
A BLACK SWAN BOOK: 9780552778190

First publication in Great Britain
Black Swan edition published 2014

Copyright © Alison Mercer 2014

Alison Mercer has asserted her right under the Copyright, Designs and Patents Act 1988 to be identified as the author of this work.

This book is a work of fiction and, except in the case of historical fact, any resemblance to actual persons, living or dead, is purely coincidental.

Biblical quotations taken from *The New Revised Standard Version (Anglicized Edition)*, copyright 1989, 1995 by the Division of Christian Education of the National Council of the Churches of Christ in the United States of America. Used by permission. All rights reserved.

A CIP catalogue record for this book is available from the British Library.

This book is sold subject to the condition that it shall not, by way of trade or otherwise, be lent, resold, hired out, or otherwise circulated without the publisher's prior consent in any form of binding or cover other than that in which it is published and without a similar condition, including this condition, being imposed on the subsequent purchaser.

Addresses for Random House Group Ltd companies outside the UK can be found at: www.randomhouse.co.uk
The Random House Group Ltd Reg. No. 954009

The Random House Group Limited supports The Forest Stewardship Council® (FSC®), the leading international forest-certification organisation. Our books carrying the FSC label are printed on FSC®-certified paper. FSC is the only forest-certification scheme supported by the leading environmental organisations, including Greenpeace. Our paper procurement policy can be found at www.randomhouse.co.uk/environment

Typeset in 11/14pt Giovanni Book by
Kestrel Data, Exeter, Devon.
Printed and bound by
CPI Group (UK) Ltd, Croydon, CR0 4YY.

2 4 6 8 10 9 7 5 3 1

For P., the paradigm shift

Acknowledgements

Special thanks are due to the following fairy book-parents: Catherine Cobain, who was intrigued by the girl in the green dress walking home one midsummer morning; Judith Murdoch, who helped me steer Anna from present to past and back again; and Sophie Wilson, for astute questions and nearly missing her Tube stop. Thanks, too, to Rebecca Winfield, Lisa Horton and Harriet Bourton. It is very reassuring to be in such safe hands.

My friends and colleagues were endlessly encouraging and supportive while I was working on this book. Abingdon people – you are the bees' knees! Thank you, too, to Helen Rumbelow, Nanu and Luli Segal, and Neel Mukherjee.

Tom and Izzy, Ian, and my family: you buoy me up, keep me going and make it all possible.

Author's note

Anna's Oxford is not my Oxford, and, like Anna herself, lives only in the pages of this book. I have attempted an impressionistic representation of the city rather than strict geographical accuracy, and anyone who looks for all the landmarks Anna mentions will not find them.

St Bart's does not exist, and nor does its north Oxford annexe; and Oxford has many pubs, but the Wickham Arms is not one of them. Shawcross village is not on any map, nor is St Bartholomew's church or its well, and no flesh-and-blood tourists have ever passed through Shawcross Hall. Deddington, Anna's hometown, is likewise an invention, as is the Garden Maze Hotel.

The chalk horse Anna visits with her friends is an imaginary beauty spot, though it bears a coincidental resemblance to the one that gives the Vale of White Horse its name. If Anna's story leaves you wanting to explore Oxfordshire, the Uffington White Horse is well worth a visit – as is Bleinheim Palace and St Margaret's Well.

My own experience of being a student at Oxford was

a gift, and I was lucky to have it; and I was especially lucky to have it when I did. I am grateful to everyone who was part of it.

So here's to the class of '91. As long as any of us are around to look back, that time isn't quite over . . .

Part One

2011

The Valley

When she turned around she looked directly at him, and he had the extraordinary feeling that she was looking right *into* him, as if she knew him and everything about him, as if she could read him like a book.

From *The End of Mr D.*, by Benjamin Dock (1978)

1

'Are you Anna Jones?'

2011

'Anna? It is you, isn't it?'

I looked up from the three-for-two display and there he was. Victor Rose, staring at me with one eyebrow raised. And no wonder, because I must have looked ridiculous. I couldn't have picked a worse time to bump into the former love of my life.

My hair was dripping, I was soaking wet, and I was carrying a hideous full-length lilac dress over one arm. It was blindingly obvious that it was a bridesmaid's dress – at least, I hoped so; what else would I be doing with a frock that was so frilly and girlish, so hopefully romantic? Even though it was swathed in wet cellophane, that wasn't enough to obscure its satin shininess.

And now I was blushing like a teenager in the presence of an idol. I realized my mouth had dropped open and shut it. I was most definitely not capable of speech.

Victor . . . in all the essential ways, Victor . . . dark-haired, dark-eyed, tall, well built, with that upright, soldierly way of carrying himself . . . but old! Well, not old, but middle-aged, with white at his temples, and bags under his eyes and lines at their corners.

He hadn't run to fat, though. He must still take care to stay in shape. Also, he'd never had the kind of bulk that goes to seed if you don't keep fit.

When I'd last stood this close to him he'd been just twenty-two. My final words to him had also been addressed to the girl he was with and to the others too, to what was left of the tight little circle we had once been. Back then, I had hoped for nothing more than never to see any of them again.

'Hello, Victor,' I said. 'How are you?'

'I'm well, thanks,' he said. 'And you?'

'Oh, I'm fine. A bit damp.'

'It's pretty bad out there,' he agreed.

'I see you've been getting in some reading material,' I said, looking down at the carrier bag he was holding. Was he wearing a wedding ring? I couldn't quite see.

'The very latest post-modern avant-garde experimental fiction . . . No, not really. *Famous Five* books for my daughter.'

'I used to love those,' I said.

'Yeah, she's a pretty keen reader too,' Victor said.

I was tempted to ask more, but thought better of it. Victor's life, and how it had turned out, was nothing to do with me, after all – I had made sure of that.

Yes, I had loved him once, but he was not the only

one I'd thought about, and missed, down the years. It had never just been about us. And now it was not about us at all, and never would be.

'It was nice to see you again,' I said, 'but I'd better be going.'

I wasn't even aware of stepping away from him, and only realized I'd backed into the table beside me when a pile of books from the three-for-two display crashed down on to the floor.

'Here, let me help,' Victor said. I folded the bridesmaid's dress and put it down on the floor. We started gathering up the books, and suddenly he was very close, close enough to reach out and touch . . .

But no, that was just a crazy impulse, the sort of self-destructive nonsense that floats through your brain like a dare. It was just the shock of seeing him out of the blue like this: someone who, for years, had only existed in memory and in dreams, who had become almost a ghost, was now kneeling on a bookshop carpet opposite me, seventeen years older than when I'd last seen him, and perfectly real. No wonder I didn't quite know what to do with myself.

Once the display of books was more or less back in place I glanced up at Victor. To my relief, my heart did nothing out of the ordinary.

'Thank you,' I said. 'I'd better head off. I'm running late.'

'Do you have to rush off?' he asked. 'Maybe we could have a coffee. Catch up.'

'I'm sorry, I can't. I only came in here because of the rain. I have to get back to work.' I glanced at my watch.

'Five minutes ago, in fact. I'd better dash. Take care, Victor. I hope your daughter likes her new books.'

I turned to go – this time taking care not to knock anything over – and was heading towards the exit when I heard him say, 'Haven't you forgotten something?'

I looked back and there he was, holding out the bridesmaid's dress.

'Thank you,' I said and took it from him.

He took an umbrella out of his carrier bag. 'Why don't I walk with you? Save you getting soaked again.'

'Oh, I'm sure it's eased off by now,' I said.

'Let's see,' he said, and we set off together towards the front of the bookshop.

It was still chucking it down. There was a random huddle of passers-by just inside the glass doors, watching the rain bounce in the puddles on the pavement.

Victor said, 'So where are we going?'

'Up towards Leicester Square,' I said.

He pushed through the door and opened up his umbrella, and I followed him out into the street. We walked along a little way together without saying anything. Then he offered me his arm and said, 'This way I get to stay dry too,' and I realized he'd been holding the umbrella over my head rather than his own.

What else could I do? It really was tipping it down. I took his arm, and there we were, strolling up the Charing Cross Road for all the world to see, as if we were still lovers, or friends, at least.

It felt good, though, that was the thing. Some people make a point of hurrying; others are too slow. Some are too short, or too tall, and you bump along and can't ever get in sync. But we walked along more or less in time, with no jolting or jarring or pulling or nudging. We had always been like that, right up until I left him at the airport in Los Angeles and flew back to start my final year at Oxford. When I next saw him after that, he had been dancing with somebody else.

'So have you got a special occasion coming up?' Victor asked.

'You mean because of the dress? Yeah. Tippy's getting married. Do you remember Tippy?'

Tippy was my half-sister. We had the same mother, and her father – my stepfather – was the only father I had ever known. We had grown up together and gone to the same secondary school, but we were not especially close. I was touched that she'd asked me to be one of her bridesmaids, but at the same time, I did wish that she could have picked a dress that was slightly less unflattering.

'I do remember,' Victor said. 'She was still at school when I met her. I can't quite believe she's old enough to get married. But I suppose she must be in her thirties now.'

'Yes, all grown up,' I said. 'Congratulations on the new job, by the way. I read about it in the paper.'

Victor had recently been appointed artistic director of the Ploughshare, a London theatre that had built its reputation by putting on new or forgotten plays with a sprinkling of star power, sometimes from Hollywood, sometimes from big TV shows. When I'd read that he had taken over, I'd felt – just for a moment – fiercely happy, almost as if it was my own triumph.

'Thanks,' Victor said, and then I found myself asking: 'Will you bring Clarissa over?'

Clarissa. Clarissa Hayes. She had always been the star draw in our little group of friends – or clique, as an outsider might have called it. And now she was properly famous: recognized around the world, an A-lister, a household name.

All I had to do was to take the escalator past the moving adverts on the Tube, or turn on the TV late at night, and there she was. Blonde, redhead, or sometimes brunette; her accent usually, but not invariably, American; dressed in a maid's uniform or a rubber catsuit or an antebellum crinoline, but still unmistakably Clarissa. It didn't bother me any more, but it was always strange to see her, like a little nudge from another life.

Victor said, 'I haven't asked.' Then, 'Anna, this is probably as good a time as any to say this, since I might not get another chance. I really am sorry for the way everything turned out.'

'I am too,' I said. 'But life moves on, doesn't it?'

'It does,' he agreed.

The smoked glass façade of Blake Fitzgerald Accountants loomed in front of us. Our time was up.

I withdrew my arm from Victor's and said, 'This is my stop.'

We had come to a standstill under the portico, left in place when the Georgian fabric of the building had been gutted. You could hear the rain hammering on it.

Victor let the umbrella down.

'So . . .' He hesitated. 'Are you Anna Jones, still? I have to admit, I have looked you up on the internet once or twice, tried to find out what you were up to. But I couldn't find any sign of you.'

'I guess I keep a pretty low profile.'

'Do you ever go back?'

'To St Bart's, you mean?'

St Bartholomew's, more usually referred to by its nickname, was the Oxford college where we'd met for the first time coming up for twenty years before. I'd only ever been back once, a few months after finals. That had been my farewell both to the place and to the people I'd known there, and I'd had no intention of ever returning.

'I know you don't go back for any of the reunions or whatever,' Victor said. 'They have you listed as a lost old member. I just wondered if you ever went to have a look round.'

'I'm not particularly interested in looking back,' I said.

'Ah,' he said. 'You're still angry with me.'

'I am not.'

'If you were, I wouldn't blame you.'

'I just don't think about it. About any of it. It is a very long time ago.'

One of the trainee tax consultants came out and stopped to put up his umbrella. He was young and cocky, a few years out of college, and obviously enjoyed spending his salary on designer labels.

He looked me up and down and said, 'Aren't you the temp? I'd get back in there quick if I were you. Nadia's doing her nut.'

'I won't be a minute,' I said.

'Time is time,' the trainee told me, 'and you're on the clock.'

His eyes flickered quickly over me and then over Victor. Then he shrugged and went off down the street.

'He's a charmer,' Victor commented.

'I'm sorry,' I said. 'I really must go. Goodbye, Victor.'

He started to say something, but whatever spell had kept us talking had been broken, and I didn't stop to listen. Instead I turned away and hurried into the building and up the escalator to the top office.

Nadia, the secretary I was working with, was waiting for me. As I came in she glowered at me and tapped her watch.

'You're late,' she said.

'I'm so sorry,' I said. 'I had to pick this up.'

I held up the lilac bridesmaid's dress. Nadia's lip curled.

'You'd better hang that up in the cupboard out of sight,' she said. And with that she pulled on her raincoat, picked up her handbag and umbrella, and strode out.

I shut the dress away as she had told me, and took myself off to the ladies' to dry my hair under the blower. It took a while – I'd let it grow over the last year or so, and there was a lot of it, though not as much as when I'd been a student, when Victor had told me he hoped I'd never cut it.

I'd had it chopped off soon after we broke up. It had been a relief to sit in the hairdresser's and see the old, recognizable me disappear.

Back at my desk, I checked the telephone system

on my computer. Oops, missed call, and there was a message.

I put on my headset and clicked on play.

It was Victor.

'This is a message for Anna Jones. I just thought I'd mention that Meg would really love to hear from you. Her email address is margaret.brierley@speedmail.com. Take care now.'

Click.

Meg! Sweet, blonde, wholesome Meg, the vicar's daughter who prayed to be good but still gave in to the urge to be bad. The one who had tried hardest to stay in touch.

I could just picture her, barely aged, a slight frown wrinkling her smooth forehead, trying to puzzle it out: *Victor, what do you think it really was, in the end, that made Anna decide to stay away? I never thought it would be forever. I really hoped she'd get over it, given time. I suppose it was just too much, everything coming all at once . . . But still, it's a shame, isn't it? Too late to do anything about it now. I just hope she's happy, wherever she is . . .*

I knew I should just delete it. But instead I noted Meg's email address on a Post-it. And then I wrote down Victor's number, which was listed on the screen in front of me, underneath it, in very small handwriting, and folded up the Post-it and shoved it in my handbag. Then I wiped the record of his phone call from the system, and got on with some work.

This was it, this was my real life: the desks, the monitors, the phones, the smell of instant coffee and microwaved lunch, the afternoon stretching ahead till hometime, the bus ride back to south London and Pete.

Pete: my boyfriend. I hadn't thought of him once throughout my encounter with Victor. But then, five minutes with an ex was no big deal. I probably wouldn't even mention it. Pete knew my time at university hadn't ended well, and I didn't much like talking about it. So why change now?

Victor was not my real life, and nor was Clarissa, or Meg, or any of my other former friends. Once upon a time I had thought they were the best, the most fun, the most interesting and gifted people I could have ever wished to hang out with. But I had not been safe with them. I had been sleepwalking towards disaster.

And now I was beyond it, and out of reach. The problem was, with Victor's phone number and Meg's email address tucked away in my handbag, I wasn't at all sure that was how I was going to stay.

2

'I am not afraid'

My first thought, from the other side of the glass front of the café, was how pissed off she looked. This did not seem like a good start to our Victor-inspired bridge-building, and I was briefly tempted to turn tail and flee, and text her my excuses. But I hesitated a moment too long, and Meg spotted me and waved, and I waved back and pushed the door open and went on in.

The other customers were all sitting at tables near the front, in the light, but Meg was sitting on a sofa halfway back, where it was dimmer, at a slight distance from everybody else. As I drew closer I saw why. There were three children more or less near her, and it was obvious they were all hers.

She stood to greet me and gave me a quick, distracted peck on the cheek, then stooped to pick up a toy and return it to the baby in the pushchair next to her. The baby promptly dropped it, and pointed at it hopefully. Meg picked it up and gave it back again, and said warningly, 'No more.' The baby looked sheepish and complied.

I was reminded of the authority she had always had, right back from when I'd first known her; if our little group had a moral centre, then Meg had been it. If Meg thought something was acceptable, the rest of us didn't fret about it; if she objected, then it was time to draw a line.

We had trusted her not so much because of her churchgoing, or because she was consistent, but because of her conviction. She had never been above interpreting the rules to fit in with what she wanted to do, and would have made a dull sort of collective conscience otherwise.

She turned to me and smiled and said, 'Anna, how lovely to see you. You haven't changed a bit!'

'Neither have you,' I said, though I didn't mean it, because of course Meg *was* different. Back then she'd waitressed at formal college dinners for extra cash and been ruthless about sticking to her weekly budget; now she had acquired a subtle, but undeniable, sheen of wealth.

She was dressed, not ostentatiously, but well, in a grey jersey tunic that draped and flattered her impeccably, and jeans that fitted as if they had been made to measure. Her blond hair was a soft and natural gold that suggested the attention of an expensive hairdresser, and she was less curvy, and more toned, than when I'd known her, despite the three children she'd had since. I wondered if she had a personal trainer. Or maybe she was just disciplined about going to the gym.

There was one other obvious difference from the Meg I'd first met at St Bart's: apart from a sleek gold bracelet, she wasn't wearing any jewellery. No cross round her neck, and no rings.

'I'm sorry to have kept you waiting,' I said.

'No, no, we were early. Ada, not on your dress. Let Mummy get you a wet wipe.'

Ada, the middle child, pouted but held her hands out to be cleaned, and then ran off to climb up on the stage at the back of the café, which was sometimes used for live music or poetry readings. I'd picked the venue; it was somewhere Pete and I had often come at weekends back in the early days of our relationship, though we seemed to go out together less often the longer we lived together.

Meg's oldest child said, 'Mummy, can I have a Coke?'

'No, Iris, you jolly well can't. The last thing you need is caffeine.'

Iris scowled and folded her arms. 'I'm bored,' she said. 'I don't like it here.'

Meg ignored Iris and settled back on to the sofa.

'I'm sorry,' she said. 'I didn't think I was going to have the children with me today.'

'That's OK,' I said, 'it's nice to get the chance to meet them.'

'I was really hoping we'd get the chance to have a good catch-up. I want to hear what you've been up to all these years.'

'Well, I want to hear all about you and Jason,' I countered, perching next to her, and hoping she wouldn't persist in encouraging me to talk about myself.

Jason, Meg's fabulously wealthy other half, had never been part of our little clique at college; he hadn't really hung out with anybody, but had spent most of his time in the computer room, occasionally surfacing to eat or go to lectures. He'd made his initial millions by selling his first internet venture just before the dotcom bubble burst.

I hadn't come across his name in the papers again until some years after the crash, when he surfaced as chief executive of an increasingly successful dating website, and was pictured with a pregnant Meg at its first birthday party. Generally, though, they seemed to go to some lengths to stay out of the public eye. Jason didn't give interviews or play the pundit, and was rarely mentioned outside of the business pages.

'I saw the pictures of you together the day after he floated his company,' I said. 'You had these amazing diamond earrings on, but he looked the same as ever. I seem to remember you were eating fish and chips on Brighton beach.'

'Yes, that sounds about right.' Our eyes met, and Meg said, 'Victor didn't tell you, did he?'

I thought back to standing next to him while the rain hammered on the portico. I hadn't given him much chance to tell me anything.

'Tell me what?'

'Jason and I have separated.'

'Oh, Meg, I'm sorry. I had no idea.'

She exhaled, and for a moment she looked thoroughly miserable, and suddenly aged. Then she composed herself, and her face smoothed and brightened.

'It's OK, really,' she said. 'It's reasonably civilized. Jason usually has the children every Saturday. He had to go to a business meeting today, which is why I have them with me. But he's very committed to making sure they don't miss out. We both are. To give him his due, he's an absolutely dedicated father.'

'That wasn't what you said about him earlier,' piped up Iris, the oldest daughter, who had settled on the armchair opposite our sofa and was entertaining herself by kicking the coffee table between us.

'Iris, what have I said to you about flappy little ears?' Meg said.

'But, Mummy, I can't help hearing. It's not like there's anything else to do. You should let us go home. At least then we could play with our toys.'

'That might not be such a bad idea,' I said.

Meg pondered for a moment. 'Really? I'm parked just round the corner, and it's not far. If you're sure you don't mind?'

'I really don't,' I said. 'It'll be nice to see where you are.'

And I did want to see. This Meg was so different to the one I'd known – glossy, groomed, worldly, wealthy – and yet so familiar, I wasn't ready to let her go just yet.

Meg's car turned out to be a people carrier the size of a small van. Once we were all in and on the move, she said, 'So, enough about me and Jason. How are things with you?'

'OK,' I said. 'Yeah, not bad at all.'

'You seeing anyone?'

'Mm, been living together for about a year.'

'What about work? Victor mentioned something about accountancy?'

'I'm kind of between jobs at the moment. I used to work in publishing, but I got made redundant a couple of months ago.'

'I'm sorry to hear that,' Meg said. 'It must be disheartening. I hope you find something soon.'

'Thanks. I'm sure I will. It's just a question of plugging away at it.'

'You'll get there.' Meg sighed. 'I suspect you're a lot more employable than I am.'

'Oh, I don't know about that.'

'No, seriously. I haven't worked since I had Iris. I felt I had to give up to look after the kids – Jason was always away so much, I thought one of us ought to be there. And who would want me now? What have I got to offer an employer? I'm brilliant at organizing kids' parties. That's about it.'

Surely there couldn't be any pressing financial need for her to find employment, given the scale of Jason's fortune? Still, she had always been so conscientious, so hard-working, I could imagine that she wouldn't like the idea of being wholly supported by an ex-partner.

Before finishing her degree she had lined up a job as a trainee manager with a food-production company. It had been a pragmatic career choice; she wanted to move to London, and that was the best offer she got. I had cut off contact with her by the time she started, so I never heard how it turned out.

'Maybe you could set up your own business,' I said.

'Maybe I could, but to be honest, I've lost my confidence. I find it hard to believe that anyone would take me seriously. I mean, who am I? I'm Jason Mortwell's ex and the mother of his three children. Who'd invest in that? At the end of the day, I'm just another middle-aged woman who's been put back on the shelf.'

'You're making it sound like you're some kind of, I don't know, trophy wife or something. You've got a degree; you had a career.'

'Had. Exactly,' Meg said. 'You might be closer to the mark than you think with the trophy-wife thing, too. You know he liked me all the way through college, but never thought he had a chance? It's funny how the power balance in a relationship can change.'

'What's a trophy wife?' piped up Iris from the row of seats behind us.

'A pretty lady who has nice clothes,' Meg said, 'but only because her husband buys them for her, because she hasn't got any money of her own.'

'Like a princess,' Iris commented.

'Exactly,' Meg said.

Then, quietly so Iris couldn't hear – I could barely make out the words either: 'Not that Jason ever conceded marriage.'

We left the main road and headed down a leafy avenue, with big properties set back behind walls and gates, and screened from view by carefully tended foliage. They were all different: mock-Georgian here, modernist glass and timber there, a Victorian attempt at a miniature castle over there.

Meg said, 'You know what, it's good to talk to you

about it. At least you haven't told me to pull out all the stops to try and get him back.'

'Why, has somebody else said that's what you should do?'

'Oh, Clarissa's full of strategies she thinks I should try. She's a romantic deep down; she wants other people's relationships to work out.'

This did not tally with my own experience of Clarissa, but I could hardly say so, and anyway, what did all that matter now?

'Victor's much more pragmatic about it,' Meg went on. 'He takes the view that once you've passed the point of no return, there's nothing you can do about it but admit defeat and acknowledge that it's over.'

She gave me a quick sideways glance as if to check whether I minded hearing Victor's views on breaking up, given that once, long ago, he and I had come to the same conclusion about each other.

I gave her a reassuring smile – I was actually quite pleased to get the chance to talk about him – and said, 'How is Victor? He seems well.'

'He is now,' she told me. 'He had a terrible time a few years back. He lost both his parents in quick succession; his father went first, and then his mother died not long after. You remember how devoted she was. Then his marriage broke up.'

'Poor Victor,' I said. 'That must have been dreadful for him.'

'He hasn't been involved with anybody since and, to be honest, I can see it staying that way.'

'I'm sure he'll meet someone sooner or later,' I offered.

'I don't think he wants to,' Meg said. 'All he really cares about is his work. And Beatrice, of course – that's his little girl. He's a fantastic father. But then he was made for it, don't you think? There was always something rather protective about him.'

'There was,' I agreed.

Beatrice. Now that was an odd coincidence. Meg would almost certainly have forgotten that it was my second name. Probably Victor had too. I had a feeling his was David, after his dad, but I wasn't sure.

Anyway, if that had been a test, I had got through it all right. My heartbeat was more or less steady, and my mouth was only a little dry. The past had been alluded to, and I'd contrived to be quite relaxed about it. Casual, even.

Meg turned on to a driveway and pulled up outside a rambling, red-brick, between-the-wars house that was probably one of the most appealing homes I had ever been invited to enter. It looked like exactly the kind of place where storybook orphans might be sent to live with an unpromising elderly relative, and find consoling magic in the grandfather clock or the kitchen garden or the cupboard under the stairs.

'My God, this place is enormous,' I said.

'I know; we're very lucky,' Meg said. 'Come on in.'

We passed through a big, cool kitchen with a red-tiled floor and spotless copper pots hanging up beside the Aga, and went into an adjoining sitting room, furnished with child-sized armchairs in sweetie-bright colours. A large wooden rocking-horse stood in one corner, next to the sort of hand-crafted doll's house that turns up in Sunday supplements at Christmastime and costs more than the average monthly mortgage; there were various toyboxes, and shelves of books and yet more toys.

Meg put Jasmine, the baby, in her playpen, and turned on the TV for the older girls. 'You can have an extra hour today, as long as you let Mummy chat to her friend,' she told them, and then she turned to me and said, 'Would you like to have a look round?'

Feeling a bit like a tourist in a stately home – curious, and self-conscious, and aware that it wouldn't do to knock anything over, since it might well be priceless and irreplaceable – I followed her into an enormous living room. It was lovely, cream and brocade and calm, with a glossy grand piano and vases of flowers and a window seat overlooking a long stretch of green lawn, but at the same time it was strangely empty and forlorn. Jason's departure had left its mark; the house smelt of scented candles, freshly cut roses, and absence.

'You could play a good game of sardines in this house,' I said.

'Been done,' Meg said, 'at our housewarming party, back in . . . oh, it must have been 2005. We just had Iris then. She slept right through it.'

We peered into the dining room with its long mahogany table, and the study, which had only a few shelves of books but plenty of proudly displayed children's drawings, then went upstairs to see the girls' rooms – pink and princessy, with a bathroom to match. Round the corner was the master bedroom, where Meg now slept without Jason in a monumental voile-draped four-poster bed.

Tucked away at the end of the corridor was yet another bedroom, painted white, with varnished floorboards; the only splash of colour was an oil painting of a sliced lemon hanging opposite the bed.

I knew that painting from somewhere. It seemed out of place in Meg's house, too bold, too fresh, too . . . too *yellow*. It suggested sharpness and a fondness for aperitifs, and a preference for exaggerated detail over harmonious impressionism, which was not much in evidence in the rest of the decor.

Meg said, 'This is Michael's room. You met him once, do you remember? Michael Hayes. Clarissa's son.'

And then I spotted the big framed photograph on top of the chest of drawers, and the tell-tale long red tendrils of curly hair lifting away from Clarissa's face and shoulders in a long-gone summer breeze. It was a much younger Clarissa, picnicking in a strappy sundress, with an equally red-haired chubby-legged toddler sitting between her bare legs and reaching for a segment of the satsuma she was peeling. Michael . . . and Clarissa, the young mum.

Next to the picnic photo was a smaller black-and-white portrait of Mandy Martin, Clarissa's sitcom-actress mother. Mandy had been styled as a 1970s version of an old-fashioned Hollywood star – pearlized lip gloss, gauzy veil, clingy dress. She looked young and fresh: younger than I now was myself.

Then I knew where I'd seen the lemon painting before. Clarissa's mother's house, where I had spent what had turned out to be one of the most magically surprising nights of my life.

Apart from that Michael's room was pretty bare. Not many books, no CDs, no sound system, no ethnic throws, no glo-stars on the ceiling or pop starlets on the walls; nothing that said *student*, or even, particularly, *young man*. All I could detect was restlessness, and the urge to be elsewhere.

Once upon a time my own teenage bedroom had given off the same message, the one that prompts parents across the land to accuse their offspring of using them like a hotel: *I need you – for now; and so I will be back, but only until I go.*

'Michael's with Clarissa in LA at the moment,' Meg said.

'So does he stay here often?' I asked.

'He lives here, pretty much. During the holidays, at any rate. He's just finished at St Edmund's – he used to board there.'

Clarissa had gone to the same exclusive London school; Victor too, a year ahead of her. They'd turned up at St Bart's already knowing each other, if only slightly. I hadn't expected that. I'd assumed that we'd all be in the same boat, all strangers, all finding our feet together. But that had turned out not to be quite true. And it wasn't a boat at all, but a haphazard, bewildering flotilla, and there was always the danger of falling out with the crew with which you found yourself, or ending up marooned, or becalmed, or stir crazy, or being ousted as a stowaway . . .

'After Mandy died we stepped up and said Michael

could come to us whenever he needed to,' Meg explained.

'Mandy? Mandy Martin's dead? I'm sorry, I just . . . I can't quite believe it. You've caught me by surprise. I had no idea.'

How could I have missed it? Mandy had once been the nation's Saturday-night sweetheart, the thinking man's crumpet, the star of a hit show. There must have been obituaries, a mention on the news. Surely *The Primrose Path* must have had a rerun on one or other of the digital channels, and even if not, it couldn't have faded completely from public consciousness.

To my horror, I felt as if I was about to cry. I told myself it was just a shock, coming out of the blue after the event.

'It was a couple of years ago now,' Meg said. 'Cancer. She was only fifty-seven.'

'I wish I'd known. I could have sent flowers or something.'

As soon as I'd said this I realized that I wouldn't have done. How could I, having broken off contact with Clarissa so completely?

'Clarissa asked for donations for the RSPCA,' Meg said. 'You know how Mandy loved her cats.'

'Yes, I remember.'

'Michael was very much affected,' Meg said. 'He'd spent a lot of time with her.'

'He's lucky to have you as a sort of auntie figure,' I said.

'I'm lucky to have him,' Meg said. 'He's stayed in touch with Jason, too. He's never seen all that much of his dad, and Jason's really quite fond of him. Oh dear, I think that's Jasmine crying.'

She shut Michael's door and hurried downstairs to retrieve Jasmine from the playpen. I followed her more slowly, still trying to compose myself.

Victor. Meg. Jason. Michael. Clarissa. Mandy.

Who next?

Meg warmed up a bottle of milk in the microwave, holding the baby over one shoulder. Jasmine emptied it and promptly drifted off to sleep, and Meg looked up at me in relief.

'She's such a good girl,' she said. 'Just as well, really.'

'You don't have a nanny?'

She shook her head. 'I have help with everything else – the house, the garden. I want to look after my kids myself. Jason's hired someone now to help out when he sees them, but that's because he's never changed a nappy if he can possibly help it. I think he's secretly scared of poo. Chief executive of an enterprise that's one of the most searched websites in the western world, and he can't cope with a bit of physical mess.'

'Well, I think you're doing a brilliant job,' I said. 'I don't know very much about children, but they seem very . . .' What was the right compliment to offer? I glanced at Jasmine, peacefully dozing in Meg's arms, and finished, '. . . content.'

'You didn't ever think you might like one of your own?' Meg asked.

We stared at each other for a moment as I tried to summon up the reply I'd used in the past when faced with this question: *No, not really, perhaps I'm just not particularly maternal*.

'I'm sorry, that was presumptuous of me,' Meg said quickly. 'It's just because we used to know each other so well. I feel as if I can ask you that kind of thing.'

I drew a deep breath and decided to tell the truth.

'It has crossed my mind, obviously. But it's never seemed like the right time, and I'm OK with that. I don't think I ever really imagined myself having children. It's not like it's this big life's ambition that I've missed out on.'

'No, that's true,' Meg said. 'I was the one who always wanted a family.'

'And you got it.'

'I got the children. I just never got the husband,' Meg said. 'Jason would never consider getting married. He was very stubborn about it. Even when we had three children. He insisted it was a stultifying convention and would wreck our relationship, which was rather ironic given the way things have turned out. It was a bit of a sticking point between us, as you can probably imagine. My dad was very good about it, and so was Brian – you remember my brother? He's a vicar too now. But I knew it bothered them. Well, it bothered me too. Still, at least it means we don't need to get divorced.'

She glanced down at Jasmine and stroked a curl of the baby's soft hair. 'I was always terrified of losing Jason the way my dad lost my mum,' she said. 'And I have lost him. But not through bereavement. He's alive and well, and so am I, and we're still not together.'

She looked up at me, and her expression was bitter. 'I

think he still can't quite believe that I'm never going to forgive him,' she said. 'But he had a fling with someone when I was pregnant. How am I supposed to trust him again after that?'

'Maybe trust is a little bit like faith,' I said. 'Perhaps you can lose it and recover it later on. I don't know. All I know for sure is that it's hard to be with anyone once someone has broken it.'

Meg hesitated, and I knew she was building up to an admission that would cost her something to say, and be uncomfortable for me to hear.

'Anna, I want you to know I'm so sorry about what happened,' she said. 'It was an awful time. Particularly for you. You were closest to it. And everything happened all at once. I know we were very young, but I don't know if that's much of an excuse. I feel bad about it. We let you down. We weren't there for you.'

'It wasn't an easy time for you either,' I said.

'It wasn't. It was a rotten way for everything to finish. When you think back to how it was at the start . . . I got the old photos out the other day, to show Michael. You know – Clarissa's boy. He's going to Oxford. To St Bart's. I shed a tear or two, I have to admit. I could tell he was rather embarrassed. Do you want to see?'

Did I want to see what we had looked like when we were still innocent? Yes – suddenly I did.

'If it's not too much trouble.'

'You want to take the baby?'

'I'm not really very used to babies.'

'Oh, she's not fussy,' Meg said. 'Any warm lap will do.'

She passed the baby into my arms and went off,

leaving me praying that she wouldn't take too long. But actually, there was something surprisingly nice about the warm, light weight of the child in my arms. By the time Meg came back and put the album on the table in front of me and took Jasmine back, I was almost reluctant to relinquish her.

'That's just the first term,' Meg said, settling next to me. 'There's plenty more, if you're interested.'

I had no photographs at all from our time at university. I'd not had a camera at the time, and I'd got rid of our formal year-group photograph, and the few copied snaps that people had given me.

But here it all was, as seen through Meg's eyes, filed away, and labelled in her clear, round, meticulous handwriting.

There was Meg's first-year room, its institutional bareness softened by fluffy cushions and pots of busy lizzies. There was St Bart's library, grand as a Gothic chapel, rearing up from the lawn opposite the exit from the beer cellar, a call to redemption for full-bladdered drinkers staggering out towards the nearest loos. There was the medieval quad, creamy-stoned and robustly proportioned, bright with Virginia creeper along one side, as self-contained and satisfactorily structured as a neatly solved equation.

And there we all were, squeezed on to a bench overlooking the river on a frosty autumn morning, happy and complete and sure of ourselves, a pack surveying its territory.

We hadn't gone to bed. We'd been talking all night. I remembered the talking, not what we'd discussed but how it had felt, being able to say whatever came into my mind, and knowing I would be listened to and someone would respond. It was leisurely, luxurious, accepting, and at the same time wildly liberating, as if something inside me that had been curled up tight, like the stem of a fern, was finally unwinding.

And then the windows had brightened – we'd been in Victor's sitting room, the one he shared with Barnaby – and Keith had said, 'Let's go for a stroll before breakfast,' and we had trooped off after him, a tall, skinny, slightly disconsolate figure in skin-tight black jeans and DM boots and an absurdly long and voluminous cape.

Keith often went for long walks on his own, and when we ventured out together he usually suggested where we should go and how to get there. It had been his idea to settle on that bench for a moment, to take in the view, and the cold breeze coming up off the river.

I was sitting right in the middle, bundled up in a very long red scarf, with Victor on one side and Clarissa on the other. Meg was next to Clarissa, laughing at whatever she had just said. Victor was debating something with Barnaby, who was wearing a tweed jacket and trying to light a pipe, a heavily built, beefily handsome young fogey with a philosophical frown and straw-blond hair.

Keith must have taken the photograph. I was the only one making a big effort to smile for him. I was beaming: I looked stupidly, fate-temptingly happy, as if there was absolutely nowhere I would rather have been.

On to the next page . . .

There we were in the main quad, underneath the arch

covered with Virginia creeper; in the Covered Market, in front of the Bridge of Sighs, sightseers who had been granted leave to stay and were no longer conscious that our visit was still only temporary. Clarissa and I, arm in arm. Barnaby giving me a piggyback. Victor looking pleased with the birthday cake Meg had baked for him as Clarissa leaned over his shoulder and pretended to blow the candles out. Me with my head on my arms on a desk in the library, sound asleep.

Clarissa and I dominated Meg's version of our history; the boys appeared only when we were there, and never without us. So I was surprised to come across a snap of Keith standing awkwardly in one of the dinosaur footprints outside Oxford's Museum of Natural History, as if half attempting to strike a pose and half wanting just to get the photo over with.

He had a cigarette in one hand and a brown paper bag in the other, and was squinting at the camera with a mildly perplexed, put-upon expression, as if to say, 'Is this really necessary?' In the next picture he had jettisoned the fag and was holding up the brown paper bag to cover his face.

'He was really annoyed with me that day,' Meg said. 'I was meant to be helping him choose you a Christmas present. He told me I was useless and didn't know you at all, and insisted on spending ages in every second-hand bookshop in Oxford.'

'I remember him giving it to me. It was still in that paper bag,' I said. 'I still have it somewhere, though I'm ashamed to say I never actually read it.'

'Don't feel bad about it,' Meg said. 'I think he rather

enjoyed scouring the shelves. I was the one who suffered for it. My feet were killing me by the end.'

'I don't feel bad,' I said, but I did.

I turned the page, and there I was with Victor.

We were sitting on opposite sides of a table in the café across the road from St Bart's; the glass window behind us was misted with condensation, and we were still wearing our coats. The way each of us was sitting mirrored the other; we both had cups of coffee in front of us, and our hands resting on the table beside them, as if at any moment we might reach out and touch.

'Young love,' Meg said.

'We hadn't even got together then,' I said, and closed the album.

'There's a gaudy coming up soon, you know,' Meg said. 'In November. I'm sure everybody would be delighted to see you, if you were up for it.'

'I don't know about that,' I said.

Oxford didn't have reunions: it had gaudies. It had a language all its own and numerous dead ones to keep alive, its own rules, its own way of doing things. Like a prism, it let the outside world in only to alter it, without being transformed itself. It was an old place that belonged to the young, who were only ever passing through, and, in my case, once gone, gone for good.

'We all miss you, you know,' Meg said. 'I've been to a couple of these things now, and it's great to see everyone. But it always makes you think about the ones who aren't there.'

'I can't really imagine going back now,' I said. 'After

all this time, it would just be . . . weird. And anyway, I'm not the same person I was then.'

'But nobody else is, either. And yet somehow or other they are. That's what's so strange about it. Anyway, I don't see why I should hide away just because of Jason. He's determined to go, and I don't see why I should make things easy for him by chickening out of it. It's bound to be awkward. Most people probably have no idea we've broken up. But they'll figure it out, won't they? By the end of the evening it won't be news to anybody.'

'Do you really think it's worth it?' I asked.

'Of course it is. It's my right to be there. I belong there just as much as he does.' Meg tapped the photo album on the table in front of us, the evidence of her belonging, for emphasis. 'And you know what, that's true for you too. We can brave our exes together. Safety in numbers. There'll be plenty of people around. It'll be easy enough to avoid Victor if you want to. Though I got the impression from him that he'd quite like the chance to have a bit of a chat with you, after all this time. Anyway, at the end of the day, what is there to be frightened of?'

'I am not afraid of Victor,' I said, though I wasn't entirely sure that this was true.

Meg pondered for a moment, then reached out and gave my hand a resolute squeeze. 'Look, maybe it's crossing a line for me to say this, but I'm going to say it anyway because if I don't, who else will? It seems to me that maybe you're still carrying around some guilt about what happened, and I think it's time you let it go.'

'Let what go?' a little voice said somewhere behind us. I turned and saw Iris, who was watching us both with wary curiosity.

'For heaven's sake, Iris, don't sneak round like that,' Meg scolded. 'How many times do I have to tell you not to listen in to grown-ups' conversations?'

'But I'm hungry,' Iris said. 'The door was open. And it's lunchtime.'

I glanced at my watch, and said, 'She has a point. I should make a move, let you get on.'

Meg said, 'Don't feel you have to rush off. You're welcome to stay and eat with us.'

'Thank you, but no, I should be getting back,' I said, getting to my feet.

'I'm really, really thirsty, too,' Iris insisted. 'I'm dying of thirst.'

'Well, you're just going to have to wait a minute, while I say goodbye to our visitor,' Meg told her.

She stood up carefully, without waking the baby, who had slept peacefully all through our session with the photo album. I followed them through to the entrance hall. At the door Meg glanced round to check Iris wasn't lurking in earshot, and said, 'I'm right though, aren't I? It's not really the Victor and Clarissa thing that's putting you off. It's all that other stuff.'

'You could put it like that.'

'There is no way you were responsible, Anna. It wasn't your fault, and there wasn't anything you could have done to stop it happening,' she said.

'I know,' I said.

'Stay in touch, won't you?' Meg said. 'Whatever you

decide about the gaudy, I'd really like to meet up again sometime. It's been great to see you. Took me right back.'

'Me, too,' I told her.

'You sure you don't want me to run you back to the Tube station? Wouldn't take a minute.'

'No, really, it's not far, and I quite fancy the walk.'

Meg gave me directions, and I turned the handle and pushed the door open wide, and stepped out of her life and back into mine.

But for some reason it didn't quite feel like mine. It was as if everything was slightly out of kilter, like a picture on the wall that has been knocked and hangs askew, and that feeling stayed with me even when I was walking up the steps to my own front door.

3

'What mere mortal could compete?'

Pete was out, and my train was delayed, so I had plenty of time to compose myself between my meeting with Meg and the next social occasion of the weekend: Tippy's hen do.

We hens were booked in for dinner and an overnight stay at the Garden Maze Hotel, in a converted Regency manor house just outside Deddenham in Berkshire, where Tippy and I had grown up. When I was a teenager Deddenham had represented everything I wanted to escape: it was safe, orderly, immaculate, comfortably modern and resolutely dull. But Tippy must have felt much more rooted there. She had lived nearby ever since she'd come back from university, and she and George, her fiancé, had ended up buying a place round the corner from our parents' house.

By the time I hurried into the hotel restaurant all the

other hens were already sitting down for a celebratory evening meal. They were all glitter and sparkle, and I felt rather out of place in my little black dress as I headed across the pastel carpet towards them.

Tippy, like Jesus at the Last Supper, but wearing a pair of flashing devil's horns, was seated at the middle of the long table. She was recounting an anecdote that had never been aired over Sunday lunch at our parents' house, something to do with being propositioned in Peru during her gap year.

I hovered at her elbow till she'd finished; she got rather unsteadily to her feet and swept me into an unusually enthusiastic embrace. The waiter appeared with a fresh bottle of champagne, and someone proposed a toast to experience, and Tippy started talking about an old boyfriend who had a nickname for his penis.

'He called it the Beast,' she explained, 'and I have to say, it certainly wasn't a beauty!'

There was general laughter, and another toast was proposed: 'To the Beast, and all Tippy's many conquests!'

I retreated to the empty place at the far end of the table, ordered some food, and began to piece together the connections between the women around me.

I recognized Tippy's gang from school, who'd been a couple of years below me. Back then, I'd been a bookworm who hung out with the Christian Union girls and fantasized about being friends with artists and bohemians, while Tippy's pals had been leggy, queeny types who were always plotting and scheming about boys. Now they were almost all married or mothers or both, and seemed less sassy and outspoken than I remembered, though I suspected they might find their voices once they'd knocked back a bit more wine.

There were a few of Tippy's past and present colleagues from the Reading department store where she worked as a manager, and her fiancé's little sister, Alexia, an art student in a macramé top, who was the youngest member of the group by at least a decade. But most of the hens were Tippy's friends from university. They were the core of the group, the most animated talkers, the ones who seemed to know all Tippy's stories already and yet wanted to hear them again, and who seemed most assured of their past and future place in Tippy's life.

I didn't want to think about my own friends from my student days; I'd spent nearly two decades schooling myself not to dwell on all that. But having seen first Victor and then Meg, it was harder than ever to exercise the old discipline, and I found myself drifting into a speculative fantasy in spite of myself.

What if it had all turned out differently, if none of the bad stuff had ever happened? Would I have been able to go out to dinner with *them* around me, and laugh and chat and reminisce, not even imagining that in some other, sadder world, such a gathering was entirely impossible?

But no . . . The truth was, I would never, ever host a dinner like this myself. I stayed in touch with some of my old colleagues from the couple of years I'd spent teaching after graduation and from my stint in educational publishing, and then there were the evening-class friends, the choir friends, and the running-club friends, but I didn't mix them. And I didn't get drunk with them. And I didn't entertain them with confessions about sex.

But while I was leaving my topped-up wine glass untouched, Tippy's hens were all getting stuck in, and by the time the main course was cleared away the volume was up and the inhibitions were on their way down. Marina, Tippy's best friend from her time at Exeter University, gave a raucous account of how she'd lost her virginity in the bushes at a Young Farmers' Club social, and then Tippy clapped her hands and said, 'Excellent! Let's have everybody's stories. My first time was Anton de Valery, New Year's Eve, in Anna's bedroom. It was all over in about a minute. I would have been terrifically disappointed, if I hadn't been quite pleased with myself for getting it out of the way.'

Then she leaned forward and looked down the table at me, and added, 'I only did it because I was mad that you'd beaten me to it.'

'Only just,' I said.

The anecdotes kept coming, rolling round the far side of the table with everybody listening and whooping, and my turn drawing ever closer.

Alexia, Tippy's arty future sister-in-law, drew slightly shocked applause for an account of a threesome involving the bass player of an indie rock band that I'd barely heard of. Then there was a small silence which was broken by Tippy saying, 'Anna, your turn.'

'It was my first boyfriend,' I said. 'Victor Rose.'

A collective sigh went round the table. Tippy said,

'Oh yes, I remember Victor. He was a bit of a luvvie, wasn't he? I wonder what's become of him.'

'I think he's doing all right,' I said.

'He did that film, didn't he? The one that didn't do terribly well. Wasn't it a road trip all told backwards, or something? Anyway, what we want is gory details. So spill the beans: when and where? And was he any good?'

The waiter came to my rescue, approaching the table with the pudding menus. A general conversation broke out about who would share a chocolate sundae with whom. By the time we had ordered, the woman sitting next to me was recalling how she'd lost her innocence while laid up in Chamonix with a broken leg, and I was off the hook. Which was a relief . . . but I couldn't help but remember a time and place when I had not yet learned to be so guarded.

That night I slept fitfully, and sometime in the wee smalls I had the recurring nightmare that I often woke from when I was away from home and in an unfamiliar bed, or just anxious about what I was doing and who I was with.

The location was always the same. I was back at Oxford, alone, on a hot, bright, silent day, and it was a pleasure to be there again, though an eerie one, because the city was entirely empty, and all its proportions had shifted. The buildings and monuments had all grown enormous, pillars and arches and great creamy stone walls reaching up towards a bright blue desert sky, criss-crossed here and there by bridges. It could have been a feverish imagining by an Old Master of an ancient classical civilization established by giants, miraculously preserved long after the last of its curators had turned to dust.

I made my way down what seemed to be the High Street. The heavy wooden gates that barred the entrance to St Bart's had disappeared. I passed through into the main quad and saw that the grass had turned to sand, and the Virginia creeper had long since died away and dried to nothing. The paving stones on the path that led around the quad's perimeter were hot under my bare feet. I turned right, into the corridor that led to the set of rooms Victor had once shared with Barnaby; the doors had vanished there too, leaving only an empty arch.

The floor was dusty with red ash, unmarked by footprints; the noticeboards were bare. Here was my task, waiting for me: a mop and a bucket, filled near to the brim with water that was miraculously icy cold. I set to work. The water I swilled across the floor quickly turned the colour of bright rust.

There was so much to do. The long corridor stretched ahead, and the patch I had started on just wouldn't come clean; I could make next to no impression on it. Suddenly I was tired, so tired; I could barely stop yawning; my eyes kept closing. Before long, despite my best intentions, my will would fail, and my body would yield, and I would sink into sleep. And then it would happen, as it did every time.

I thought I felt someone watching me from behind, and turned to see no one at all, just a shifting shadow glimpsed out of the corner of my eye, just beyond the archway.

And then I found myself in my first-year student room, as bare and tidy as it had been when I moved in, empty apart from the single bed, the desk, the chairs and the built-in wardrobe. The window looked out on to a box-hedge maze, the foliage dark green and glossy under a grey and cloudy sky; it was drizzling, and there was a smell of river water in the air.

I shut the door and locked it, and lay down on the bed to sleep.

And then I rose up and hovered somewhere near the ceiling, looking down at my curled-up body. I hadn't been aware of it while I was wandering around, or attempting to mop the floor, but I saw now that I was wearing a green silk dress with a full skirt. My ball dress, shiny and perfect and brand new. My hair spread right out across the pillow behind me and reached down towards the floor – how had it got so long? It had a youthful heaviness and curl that I remembered but hadn't quite realized it had lost, and not a hint of white.

And then the door swung open, and a man whose face I was not permitted to see came in and gently, tenderly, stroked my hair away from my face and neck, and then lifted his other hand, the one with the knife in it, and cut my throat.

I shuddered into wakefulness. Still here, still breathing, still alive. I touched my hand to my neck: no blood, no damage done.

Just a dream.

It was intensely dark, much darker than the bedroom I shared back at home with Pete. It took me a moment to remember that I was in a hotel, in a twin-bedded en suite overlooking a garden maze – so that was where the maze in the dream had come from – and the curtains were long and muffling and heavy, unlike the ill-fitting blind back home that failed to keep out the orange glow of the streetlight in front of the flat.

My breathing slowed; my heart rate eased. In the other bed, my room-mate – Alexia, the young student groupie, Tippy's future sister-in-law – continued to sleep peacefully. Perhaps, if I was going to be awake for the rest of the night, I could creep into the bathroom and read without disturbing her . . . but no, the fan would go on. I listened to her slow, steady breathing, and waited to drift off.

And then I was no longer in the Garden Maze Hotel, or at home in the first-floor flat in Nod Hill Road. I was in a big, soft bed somewhere else, somewhere high up, and as I dozed I could make out the sound of rain on glass, and wind in the trees. Was it woodland, or a park? When morning came I would draw the curtains and see.

There was someone sleeping next to me. A big, warm, peaceful body. Sometime soon, in due course, we would both wake, and we would fix breakfast, and then we would plan our day. There was no particular rush, though; we had all the time in the world. And I was so tired; my body ached as if I'd just been through some kind of ordeal, a test perhaps, or a performance or a confrontation, or even a trial. But it was over now, and I was safely home, and free.

The dream was so comforting I was reluctant to surface from it, but the next time I woke I was back in the hotel, and there was just enough light filtering in round the heavy curtains to show that it was morning; the intense blackness of the night had faded to a muted grey. My room-mate was still soundly asleep, though. I'd left her in the bar with the others when I turned in the night before; they had all probably stayed up late.

I got up as quietly as I could, pulled on my swimming costume and put my T-shirt and shorts on over it, found my sandals, grabbed my washbag and towel and stole out to start the day.

It was just past seven, too early for the restaurant to have opened for breakfast, although I saw a maid pushing a trolley laden with trays, each one adorned with a single red rose. I went past the treatment rooms and through the changing area to the pool, which had been done out in a mock-Roman style, with white mosaic tiles and decorative fluted pillars flanking the edge of the pool. The light was greenish and subterranean; there were no windows or skylights. In the old days, when the hotel was a private house, this had been a ballroom. It had never been intended to be seen by day.

The water had the glassy stillness of a pool that has been empty long enough for every last ripple to fade away, so that the surface is restored to a perfect, unbroken plane. I dumped my stuff on the poolside, kicked off my flip-flops and was just about to pull my

T-shirt off over my head when someone said, 'Good morning, early bird.'

I turned and saw a woman lying on a sun-lounger a few pillars down, cocooned in white towelling; she was wearing a pristine hotel dressing-gown with matching slippers and turban. She had a perfectly circular slice of green cucumber covering each eye, and a thick white paste slathered on to her skin. If it hadn't been for her voice, I wouldn't have known who it was.

'You're up pretty early yourself,' I said. 'How's your head?'

'Oh, fine,' Tippy said. 'Really, I feel OK. Anyway, I'm about to blast all the toxins out of my system. I'm going to have the bridal body wrap. You have to spend three hours coated in algae with cling film over the top, but at the end of it you've lost three inches of body fat.'

'Three inches off where?' I asked.

'Off everywhere,' Tippy said crossly. 'Sarita's doing it. She's the resident beautician here. She's quite famous, you know. I booked in the minute I knew we were coming here, and even then I was lucky to get an appointment.'

She plucked the cucumbers off her eyes and laid them carefully on the white plastic arm of her sun-lounger, and reached into the raffia bag at her side to pull out a magazine.

'Look,' she said, reaching across to show me. 'Your old mate uses her. I'd say that's quite an endorsement.'

I glanced down at the spread that Tippy wanted me to see. And there was Clarissa Hayes, my A-list former friend, strolling along the beach in a white bikini, sunkissed and carefree, her face mostly hidden by a huge pair of sunglasses, her curly red hair blowing a little in the breeze. She'd always had the knack of wearing white, even before she was famous – the knack being not to care if it gets dirty.

'See?' Tippy said. 'It says here: "Went to the Garden Maze Hotel in Berkshire for a spa break, including treatments from celebrity beautician Sarita, before catching some rays in Biarritz."'

'She certainly looks good on it,' I said, taking the magazine. Tippy lay back again, and put the slices of cucumber back over her eyes.

'After you went to bed last night some of the girls were asking about you, and I told them you'd gone to Oxford and been pally with Clarissa Hayes,' she said. 'They thought I was having them on. She's incredible, isn't she?'

'She is,' I agreed.

'I suppose it must be weird, now that she's so famous. I bet you sometimes wish you'd stayed in touch.'

'Not really.'

'Oh, I know it wasn't great, how it all turned out. But just think, if you could have got past all that, maybe you could have been right there, strolling along the beach with her. Celebs do sometimes have non-famous friends, don't they? I expect it works all right as long as you know your place. I mean, what mere mortal could compete?'

'I've never been very keen on knowing my place,' I said.

I reached across and put the magazine down on the

arm of Tippy's sun-lounger, then shed my shorts and T-shirt and dived into the pool.

When I surfaced Tippy was sitting up, and one of the cucumber circles had fallen off into the gunge on her cheek. She was staring at me through the one eye that could see as if speculating about why exactly I had been so pig-headed about refusing to bury the hatchet with Clarissa Hayes. I waved at her and she managed a baffled smile in return. I slid back into the water, and ten lengths later, I looked up again and saw that she had gone.

I climbed out. The magazine was lying on the floor, and I couldn't resist the temptation to pick it up and have another look.

It was splotched with damp from the splash I'd made going into the water, as if someone had been crying over it. I perched on Tippy's sun-lounger and studied the picture of Clarissa more closely, as if it might hold a clue, some tiny piece of vital evidence that I'd missed.

There was a man with her in the photo. Not a lover, surely. He looked very young, and was walking along at a slight distance, as if he wasn't entirely sure he wanted to be associated with her. So who was he?

'Making Hayes while the sun shines.' How many times had I seen variations on that headline?

> Clarissa Hayes enjoyed a well-earned sunshine break after filming wrapped on the latest instalment of the Ultramen superhero franchise at the West Heath film studios in Berkshire. She was not joined by film director hubbie Artie Janx,

> but instead enjoyed a spot of quality time with her 17-year-old son from a previous relationship, who will soon take up a place at his mother's old college at Oxford University.

Michael again. Mooching along in an oversized shirt and shorts, he was obviously barely out of adolescence, whereas Clarissa had always been poised and self-possessed, as if she was already feigning indifference to the cameras. It was hard to believe that when I'd first met her she'd been about the same age as her son was now.

> 'I'm delighted that Michael's going to be following in my footsteps,' Clarissa told waiting reporters before boarding *Disco Inferno*, the 100-metre-long yacht of the fashion designer Salvatore Braganza, with whom she and Michael are staying. 'But I shall have to fight the urge to keep checking up on him. I've always been very protective of Michael, and we all know the kind of things students get up to.'

'You don't know the half of it,' I told the Clarissa in the picture.

The words hung in the air like a threat, or maybe a promise. I dropped the magazine on the sun-lounger and retreated to one of the cubicles that lined the wall behind me to strip off and towel myself dry.

When I emerged I still had the place to myself. The ripples I'd left on the surface of the water were beginning to die away, and the pool was almost smooth again, as if I'd never been there to disturb it.

It had rained most of the summer, but Tippy was in luck. When her big day came round, a week after the hen do, it was dry and breezy, with stretches of blue sky between the fast-moving clouds.

As we bridesmaids lined up behind her to go into the church, Marina, the matron of honour, observed that the weather needed to hold just long enough for the photographer to finish the outside shots. And sure enough, it wasn't until the last group picture had been taken – it was of all the hens – that I noticed a pinprick of damp on my lilac satin dress, and looked up to see the sky full of looming clouds.

Pete was hovering nearby, looking ill at ease. He hadn't been looking forward to this occasion much; he found Tippy strident and my stepfather overbearing, and we'd once had a particularly unpleasant row because he'd described my mother as a doormat.

When I rejoined him he told me, 'You go in if you want; I'm staying out for a bit.'

'No, good idea, let's make the most of it. I wouldn't be surprised if it starts chucking it down before too much longer,' I said.

We made our way to a nearby bench, where Pete lit up and we looked out in silence at the green landscaped curves of Deddenham Golf Course, a favourite haunt of my stepfather, where the reception was being held.

I thought about how happy we'd been back when we were first seeing each other. After the inconclusive dates and flings of my late twenties and early thirties, it had been a surprise to me to be so comfortable with someone. I had decided to take a chance on living with him even though I couldn't bring myself to tell him everything, and it wasn't really fair to attempt to go from intimacy to domesticity without disclosure.

We had met at work, where he was in the IT department; he'd asked me out after we got chatting at a colleague's leaving do. He was big but gentle-seeming, a combination that appealed, and I had thought, *Can't do any harm. Why not try?* Now he had a new job he didn't like and I had no job at all, and we seemed to be in the doldrums romantically as well.

It didn't help that our little rented flat was really too small for two – I'd lived in it by myself before the friend Pete lodged with decided to get married, and asked him to move out. We'd been talking about moving somewhere bigger before I got made redundant. But deep down, I knew the problem wasn't lack of space. Maybe we just didn't have it in us to last, but it also didn't help that there was so much I was keeping from him.

'You don't seem to be having that great a time,' I said. 'Are you OK?'

Pete swallowed. 'Actually, there is something I was wanting to talk to you about—'

But then Tippy's friend Marina came over to us and said, 'Anna, Tippy told me to come and get you. She wants all the single ladies. It's time for the scrum!'

I glanced at Pete and said, 'I'm not really single.'

'Come come, no excuses,' said Marina, with the brisk

authority of the married person who has earned her exemption from such humiliations. 'It's traditional.'

And so Pete and I got to our feet and followed her to where Tippy was waiting, with a motley assortment of single women of various ages – including Alexia, my room-mate from the hen do, now officially Tippy's sister-in-law – lined up in giggling embarrassment in front of her.

I joined them. Someone called out, 'No cheating!' Tippy flashed me a look, turned her back, and hurled her bouquet of white and pink roses up into the air.

We all watched it rise, then arc downwards, straight towards me. I stepped back just in time, and Alexia lunged forward and grabbed it. The others crowded round to congratulate her and she smirked and said, 'I'm not actually seeing anyone right now, but maybe it's a good omen.'

I looked around for Pete, but he had disappeared. Tippy tapped me on the shoulder and said, 'I meant that for you.'

'I don't actually want to get married. Not right now, anyway.'

'Every woman wants to get married,' Tippy said.

Mum came over. I'd been hoping she would relax and enjoy herself when Tippy's big day finally came round, but she still looked fraught, her worried expression contrasting oddly with the jaunty hat she had, after much deliberation and only with Tippy's express encouragement, summoned up the nerve to buy.

'I think they're ready for us to go in for dinner,' she said.

As we filed in to take our places for the meal, I found myself thinking about what Tippy had said. Me getting married to Pete? It seemed (*a*) like something that was never going to happen, and (*b*) all wrong. But why? It wasn't as if I had a principled objection to matrimony.

I had been telling myself that we were in a sticky patch, but what would our life together be like when we were out of it? Perhaps we were only stuck because neither of us had found the courage to be free.

When the speeches were over we all gathered round the dance floor to watch Tippy and George, her new husband, strut their stuff.

Pete had gone off somewhere again. Part of me wanted to go in search of him, but I also didn't want to miss Tippy's big romantic moment. As the *Dirty Dancing* theme tune blared out, George, judging by his strained expression, was feeling the pressure, but Tippy, who had hired an instructor to coach them through the routine, looked magnificently happy. As I watched them I found myself thinking, not about Pete, but about someone else entirely.

My reverie was interrupted by Mum whispering loudly in my ear, 'Anna, could I have a word?'

I nearly jumped out of my skin. She put a finger to her lips and nodded towards the exit, and I followed her out.

It was noticeably colder outside, and the air was still and heavy, as if the threatened downpour was finally on the way. Pete was hunched up on the bench we'd shared earlier in the day, looking pale green. Mum said, 'Anna, I think you should take him home.'

I said, 'My God, Pete, are you all right?' and hurried over to sit next to him.

A female voice said, 'It's not my fault if he's a light-weight,' and I looked up to see Alexia, who had won the bouquet.

'I think the less said about this the better,' Mum said. 'I'll make your apologies, Anna. Let's get you back to your parents, young lady.' And she took Alexia by the arm and steered her back into the hotel.

'Pete,' I said, 'please tell me you didn't just try to cop off with Tippy's new sister-in-law.'

He straightened up, groaned, and let his head fall back towards his knees. After a while he said, 'Anna, I feel really terrible. Please don't give me a hard time. Not now.'

'Just tell me what happened,' I said, 'or I will walk off right now and leave you here, and you can fend for yourself.'

There was a pause. A long one. A regular beat began to pulse out from the clubhouse; the disco was under way.

Pete eased up his head but didn't meet my eyes. He said, 'No, nothing like that. I just had a spliff with her. Jesus, it was fucking strong.'

'No! You've got to be kidding. Oh, Pete . . . you just can't do that kind of thing with my family around.'

'But they weren't around,' Pete said. 'They were all inside. I thought it might help me relax a bit. Get me through the rest of the do. Anyway, it was Alexia's idea.'

He looked more sorry for himself than contrite as he went on, 'I know you don't do it yourself, but you've never minded me having a smoke now and again.'

'How come my mother found you?'

'I think she was looking for me. She's never liked me.'

'Yeah, well, she definitely doesn't like you now.'

'It's worse than that. I . . . threw up in front of her.' He cleared his throat. 'On her, actually.'

'On her?'

'Kind of on her shoes.'

'My God.' I thought for a moment. 'Literally on her shoes? Or just at her feet?'

Pete cleared his throat. 'Well, there was a bit of spatter.'

'Are you all right now? You still look a funny colour.'

'Don't be like that,' Pete said. 'Don't be all nice about it.'

He stood up, and I recognized in his face the peculiar cold anger that goes with deflecting the blame on to someone else for a mishap that's your own fault.

'Here's the thing, Anna,' he told me. 'This is what I was trying to say to you earlier, and I've wanted to tell you for a while, but the right moment just never seemed to come along.' He jabbed a forefinger in the direction of the clubhouse. 'There is no way you and I are ever going to be doing that.'

'That's OK, I don't want to get married either.'

'That's not what I meant,' Pete said. 'I know you're trying to pretend nothing's wrong, but you can't. The thing is, Anna, the thing that's wrong – it's not the flat, it's not my work or your work, it's you. Living with you is like sitting around with a bomb in the room and waiting for it to go off. It's tiring, and I'm not sure I want to do it any more.'

'That's ridiculous, and also, I don't see what it has to do with you getting drunk and stoned at my sister's wedding and throwing up on my mother.'

'You see? You can't talk about it. You're never going to tell me what's really going on in that head of yours.'

'I think we should get a cab and go home,' I said, 'that is, if you think you can make it without being sick again.'

We didn't talk on the way to the station; the only sound I registered was the squeak of one of the windscreen wipers as it swept away the steadily thickening drizzle. *A bomb in the room?* Surely he didn't mean it? It was just a stray, stoned, stupid comment. And if he did, what kind of a weird double life had we been maintaining all this time, pretending that everything was normal?

On the train back to Waterloo he fell asleep. Seeing him dozing, his features smoothed into innocent unconsciousness, the dark window next to him streaked with rain, I found it was no longer possible to feel angry with him. Instead – and this was just as surprising to me as the moment when Pete had said *a bomb in the room* – I was *pleased*.

I knew that what Pete sensed about me, but had never said until now, was true. I *was* a threat. To someone, but not to Pete: to someone who, perhaps, had cause to be afraid.

And if that was so, perhaps I could afford to be bold.

I wanted to see Victor again. Of course I did. Why shouldn't I seek him out in the place where we had first met? I belonged there as much as any of them; why should I be the one who was scared to show her face?

It had taken a year of dating for me and Pete to move in together, but it only took a fortnight for him to find somewhere else to go.

Those two weeks were horrible. Pete was cold and resentful, and I was guilty and tearful, and nothing could hide the truth from either of us any longer, which was that we had ended up using each other as a kind of mutual prop, a least worst alternative to loneliness, and what we were losing now was not love so much as the idea of ourselves as loveable.

But then Pete was offered the chance to house-sit for a friend at short notice, and by the time his last day came round we had arrived at a kind of truce. We were, after all, in the same position: stepping out from the apparent safety of the relationship, ready to find out what might, or might not, be waiting for us.

I ended up helping him pack up his stuff, and by the time we'd finished it was evening. The living room didn't exactly look bare now we were done – the bookshelves were still full to capacity – but there were several new and surprising empty spaces, including the patch on the table where Pete's laptop had once stood. I foresaw myself becoming a regular at the local internet café in the near future, unless I finally got lucky with one of my job applications and could afford to buy a computer for myself.

We ate our last takeaway curry together, and when I came back from clearing the table Pete was sitting on the sofa in front of his DVD of *Dawn of the Dead*, and flicking through a pile of unopened post.

I sat down next to him and said, 'Looking for anything in particular?'

'You could bin most of it, I reckon,' Pete said. 'Load of junk. But this looks like it might be important.'

He passed me a large creamy envelope, addressed by hand.

'Another wedding, is it?' he asked.

'No, a reunion.'

'What, a school reunion?'

'No, college.'

I'd emailed St Bart's with my address the night we came back from Tippy's wedding, but by the time my invitation to the gaudy arrived doubt had set in. I was breaking up with my boyfriend; surely I couldn't be in that much of a hurry to put myself in a position to meet up with another ex? It wasn't exactly respectful . . . what if it was all just some kind of sad rebound fantasy?

'Really? You're not going to go, are you?' Pete said.

'I'm thinking about it. Why shouldn't I?'

'Well . . . you've never mentioned any friends from there. You never even wanted to talk about it. I mean, I have actually seen you wince when somebody asked you about it.'

'That is not true,' I said; then, 'OK, it has been a bit of an uncomfortable subject. I did have friends there, good friends, or so I thought, but then . . . it all kind of went wrong.'

'Oh.' Pete shrugged. 'Well, I can see why you cut your losses, then. So why go back now? Don't take this the wrong way, but you always run a mile from a potential row, given half a chance.'

I looked away, towards the bay window, the reason I'd wanted to live here. There was no blind, so it was never covered, and the scattered lights shrinking and receding towards the horizon gave the room a sense of depth, and of being a vantage point.

Without it, the flat would have felt far more claustrophobic. Probably we wouldn't have lasted even as long as we had.

'I guess I want to see the old place again,' I said, turning back towards Pete.

'Fair enough,' he said, and put the heap of junk mail down on the sofa between us.

'Also, I want to see my friends again. Despite everything that happened, for a time they were the best friends I ever had.'

But Pete was engrossed in the film, and gave no sign of having heard.

On the TV screen, the living had barricaded themselves into a shopping centre, but they were far from safe. Shadowy hands rattled against panes of dark glass. The undead were coming.

I tore the envelope open and drew out the smooth white card, printed with silver lettering, and the accompanying letter giving details about the evening, setting out the cost of attendance, and asking questions: could I name three people I would like to sit near to, was I vegetarian, did I want accommodation in college for the night?

Well, did I? Would I even be able to sleep? If I had nightmares about St Bart's when I was away from home, what would I dream of when I was back there for real?

But, damn it, what could possibly happen that was worse than what already had?

There was a fee for attending. It wasn't too steep, though. I got up to fetch my chequebook, and left Pete entranced by the spectacle of fear finally being faced.

4

'Open the box'

Saturday night was hotting up. To start with, the bus from the station trundled towards the centre of Oxford past scenery that could have belonged to any British city: an Irish theme pub and a comedy venue and Lebanese and Chinese and Japanese restaurants, and the nightclub that I had gone to just once, in my very first week in college. Even at this early hour of the evening there was a queue building up outside: girls with bare legs despite the cold and huddles of boys waiting to impress them, attended by bored policemen in yellow high-vis jackets.

At Carfax crossroads I caught a glimpse of the main shopping street, all lit up with Christmas lights – it had been pedestrianized since my time – and then we were moving on towards St Bart's, in the old medieval heart of the city, and I could feel myself slipping back into the past. Not just my own past, but a collective history, shared by the people I had known here and everyone else who had come to see the place for themselves, whether they were here for a day or for years.

I got off at the bus stop opposite the college: the exact spot where I'd had a chance to avert the oncoming catastrophe, and had let it slip through my fingers. I had been too late then, but only by minutes; I was more than seventeen years too late now, and the midsummer evening of the ball, the last night I had spent in Oxford, was long gone.

As I made my way across the High Street I told myself that it would be fine once I was safely in and had taken my seat in the hall for dinner. Pleasantries, do-you-remembers, how-are-yous: that was all that would be called for. It was a formal occasion, and there was nothing to worry about, because what could possibly go wrong?

The doors were shut across the arch of the main entrance, as if barring access to a castle inhabited by a particularly sought-after princess, or defending the lair of an ogre and his treasure. I pushed at the smaller, man-sized entrance cut into the fortified wood; it gave way, and I stepped into the short passageway that opened out on to the main quad.

A square of dark grass stretched out in front of me, surrounded on all sides by old pale stone walls, three storeys high, with crenellated parapets and windows looking down: the castle's keep, the inner sanctuary. *It hadn't changed.* Of course it hadn't. Why would it? It looked much the same to me now as it would have done to a monk in the Middle Ages, a cavalier, a top-hatted Victorian dandy fresh from his grand tour of Europe, a Bright Young Thing; and to Clarissa's son, too, just a month or so before.

That was the point of it: it was there for the record. It was a repository of memories, a golden, ghostly half-way house where newcomers could delve into what their predecessors had learned and left behind.

I turned right, into the bright space of the porters' lodge, where a portly uniformed man was sitting behind a glass window, watching the grey-and-white footage from the CCTV cameras. He turned to greet me and said, 'It's Jones, isn't it? Anna Jones?'

'How did you know?' I said. I didn't recognize him, not in the slightest. He was heavy-jowled and grey-haired; although he was being affable now, I imagined he could probably do a fearsome job of breaking up a student party.

He nodded towards the big framed photograph on the desk in front of him. I'd once had a copy of the same picture, but had got rid of it. It showed the whole of my year group on the day we'd matriculated, and been formally admitted to the university as freshers.

'Aide-memoire,' he said. 'Also, I never forget a face. We know who our people are. Welcome back.'

He gave me a key and told me where I was going to sleep that night, and I thanked him and turned away on to the path around the perimeter of the quad. I reached the archway in the far left-hand corner – still, as I remembered it, festooned with Virginia creeper – and went through into a smaller quad, edged on one side by metal railings that fenced off a garden students were not permitted to use. I passed through another arch in an old stone wall and crossed the familiar cobbled lane. I had expected this part to be hard, but actually, it was easy; it all seemed perfectly safe, even welcoming. And there it was, the 1960s block I'd lived in as a fresher, all boxy glass windows and concrete and echoing hollow stairs.

I'd been on the first floor then, but which staircase? I couldn't be sure. There was no one else around; I was running late, they'd all be at the drinks reception already. I made my way to the room I'd been allocated and let myself in.

In all its essentials it was exactly the same as the room I remembered: the desk, the shelf, the pair of chairs, the alcove with its single bed next to the wardrobe unit with the basin and mirror. It was even painted the same shade of muted orange, though it must have been redecorated several times since I'd been resident somewhere up or down the stairs, and along the hall.

I dumped my overnight bag, shed my coat, and checked on my reflection. I had my black dress on, my hair was up, and although I didn't bother much with make-up these days, I was wearing red lipstick. In the dim light from the overhead bulb, my face was pale and shadowy, and my lips and hair and eyes were dark and shining.

'Time to go,' I told myself.

I slipped the key into my clutch, let the door shut behind me and returned the way I'd come.

It was going to be a frosty night, but I didn't feel the cold as I made my way back to the main quad and the archway that led to the hall and the upstairs room where drinks were being served. I felt as light as a feather, or a ghost, and as if I was being drawn effortlessly on and along the corridor and up the spiral stairs.

It was easy to tell which was the right door; I could hear the hubbub already. I went on through, and found myself standing on the edge of a crowd of vivid strangers. They were laughing, gossiping, embracing, delivering anecdotes, the men all in dark suits and bow ties, the women in lace and silk and velvet dresses.

And yet, they weren't strangers at all . . . everywhere I glanced, I recognized someone. Twenty years had changed and disguised them all, and yet their younger selves became more clearly visible the longer I looked.

There was Violet Tranter, one-time women's officer, wearing her signature shade of purple; Mark Flask, who had once snogged Violet in the bar without caring who saw, and was now politely exchanging news with her; ladylike Sophie Adamson, who had briefly gone out with Barnaby, slim and pretty in rose-pink silk; Inga, my blonde former neighbour with the vigorous sex life, chatting charmingly to Jason, the bashful internet millionaire.

Wherever Jason was, Meg was likely to be as far away as possible. There was a waitress standing just inside the door with a tray of glasses of champagne; I took one and was about to slip into the throng when I heard someone next to me say, 'Hello, Anna.'

I turned and saw Victor.

He was watching me carefully, and not smiling. He didn't look pleased to see me, exactly, but he didn't look hostile or embarrassed either. He looked . . . serious.

But, more than that: interested. As if I might have something to say that he would want to know: some item of news, a fresh insight, an old secret. As if I belonged to a story he'd put to one side long ago, but still remembered on occasion, and hoped to hear the end of.

I managed to say, 'Hello, Victor.'

A waitress approached us with a bottle of champagne and topped up Victor's glass. As she moved on he held it up to me for a moment, then brought it to his lips and drank.

What was he thinking? *Shame how everything turned out? If only we'd handled things differently?* Or maybe, *Pity we can't all be here tonight, here's to the one who's missing?*

'Thank you for giving me Meg's email address,' I said. 'I met up with her back in the summer.'

'Yes,' Victor said, 'I heard.'

'We've tried to get together a couple of times since, but her kids keep getting ill. It seems like she's had a rough time of it. I was sorry to hear about her and Jason.'

'He's here, you know. I don't think they've actually spoken to each other yet. Still, I think Meg will be OK. She seems very calm about it all.'

I wondered if Meg had told him about me and Pete, and Pete vomiting over my mother's oyster-coloured silk shoes at Tippy's wedding.

'I should go and look for her, say hello,' I said, but made no attempt to move.

'It's good to see you again,' Victor said. 'I'm glad you decided to come, in the end.'

Our eyes met, and I realized how close together we were standing. We weren't touching, but it almost felt as if we were. My heart rate speeded up a notch.

'I'm glad too,' I said.

A bell rang. I was reminded of the people talking all around us, even as they hushed to hear the announcement. It was time to go in to dinner.

Victor gave his head a little shake, as if trying to wake up. He said, 'You just made it in time. Should we go down?'

I nodded, and we turned to join the others filing through the door and down the stairs into the hall.

We must have been slow off the mark, because even though we were standing close to the exit, we ended up in a queue, and were pressed together by the others crowding around us. I caught snatches of other conversations: Leila Vetch describing her attempt to keep hens in her back garden; Sophie Adamson telling someone about the entrance exam for her son's prep school; and Tim Rosewell, the physicist, explaining, not for the first time, about the philosophical experiment involving Shrödinger's cat.

When we reached the hall people were already taking their places at the long lines of heavy tables and benches in front of us. Apart from the shining silverware and crystal, everything was dark old wood: the parquet floor, the panelled walls, the vaulted ceiling that rose high above us, as if we were in a cathedral. A scholarly kind of cathedral, though: the clusters of candles lined up down the middle of the tables reminded me of study lamps on banks of reading desks in a library.

As we studied the seating plan, which was pinned up on a board displayed just inside the entrance, Violet drew level with me and said, 'Anna, good heavens, is that really you?'

We had been friendly in our first term, but after that we'd both taken to spending time with other companions, though we had never expressly fallen out. Always noted for her impressive bosom, she'd become softly, voluminously fat, and the dress she'd chosen was drapey and swathing, rather than the snug, poured-in style she would have gone for in the old days. The effect could have been maternal, but somehow wasn't; her eyes were too sharp.

'It's good to see you, Violet,' I said. 'How are you?'

'Oh, I'm fine, thank you, yes, and delighted to be back here, of course. My goodness. Don't you look well! I don't think I've seen you since we left.'

'No, this is the first time I've been back.'

'So where are you?' Violet asked, turning her attention to the seating plan. It alternated men and women. I was between Tim Rosewell and Mark Flask, and diagonally opposite Meg.

'That's me,' I said, pointing.

'Ah, we're nowhere near each other. Are you staying tonight?'

I nodded, and Violet said, 'Excellent, let's have a good old catch-up later,' and hurried off.

Victor had already gone. As I went to sit down I spotted him on the opposite side of the room, well out of reach. I told myself I shouldn't be surprised, or disappointed, that he was nowhere near. I'd been asked to name three preferences; I'd played it safe, and I'd got exactly what I'd requested.

Meg gave me a little wave and held up her evening bag and pointed at it, and then at me, as if to say, 'I've got something for you.' Then everybody around me started getting to their feet, including Meg, who put down her bag and demurely clasped her hands together and closed her eyes.

This was how these formal meals always started, with a Latin grace read by the Master of the college, a dignitary whose portrait would, in time, join the gallery of the great and good looking down at us from the walls. Next to me, Mark, the teacher, was looking respectfully down, while Tim, the physicist, was staring moodily into the middle distance, as if contemplating the inevitable absurdity of human beliefs in the face of an infinitely mysterious universe.

Then there was a slight but general stir, as if the focus of attention in the room had shifted. Meg kept her eyes discreetly shut, but both Mark and Tim turned to look, and I did too.

It was Clarissa, making an entrance, as she always had, with the confidence that comes from not caring if you're interrupting anything, blended with a hint of defensive irritation, as if she both fully expected to be stared at and found it tiresome.

She had gone blonde, and was wearing a strappy gold dress that exposed her back and arms; her outfit might have been purposefully designed to encourage you to wonder what she would look like without it. Her skin had an unnaturally perfect sheen of health, as if she'd been grown in a vat, and had never been exposed to ordinary, dulling wear and tear. And she was tiny – thinner, if anything, than she had been twenty years ago – though she was also taller than I had ever seen her, thanks to a pair of impossibly high-heeled shoes.

The Master, who was still reading the grace, hesitated for a moment, and then ploughed doughtily on as Clarissa teetered across the hall towards Victor, and out of my line of sight.

Meg had become restive; one of her eyes opened in spite of herself, and she forced it shut again. The minute grace was over she had a good long look over her shoulder. Then she composed herself, adopted a sprightly smile, and started chatting to Damon Adkin, a still-muscly ex-rower who now did something in the City.

I waited till she was too deep into conversation to notice, and craned my neck to see what exactly it was that had bothered her.

There was Clarissa's bare, perfect back, Victor to one side of her, and on the other . . . Jason, Meg's multi-millionaire ex. On the far side of the table I could just make out the straw-blond shock of Barnaby's hair.

Presumably Clarissa had expressed her three preferences too, and Meg had not been one of them.

Mark Flask ate the fish mousse starter but left the garnish, and so I did the same. We made small talk about the school where he worked and my own brief experience of teaching, and in due course he moved on to Maria, his other neighbour, a winsome Greek-Cypriot flautist whom he had once been rumoured to be besotted by, but had never actually dated.

On my other side, Tim Rosewell was discussing the potential power of the Large Hadron Collider to destroy the entire universe. I slipped out to find the nearest ladies', and one of the waitresses directed me to the washroom next to the hall, which was barred to students but was available to us now.

It was grander and roomier than the usual college facilities, lit by sconces set in the flock-wallpapered walls, and furnished with a small chaise-longue upholstered in gold. There, standing in front of one of the basins, was Clarissa, smoking a cigarette and watching herself in the mirror.

'I have a feeling that's not allowed in here,' I said.

Clarissa took another drag and exhaled thoughtfully.

'But it's freezing outside,' she said. 'Sure you don't want one?'

I shook my head. She put hers out and tossed the stub into the bin underneath the basin.

'There. Better now?' she said.

'You didn't have to do that on my account.'

'You never used to be so disapproving. I seem to remember you were rather naughty yourself, once upon a time.'

She opened her handbag, took out a jewelled powder compact and started to dab at her nose.

'I expect you've heard that I'm about to get divorced again,' she said.

'I'm sorry to hear that. I didn't know.'

She closed the compact with a snap and dropped it

back into her bag. 'I haven't exactly had much luck in love, have I? You probably think that serves me right.'

'No, I don't.'

'Well, you should.'

And then she was gone, leaving behind only a lingering smell of cigarette smoke, and a trace of perfume that smelt of jasmine in the summer dark, and reminded me of that other evening, the night of the ball, when the heat had lingered on long after the sun had gone.

Back at the table I found that the main course had arrived: meat and two veg, nothing to challenge my hazy grasp of dining etiquette, which, in the old days, I would already have been too tipsy to worry about. Mark was listening reverently to whatever his old crush was saying, and Tim had run out of chat about the Large Hadron Collider and was gazing rather sadly at his empty wine glass.

I told him I had overheard him talking about Schrödinger's cat earlier, and it had taken me right back to being stoned in somebody's room late at night, and not having a clue what he was on about. Like a football fan faced with someone who had admitted complete ignorance of the offside rule, he proceeded to attempt to explain.

'Here's what it boils down to,' he said. 'If the cat is in the box, how can you tell if it's dead or alive? You can't. Unless you open the box. But what if the act of opening the box changes what there is to find?'

I reached for the nearest bottle of wine and topped up both our glasses.

'If the cat's dead,' I said, 'it doesn't make a blind bit of difference, at least not from the cat's point of view.'

'Well, no,' Tim agreed gravely. 'But as a cat lover, I would always advocate opening the box. Just in case.'

By the time we got to coffee we had covered black holes, the Big Bang and the nature of anti-matter, while Mark's conversation with Maria had become increasingly intimate and intense. As the meal drew to its close I noticed that Meg had joined the cluster of fans who had gathered around Clarissa; clearly they had all now drunk enough to abandon any pretence of indifference to the one bona fide A-lister in the room. I couldn't see Victor or Barnaby.

At Tim's suggestion he and I headed out of the hall together, along the corridor and back out into the main quad, and down the stone steps that led into the college bar, which was housed in a vaulted cellar.

Just one drink . . . then I could go back to my room. And in the morning I could slip away. There was no real need to stay for breakfast.

We went over to join the queue at the bar, and then Maria came down the steps, apparently unaccompanied by Mark, and Tim went over to say hello to her. She gave him a grateful smile and reached forward to adjust his bow tie, and I wondered if he was the one she'd really liked all along.

As I stepped away from the bar with my bottle of beer Violet Tranter rounded on me and said, 'Anna, you lady of mystery, what have you been up to all these years?'

She swiftly established that I was boyfriendless, childless, and without permanent employment. Meanwhile, I learned that she had become a child psychologist, was married to an engineer who specialized in sausage casings, and lived with him and their three sons – aged six, four and three – in an eighteenth-century cottage with slight damp issues.

'But it must be such fun, still being young, free and single,' Violet commented. 'You can please yourself, can't you? No responsibilities, no ties, you can jet off whenever and wherever you like. So do you see much of Clarissa these days?'

'No. Not in the flesh, anyway.'

Violet lowered her voice and leaned in. 'She's had some work done, don't you think?' she said. 'If I hadn't known who it was, I wouldn't have recognized her, and not just because she's gone blonde. Still, it can't be easy to resist the pressure. The film industry is so desperately chauvinist.' She shook her head, and I recalled that back in our student days her feminist beliefs had earned her the nickname of Violent Ranter.

'She's not been having the best of times, poor thing, has she?' Violet went on. 'What with her husband going off with that girl who used to do the underwear ads. Not to mention the spell in rehab. I hear she's thinking about jacking it all in and coming back to Blighty, maybe doing some kind of further degree.'

Leila Vetch joined us, and Sophie Adamson too, and they started talking about which of Clarissa's films they'd seen. I spotted Meg coming down into the bar, made my excuses and picked my way through the crush to greet her.

'Are you all right?' I asked, but it was obvious that she wasn't.

'Bloody Jason,' she hissed. 'First he's all over Clarissa, and then he moves on to Magdalena Dale!'

Magdalena had been one of the acknowledged beauties of our year, second only to Clarissa in popular lust, a full-lipped, smooth-faced Latin sexpot with a Colombian model mother and a Yorkshire loo-roll magnate for a father. Keith had once told me she was the ideal woman, and plenty of others had felt the same way.

'I'm sure it's not whatever it looked like,' I said, but Meg was not to be consoled.

'What it looked like was Jason rubbing my nose in it,' she said. 'I mean, I always knew he had a soft spot for Clarissa, what man wouldn't? But he doesn't have to make it so bloody obvious. And as for Magdalena . . . She wouldn't have gone anywhere near him in the old days. Before he made his money.'

'Let me get you a drink,' I said, but then Magdalena Dale came down into the bar with Jason just behind her, and Meg fell silent.

Magdalena turned and waited for Jason to reach the end of the stairs, and then they went together to the bar. Jason said something to her and she laughed, and then he glanced, not quite casually, over to where Meg and I were standing to see if she had noticed.

Meg said, 'Did you see that? Bastard. He did that deliberately. He's trying to make me jealous.'

Then Jason reached out and casually rested his hand on Magdalena's waist, as if propelling her towards some destination that he had in mind but she was still oblivious to. Meg's mouth dropped open. Then she turned and bolted up the stairs and out of the bar.

There was a slight hush, and I realized that everyone around me had noticed what had just happened, and knew why. As I hurried up the stairs they returned to their conversations, as if satisfied that Meg was being taken care of. But when I emerged on to the main quad I found it dark and deserted; she was nowhere to be seen.

Acting on instinct, without really stopping to think, I turned back into the passageway that led to the hall and pushed open the door to the college chapel.

For a moment I was dazzled – the lights were all on, and it was surprisingly bright, compared to the subterranean gloom of the beer cellar. Then I saw that she was sitting in the front pew to my right, by the black-and-white-tiled central aisle that ran from the entrance to the altar. She was bent over as if her insides hurt, and she was crying.

I sat down next to her and passed her a tissue from my bag, and she straightened up and blew her nose.

'I feel so stupid,' she said after a while. 'I thought I could handle this. Now I see I can't.'

'You are handling it,' I said.

'No I'm not. I'm sobbing in the college chapel and wondering if God is punishing me for having three children out of wedlock. That's not handling. That's falling apart.'

'What happens in private doesn't matter,' I said. 'Nobody can see you. Nobody will know.'

'It does matter, because Jason knows. You saw him. He did it quite deliberately. He was goading me. I suppose it's definitive proof, if any were needed, that he's decided he can do better than me. He's ready to trade up.'

'Why would he try to provoke you if he didn't still have feelings for you?'

'Because he can't bear to lose, and all he wants now is to win. It's about power, pure and simple. It's got nothing to do with love. Though I wouldn't put it past him to try and get back into bed with me at some point. I'm sure there's nothing Jason would find more satisfying than a revenge fuck.'

'Why would Jason want revenge? Surely, if anyone's going to be trying to get their own back, it would be you.'

'Because I slept with someone else first,' Meg said. 'It was a one-night stand. That's all it was. My tennis coach. I was such a fool. I was flattered, I couldn't believe someone that young and fit could find me attractive . . . I could have carried it on, but I didn't. I stopped the lessons straight away. Jason had no idea. He teased me about it. Went on about my fitness fads and how I kept chopping and changing. When he found out he had our court taken up, and then he had an affair with his secretary, and after that he was on a roll. If only I hadn't told him. I kept it to myself for ages. But then I was pregnant, and full of hormones, and I wasn't thinking straight. I just felt so guilty, and so ashamed, I couldn't bear to keep it to myself any longer.'

'He must feel guilty too,' I said. 'And I'm sure he still cares for you, however muddled it all is.'

She reached out and squeezed my hand. 'You know, when we left, I honestly thought I'd never hear from you again. I rang your house so many times it was embarrassing.'

'I felt guilty,' I said. 'That makes people do strange things.'

She withdrew, opened up her handbag and brought out a brown A5 envelope.

'Before I forget,' she said, 'I brought this for you.'

It wasn't sealed. I opened it and peered inside. She'd made copies of the two photographs of Keith I'd seen in her album on the day she'd invited me into her house: Keith in front of the Museum of Natural History, frowning, and then holding the brown paper bag up in front of his face.

'Now you see him, now you don't,' I said. 'Thank you.'

'I miss him too,' she told me.

'What will you do now?' I asked her. My eyes were hurting and I had to blink hard to keep them from oozing tears.

'I'll stay here for a while, I think. And then I'm going to drive home, and when I get there I'm going to have a very stiff drink.'

'I should probably call it a night too,' I said.

I could have bailed out then and there and asked her for a lift back, but that didn't even occur to me. I didn't head towards my room, either. Instead I went back down to the beer cellar.

And as I reached the bottom of the steps I saw,

standing right in front of me, the one person I really didn't want to talk to. 'Anna,' he said, and loomed forward, as if half expecting to kiss me.

'Excuse me,' I said, and made to go round him.

He grabbed my arm – I could smell the drink on his breath – and said:

'That's not very friendly, is it? I mean, come on. I saw you chatting away to Victor earlier, so why not me?'

'Let me go,' I said, and he did, but he was still blocking my way.

'If you're looking for Victor, I think he was last seen escorting Clarissa to her limo,' he said.

'Don't ever touch me again,' I hissed at him. 'Don't even come near me.'

As I turned away he said, 'For God's sake, Anna, why can't we just let bygones be bygones? I'm trying to talk to you here.'

He was pleading as well as angry, and – yes – a little afraid. *Tell me it's OK, that you're OK and I'm OK and it was OK and nothing really happened, go on, exonerate me, or at least pretend . . .*

'I have nothing to say to you,' I told him, and retreated back up the stairs.

Main Quad was dark, icy cold and quiet as a sanctuary. I was just about to disappear in the direction of my room when I heard Victor calling out my name.

Part of me wanted to keep going, but I forced myself to stop. As he caught up with me I realized I was trembling. I hoped he wouldn't be able to see.

'Are you turning in already?' he said.

'Yeah, I'm pretty tired.'

'You couldn't be persuaded to go for one last drink, for old times' sake?'

'I've already been. Meg's decided to go home. She was upset with Jason.'

'I'm not surprised,' Victor said.

'Has Clarissa gone?'

'Yes – she has an early start. You've just been in the bar, then? Is Barnaby down there?'

'Yes, I think so. It's pretty packed. You should go mingle.'

He hesitated. 'Perhaps I'll see you in the morning,' he said finally.

'Perhaps,' I said. 'Goodnight, Victor.'

I walked away through the arch into the next quad, leaving him behind, and did not allow myself to look back.

When I reached my room I didn't hurry to get ready for bed; I assumed sleep would take a while to come. As I laid my head on the pillow and closed my eyes my heart was still beating hard and fast, and I thought I would be lying awake for hours.

But then I found myself going down into a cellar, not unlike the one that housed St Bart's college bar, though this wasn't a space with a social function. It was an archive.

I was not alone. I had a companion: tall, thin, tense, cloaked. Keith had turned up to serve as my guide.

'You took your time,' he observed. 'You'll find all the things you've lost down here. It's where they end up.'

And sure enough, there, hanging up on a rack, was

the costume I'd put together for that first-term trip to see *The Rocky Horror Show*; my black academic gown; and, just visible beyond the other clothes, the green dress I'd worn to St Bart's college ball on my twenty-first birthday.

'There are a couple of other rooms,' Keith said, 'if you want to explore.'

'I don't know,' I said. It looked dark, and I wasn't sure I fancied it; it seemed sensible to stay close to the stair-well.

'You never know what you might find,' he said, holding out a book in a green hardback cover. I took it and opened it, but all the pages were blank.

'This isn't much good, is it?' I said. 'Look, it must be damp down here, it's got mildew on it.'

'That happens when things get neglected,' Keith said.

I noticed that his cape smelled of dirty river water, and he turned his face so I could see the side of it that was livid with mould.

'I wish I'd never let you go,' I said.

'I know,' he said, and the look in his good eye was infinitely regretful.

'I miss you,' I told him.

'Course you do,' he said. 'And so you should. Watch your step on the return journey, won't you? It can be slippery, and we wouldn't want you to fall.'

He went off whistling into the gloom. I found myself alone and empty-handed, and there was nothing for it but to retrace my steps, and begin to climb back up to the light.

Part Two

1991–2

The Foothills

She said, 'Hello, Mr D. Do I look familiar to you?'
'All young people make the mistake of thinking they're untouchable,' he said. 'I was like that, once. So maybe you remind me of me.'

From *The End of Mr D.*, by Benjamin Dock (1978)

Part Two

1991–2

The Foothills

5

'Have you left anyone back home?'

1991

As we reached the ring road Oxford came into view, a cluster of white towers rising above the green swell of trees. It looked like a ghost citadel, or a mirage, an oasis that would always keep its distance, no matter how close you approached.

The last time I'd been to the city had been for my interview at St Bart's with Dr Kaspar, the English tutor. An alarming presence in a jewel-coloured silk jacket, she had regarded me all the while with the calculating detachment of a racehorse trainer assessing a potentially promising foal. Oxford then had seemed big, and cold, and white, and daunting, a fantastical assembly of great halls and secret corners and traps for the unwary. Now it looked soft and promising and unreal, a place you might read or dream about.

'Thank God, we're nearly there,' said Mum, who was driving.

'Yeah, not long now,' I said.

Usually Gareth took the wheel on long journeys, but today he was taking Tippy to play in a hockey match, and so it was just me and Mum, the way it had been in the beginning, before I found Gareth – who had been her boss before I came along – sleeping in her bed one morning, and was shooed out of her room.

When they married I changed my name, and became Anna Jones instead of Anna Sands; but I never called Gareth Dad. Mum made it clear to me that I didn't have to, but I suspected later on that he would have loved it if I had. I felt guilty for not giving him what he wanted, but by then it was too late, and anyway, Tippy had come along, and 'Dad' was her very first word.

Gareth taught Mum to drive and bought her a car, but all these years later, Mum was still a nervous driver and usually stuck to local roads. I hadn't realized quite how anxious she was about the hour-long journey to Oxford until we set off.

We'd barely spoken on the way; she was sitting so rigidly, and clutching the wheel so doggedly, and concentrating so hard on the road, that my own shoulders and back ached in sympathy. Having just failed my test, I was in no position to take over. I had the road map open on my lap, and had been guilty of a couple of misdirections, which made me feel even worse.

As soon as we descended towards the city's outskirts we ran into traffic. Half an hour later the distant white towers had turned into Victorian terraces, intermittently decorated with B & B signs, and we were creeping forward in a long line of cars and buses while cyclists serenely overtook us.

There were students all around us: girls with long skirts and hair wobbling along on their bikes, determined, pained-looking boys jogging in tight tracksuits, and the occasional couple strolling along arm in arm as if the whole place, if not the world, belonged to them.

As we finally got past the tiny roundabout we had been queuing for and reached the High Street, I folded up the map and said, 'I hope it'll be easier on the way back.'

Mum didn't reply. She was gripping the steering wheel as if both our lives depended on it.

'OK, slow down, St Bart's is coming up,' I said. 'That's the turning, on the left.'

We ventured under the narrow archway that preceded the main gates, and bumped over cobbles past a stretch of gabled Georgian housing fronted by a small lawn. To the right was an old stone wall overhung by wisteria; on the left was a boxy concrete building with big square windows, and, underneath it, four parking bays, the first three of which were occupied by a muddy Land-Rover, a black Mercedes with tinted windows, and a grimy, dented Mini.

Mum parked, drew a deep breath, turned to me, and said, 'Ready?'

'Yeah, I guess so. I mean, as much I can be.'

'You will phone, won't you? Let me know how you're getting on.'

'I'll phone,' I promised.

A girl with a mass of red curly hair got out of the Mini and set off across the cobbles. She looked as if she knew exactly what she was doing, and I immediately wanted to follow her.

'I guess I'd better go and let them know I'm here,' I told Mum.

'Want me to come with you?'

'No, no, don't worry,' I said. 'You sit tight. I'll be back in a mo.'

I got out of the car and left her gazing fretfully at the fine drizzle falling on the windscreen. I had a pretty shrewd idea what was going through her head: visions of me stumbling into all kinds of disasters – unwanted pregnancy, or drugs, or getting in with a bad crowd.

I hurried the way the girl with the red hair had gone, through the archway in the old stone wall, past a railing covered with honeysuckle and tumbling fronds of jasmine. The main quad was through yet another archway, hung with tendrils of bright green Virginia creeper. And there was the redhead, reading something written on a blackboard propped up on the pathway.

She was wearing army boots and a green serge army greatcoat; she wasn't tall, and without the hair, the clothes would have seemed too big for her. She stepped forward and disappeared, and I came to a halt at the spot where she had vanished.

The blackboard said 'Freshers here!' in big, forceful, slapdash letters. A dagger-like arrow pointed towards a black door, which was slightly ajar. Beyond it was a gloomy, wood-panelled room, and the girl with red hair, standing with her back to me.

Facing both of us were two boys, one big and hearty-looking and fair, the other long-faced and dark-haired and wry. The blond boy was standing in front of a long trestle table; the dark-haired boy was seated behind it.

'Welcome to St Bartholomew's. Pleased to meet you, Clarissa,' the blond boy was saying, holding out his hand for the redhead to shake. He didn't smile; he was frowning slightly, as if she was an important puzzle he was required to solve.

For a moment I wondered if he was some kind of college official – he was wearing a blazer and cords, and seemed more formal than you would expect a student to be, even a little pompous. But then he went on, 'I'm Barnaby Stour, Victor's room-mate. I lucked out and came top of the ballot, so we ended up with the very best second-year rooms in college. You must come round and check them out.'

'I'm sure I will,' Clarissa said.

Close up, she was as pretty as a china doll, made up and accessorized as a New Age festival-goer. Her green eyes were heavily rimmed with kohl, and her pert little nose was decorated with a small silver stud.

She went over to Victor and picked up the book lying on the table in front of him, examined the cover, and flicked through a couple of pages.

'Are you studying this?' she asked.

'I will be,' Victor said. 'I was thinking I'd like to direct it sometime.'

'Hah! I suppose you'll want Clarissa in it,' Barnaby muttered.

'I wouldn't even if you did,' Clarissa said. 'I've had enough of all that kind of thing.'

'Clarissa was a bit of a star at school,' Victor commented.

'I can imagine,' Barnaby said. 'After all, you've got the pedigree, haven't you?'

'Maybe I do, but that doesn't mean I have to trade on it,' Clarissa said. 'Anyway, I think the world can do without another actress, don't you? I've decided I'm going to be a writer.'

'There are a fair few of those around, too,' I said, and for a moment they all stared at me.

Barnaby was the first to turn back to Clarissa. He appeared to have decided to treat my comment as an unwarranted interruption, but Victor smiled faintly and said, 'Touché.'

For a split second I thought Clarissa was offended. Then she smiled and shook out her hair – the scarf holding it back off her face was trimmed with tiny bells that chimed when she moved – and said, 'Well, I'm not scared of a bit of competition.'

She gave Victor his book back, and I said, 'What is it?'

'*The Changeling*,' Victor said, holding it up for me to see.

'It's a revenge tragedy, isn't it?' I said. 'The heroine ends up being seduced and corrupted, and turns into a murderess.'

'Hark at you,' Barnaby said. 'I'm guessing you're another English student. Well, don't be fooled by Mr Rose here.' He nodded towards Victor. 'Mostly, he doesn't do a scrap of work, he just runs about putting on plays, and once in a while he stays up all night in a great lather to write an eight-page essay. Not like us classicists, who actually have to put some effort in. Anyway, Clarissa, seeing as you two already know each other, Victor should show you to your room and get you settled in.' He said this with a look for Victor that I thought meant the exact opposite.

'Oh, Victor will keep, won't you, Victor?' Clarissa said. 'Why don't you take me, Barnaby?'

Barnaby gave her a little bow. 'I'd be delighted.'

'I wonder what my boyfriend is going to make of this place,' Clarissa commented airily, and Barnaby's face fell.

'I'm sure he'll find us all very welcoming,' he said coldly.

Victor suppressed a smile as he leaned forward to check the list lying on the table next to his book. He rummaged in a cardboard box of keys, took one out and passed it to Clarissa.

'Rhys House, staircase two, room three,' he said.

Barnaby escorted Clarissa out of the room. Victor turned to me and said, 'And you are?'

I told him my name, and he checked it off on the list and started hunting through the box for my key.

'You know Clarissa from school, then,' I said.

'I was in the year above her. But I know her family from way back. Before her mother made it as an actress she used to sing on cruise ships, and my dad was her accompanist.'

'Small world,' I said.

'Sometimes,' he agreed.

'Who is her mother, anyway?' I asked.

He said, 'Mandy Martin,' and my failure to place the name must have been obvious, because he went on, 'She's a sitcom actress, or she used to be. Quite well known. She was in something called *The Primrose Path*. It used to be on Saturday nights in the eighties.'

Now I remembered, but only just: the image that came to mind was of a dizzy comic blonde, pretty and pert, with a tautly trousered rear. I'd never really paid much attention to what was on the box; I'd always had my nose in a book.

'Is that what Barnaby meant about Clarissa's pedigree? I thought maybe she was some kind of aristocrat.'

'I suppose he did, in a way,' Victor said.

He got to his feet and held out my key, and I took it. Our fingers touched, though only for a moment. I wondered what it was like to be the one who knew where he was going, who was in a position to show someone else around.

'Come on,' he said, 'let's go find your room.'

We walked back across the main quad to the parking spaces in silence. It seemed an important moment, walking alongside this tall, courteous boy, heading towards my new room in this strange place where I was now to live. There was plenty I could have asked him, about life in college, the course, the tutors, but I was suddenly shy.

As we emerged on to the cobbled lane I spotted Barnaby and Clarissa heading towards the Georgian houses that Mum and I had driven past on our way in. They weren't all that far ahead; maybe Barnaby was walking extra slowly to spin out his chance to impress Clarissa.

We carried on towards the modern block just beyond the parked cars. As we skirted Clarissa's Mini I caught sight of Mum in the front seat of our estate car; she looked as if she'd been crying. I gave her a little wave, and shook my key and pointed upwards to indicate that I was going up to my room, and she gave me a wan smile in return.

'Was that your mother?' Victor asked, holding the door open for me.

'It was,' I told him. I passed through and he followed; the door shut behind him with a heavy clang.

As we began to ascend a flight of wooden stairs I said, 'My stepdad would have come, and my sister, but she has a hockey match, so that's where they are.'

God, how banal I sounded! How to make myself a bit more compelling? I didn't have a celebrity mother, I wasn't eccentric like Barnaby, and it had never occurred to me to put on a play, as Victor seemingly did all the time.

It was true that there was one mystery in my life: the space on my birth certificate that said 'Father unknown'. I had now seen it with my own eyes; I had asked Mum if I could when I was sorting out my paperwork to take to university – my national insurance number card, my first bank statements – and she had fished it out of the desk and allowed me to look it over before taking it back and filing it away.

'I'd better hold on to that, I think, you might lose it,' she had said. Her face had taken on a shuttered, go-no-further look, and I didn't have the heart to start asking questions she plainly wouldn't want to answer.

We came to another landing and he walked over to the alcove on the far side, nodded at the middle door of three, and said, 'This is you. Hanover Buildings, staircase two, room six.'

And there was my name, written in gold lettering by the door: *A. B. Jones*. Anna Beatrice Jones.

I'd been named Anna after my mother's mother, who had died the year before I was born, leaving Mum without any living family until I came along. I'd asked Mum once about Beatrice, and she'd said, with the special defensiveness that made it so hard to question her about anything, 'I just liked the name. Why, do you object to it?' I had instantly felt guilty, and assured her that I liked it very much.

Mum had Gareth now, and Tippy. It wasn't as if I was leaving her on her own.

'You'll be all right here,' Victor said. 'I had a room just upstairs last year. It can get a bit noisy, but it's pretty friendly. This is where they put all the freshers.'

'Apart from Clarissa.'

'Well, yes, there's always a bit of overspill.'

I put the key into the lock. It turned suddenly and I lurched forwards into the empty room.

Victor asked, 'Can I help you bring your stuff up?'

'Oh no, it's OK, I can manage, thanks.'

'Then I'll leave you to it,' he said. 'I'll see you around, no doubt.'

And with that he was off, his tread rattling and echoing on the wooden stairs.

I thought of him calling round on Clarissa later, maybe with Barnaby in tow, and as I made my way down to the car to get my stuff out of the boot, I tried to picture the person I might become if I could join them. At the very least, I would be a more vivid version of myself, and this would happen quite naturally, without effort; their self-belief would be contagious.

Mum got out of the car and said, 'Who was that boy who was with you?'

'Oh, just one of the second years. There are a couple of volunteers showing the freshers where to go. My room's really nice. Big, too.'

'Have you got a mirror in there?'

'Yeah, there's a mirror.'

'Full-length?'

'No, just a little one.'

'That's something, anyway,' Mum said. 'You won't want to be wandering round the corridors with sleep in your eyes.'

She glanced across at the Mercedes and the Land-Rover parked in the neighbouring spaces.

'After all, when it boils down to it, however clever people are meant to be, they do tend to judge by appearances,' she observed, and opened up the boot of the car.

She looked down at my possessions – the box of books I'd selected to highlight my literary tastes, the duvet, the kettle, the holdall full of sensible clothes – and folded her arms.

'You know what, Anna,' she said, 'part of me just wants to take you straight home again. But what can I do about it? You're eighteen years old.'

She pulled the holdall out and lugged it off in the direction of my new room.

That evening, viceroys and ministers and judges looked down from age-darkened portraits as I sat at one of the long tables in the hall at St Bart's and chewed my way through a jacket potato that was almost, but not entirely, cold.

I'd ended up sitting with a pack of other freshers, next to a PPE student called Violet, who was wearing a fluffy amethyst jumper. At least I wasn't having any problems remembering her name. On my other side was a slightly spotty fellow English student called Mark Flask, who was explaining the reasons behind his A-level choices when the table opposite us cleared and I caught sight of Victor, who was facing away from me on the other side of the room.

There was something very attractive about the upright way he was sitting, the squareness of his shoulders, the neat shape of his head and ears. I could imagine running my hand up the back of his neck and into his hair, how it would first resist but then yield like the pelt of an animal stroked the wrong way and then smoothed. It was lucky that I could watch him with impunity; the only way he could catch me would be to turn round and look straight back.

And then he did – perhaps spurred by the instinct that tells us when we are being observed, or maybe coincidentally. I immediately dropped my gaze to my plate.

'So then I got my four A grades, and I had English AS as well, and I decided to take a year out and reapply,'

Mark explained. I mumbled something in response, and he started talking about interrailing.

Victor was sitting next to Barnaby, deep in conversation. Clarissa approached them, carrying her tray, with two other diners following her: a tall, thin boy with lanky shoulder-length hair and skintight black trousers, and a rosy-cheeked, sweetly pretty girl with bright blond hair, teetering along on purple spike heels that gave her the look of a child playing dressing-up.

Clarissa put her tray down opposite Victor and Barnaby and gestured towards her companions as if introducing them. The skinny boy said something, and they all laughed uproariously.

'So where did you go to school?' Mark asked.

'Oh . . . nowhere you would have heard of. A girls' school in Reading, called the Evenlode.'

'All girls?'

'A-ha.'

'Even in the sixth form?'

'Mm, yes.'

'That must have been . . . rather boring,' Mark said. 'We had girls in the sixth form. It definitely perked things up a bit. I mean . . . suddenly there was something nice to look at. Not that I'm being chauvinist or anything,' he added hurriedly.

'I know. I expect we would have perked up too, if we'd had some boys around,' I said.

'Are you guys coming down to the bar later?' Violet asked, leaning across to address both of us.

'You up for it, Anna?' Mark asked. 'Get a few beers in? Start as we mean to go on?'

'Sure,' I said.

'Excellent. Let's all get down there for eight o'clock. Safety in numbers,' Violet said. 'I expect it'll be packed out with second years, all acting like they own the place.'

What on earth was going on at Clarissa's table? The blonde girl had started *singing*. Up and up the scale, impossibly, dizzyingly high . . . She hit a crazy top note without faltering and stopped in a sudden hush.

Clarissa said, 'It's a hit, ladies and gentlemen,' and began to clap, and the others around her began to applaud too.

Violet raised her eyebrows. 'I think there's a bit of *showing off* going on in here tonight,' she said. 'Mark, what's the name of the boy who's living next to you? Was it Tom? Tim? Something like that. The quiet one who's doing physics. Will you try and drag him down to the bar as well?'

'I'll try,' Mark said, without any great enthusiasm.

'That's the spirit,' Violet said.

I attempted another mouthful of lukewarm jacket potato into my mouth, and heard Clarissa calling out, 'Truth or dare! Who's next?'

Later that evening I made my way down to the beer cellar, along with Violet, Mark, Tim the physicist, a shy Greek-Cypriot girl called Maria who was studying music, and a rag-bag of other freshers. A group of older boys had stationed themselves at a table just inside the entrance, and I felt them sizing me up as I walked past.

We joined the tail end of the queue waiting to be

served. Looking round, I spotted Victor, with Clarissa next to him, standing by the pool table. There was something soft and remote about them, as if they were part of a tableau glimpsed through a window, subject to different and more forgiving lighting.

Victor offered Clarissa a cigarette; she took one, and so did he. He clicked open a lighter and held it out to her; she inclined her pursed lips towards the flame, then straightened up and exhaled, and flashed him a brilliant, unmissable grin.

The skinny boy and the blonde girl were nearby, but weren't paying Victor and Clarissa any particular attention. They were busy playing pool. The boy leaned forward to take a shot, and then stood up and shook the hair back from his face. Our eyes met. He didn't smile; his expression was distant, though certainly not hostile – if anything, it was nervous. He was the first to look away.

'Do you know that boy?' Violet said. 'That thin one who's all in black.'

'No, who is he?'

Violet sniffed. 'He looks a bit *druggy*, don't you think? I mean, enough people want to come here. The least we can do is take it seriously and not go mucking around with *illegal substances*. And you know any one of us could be thrown out *just like that*.' She clicked her fingers.

'I always wonder what people like him end up doing out in the real world,' Mark commented.

'Oh, I dare say he'll end up all nicely scrubbed up and in a suit, and carrying a briefcase to meetings,' Violet said. 'You see that blonde girl who's with him?

The sweet-looking one? You're not going to believe this, but she's actually engaged. Can you imagine that? At eighteen, when she's got a place here and the world is her oyster. Obviously it's not going to last.'

'Maybe she's in love,' I objected.

Violet made a small scoffing sound. 'There's love, and there's timing, isn't there? Her father's a vicar, which *may* be something to do with it. Meg's very nice, don't get me wrong – she's my next-door neighbour in Hanover Buildings. She's a chemist; seems a sensible sort, apart from the engagement. Shame she's been commandeered by that loud red-haired girl. Still, maybe it won't last. Did you make it to the freshers' tea?'

'No, I was too busy unpacking,' I said.

I had wanted to go; it had been mentioned in the advance information as an ideal first chance to meet fellow students. But Mum had insisted on helping me get settled, and then had not been in all that much of a rush to hit the road.

'You didn't miss much,' Violet said. 'It wasn't all that well organised; quite a long queue, and not nearly enough sandwiches. I went with Meg, and that other girl – Clarissa, I think it is – spotted the engagement ring and asked her about it. Next thing I knew they'd gone off together and Clarissa was introducing Meg to that boy in the black leather jacket. Heaven knows what Meg's fiancé is going to make of her new friends.'

As we moved away from the bar with our drinks Mark singled me out and started telling me about a girl he'd met while he was teaching abroad during his year out. He wasn't explicit about the nature of their relationship, but I got the impression he wanted me to think they had been lovers.

Then he said, 'So have you left anyone back home?' and the first person who came to mind was my mother.

'I haven't got a boyfriend, if that's what you mean,' I said.

'That's good, I think,' he said. 'No ties. You can really throw yourself into college life and all it has to offer.'

Barnaby walked past with a tray of drinks. When he reached the pool table Victor and Clarissa and the other two each took one. He said something to Clarissa, and she put her pint down and took Meg's pool cue and nodded as if to say, 'Do your worst.'

'Come on then, Keith,' Barnaby said carryingly to the skinny boy in black. 'Hand it over. Let me show you how it's done.'

Keith relinquished his cue and Barnaby readied himself for his first shot with an expression of slightly absurd seriousness, as if this was not a game at all but a test of his ability to impose his will on the world around him.

Mark glanced over his shoulder to see what I was looking at.

'Do you fancy a game later?' he asked.

'I don't know how to play.'

'I can teach you. It's easy. You'll get the hang of it soon enough.'

'I don't know. I'm not sure if I want to make a fool of myself in front of everybody.'

'Oh, I'm sure you wouldn't. And anyway, this is all about attempting new things, isn't it? Finding out what you like, what you don't like, what you're good at, what you're absolutely bloody terrible at and should never attempt again?'

Clarissa clapped, presumably in acknowledgement of Barnaby's prowess. The others were watching him too; only Victor looked unsurprised.

'I guess you're right,' I told Mark. 'It's a case of *carpe diem*, isn't it? If there was ever a time to try something out, it's now.'

Mark beamed at me. 'Attagirl,' he said. 'To new experiences,' and we chinked glasses.

'To new experiences,' I agreed.

Victor was saying something to Clarissa, and Keith was watching me again. A rogue boy, a bad boy, the sort my mother wouldn't want me to associate with . . . but look who he was friends with. He was standing right next to Victor, which was exactly where I wanted to be.

I angled my arm so that my glass was lifted towards him, dipped my head in acknowledgement, and did my best impression of Clarissa's dazzling smile.

6

'Fifth-week blues'

My social life over the first few weeks of term consisted mainly of group activities organized by Violet: a trip to a nightclub, a curry, a film. There was an awkward moment, during the second week, when Mark Flask told me he thought he was in love with me, but he seemed to get over his infatuation very quickly, and I suspected he'd simply transferred his affections to somebody else.

Even though we were studying the same subject, I had very little contact with Clarissa. I never saw her in the library, but knew from Mark, who had her as a tutorial partner, that her essays were always good. 'Of course they are,' he said bitterly. 'She has Victor's from last year, and all the questions are exactly the same. She just takes what she needs and roughs them up a bit.' She had apparently offered to lend Mark Victor's essays too, but he had declined.

Clarissa's willingness to purloin Victor's work shocked me a little initially, but not when I stopped to think about it. I had to admit, if Victor had offered me his essays, I wouldn't have turned him down. Though perhaps my reasons for wanting to have Victor's work to hand would have been slightly different to Clarissa's.

I did get the chance to study Clarissa at close quarters during our weekly Anglo-Saxon lessons, though I learned only that she was a prodigious doodler, and rarely spoke up if she didn't think there was anything to be gained from doing so. I always saw her after my weekly tutorial with Dr Kaspar, too. These sessions were held in Dr Kaspar's room off the main quad, and involved being subjected to an alarming interrogation designed to establish whether we had given due attention to everything on the reading list.

My tutorial partner was Leila Vetch, a very tall vegan who wore pink dungarees and was rumoured to write poetry about the moon; fortunately, she was also sharp-witted and co-operative, and we soon became adept at covering each others' backs. Clarissa and Mark had the slot before us. Mark tended to emerge first at the end of the allocated hour, red-faced and sweating, and would give me a signal to indicate just how bad it had been: a thumbs down, a pretend retch, a finger drawn across the throat. Then Clarissa would sail out, and Mark would thump down the stairs after her, and Leila and I would be in.

Once when I came down from my tutorial and said goodbye to Leila I saw Clarissa falling in with her friends, who were waiting for her just outside the porters' lodge. I noticed Victor first, but they were all there: broad-shouldered Barnaby in a tweed jacket and a fedora; Meg, wearing a sensible navy-blue coat and high-heeled boots covered with buckles, which would not have looked out of place on a bondage queen; and Keith, dressed as ever in black.

As I walked round them Clarissa launched into an uncannily accurate impression of Dr Kaspar, complete with clipped voice and eaglish stare.

'And then she said: "That is a most unusual interpretation."' The pause lengthened almost to breaking point. '"You *almost* had me convinced."'

I turned away into the room of pigeonholes for student post, opposite the entrance to the porters' lodge, and found I had a phone message from my mother: *Please ring re Saturday to confirm arrangements.*

When I came out Clarissa and the others were still there, and Clarissa was saying, 'I could hardly tell her I hadn't actually read *Mill on the Floss* because I'd spent the weekend in London with my boyfriend. But we did have a rather pointed discussion about love and duty. I think Dr Kaspar may have telepathic powers.'

As I passed them again Victor didn't take his eyes off Clarissa. But Keith did, and the look he gave me was questioning, maybe even inviting. I smiled at him, but hurried on towards the corner of the quad that led to the computer room and, tucked away down the same corridor, the cubby-hole with the payphones.

I knew that Mum would be waiting to hear from me, just as I knew that she had been worrying about me, and, when we met, would be checking anxiously for warning signs that I was heading for trouble of one kind or another: academic trouble, drugs trouble, money trouble – and boy trouble most of all.

I hoped to be able to reassure her; I'd had no romantic encounters whatsoever, not so much as a drunken snog. I felt different – hardier, and more sure of myself – but this hadn't manifested itself in any unusual, or even conspicuous, patterns of behaviour. It was as if I had grown new roots, but there were no signs as yet of green shoots above ground, and no obvious promise that my transplantation was about to bear fruit.

When Saturday came my family arrived half an hour early; I'd only just finished drying my hair. Gareth stood back so my mother could move in for the first embrace, and after we'd held each other she pulled back and said, 'You've lost weight. Are you eating properly?'

'Yeah, the food's fine. I've just been busy, I guess.'

Gareth embraced me, and Tippy hung back but gave me a small nod of acknowledgement and a muttered 'Hi'.

'It is so beautiful here,' Mum observed, going over to the window seat.

'It's not exactly the best day to see it,' I said.

It was murky and rainy outside, as it had been for weeks. Various colds and chills had been working through college – it seemed we picked up germs off each other as efficiently as we circulated gossip – and there had been long queues outside the nurse's room in the mornings.

'No,' Mum agreed. 'Still, there is something magical

about it, isn't there? I suppose you get used to it, being here all the time.'

I shook my head. 'No, I honestly don't think I'll ever take it for granted. It always feels like it could vanish at any moment.'

Tippy was standing by Gareth, looking at the official photograph of my year group, which was propped up on the shelf over the desk. She took it down so she could have a closer look, and said, 'Are you in this? I can't see you anywhere.'

I joined her in scanning the rows of faces: some smiling, some not, some caught out with odd pouts or closed eyes or unfortunate leers. The photograph had been taken to mark our formal admission into the university, and we were all dressed in the waiterish black and white uniform and short black academic gowns that we would also wear for finals, just before we left.

'That's me,' I said, pointing. I was standing near the front, between Leila Vetch and Malcolm Pye, a plump historian with a fondness for quoting Monty Python. My expression was hopeful but unfocused, and I'd tied my hair back, which made me look closer to Tippy's age than my own.

'Let me see,' said Gareth, getting to his feet.

He studied the faces for a moment, then said, 'So where's Mandy Martin's girl, then?'

I pointed out Clarissa, and he said, 'What's she like?'

'I don't really know her.'

'That figures,' Gareth said. 'I suppose she's going to stick with her own kind, isn't she?'

'What do you mean?'

'You know, showbiz people. Well-connected. Ones with titles and so on. There must be a few of those.'

'Actually, her friends aren't really like that,' I said. 'They're . . .' What were they, really? 'Characters,' I finished lamely.

It was true that Barnaby had gone to a well-known boys' public school, while Victor and Clarissa had both gone to a London school that seemed to have an abundance of ex-pupils at Oxford. I didn't know about Meg and Keith.

But anyway, it seemed to me that they were friends not because they had shared backgrounds and prejudices and tastes and were able to reinforce each other, but precisely because they were different, and drew strength from their variety.

'So who's your boyfriend, then?' Tippy said.

'I don't have one,' I told her.

'No way,' Tippy said. 'I thought you were exactly the sort who'd lose your virginity in the first term.'

'Tippy, don't be vulgar,' Mum protested.

'Seriously,' Tippy persisted, 'have you not even got a body piercing? A tattoo? What kind of student are you?'

'A good one, I hope,' Mum said, leaving the window seat and coming over to look at the photograph.

'Yeah, too damn good to be true,' Tippy muttered.

Mum took her glasses out of her handbag and studied the faces closely.

'I hope you know you're welcome to invite your friends home anytime you want to, Anna,' she said. She sounded almost pleading.

'Thanks, Mum, I'm sure I will,' I said, but she didn't look convinced, and I could barely imagine returning to the hush and privacy and comfort of home myself, let alone taking anyone with me.

As I put the photograph back on the shelf there was a loud knock on the door, and Mark Flask called out, 'Jones, are you there? I've come to borrow a bra!'

Tippy's ears suddenly pricked up; Gareth looked shocked; my mother merely raised her eyebrows, as if this was much more the kind of thing she had been expecting.

'My family are here,' I called out before he could say anything else.

I opened the door a crack – not too wide, I didn't want him bursting in – and his mortified face peered through.

'Should I come back later?' he said.

'We're going to be out most of the day. I'll find you at dinner,' I told him. 'And anyway, can't you borrow one of Violet's?'

'It's not for me, it's for Tim. We thought he might be about your size,' Mark said. 'Anyway, I'll see you later.'

'I thought you said you didn't have a boyfriend,' Tippy said as I closed the door.

'I don't,' I said, and thought of Victor. Ha! If only.

'Woo-hoo, you're blushing,' Tippy pointed out.

'Mark's just a friend,' I told her. 'A group of us are going to *The Rocky Horror Show* tonight.'

'Isn't that about transvestites?' Gareth said with a frown.

'It is,' Tippy said. 'It's also an excuse for girls to dress up like sluts.'

'Tippy, please,' Mum said faintly. 'Anna, when do you think we might go out for lunch?'

I checked my watch. 'We could go now, if you like,' I said. It was just before noon, a bit early, but at least this way we'd definitely get a table, and I was suddenly ready to get out of St Bart's.

As we went out Mum said, 'I hope your neighbours are considerate, and you don't get people banging up and down the stairs all hours. I should think it could be quite difficult to get a good night's sleep.'

I thanked my lucky stars that Inga, my Swedish neighbour, hadn't just been in the throes of one of her sex sessions with the captain of the first eight.

'I'm usually out as soon as my head hits the pillow,' I said, and led the way out on to the High Street.

I'd asked around to see where was considered a good place to take visiting parents, and in the end I'd opted for the Wickham Arms, a city pub with a hall of fame of past patrons displayed on its dark green walls: poets, politicians, sporting heroes. I didn't recognize half of them myself – they were mostly middle-aged men, more or less scruffy; they could have been anybody – but they looked important just by virtue of being framed. Captured in dim corners and on banquettes, their features both emphasized and softened by the shadowy, forgiving light, they were turned from everymen into art.

The moment we stepped inside, though, I wondered

if I'd made a mistake. If I could keep my family life separate from the world of St Bart's, I might just be able to slip from one to the other and back again. But no – here we were, at one remove from the college domain, and St Bart's had beaten us to it.

There was a long table just inside the entrance, and Clarissa, Victor, Barnaby, Keith and Meg were sitting around it. I could hear them quite clearly from across the room as we came in. Keith was saying, 'I'm sorry to moan, everybody, but I want to remind you all, I feel awful.'

He was huddled in a big dark cape I hadn't seen before, and looked watery-eyed and wretched.

'It might help if you'd stop smoking,' Meg said as Keith blew his nose.

'It's the fifth-week blues,' Victor said. 'Halfway through the term, everybody's tired, people begin to flag, and they come down with things. Or they suddenly start doing things they shouldn't.'

I steered my family into the non-smoking room, which was empty apart from an elderly couple sitting by the window. Gareth chose a table and I went back out to pick up a couple of menus. When I emerged into the main body of the pub, though, I went straight over to where Victor and his friends were sitting.

'Hi, all,' I said, and was pleased to hear that I sounded more casual than I felt, having barely spoken to Victor since we'd met. 'Is it a special occasion?'

'We're about to be introduced to Meg's fiancé,' Clarissa said. 'He's a bit late, isn't he? I thought he was meant to be here at noon, and it's quarter past already.'

'We'll mark him down for it,' Barnaby said.

'You're not to keep any kind of score,' Meg scolded. 'Poor Freddie, he's probably just lost.'

'So you're here with your folks, Anna?' Keith said, and I nodded.

'Another characteristic of fifth week,' Barnaby commented. 'The family visit. Not that I mean to imply that it's at all related to the blues.'

'I'm not blue,' Meg objected. 'I'm perfectly happy, thank you very much.'

'Course you are,' said Clarissa and started humming the Wedding March.

'I'll leave you to it, then. Have a good lunch,' I said.

Victor smiled and said, 'You too,' and I felt the blood rush to my face and hurried to get the menus before I gave myself away.

This was crazy. I was absolutely elated, and for no better reason than that Victor had spoken to me.

As I went back into the non-smoking room the elderly couple came out, holding hands. The gentleman dipped his head and touched the brim of his hat in acknowledgement, and the lady gave me a bright-eyed, appreciative look, as if I'd just done something splendid, and she was delighted to be in the know.

They passed me and headed towards the exit to the street, and I went to join my family.

The meal started off well enough. Gareth quizzed me about rowing, which I was already planning to give up the following term, though he was so pleased that I'd started I didn't share my decision to quit. I also decided not to tell him about the review I'd contributed to one of the student papers: 250 words on a Mongolian film that had been on at the Phoenix Picturehouse.

I had been very happy to see my name in print, but the paper's editors seemed to think I had been insufficiently scathing, and had not allocated me anything to write for the next issue. Anyway, I suspected Gareth would perceive both film reviewing and Mongolian arthouse cinema as being on a hiding to nothing.

Tippy picked at her food and looked bored; Mum listened with polite interest and a hint of scepticism.

Then Gareth said, 'So what are your marks like? You managing to stay up there at the top of the class?'

'We don't actually get official marks for our weekly essays,' I said. 'They're more like material for discussion. Our degree results go on six days of exams right at the end.'

'Sounds like an odd kind of system to me,' Gareth said. 'Of course, it's not just about the academic stuff. It's all about networking, a place like this, isn't it? You play your cards right, the people you meet here, the friendships you make, will stand you in good stead for the rest of your life. You might want to bear that in mind.'

'I will,' I promised.

Gareth nodded and beamed at me. 'If anyone had told me, back when I was starting my apprenticeship, that one day I'd be coming here to take my daughter out for lunch . . . well, I wouldn't have believed it.'

'You'd better make the most of it then, because I don't see myself wobbling over the cobbles on a pushbike,' said Tippy.

'Maybe you're more like me,' Gareth said.

'Well, duh,' Tippy said, with a tiny roll of her eyes. 'Of course I'm more like you. We're actually *related*.'

Silence. Gareth stared at Tippy in dismay. My mother laid her cutlery very softly and quietly on her plate.

For once, she looked neither worried nor uncertain. She wasn't even angry. It was as if she'd been brooding for years about when and how this particular unpleasantness would surface, and was glad finally to have the chance to square up to it.

'Tippy, that was very . . . insensitive. I think you had better apologize, and then we need say no more about it,' she said.

'Why should I say sorry?' Tippy protested. 'And who to, anyway?'

'To your sister, and your father,' Mum said, 'and me too.'

'But she's not my sister! She's my *half*-sister. And he's not her father,' Tippy said, thumping the table for emphasis. 'She doesn't even call him Dad! I'm sick of us tiptoeing round this all the time. Why does it have to be such a big secret? I mean, does anybody actually know who her real father is? Do you?' She looked from me to Gareth, and then at Mum. 'Does anybody?'

'You should be careful what you imply about me,' Mum said, and her tone was so formidable, and so icy, that Tippy's indignation was no match for it.

Gareth cleared his throat, and said, 'All I meant was that perhaps, Tippy, you're not much of a one for school, which is what I was like. It didn't really click until I was out there earning.'

Tippy's resentment appeared to ebb away just as quickly as it had flared up. 'I just thought maybe we could all do with being a little bit more open,' she said, and fell to studying the tablecloth.

'I agree,' I said. I looked at Mum. 'I want to know who he is, too.'

'Anna,' Mum said, 'this is neither the place nor the time for this discussion.'

'There will never be a place or time for it,' I said. 'It's obvious that you don't want to tell. I know you would prefer it if I didn't want to find out. You probably think you're protecting me. But if I don't know who he is, how can I be sure who I am? Everybody needs to know where they come from.'

'You do know,' Mum said. 'We're right here.'

'All I want is a name,' I said.

'No you don't,' Mum said. 'You want a story. And I said, not now.' She stood up and tucked her chair neatly under the table. 'I'll ask for the bill, and Gareth, would you take care of it, please? I'm going to wait in the car. Tippy, you can come with me.'

Tippy obediently followed her out.

'Is that it?' I said to Gareth. 'You're all clearing off home now, because the big forbidden question finally got asked? Just what exactly is it you're so afraid of?'

He shook his head. 'I did try to tell her,' he said.

'Tried to tell her what?'

'That you would be thinking about it. Even if you didn't let on.' He leaned across the table and said, 'That man, the one you're suddenly so interested in, he didn't want to know, Anna. He told your mother to abort you, and he got married to someone else.'

He was speaking quietly but very clearly, which seemed to have the effect of amplifying every word he said, and hushing the other diners who had come in since our arrival: a pair of middle-aged women, a young family, a solitary bearded man, all strangers now well placed to hear what I didn't want to hear myself.

'He was a despicable, self-serving, ruthless, idle little shit with a lot of very nasty friends, and you're infinitely better off without him, believe me,' Gareth went on. He straightened up and folded his arms. 'Go on then, ask me. Say it. "I want to know who my father is."'

I stared at him. He went on, 'You can't, can you? You can't call him that. Because he isn't. He isn't anything.'

The waitress came in with a slip of paper. She gave it to Gareth and said, 'Your wife asked for the bill.'

'Thank you,' Gareth said.

The waitress went out again, and he got a wad of notes out of his jacket pocket, eased a couple out of the money-clip and laid them down on the table. Then he looked up at me as if something had just occurred to him.

'I have a question for you too,' he said. 'Who pays the parental contributions to your maintenance while you're here?'

'Is that a threat?'

'Not, of course not. More of a reminder. Look, I'll make a deal with you. If you still want to know when you're twenty-one, when you've finished your degree, and come properly of age, I'll tell you about him then.'

'Are you serious?'

'I am.' He shrugged. 'It's only three more years. Hopefully you'll be a bit more mature then, a bit better able to handle it.'

'Will you say anything about this to Mum?'

'I should think she'll be relieved not to have to handle it herself.'

He held out his hand across the table. I hesitated – was this wise? Was this the best I was going to get? But Mum had been so cold and angry – she must have been very badly hurt, to become so unlike herself . . . This way, I could find out without ever having to broach the subject with her again.

I held out my own hand in return. Gareth's touch was warm and firm, and he smiled at me as if it was a deal well done.

'Come on, then,' he said, getting to his feet and pulling his coat on. 'You should say goodbye to your mum and Tippy. Make nice. We don't want a lingering nasty atmosphere in the house when you come home for Christmas.'

As we walked out, I saw that the table by the door was empty. The crowd from St Bart's had moved on too, with or without Meg's fiancé. Which was just as well, because if they had still been there I would have been sorely tempted to ask if I could join them, and to let Gareth make his way back to the car on his own.

That evening, when I was in the college bar after seeing *The Rocky Horror Show*, Keith came in to get a packet of cigarettes from the machine, and I just happened to be standing next to it.

'Nice costume,' he said, pushing a couple of coins into the slot.

'Thanks. I could say the same to you.'

He glanced down at his cape. 'It's keeping me warm in this freezing bloody place,' he said.

'Nobody asked to borrow it off you for the show?'

'Nah. You had a good night?'

'Yeah, really good, thanks.'

'You all right?'

'Me? Course I am. Why wouldn't I be?'

He shrugged and stooped to collect his selection. 'Just asking.'

'Actually . . . I'm not that great. Maybe it's the fifth-week blues.'

'You're welcome to come back to mine if you want to talk about it,' he said, 'or even if you don't. Have a cup of tea. Or coffee. Or whisky. Or a smoke. Or even a cold cure. Plus I have custard creams.'

I looked around at my companions. Mark had his arms wrapped round Violet; his mouth, which she had carefully painted with her Juicy Plum lipstick, was smeared where they'd been kissing. Tim, also perhaps emboldened by his make-up – he'd turned down the opportunity to wear my bra, but had allowed Violet to apply his eyeliner – was busy chatting up Leila Vetch. They were all having a great time; they probably wouldn't notice I had gone.

'OK, you're on,' I told Keith.

He turned away towards the stairs, and I followed him up and out.

7

'The point of a dare'

When I came to the next morning my bed was harder and narrower, and the wardrobe had turned darker and plainer and flatter, and was closing in on me like a wall.

As I attempted to get out of bed my stockinged foot slid into something soft and sticky, and I realized what the rank smell was; I'd been sick on the carpet. And I wasn't in my room at home at Topaz Close. I was at St Bart's.

I turned on the fluorescent light above the basin and mirror unit built into the middle of the wardrobe. Not a pretty sight: I looked like a zombie without the blood.

My hair, which I had backcombed and put up, was now loose and matted, as if it had been beaten with a whisk. My make-up – kohl-rimmed eyes, scarlet mouth – was no longer a bold mask, but was smudged around features that were recognizably mine. I was still wearing my costume from the outing to see *The Rocky Horror Show,* but my short black skirt had acquired a small but noticeable cigarette burn, and the white shirt I'd knotted over my black bra looked distinctly the worse for wear.

Still . . . and this was the odd thing . . . I felt *good.* Good *and* bad at the same time, as if I'd been both purged and poisoned. Whatever I'd done the previous night – and it was pretty hazy in parts, as if it had been edited into a series of jump cuts and surprising juxtapositions – I didn't regret it.

I drank some water, which had the effect of making me want to be sick again, and cleaned my face.

So, there had been the performance . . . the Time Warp, between Violet and Leila, lined up behind a row of red velvet seats . . . and then back to St Bart's, where I'd been gripped by a kind of giddy recklessness, a longing to break through, but where else was there to go?

And then Keith had come along. Which had seemed like a boon at the time, but in the cold light of day I wished he hadn't been quite so generous with his hospitality.

The whisky . . . the smoking . . . Clearly I wasn't cut out for Keith's idea of a quiet night in.

I stripped off and got into my dressing-gown and went out of the bedroom alcove into the main part of the room. The curtains were drawn. Had I been sufficiently compos mentis to do that? Or had someone else done it for me? I pulled them back. Outside it was grey and dull, but definitely daytime.

My watch was still on my wrist, even though I always took it off before going to sleep. Half-past nine.

Just twelve hours since I'd met Keith by the cigarette machine.

I dived across the corridor into the bathroom and grabbed some paper towels to clean up with. I didn't bump into anybody, thank God. It wasn't until I came back in that I saw the note waiting for me on my desk.

It was written in round, artful handwriting, and it said:

Hello, hope you are not feeling too bad this morning. Come and see me when you're up.
Love and peace
Clarissa x

I showered and washed my hair and put on my regular, unrevealing clothes – jeans and a jumper – and made my way to Rhys House to call on my good Samaritan.

I knocked quietly, in case she was still sleeping. The door opened a crack and a lurid green face appeared on the other side. It took me a moment to work out that it was really Clarissa I was looking at.

She was wearing an orange kimono and a face mask, the sort that cracks when you smile, and her hair was twisted up and secured in place with a pencil.

'Quick, come on in, for God's sake,' she said, waving me in, and the minute I was through the door she shut it behind me.

Her room was dim and smelt of sandalwood. The blind was down, a candle was burning, the reading light was on, and there was a letter lying on the bed.

'Just going to wash this gunk off my face,' she said.

She went over to the basin, turning her back to me, and started rinsing the dry clay off her skin.

I perched on the bed, which was covered by a rumpled quilt patterned with a tiny print of gold and yellow songbirds; it felt like silk. The letter Clarissa had just been reading was three pages long, well thumbed, in emphatic, spiky handwriting: *fucking dead-end job . . . provincial shit, I keep asking myself why I'm here . . .*

It must be from Des, her boyfriend. But he sounded like a bit of a moaner – I'd have expected her to be with someone glamorous and successful, not an angst-ridden self-doubter. Still – who knew what someone else would find attractive?

Clarissa took a dark red towel off a drying rail by the basin and patted her face dry.

'That's better,' she said, replacing the towel. 'You must think I'm monstrously vain, but I promise you, I'm not really one of those girls who's always fussing about beauty treatments. I just had to use that stuff up.'

She came over to sit next to me on the bed, spotted the letter, and swiftly scooped it up. 'Oh God, you haven't been reading this, have you?'

'Um . . . My eye may have fallen on a couple of lines . . . I'm sorry. I didn't mean to pry.'

'Just so long as you didn't see anything too hair-raisingly obscene,' Clarissa said, and shoved the letter in the top drawer of her bedside table, which looked as if it was crammed with similar missives.

She took a big framed photograph off the bedside table and passed it to me; it showed her sitting on the edge of a stage with an intense, unsmiling young man next to her, traditional red theatre curtains drawn across the proscenium arch behind them.

'Desmond Cox, the love of my life, destined to be one of the greatest actors of his generation . . . though I do sometimes wish he wasn't quite so single-minded about preserving his artistic integrity. The problem is, he's absolutely incapable of just closing his eyes and thinking about the money,' she explained.

In the photo, Clarissa was beaming meltingly at the camera, the very image of the contented young lover; Desmond looked preoccupied, as if he had plenty else to be getting on with, and had agreed to pose in order to humour her.

'You look great together. Very loved up,' I said.

'We are,' Clarissa sighed. 'I miss him terribly, but what's a girl to do?'

She put the photograph back next to the candle, loosened her hair, and took off the kimono. Underneath she was wearing a silk camisole and matching knickers, which had probably cost more than the entire contents of my underwear drawer. She was slim, but strong and supple-looking too, like a dancer; she seemed entirely unselfconscious and knowing at the same time, as if she was acutely aware of every movement and how it would appear, but without thinking about it – as if she didn't even *need* to think about it. She hung the kimono on a hook on the door, and started rummaging through her wardrobe.

'You attracted plenty of notice in your outfit last night,' she commented. 'I had no idea you were such a minx. It's just as well we were around to make sure you got safely back to your own bed.' She took a grey T-shirt off a hanger and put it on, then pulled on a pair of leggings.

'It was only fancy dress.'

'Sexy fancy dress,' Clarissa insisted. 'You should get those legs out more often. It was quite a transformation.'

'I remember being in Keith's room, and you turning up, but after that it's all a bit foggy,' I admitted.

Clarissa stepped into a floor-sweeping black skirt and added a huge mohair jumper; her body had now all but disappeared under layers of clothing. She peered into the mirror over the basin, put in her nose-stud and started to line her eyes with kohl.

'You two were having this big heart-to-heart about your favourite books,' she said. 'I could hardly get a word in edgeways. So then I said I was going to head back to Rhys House, and you said you'd come too, and you stood up and promptly fell over, and we realized that maybe it had all been a little too *much* for you.'

'Thank you for getting me back to my room,' I said. 'I hope it wasn't too difficult.'

'Oh, we managed between us, it was fine.'

'What, you and Keith?'

'Keith? Flyweight Keith? Are you joking? He is not the man you need when it comes to manoeuvring drunk girls upstairs. No, I sent Keith to get Victor. Barnaby might have done at a pinch, I suppose, but I wouldn't *quite* have trusted him not to try to sneak a peek down your bra. Whereas Victor is so thoroughly determined not to get involved with anyone this year, he's virtually a eunuch. You could put him in charge of a whole harem of prancing virgins and their honours would all remain unsmirched.'

Oh God! I did remember, though only just, as if from a dream . . . Victor looking down at me with those dark eyes, slightly perturbed but, at the same time, with a hint of a one-sided smile.

'Did he . . . carry me?' I asked.

'Fireman's lift, darling. All the way across Main Quad and back to Hanover.' She started laughing. 'No need to look so appalled, I'm only kidding. We managed to sort of prop you up between us, so don't worry, I don't think anybody realized what a state you were in.'

She sat down next to me on the bed and wriggled her toes into a pair of rainbow-striped socks, and I tried to banish the thought of Victor struggling to lug me up to my room and get me off his hands.

'Why doesn't Victor want to get involved with anyone?' I asked.

'Heartbreak at the end of his first year, didn't you know? He was going out with Eleanor Gordon – you must have seen her around, pretty, ringletty, she does Classics, like Barnaby – and he cast her as Rosalind in his *As You Like It*, which was part of the Oxford Summer Shakespeare Festival, and then she got together with this rather good-looking chap from some other college who was playing Orlando, and that was that.'

'Poor Victor,' I said.

'I know, I do get the impression he was rather devastated. Now he's determined to focus purely on directing. He's even worse than Des. Tunnel vision. Relationships are a distraction, girls are sent by Satan to tempt you into abandoning your creative path, love is for people who don't love their work, and so on and so forth. Whoever goes out with him next is going to have a complete nightmare, poor girl. So he and Barnaby are the eternal bachelors – for now, at least.'

She laced up a pair of cherry-red Dr Marten boots and went on, 'Poor old Barnaby wants a Miss Joan Hunter Dunn type. You know, someone who could put a bit of spin on her backhand and give him a good run round, but those sort of hearty sporty girls find him a bit odd and intense. Anyway, they've got dozens of rowers and rugby lads to choose from.'

'I suppose the odds do work in the girls' favour,' I agreed.

St Bart's had not been quite the last of the formerly all-male Oxford colleges to take in girls, but it had not been far off. About a third of the students were now female. It didn't exactly feel as if we were in a minority – in some subjects, like English, we had more or less taken over – but we were certainly surrounded by potential boyfriends.

'It'll all come right for Barnaby one day, when the women he knows stop wanting boyfriends and start looking for husbands,' Clarissa decided. 'You know he grew up in a manor house in Norfolk. That'll help, I expect.'

'I wonder what it's like.' I was thinking that it might be rather nice to pay a visit sometime.

'You know Victor's never been. He says Barnaby

loathes his father and wants to keep his college life as separate from home as possible. He doesn't seem to have much to do with people he knows from school, either. I guess he wanted a clean slate when he came here. Do you want to come for breakfast?'

'Sure, yeah, I'd love to,' I said, hoping I'd be able to keep it down. 'I'd better go get my coat and purse. Shall I see you down at the exit?'

'I'll come with you,' Clarissa said, shrugging on her big army greatcoat, and picking up a battered leather satchel.

She stooped to blow out the candle on the bedside table, and we went across to my room together. She followed me in and looked around at the posters I'd put up on the walls: Klimt's *The Kiss*, golden, gleaming, and delicate, and pre-Raphaelite girls coming down the stairs.

'What a romantic you are,' she said.

'I thought I was a minx.'

'A romantic minx.'

We went out together and headed towards Main Quad. The air was cold and everything looked white and clean. Despite the previous night's excesses, or maybe because of them, St Bart's seemed brighter and more promising than ever, as if I'd been adrift on the currents, a mere spectator, and had finally come down to earth.

Without Clarissa's help, I never would have found Keith's room again. It was on the far side of the library lawn, tucked away off a long, featureless corridor in the block where we had our Anglo-Saxon classes.

'It's handy for Keith, because it means he can just roll out of bed and into his maths seminar, and he does not like to get up early,' Clarissa said, and knocked vigorously at the door. Clearly, whether he was awake or still asleep, she intended to be answered.

After a moment Keith opened up. Behind him I glimpsed the room where we'd bonded the previous night. There were books stacked up by the bed, a sound system and an old grey trunk in one corner. Apart from that it was mostly bare, apart from the whisky bottle, the overflowing ashtray, the box of tissues and the biscuit tin on the desk. The only dash of colour was a faded red-and-black zigzag duvet cover that looked as if his mother might have chosen it for him back in the mid-eighties.

Keith squinted at Clarissa, and then at me. 'You look full of beans,' he said.

'Anna clearly has an ox-like constitution,' Clarissa said. 'Nevertheless, we need to get some coffee into her. Today I am your pied piper, and Barnaby and Victor are our next stop.'

She led the way back across Main Quad, up a staircase and along to a door with two names over it: *B. G. A. Stour* and *V. Rose*.

'This is the sitting room,' she explained. 'Barnaby's bedroom is next to it, and Victor's is upstairs.'

She knocked, and said, 'I bet you Victor's gone out for a run, and Barnaby's still snoring.'

'What are you doing up?' said a voice from somewhere behind us.

It was Victor, who was coming along the corridor carrying a towel and wearing a dressing-gown and slippers, his hair still wet.

'Thank you for helping me last night,' I said.

'You need to look after yourself, you know. There might not always be someone around who's going to do it for you,' he said.

I might have felt sheepish, or foolish, or even ashamed of myself – and perhaps some part of me was – but more than anything else I was touched by the note of concern in his voice. He was looking at me quite closely, as if . . . certainly not as if he despised me, or found me laughable. There was curiosity there, certainly, and softness, too. You might almost say *tenderness*, mixed up with something a little more wolfish.

At any rate, it seemed that I'd well and truly got his attention.

'I suppose you'd better all come in,' he went on. 'Try not to be too raucous, though. Barnaby might not thank you if you wake him up. It was the Classics dinner last night.'

He unlocked the door, went into the darkness beyond it and flicked on the lights. Then he went off to get dressed, and Clarissa decided to go and see if Meg and her fiancé wanted to come out for breakfast, and I found myself alone with Keith in a big, oak-panelled room with a view of the High Street, and dark, well-worn furniture that made me think of a gentleman's club.

We settled on the big leather Chesterfield sofa, in front of an abandoned chess game laid out on a coffee table. Keith's thin white hand appeared from underneath the folds of his cape, clutching a handkerchief; he blew his nose, and the hand and the handkerchief disappeared again, and he tucked his knees up under his chin so he was just a pale face atop a triangle of slightly damp-smelling second-hand wool.

'Kill or cure,' he commented. 'I do actually believe my cold is on the turn today. So do you actually remember what we talked about last night?'

'Course I do. I told you I'm infatuated with Victor, and you told me you're obsessed with Magdalena Dale.'

Magdalena was an impeccably groomed brunette who had supposedly attended a Swiss finishing school, a type of educational institution which I had previously believed to be entirely fictional, like the Chalet School and Malory Towers. She owned cashmere cardigans in a rainbow assortment of colours, and knotted them around her shoulders on mild days with a casual elegance that did not seem at all English.

'Of course she barely knows I exist,' Keith had said. 'And why should she? She's not going to be interested in a skinny weirdo like me.'

Having already confided in Keith about my feelings for Victor, I had been duty bound to commiserate, but even through the bonding, sentimental haze of alcohol it had occurred to me to feel slightly piqued. After all, it would have been rather gratifying to be the object of such admiration myself.

'You won't tell the others, will you?' Keith said.

'My lips are sealed.'

'We're in the same boat, in a way, aren't we? I thought

we did a pretty good job of changing the subject when Clarissa turned up. Do you remember?'

'Sure I do. The big books talk. You prefer your authors male, cerebral and ambitious, with a dash of cult. But you also read stacks of pulpy crime fiction and pride yourself on hunting out writers nobody else has heard of. I like stories about resourceful orphans, which is what all good heroes and heroines are, even if they have parents still living. Neither of us insists on happy endings, and the only book we both really love is *The Catcher in the Rye*.'

'And there was me thinking it would all have been wiped away by the sheer excitement of having Victor escort you to your bedroom.'

'With Clarissa in tow,' I reminded him.

'Nobody tows Clarissa,' Keith said. 'She tows us.'

'Why didn't you apply to study English, if you love reading so much?' I asked him.

He shook his head. 'That's a typical arts student question. You always assume that it has to be one or the other. This way, I can do both.' He looked stricken. 'And, to be really honest, my parents thought maths would be a better idea.'

'Ah. Yes, my stepfather wasn't at all sure about me doing English.'

'Is that who was with you yesterday? He must have got over it. He looked very proud of you.'

'He was at the beginning. Not so much at the end.'

'Really? Why, what happened?'

'I kind of waded into a really sensitive subject.' I shook my head. 'I don't know what got into me.'

'You can tell me if you want,' Keith said. 'I'm good with secrets.'

'It's not really a secret,' I said. 'It's more of a mystery. I've never met my real father. I don't actually know who he is.'

'Do you want to?'

Well, did I? Part of me was impatient and wanted my question answered now, not later, and chafed at being made to wait – and another part of me was resigned, even a little relieved.

'I don't know,' I said. 'It sounds like he might be a bit of a low-life. I think I preferred it when I could imagine that he might be anyone. Anyway, my stepfather said that if I still wanted to know in three years' time, when I'm twenty-one, he'd tell me then. So that gives me some time to think about it.'

Keith nodded matter-of-factly, as if this was a perfectly reasonable arrangement.

'A cooling-off period,' he said. 'So your stepfather's going to do the telling, then, is he? Not your mum?'

'He is. Actually, I think that's for the best,' I said. 'It makes him angry, but it hurts her. I don't want to put her through that if I can avoid it.'

'Well, obviously it's up to you what you decide to do,' Keith said. 'But the way I see it is: you're your own person, the person you decide to be, in the here and now. At least, that's how I think of it. I'm adopted, and I don't ever want to track down my birth mother. I know she couldn't cope with me, for whatever reason, and decided to give me up, and that's enough, as far as I'm concerned.'

'You're not even a little bit . . . curious?'

'No,' Keith said flatly. 'Not even a little bit. I think my parents would be devastated if I did, and it seems very unfair to do that to the people who have looked after me all my life, pretty much, or at least as far back as I can remember. After all, they've always been fair to me. My sister's their biological child – they adopted me and then all of a sudden my mum got pregnant – but they didn't suddenly turn round and decide to give me back because things had finally turned out the way they wanted in the first place.'

'My sister's the child my mum had with my step-father,' I said. 'She was with us in the pub yesterday.'

'I had a funny feeling you and I might get along,' Keith said, 'and you have to admit, we do have one or two things in common.'

'I suppose we do,' I agreed, and was suddenly tempted to reach out and hug him – the impulse came out of nowhere but was very strong, as if only an embrace would suffice to confirm our newfound closeness. But then the door burst open and Barnaby bounced in, dressed in cords and a big, cuddly-looking Aran jumper, his hair damp and tufted where he'd combed it.

'I say, sorry to interrupt,' Barnaby said. 'You look like you're having a bit of a moment.'

'I think the moment is now over,' Keith said.

Barnaby settled into the armchair opposite us and regarded us both curiously for a moment, then picked up a pack of cards off the coffee table and began to flip them expertly back and forth from one hand to the other.

'If you're thinking that Keith and I are a couple or something, we're most definitely not,' I said.

'None of my beeswax,' Barnaby said. 'Just my usual rotten timing. I used to do it to Victor all the time, when he was seeing Eleanor.'

The door opened again, and Victor came in.

'Morning all,' he said. He settled in the armchair next to Barnaby and asked him, 'How's your head?'

'Bloody awful,' Barnaby said. He put the pack of cards down, surveyed the chess board and told Victor, 'It's your move, you know.'

Victor leaned forward and studied the chess board. 'I have a horrible feeling this is just staving off the inevitable,' he said, and moved his knight.

'No,' Barnaby said, 'I don't think inevitable just yet. Do you play, Anna?'

'Not chess,' I said.

'Barnaby is teaching us all how to play poker,' Keith said.

Barnaby took one of Victor's pawns. 'Meg is the best,' he said. 'You'd think it would be Clarissa, but she gets bored and loses concentration. Victor hates it when he's losing, and you, Keith, don't care enough about winning. Maybe you'll join us next time, Anna.'

'I'd like that,' I said.

Victor looked up at me and smiled and said, 'Anna's such a dark horse, I think the rest of us had better all look out.'

I was so sucker-punched by the smile that I completely missed the next part of the conversation, and only tuned back in once Clarissa and Meg and Freddie, the fiancé, turned up, and we were finally heading, en masse, out of St Bart's and to the café on the other side of the High Street for breakfast.

When we'd all finished Clarissa said, 'Let's go for a drive.'

Keith asked, 'Where did you have in mind?'

'Surprise,' Clarissa said, tapping her nose.

'We'd have to take two cars,' objected Meg.

Freddie had a proprietorial arm draped round her shoulder. He was dark and neat-featured and good-looking, and Meg was clearly very proud of him. She hung on his every word with absolute devotion, and kept glancing at him in adoration, as if she couldn't quite believe her luck.

She looked . . . *wifely*. She was wearing a long, modest dress with buttons down the front, and blue eyeshadow; the bondage boots had gone, and she had black Mary Janes on instead.

'Freddie, do you think you can follow me?' Clarissa asked.

'Course I can,' Freddie agreed. 'What do you say, Meg? I wouldn't mind getting out of town a little bit, taking in some of the scenery.'

'Of course, if that's what you'd like to do, darling,' Meg agreed.

'I'm game,' Barnaby said.

Victor and I exchanged glances – just that was enough to set my heart racing – and Victor said, 'Then what are we waiting for?'

But somehow Keith ended up sitting between me and

Victor in the back of Clarissa's Mini, while Barnaby, who was the biggest, went in front. Freddie's Fiesta pulled up alongside us, and Clarissa quickly conferred with him and Meg, then got in the driving seat and manoeuvred her way out of the side road where she had parked and on to the High Street.

I said, 'This is a bit like being a kid again. But way better than being in the back with my sister. She used to do everything she could to wind me up, then make out that she was being good as gold.'

'Oh, poor you,' Clarissa said. 'I always feel sorry for people who have siblings. It strikes me as bad luck to have to share the limelight right from the start.'

Barnaby leaned round and glanced questioningly at Victor, who said, 'It's all right, I don't mind.'

'Don't mind what?' Clarissa asked.

'Clarissa, maybe you should drop it,' Barnaby said. 'Change the subject.'

'Why are you behaving like I've put my foot in it? You haven't got any sisters or brothers, have you, Victor?'

Victor hesitated. 'I never quite know how to answer that question.'

'How about "Yes" or "No"?' Clarissa said. 'I thought you said you were an only child.'

'I might have said that,' Victor said. 'I sometimes do. It's easier.'

'Why would you say it if it isn't true?' I asked him.

'Because I did have a brother. He had . . . problems. Various problems. He's dead now.'

'I'm sorry,' I said, and Clarissa said:

'But that's terrible! What happened to him?'

'He had to have heart surgery, and it didn't work out. He was five. I was seven. He had been in and out of hospital, and that time he didn't come back.'

'Why didn't you say something before?' Clarissa wanted to know.

'I've had years to get used to it, but other people haven't, and they often don't know how to react,' Victor said. 'It can be a bit of a conversation killer. Especially when you're making small talk about school and gap years and A-level subjects.'

'But you told Barnaby,' Clarissa pointed out.

'Yes, and Barnaby doesn't insist on talking about it.'

After a pause, Keith said, 'So where are we going?'

'You'll enjoy it much more if you don't know,' Clarissa told him.

'Freddie knows,' Barnaby objected.

'Freddie needs to know,' Clarissa said firmly, and we drove on in silence.

We circled the city, then turned off the dual carriageway and within minutes were on a winding country lane, with fields stretching to the horizon on either side. We seemed to be heading into the middle of nowhere, and I was beginning to wonder if Clarissa had taken a wrong turning when we reached the end of the lane and she pulled up in a lay-by opposite a farmhouse.

'Is this it?' I asked.

'You're all very impatient, aren't you?' Clarissa said. 'Not much longer, I promise, and all will become clear.'

Freddie parked behind us, and we all got out and followed the path that skirted the boundary of the farmhouse garden. A young billygoat came up to the wall and fixed its eyes on us with philosophical objectivity, seeking neither to wheedle nor to intimidate, but to see if we meant food or something else. His two companions ignored us and carried on nosing through the weedy grass in their pen.

Victor said, 'What is this place?'

Clarissa didn't answer. Instead she passed through a gate and disappeared beyond the dense wall of greenery that screened off whatever it was that came at the end of the path.

Victor went after her, and I followed them and found myself in a tiny graveyard, dotted with crumbling and illegible stones, and encircled by huge, ancient yew trees that dwarfed the church itself, which was an inconspicuous building with a low tower, not much bigger than a chapel.

The earth was buckled by roots, and dry and sandy at the feet of the trees. A canopy of leaves sheltered the little congregation of the dead from the wind, the sun and the rain. It was as if we were already inside, if not a church, then some other protected space. The light was softened into shades of shadow, the breeze that had been picking up outside was quelled, and even the bleat of the neighbouring goats and the rattle of their bells didn't penetrate.

Clarissa was standing on the far side of the churchyard, looking down at something. Suddenly she threw something small and bright and round so that it fell towards the spot she'd been staring at. It seemed not to strike earth but to sink beyond it.

Victor joined her, and as I approached I saw there were two lines of bricks set into the ground in front of her, the tops of parallel walls on either side of a series of steps leading down into a dark hole. The bottom steps were damp and bright with pennies.

As the others came over Clarissa said, 'It's St Bartholomew's well. An ancient site of healing and pilgrimage. The church is named after it.'

'What did you wish for?' I asked Clarissa.

'If you tell, it doesn't come true.'

'Honestly, you pagans,' Meg said. 'You won't countenance the miracle of the bread turning into the body of Christ, but a magic well is just fine.'

'That spring was regarded as magic long before it was St Bartholomew's,' Barnaby observed.

'And I suppose you think that means both beliefs are equally superstitious,' Meg said. She linked arms with Freddie and went on, 'Let's see if we can have a peep inside the church. It's a gorgeous little place, don't you think? Really characterful.'

'Twelfth-century, by the look of it,' Barnaby commented.

'Shame it's so small,' Freddie said. 'I don't think it'd do for us.'

They went off to try the door, which turned out to be locked. Barnaby followed them and stood at a slight distance, studying the church as if committing its architecture to memory.

Victor rummaged in his pockets and brought out some small change, and then cast down a copper coin to join the rest. His face was mute and serious. Whatever he had wished for was something he really wanted. I wondered if he would ever tell me what it was.

'Your turn, Anna,' Clarissa said.

'I left my purse in the car,' I said.

'Here,' Victor said, and handed me a 10p piece.

I held it ready and closed my eyes.

What to wish for?

What I asked for, in the end, was this: *Love that lasts.*

My coin tumbled down into the darkness and was lost alongside Victor's and Clarissa's, and all the other tokens of things that people hoped to find.

When I looked up I saw Keith was watching me. I said, 'Do you want to make a wish?' but he shrugged and shook his head.

'We malcontents don't make wishes,' he explained. 'We brood bitterly and shake our fists against the gods,' and with that he went off to lean against the crumbling wall and watch the goats.

Clarissa urged us back into the cars, and we were soon on the dual carriageway again.

'Where now?' asked Keith.

'You'll find out in a minute,' Clarissa said.

Drops of rain began to streak the windscreen as she turned on to a deserted single-track road that snaked round the foot of a hill. We came to a halt in a near-empty car park. Freddie pulled up next to us, and we all set off up the footpath that led to the summit of the hill, with Clarissa leading the way.

The wind was much stronger here, and whipped Clarissa's hair into a frenzy. We passed a couple of other walkers on their way down: hardy, hearty types in padded jackets, one with a dog. Nobody else was going up, which was not all that surprising, given that it looked as if it was about to pour.

When we got to the top I saw why Clarissa had brought us here. The long lines of an ancient chalk horse were etched into the far side of the hill, and we had all of the view beyond it to ourselves.

All of us were silent. Freddie pulled Meg in close, and Clarissa lifted her arms up to the sky and slowly let them fall.

Above us heavy clouds whipped across the sky. Below us the hill, crossed by the lines of the rushing creature that had been marked on it millennia ago, flattened out towards the car park, then stretched out through fields and tracts of woodland towards the horizon. Not much interrupted the rolling sweep of the land; here and there the spire of an unknown village church protruded, and a remote radio mast was a thin black line against the sky. On the far side of the valley, a cluster of pale towers rose above the surrounding trees.

'Look,' Victor said, pointing. 'Oxford. It looks so idyllic at a distance, doesn't it? Exactly how people imagine it.'

The scream seemed to come from nowhere; I froze, and then realized it was Clarissa. She had cupped her hands to her mouth and was howling into the wind.

'That's quite a pair of lungs you've got,' Victor told her.

'You should try it,' she said. 'Works wonders.'

'I don't go round emoting,' Victor said. 'You know that.'

'Quite,' Barnaby commented. 'We leave the emoting to you ladies.'

'The noisy emoting, anyway,' Keith agreed.

'Then how about you, Anna?' Clarissa turned to me with a challenging look.

'Me? No way.'

'Why not? There's no one here.'

'You're all here.'

'Think of it as a dare,' she said.

And so I did. What came out of me was a terrible sound: shrill, desperate, and full of rage. When I stopped, they were all looking at me in astonishment.

'Fuck me,' Victor said, 'she's a banshee.'

Clarissa cleared her throat. 'I think we'd better make a run for it,' she said. 'It's about to pour.'

We scrambled down the hillside as the rain started in earnest. By the time we reached the car park we were all soaked, and Clarissa's hair was darkened and streaming.

I climbed into the back of the Mini, which promptly began to steam up. Clarissa started the engine, got the blower on, and passed me a rag to wipe the back windscreen.

As I gave it back to her I said, 'What was with the screaming?'

'You did it too,' Clarissa said. 'Don't you feel better?'

'I think we all feel deafer,' Keith said.

'It's just not the kind of thing I normally do,' I said.

'That, my darling, is the point of a dare,' Clarissa said.

'I thought I was meant to have the option of truth,' I said.

'Not necessarily,' Clarissa said. 'Only if you fail on the dare.'

'So what has everyone else done for theirs?' I said.

'Meg sang in the hall on the first night. Barnaby had to let me and Meg teach him how to dance. Victor and I climbed into the Meadows after the gates were locked and had a walk in the moonlight,' Clarissa said. 'They're very high, you know, and spiky on top. I'm still amazed we managed to get in and out without doing ourselves a damage.'

'And what about you, Keith?' I asked.

'Keith had to invite someone he'd never talked to back to his room,' Clarissa explained.

'That was me, I suppose,' I said.

'Correct,' Clarissa said. 'Well, you did ask. It turned out rather well, don't you think?'

'No one went for truth, then,' I said.

'No,' Clarissa agreed. 'In the end, no one did,' and she started the drive back to Oxford.

8

'Bookworm and Superhero'

'If this is our moment of fame, I don't think much of it,' I said to Keith.

It was December, the eighth and final week of our first term, and dark and icy outside; the cold had soaked into the creamy stone of St Bart's as if the college itself was chilled to the bone. We were sitting at either end of Keith's bed, our legs underneath the covers for warmth. Resting on the red-and-black zigzag duvet between us was a large mathematics textbook, a packet of cigarette papers, the handleless mug Keith used as an ashtray and a badly photocopied sheet of A4 paper that he had just found in the toilet on the landing outside, and brought back for me to peruse.

It was the college Bogsheet, an occasional gossip report put together by a boy – it was invariably a boy – who had been elected to produce it:

As Christmas draws closer, who do we expect to see indulging in flagrant PDAs (Public Displays of Affection – do keep up), with or without the excuse of mistletoe?

The Bogsheet has observed, from afar, the development of an oh-so-close friendship between a high-flying college thespian and a certain flame-haired first year. We hear rumours that she has a boyfriend, who necessitates frequent trips to London, and are reminded of the character from *The Importance of Being Earnest*, who invented an invalid friend called Bunbury as an excuse to get away. We say: let no Bunbury stand in the way of true love!

Santa need not look too far to find another likely couple in need of a little aphrodisiac assistance. Usually a superhero has to don his costume in order to get the girl, but if this black-clad crusader really wants to get it on with the brainy brunette bookworm of his dreams, he should probably get rid of his cape.

'You mustn't let it bother you,' Keith said, lighting the joint.

'It doesn't,' I said.

'They really are just friends, you know.'

I sighed. 'You think?'

'Anna, she flirts with everybody. Male, female, old, young. Even me. You, too. It's the only way she knows how to interact. I think it's pathological. She really can't help herself. The only way she can turn it off is to stick her nose in the air and try to ignore people. Otherwise, she's giving it all she's got, all the time. I bet she even does it with your tutor.'

'She certainly does work the charm with Dr Kaspar,' I agreed.

'I think she thinks she needs to,' Keith said. 'Being pretty isn't enough for her; she wants everybody to think she's brainy too, which is tough with so many eggheads around. I suspect she's got you down as competition on that score. Your tutorial partner apparently keeps telling everybody about how good your essays are.'

'Really? Well, that's nice to know.'

I took the joint from him, inhaled, and began to feel a little better.

'The funny thing is, sometimes I really do get the feeling that Victor fancies me,' I said. 'But if anything *did* happen between us I'd be absolutely terrified. I mean I wouldn't have the least idea what to do.'

'Really? You mean you've never done it? Well, don't expect too much, is my advice.'

I passed him back the joint. 'So it was a . . . disappointment?'

'I suppose the circumstances weren't ideal. I'm not in a rush to do it again . . . unless Magdalena comes begging, of course.'

'So, er, who did you . . . ?'

'The babysitter. Don't look so shocked, it's not as bad as it sounds. I was fourteen and she was sixteen, and I think she thought she was doing me a favour. She decided to seduce me on the sofa while *Ghostbusters* was on the video. I couldn't stop worrying about what would happen if my little sister woke up and came downstairs, though. I kept thinking about how we could explain it to her, and what we'd have to say to make it all right. So it was a pretty strange experience. I mean, not unpleasant, just a bit odd. I've still never seen that film the whole way through.'

'It sounds very off-putting,' I observed.

'It was,' he agreed. 'When I went out with someone else later on I was really worried it would spoil things, so I wouldn't do it even though she wanted to. Which turned out to be a big mistake. We held hands a lot and I wrote poems for her, and then she dumped me and lost her virginity to Kevin Shale.'

He offered me the joint, but I shook my head. I was feeling faintly giddy, and my grip on myself was beginning to loosen. Everything around us had become both hazy and extraordinarily vivid, and hummed with significance, as if it all had a message for me, if only I could tune into it.

Keith dropped the joint into the handleless mug. 'I ♥ Los Angeles', it said. That was where Clarissa's father lived, and it had once been hers, till she broke it and Keith asked if he could have it. He was always a careful custodian of things other people didn't want.

'In my experience, suffering unrequited love is significantly less painful than trying to have a proper relationship and screwing it up,' Keith told me. 'I went out with Tanya for all of six weeks. It was a summer thing, we were both kids really: what did I think was going to happen? And yet when it was over I was absolutely beside myself. I behaved like a bloody idiot, to be honest. That was when I did this.'

He shook back one of the sleeves of his jumper, turned his hand so his palm was facing upwards, and held it out for me to inspect. The inside of his wrist was criss-crossed by a series of thin white lines. Then he withdrew his hand and let it fall to his lap.

'It hurt like hell, which is why I only did one of them,' he said. 'I did it in the bath, one night when nobody else was around. Then I thought better of it. I had to get out and put something on, which wasn't easy, as you can probably imagine. We lived round the corner from the hospital, so I walked to A & E. I was dripping blood everywhere. It was pretty disgusting. Then they stitched me up and sent me home. When Tanya found out she just avoided me even harder. I still see her around sometimes, though. Last time I bumped into her she was the size of a house and had twin toddlers on a lead. I think she's probably happy. It was hard to tell.'

I reached out and took both his hands in mine, and said, 'You must promise me you will never do anything like that again.'

'Don't you ever even think about it, either,' he told me.

'I won't,' I said.

'Nobody else knows about that, by the way.'

'Then it's between you and me,' I told him.

I let his hands go, and he said, 'Let's talk about something else,' and picked up the Bogsheet.

'Do you know who this is? "Frisky fresher couple

found indulging in a carnal act in the laundry room, giving a whole new meaning to washing your dirty linen in public?"'

I did not know, but began to speculate in order to oblige him, and the rest of our conversation that night was resolutely frivolous. Later, though, when I was alone in my own bed, the only way I could dispel the darkness of what he had told me was to turn on the light and read until dawn.

And that was the only lasting consequence of the Bogsheet: I now knew about Keith's scars, and the others did not. Meg, who had been lampooned in a previous issue for the double lilo she'd bought to accommodate her fiancé, was indignant on our behalf, but Barnaby pointed out that it was nearly the end of term and everybody would have forgotten who was meant to be in love with whom by the time we came back. Clarissa shrugged off the speculation about herself and Victor as if it was only to be expected that her peers would conjure up imagined passions for her, and Victor, who hadn't read it and was oblivious to what it implied until we told him, was much too excited about his forthcoming play to care.

He had pulled off quite a coup, persuading Oxford's Theatre Royal, which never usually staged student shows, to take on the production of *Doctor Faustus* he was planning for a week's run in the summer term. Oddly, it was Clarissa who was coolest about this achievement, commenting disparagingly that he might get a mention in the local press if he was lucky, but he shouldn't expect miracles in terms of getting coverage in the nationals. She then made a point of bigging up her boyfriend Desmond's latest creative venture, a one-man show that he'd written and planned to direct, produce and star in; and I thought, *She's making a real effort to be loyal*, and preferred not to wonder what might happen if she ever tired of the attempt.

Term ended and one by one we dispersed back to our other lives, to the places that we still thought of as home but which, over the course of the previous eight weeks, had gradually become less vivid and real to us than St Bart's, the one-time dream that we now could not quite imagine ourselves outside.

Meg was the first to leave. Her father, the vicar, drove up in a battered old estate car, with her little brother in the passenger seat – though he was not so little, and, like Meg, was fair-haired and good-looking, liable, I imagined, to find plenty of temptation coming his way, though perhaps he would care less about trying to be virtuous than his sister. I helped take Meg's stuff down to the car, and saw that her father put the deflated double lilo Meg had shared with Freddie into the boot without comment; seemed genuinely delighted to be taking her back home.

Barnaby was next, catching a train back to his parents' manor house in Norfolk – moatless, he assured us, and in desperate need of a new roof. The rest of us lingered on. We were allowed to stay for another couple of weeks, unless our rooms were needed for conference delegates, and Keith and I were planning to remain for as long as possible, on the pretext that we were using Oxford's numerous libraries to further our studies. In reality, though, we were just reluctant to leave.

By the middle of the following week the college was unusually quiet. Its corridors were empty, there were no more meals served in the dining hall, the bar was closed, and you could take your pick of seats in the library. Clarissa offered Victor a lift to London, and Keith and I stood rather forlornly by her Mini as she loaded it up in readiness to leave.

'*Au revoir*, then,' she said once she was done. 'I'll see you all in a couple of weeks.'

She had invited us all to see her boyfriend's play in the holidays, and stay over with her afterwards. We were all going apart from Meg, who was going to miss out on the get-together because she had to spend time with her future in-laws. I felt rather sorry for her; I couldn't imagine that they would be as much fun as hanging out at Clarissa's.

'Have a good Christmas,' Victor said to me, and then, to my complete surprise, he pulled me into a slightly clumsy embrace and kissed me on the cheek.

As he let me go I felt myself turn scarlet. I muttered, 'You too.'

Clarissa, who had already started the car, wound down her window and said, 'Come on, Victor. Time to go,' and Victor said a quick goodbye to Keith and ducked into the passenger seat.

Clarissa reversed out of her parking space and bumped the Mini forward over the cobbles as Keith and I waved, and a moment later they had disappeared from view. Then Keith turned to me and said, 'If I poured water on you now, you'd sizzle.'

'He just caught me by surprise.'

'It's all right,' Keith said. 'You don't have to pretend to me, remember? I'm the one who knows.'

Early the next morning Keith knocked at my door and announced, 'I'm going to walk to Witcherley Lock. Do you want to come?'

'Where's Witcherley Lock, and why do you want to go there?'

He brandished a slim pamphlet that looked as if it had been acquired from the city's tourist information centre. 'It's not far. Six miles round trip. The fog should have cleared by the time we get there.'

'Fog?'

'The mistiest mornings often turn out to be the brightest days,' Keith said firmly, and so I acquiesced and we set off.

He walked at quite a pace, and I had to hurry to keep up. He led me down a narrow lane that took us away from the High Street, cut between the colleges of St Thomas and St James, and opened up on to the Meadows. Gliding forward through the whitened air, his long cape barely stirring as he walked, he looked like a fixture of the place, as much a part of the landscape as the gargoyles that decorated the west side of St Thomas's, or the tall gates that barred the way into the Meadows at night.

The tree-lined walkway down to the river was more

than wide enough for two abreast, and we had it to ourselves. The colours of the Meadows had faded from the bright jamboree of autumn; what was left was a palette of light and dark – the hazy sky tinted rose by the late dawn, the clusters of stark black branches obscured by the clouds that had drifted down to earth, and just ahead of us, a glimpse of fast-flowing grey water.

We strolled along without speaking until we reached the towpath. I was thinking about Victor: what he was doing that very minute, what he was thinking about – rehearsals for *Doctor Faustus*, most likely – and what his Christmas would be like.

He had said that his father, who had Alzheimer's, was increasingly muddled and forgetful. Him being at home was a chance for his mum to have some respite, but she was still always encouraging him to travel, to go off and meet new people, to pursue his ambitions. She didn't want him to be tied down or held back; she wanted him to be free.

No wonder he was so driven. And yet surely even Victor sometimes tired of always planning for his future, and felt the lack of a lover to share the present with?

'Shall we stop at the vantage point?' Keith said, and we settled on the bench where, weeks before, when the trees still had their leaves, I had sat with Barnaby and Victor and Clarissa and Meg. Keith had taken a picture of us with Meg's camera and said, 'There, that's one for the album. The posse is now officially immortalized,' and Clarissa had said, 'I hope not, given that we're all disgustingly hungover and look like death warmed up.'

As we looked out at the river Keith said, 'It's beautiful, isn't it?'

It was cold, but not freezing; the sun was already beginning to suck up the fog, and I'd been moving fast enough to stay warm. There was no real reason for the chill that ran down from my head to the base of my spine.

'It is,' I agreed.

'I have something for you,' Keith said.

He brought something wrapped in brown paper out of the messenger bag he was carrying under his cape, and handed it over. It was a book, a plain green hardback, a little worn. I opened it and saw, on the first page, his name and mine, and a kiss.

'Happy Christmas, Anna.'

'You shouldn't have,' I said. 'I feel bad. I haven't got you anything.'

'It's a gift,' Keith said. 'That means you're not obliged to give me anything in return. Anything at all.' He held out his hand. 'Here, let me put it back in my bag. But don't let me forget to give it to you later.'

I reached out to embrace him. 'Thank you, Keith. I'll treasure it.'

Up close, the heavy wool of the cape smelt of old damp. I let him go, and he took the book from me and put it back in its paper bag, saying, 'I'll be interested to know what you think of this. I didn't expect all that much of it, and then it kind of crept up on me. I think for me it really illustrated what fiction is for – that it's a place for the things you just can't do in real life, for whatever reason. Or don't want to do. But you'll see what I mean when you read it.'

'I look forward to it,' I said.

He put the book back in his bag, and we got to our feet and set off again towards the lock.

9

'The love bubble'

When I arrived at Clarissa's house I was embarrassed to realize that I was actually half an hour early, despite having spent what felt like forever wandering around clutching my London *A-Z* and looking for the address. I'd been so keen to arrive that I'd caught the train from Deddenham much earlier than I needed to.

Fourteen Culhearn Mews turned out to be a boxy, 1960s building, not unlike the block I lived in at college, all wood cladding, concrete and expanses of glass. Heavy curtains had been drawn across all the windows, allowing only an occasional chink of yellow light to show through. I rang the bell, and a moment later the door opened and I found myself face to face with one of the small-screen icons of my childhood.

Even though I didn't particularly remember watching *The Primrose Path*, Mandy Martin's sharp green-eyed gaze and heart-shaped face were intensely familiar, as if she was a long-lost aunt. She was smaller than I would have expected, as if time had shrunk her, although actually she had aged very little. Her skin was very finely lined around her eyes and mouth, and there was a crispness to the line of her jaw and the cut of her hair that suggested assiduous maintenance.

I introduced myself, and she shook my hand – hers was littler and frailer than mine, but her grasp was disconcertingly tight, so I was left feeling both oafish and slightly crushed.

'I can't say I've heard a lot about you,' she said, standing back to let me in. 'Clarissa does her best not to tell me anything.'

I found myself in a small, chocolate-brown corridor, with shaggy carpeting and textured stripes on the wallpaper. A series of framed photographs of Mandy ascended parallel to the stairs. There was Mandy posing in tennis whites, looking cute; Mandy in profile, wearing a strapless red silk dress with a skirt as big and pouffy as a parachute, plus matching lipstick; Mandy in black and white, her cheekbones lit up like a diva's, eyeing the camera through a wisp of polka-dotted veil.

'You won't see any pictures of Clarissa, at least not recent ones,' Mandy said. 'She won't let me. The other friends aren't here yet, and she's in the bath, so why don't you come on up and have a glass of wine with me? You look like you could do with warming up.'

I followed her upstairs into a lounge done out in shades of tobacco and citrus, with a large gold-framed oil painting of a cut lemon dominating one wall. The room was filled with big, bold, confidently mismatched pieces of furniture: an orange cocoon chair, a long,

L-shaped white sofa, a tall lamp with an arched steel spine and a bulbous shade. So this was what Clarissa had grown up with. No attempts at quiet good taste, nothing antique, but plenty of colour, and a fondness for eye-catching possessions.

We went through into the kitchen, which was white and aquamarine with scattered tiles in geranium red; it was like stepping into a child's drawing of sunset at the seaside. A sleek Burmese cat sidled out, giving Mandy a reproachful look as if to say: 'Look what you dragged in.'

Mandy indicated that I should take a seat at the white Formica table. She handed me a large glass of red wine and sat down opposite me.

'So, while I've got you on my own, do tell me,' she said, 'is there any hope for my daughter?'

'I'm sorry, I'm not quite sure what you mean.'

Mandy glanced across to check the door was shut. She dropped her voice and said conspiratorially, 'I was sure Clarissa would meet someone new when she went to Oxford. I know my daughter very well – as well as I know myself; we are much more alike than she would care to admit. New town, new man, right? That's how it goes. So who is he?'

I was so taken aback by this brutal appraisal of Clarissa's character that I couldn't think of anything to say. Mandy raised her eyebrows and nodded ruefully: 'News to you? It's true, I'm afraid.'

'I think Clarissa's a very loyal person, actually,' I objected.

'I thought perhaps the new chap might turn out to be

one of these boys who is coming along to this ghastly play tonight,' Mandy said. 'It would be so like Clarissa to invite the replacement along to see the old love interest make a fool of himself.'

She got up, picked a piece of paper up off one of the worktops, and slapped it down on the table in front of me.

It was a flyer for Desmond's play, *Now, Gods, Stand up for Bastards!*, which was on at a local pub theatre. Below the title it said, in large type, 'WRITTEN, DIRECTED BY AND STARRING DESMOND COX', and above the title were two pictures of Desmond, presented as if shown on a split screen. In one he was dishevelled and punky-looking, and in the other he was wearing a bowler hat. The rebel must have been meant to look angry and heroic, and the conformist was surely supposed to appear villainously smug, but actually Desmond's expression in both images was pretty much the same.

Clarissa had told us that the play was about a struggling actor, the illegitimate son of a critic who refuses to acknowledge his son's brilliance. Desmond was to take on both roles. As far as I knew, Desmond's dad, whom Clarissa dismissed as 'very rich, something to do with plastics', was not planning to see the show. Neither was his mother, who had been happily married to his father for many years, and had interpreted the play's subject matter as a deliberate slur on their family life.

'I suppose he must have felt very pleased with himself, getting a swear word into the title,' Mandy said.

'It's a quote from Shakespeare,' I said, 'from Edmund in *King Lear,* when he says he's just as good as anyone else, even though he's illegitimate, in fact he's probably better—'

'I know where it comes from,' Mandy snapped. 'I was an actress for many years. Please don't assume that you know the works of our greatest playwright better than I do, just because you happen to be studying English at Oxford.'

'Clarissa says Desmond's going to get all the way to the top,' I said, hoping this would turn out to be safer ground. 'She's always going off to visit him, and she talks about him all the time. I think she really is in love with him.'

Mandy rolled her eyes. 'He's an excuse for not having a go herself,' she said. 'God knows, she's had plenty of chances. When she was little she was always getting asked to do commercials, and she refused point-blank. When she finally did a play at school she didn't even tell me – I found out about it when an agent rang up here wanting to represent her. Clarissa hadn't invited him or anything, he was somebody's father. But she swore blind she was never doing it again. And then she started seeing Desmond.'

'I think she wants to be a writer. Or that's what she said the first time I met her.'

'Oh, that's just a whim. If she hasn't dropped it already she soon will, once she's had a bit more of a chance to realize what the good stuff is like, and has given up imagining she might be able to emulate it. It's so obvious what she ought to be doing, sometimes I do ask myself if she's just avoiding it to annoy me. The funny thing is, we go to the theatre a lot. She's quite happy watching.'

Clarissa burst in. She was wearing her kimono, and her hair was loose and damp, its long tendrils tightening into corkscrew curls as they dried.

'What are you two talking about?' she demanded, and then, without waiting for an answer, 'Anna, why don't you come down, and I'll show you my bit of the house. You can chat to me while I get ready. Bring your glass of wine.'

I glanced back at Mandy just as I was about to leave the room. She was still seated at the table, staring into space with an expression of frustrated longing, as if she'd just been thwarted in love.

'It was nice to meet you,' I said, but she showed no sign of having heard, and I got the feeling she had already forgotten I was there.

I couldn't really tell whether Desmond's play lived up to Clarissa's hopes or down to her mother's expectations; I found it almost impossible to concentrate. Part of me longed for it to be over with, so we could all escape the stuffy pub basement and have a drink. At the same time I was in no rush to go anywhere, and that was because I was acutely aware of Victor.

He was sitting just the other side of Clarissa, attentive and alert, and not, I thought, because of the performance going on a couple of rows in front of us. I felt as if I was being appraised with just as much interest as anyone was paying to Desmond. Perhaps it was wishful thinking, but Victor seemed just as conscious of me as I was of him.

Our mutual awareness snaked between us in the

gloom, a shared illumination that tactfully bypassed Clarissa, who was hunkered down in her seat, half hiding behind her hair. I guessed she didn't want to put Desmond off by catching his eye, and perhaps she was nervous for him; or maybe she, too, was not finding the play especially gripping. I could just make out Barnaby's profile on Victor's other side – he was leaning forward, and appeared to be concentrating hard; next to me, Keith was slumped in his seat, so still he could have been asleep.

Finally, there was a small, solid silence that let us all know the play was finished.

Victor said something to Clarissa – it must have been complimentary, because she nodded and looked pleased. Then he joined enthusiastically in the general applause. Desmond took first one bow and then another. And at last I was free to go to the bar and see if Victor would flirt with me.

Maybe it was because we were out of our usual environment, or maybe it was because Meg, who usually had a sobering effect on the rest of us, was absent, but none of my friends were quite their usual selves that night. Or rather, we were all trying to be our usual selves, and were overshooting the mark. As the evening wore on we became increasingly hectic and self-conscious, as if we'd been apart longer than a mere few weeks and were trying to recapture the way we'd once got along, or were new acquaintances trying to be memorable to each other.

By the time Desmond joined us we were on to our

second round of drinks, having spent the first round teasing Barnaby for admitting he hadn't been able to make head nor tail of what the play was on about. To my surprise, Desmond seemed quite happy to take a back seat in the conversation. He didn't show any signs of being particularly keen to get to know us, or of being eager to make a good impression, or even of finding us objectionable and wishing he had his girlfriend to himself. Perhaps worn out by the demands of the show, he appeared to be content to be bought one pint after another, and to say very little.

When the bell rang for last orders, Clarissa turned to him and said, 'You will come back with us, won't you? You know you can easily stay out of Mum's way.'

Desmond pulled a face. 'Please,' Clarissa said, gesturing round at the rest of us, 'you know I can't come back to yours tonight,' and then put a hand on his thigh – or somewhere near to it – underneath the table.

'OK, OK, I'll come.'

On the half-hour walk to Culhearn Mews Clarissa, Barnaby and Desmond took the lead, and I fell in behind them, between Victor and Keith.

No, I definitely wasn't imagining it – the private hum of attraction between me and Victor was still there. I thought it wouldn't do to be too obvious, so I made a point of talking to Keith. Victor kept quiet, but I knew he was listening, and I knew something was going to happen, but I had no idea what.

As soon as we were settled in Clarissa's basement sitting room she produced a bottle of whisky and insisted that we play a drinking game. When Desmond got up and said he was going to bed she barely seemed to notice, and made no move to follow him, even though she had been so keen for him to come back with us. He took this in his stride, as if it was nothing new for her to blow hot and cold; and as she distributed the glasses and poured us each a measure, it occurred to me that she might one day be equally capable of electing to ignore one of us.

The game Clarissa decided we should play was 'I never have', where one person reveals something they have yet to experience – shoplifting, or skinny-dipping, or dialling 999, or burying a pet in the back garden, or making spaghetti Bolognese – and anyone who has done it, whatever the it is, has to drink up. Keith rolled a relentless supply of joints, having been assured by Clarissa that Mandy had smoked too much of the stuff herself in her younger years to object, and Victor, who could usually be relied on to turn in soon after midnight, showed no signs of being ready to sleep.

Soon after one o'clock we realized that Barnaby had disappeared, and Clarissa found him snoring gently in the corridor outside her bathroom.

'So that's him out,' she commented, returning to her place next to me on the sofa. 'Who's next?'

'Maybe it's a sign that it's time to call it a night,' Keith commented. He had sunk so deeply into the beanbag on which he was resting that he appeared to have melded with it; his eyes were half shut, and he looked well on the way to dozing off himself.

'Oh come on,' Clarissa said. 'Victor, it's your turn.'

'All right, I've got one for you,' Victor said. 'I've never seen one of my parents on national television.'

'There you have me. I've certainly ticked that one off, many many times,' Clarissa said, and raised her glass to her lips.

'I can't say whether I have or not,' I said.

Keith's eyes opened a fraction. Clarissa said, 'This game only permits yes/no answers, I'm afraid. "I don't know" is not a valid option.'

'"I don't know" happens to be the truth,' I said. 'I don't know who my dad is. He could be anybody. I could have seen him on the telly. I might even have met him. But if I have, I'm none the wiser.'

'What, are you a test-tube baby or something?' Clarissa asked.

'No, my mum just never told me who he is. She got together with my stepdad when I was still quite little, and the other one was never around. I think he was probably a bit of a shyster. At any rate, I think it's fair to say that he's never come looking for me.'

Victor asked, 'Are you ever going to find out?'

'Yeah, just not yet, in a couple of years' time,' I said. 'I'm not in any big rush.'

'How can you stand not knowing? I know I couldn't,' Clarissa said.

I shrugged. 'I've lived with not knowing for a long time. It's more scary to make the change than to carry on the same.'

'I'm glad you said,' Clarissa commented. 'I think we should know these things about each other.' She glanced around the room as if to reassure herself that she had not been alone in her ignorance; Keith, who was staring at his boots as if they were particularly fascinating, did not meet her eyes, and she homed in on him straight away. 'You knew all about this, didn't you? How come she told you and not us?'

Keith's eyes flickered open. 'Timing, I guess,' he said, and something about his tone made even Clarissa think twice about pressing the point.

After that, as if by unspoken agreement, we gave up on the drinking game; Clarissa, who had been the one goading us on, seemed to have lost the heart for it. By and by she yawned and said, 'I must love you and leave you. Anna, do you want to sleep down here or in the living room?'

'I'm afraid I am absolutely physically incapable of stirring from this beanbag,' Keith said.

'OK then, it's all yours down here, boys, but don't be surprised if Barnaby comes blundering in later on, looking for a more comfortable spot,' Clarissa said.

She led me upstairs to the lounge and made me up a bed on the sofa. After she had gone I took off my jeans and got under the duvet she had provided me with. I felt absolutely wide awake; I couldn't imagine how I was ever going to sleep.

I made a start on the book Keith had given me for Christmas, but I just couldn't get into it. It was a short-story collection, published back in the 1970s; I had never heard of the author. The opening pages were about an alcoholic enforcer called Buster Dibbs, and I had to go over them several times before I could make any sense out of what was happening.

Scarcely ten minutes later there was a soft tread on the stairs and Victor appeared. He'd taken off his shoes, but was otherwise still fully dressed.

'Sorry to disturb you,' he said. 'I saw the light was still on, and I thought I'd just sneak up and get a glass of water.'

'Don't worry,' I said. 'Would you get me one too, while you're there?'

He went obediently off and when he reappeared I put my book aside and patted a spot on my duvet just next to me. He handed me a glass. We both sipped. I put my glass down. He kept hold of his.

'You're not sleepy?' he asked.

'Not at all. It's the excitement of being in a strange place, I guess.'

There was a pause. He didn't look at me. He was so close I could make out his pores, the individual hairs in his brows, the flecks in his irises. I wanted very much to touch him, but even more than that, I wanted him to touch me.

'It's been quite a night, hasn't it?' I said. 'What did you think of the play?'

'Honestly? I think Desmond could do with a better director.'

'But you didn't tell Clarissa that.'

'It wouldn't have been very diplomatic.'

'So what did you tell her?'

Victor swallowed another mouthful of water, then put his glass down. 'You have to say something, don't you? I said, "He's really good. I'm jealous."'

'Are you?'

'No,' he said.

He looked at me and smiled, and then we kissed, a bit awkwardly at first. What seemed like it was going to be a short kiss turned into a long one. Then he broke off and looked at me regretfully.

'We can't do this here,' he said.

'Can't we?'

'We can't,' he told me.

'I don't want you to go.'

'I don't want to go either.'

'Then don't.'

I reached out and flicked the switch on the standing lamp, plunging us both into darkness. I lay down and reached up to him; the pale streak of his face loomed above mine in the darkness as he hesitated. Then he settled down on his side next to me, propped up on one elbow.

He stroked my hair. 'I've wanted to do that for a long time,' he said. 'You have beautiful hair. I hope you never cut it.'

'I don't intend to,' I said, and yawned. 'That's weird. I suddenly feel sleepy.'

'That's all right,' he said. 'Go to sleep then.'

'I've never actually slept with anyone before. In either sense. I mean, not in the sex way, and not literally, either.'

'Then I'm honoured,' Victor said, and that was the last thing I heard him say before I was out, not quite like a light, but more a slow drifting down into the darkness, as if I was being gathered in.

*

The first thing I saw when I opened my eyes was the glistening inside of a very large, acid-bright cut lemon. It took me a moment to work out that I was looking at the painting that hung opposite the sofa in Clarissa's living room, and it was morning; daylight was creeping in through a chink in the yellow curtains.

I was alone, and there were voices coming from the kitchen: a man and a woman.

'Go on, that's it, just chuck it all in,' the woman said, and a machine whirred.

I got to my feet, combed my fingers through my hair and went to see who was up.

Barnaby was leaning over the kitchen worktop, detaching a jug of vile-looking green fluid from a blender. There were carrot tops and remnants of green vegetables – unidentifiable to me, but no doubt powerfully healthy – scattered across the chopping board next to him.

Mandy turned to beam at me. 'Anna! Well done, you're just in time to try some of our carrot and kale special.'

'I might pass on that, actually, but if there's any chance of coffee – instant would be fine . . .'

'Oh, please, no! Let me fix you a decent breakfast. It's such a pleasure to have the chance to satisfy my maternal impulses – Clarissa just tells me not to fuss. She was quite chubby as a little one, you know. She really has to watch what she eats.'

Quarter of an hour later Barnaby and I were both tucking into bacon and eggs when Keith and Victor came in.

'That smells amazing,' Keith said. 'Mandy, you're a wonder.'

'It's nice to be appreciated,' Mandy said.

Victor sat down next to me and said, 'So how did you sleep?'

'Very well, thank you,' I said.

'All right for some,' Barnaby said. 'Muggins here ended up sleeping on the floor because his so-called friends had taken all the best spots.' He glanced at Mandy to make sure she was still fully occupied with Keith, and asked in a low voice, 'So what did you all make of last night?'

'Definitely one to remember,' Victor said. 'Though not at all what I was expecting. What did you think, Anna?'

'I'd go along with that,' I said.

'That Desmond chap's a bit of a pillock, isn't he?' Barnaby observed in a whisper that was slightly too loud to be discreet.

At that moment the door was flung open and Clarissa came in, wearing her peach-coloured kimono. Her hair was more wildly curly than I had ever seen it, and she had a conspicuous lovebite by her breastbone.

'Would you believe it, Desmond wants breakfast in bed,' she said.

Then she stopped in her tracks and looked round at us all: Barnaby gaping as if he'd been caught red-handed, Victor smiling, me blushing, Keith standing next to Mandy but watching me, and Mandy looking round to try and figure out what was going on.

'What did I miss?' Clarissa said.

'Oh, nothing much,' Victor said, 'just talking about last night.'

'I feel quite worn out by it all,' Clarissa commented. 'What's this? It looks like a mad science experiment.'

She leaned across the table, poured the last of the liquidized carrot and kale into a glass and held it up to the light: it was a murky opaque green and looked more like poison than a remedy. She sipped it, pulled a face and set it down on the table.

'That's gross,' she said. 'Someone's a glutton for punishment. Anna, is that coffee? That's much more like it. I'm definitely having what you're having.'

Oh no you're not, I thought. My knee was touching Victor's under the table.

I pushed the cafetière across the table towards her, and said, 'You're in luck. I think there's enough for Desmond, too.'

Just before he left Mandy's house, Victor asked me for my phone number. I didn't have to wait long for him to call; he phoned me the very next day, soon after I'd got back to Deddington.

'It was a good evening, wasn't it? I just wanted to say thank you,' he said.

'Shouldn't you be saying that to Clarissa?'

'Not in quite the same way. No. No, I think the person I really want to thank is you.'

'You're very polite,' I said.

He laughed. 'Not always. I'll see you in college, OK?'

'I guess you will,' I said.

'Not long now,' he told me. 'I'm going back on the Sunday before term starts. You?'

'Same,' I said.

'Would you like to go out for a drink?'

'Are you asking me out on a date?'

'I don't date,' he said. 'Dating is for adolescents in American teen movies. Sometimes a drink is just a drink. Sometimes maybe it leads to something else, but wouldn't it be dull to categorize it in advance?'

'I just like to know where I am,' I said.

'I find it's more interesting to think about where you might be going,' he said. 'I'll call for you at eight.' And he hung up, leaving me staring at the phone in my hand in astonishment, as if it had just performed a magic trick.

Sure enough, at the appointed time, he knocked on my door in Hanover Buildings.

I asked him in. He shut the door. He put his arms around me and we looked at each other.

He shook his head and sighed. 'You're making this really quite difficult,' he said.

'I am?'

'It's cold out,' he said, touching his hand to my cheek – it was so icy that I flinched. 'Why are we going anywhere?'

'We don't have to,' I said.

'I was hoping you'd say that.'

I took his hands and slid them under my jumper. He made an odd little gasping sound, as if I was the one who was surprising, uncomfortable even, to the touch.

'I've been wanting to do this for a long time,' he said.

'Good, because I have too, and it's been driving me slightly crazy,' I told him, and then I led him towards the bed.

I'd acquired Clarissa's fondness for candles, and had one standing ready by the washbasin. Victor sat on the bed and watched me as I lit it, and turned out the overhead light, and for once his expression was not at all teasing. Then he stood up and faced me, and we undressed each other quickly and with ruthless efficiency.

He was more taut and muscled than I would have expected. Next to him, I was soft, and my skin was very white in the candelight. His was tawny, but smooth, almost hairless.

'You know I'm a virgin,' I said.

'We don't have to rush this. We don't have to do anything.'

'I suppose you do know a lot about me,' I said.

'I do,' he agreed. 'I know about Jean-Paul, the boy you got to second base with on the French exchange trip, and I know about Charlie who kissed you at the sixth-form barn dance, and that other one who asked you out over the tills at the garden centre. I prefer not to think about them, to be honest. It makes me feel slightly murderous, which seems wrong, because I'm sure they're perfectly harmless. But anyway, I don't want to think about them now, because all I really want is to make you come.'

'You're welcome to try,' I told him.

'Then I think you should lie down,' he said, and I did as I was told, and he took up his place on the bed next to me and propped himself up on one elbow and said, 'This is more like it.'

He started to touch me. I wasn't expecting anything much to happen, though I was quite willing to be accommodating. But I found I didn't need to be, because he wasn't trying to break me in; what he wanted was a response, which was exactly what I was giving him. I was submitting, not to his will, but to my own; and then, to my astonishment, I realized I was about to lose control completely.

I really was falling – falling into an oblivion that was both mindless and violently alert – and I was nothing to do with it any more; my body had taken over, and was twitching and jerking and stretching itself out as if I'd been given an electric shock, or had something in me that I was trying to shake out. And then it was over, and I was boneless and monolithic, an old totem on a faraway shore, and he leaned over and planted a kiss on my lips and said, 'Wherever you are now, that's where I'd like to be.'

Later on we agreed that we were hungry. Victor checked the time: it was coming up for midnight. We decided to dress and go out and get something from the kebab van just outside the college gates.

'Classy,' I said, pulling on my underwear.

'Always,' Victor said, buttoning his shirt. 'Don't say I don't know how to show a lady a good time.'

We hurried out into the cold and starry night, across

the main quad, through the front gate and on to the High Street. Despite the late hour, or perhaps because of it – there was nowhere else to go that was open – there were two or three people already lined up, waiting for food.

As we approached something caught my eye: the glint of a thin white face, turned towards us, then a stirring of fabric, like a dark flag. A tall cloaked shape detached itself from the queue and walked quickly and soundlessly away from us down the High Street.

'I think I just saw Keith,' I said to Victor. 'But if he saw us, he didn't want to let on. He looked like he couldn't get away fast enough.'

'Probably just trying to be tactful,' Victor said. 'Anyway, he's all for it. I said something about you to him that night at Clarissa's, and he told me to go up and see if your light was still on.'

'What about the others?'

'I'm sure they'll all be delighted for us, and if they're not, they'll soon get used to the idea,' Victor said, and pulled me in closer.

When I woke the next day and rolled over Victor's eyes were already open and gazing steadily back at me. I had always thought of them as brown, but on closer inspection they were green with brown flecks that were almost golden, the colour of amber.

'You really are beautiful when you're asleep,' he said. 'No more than when you're awake, of course, but it's a perspective on you that I'm grateful to have had.'

'I can't quite believe you're here,' I said. 'I've been

thinking about this for so long, and hoping it would happen, but I was never quite sure whether you liked me. I mean, I knew you liked me – I just wasn't sure if it was this kind of like.'

'I think it was when we went to see the white horse on the hill – that was what did it,' he said. 'I saw you properly, and after that I couldn't unsee you. You watch everybody, you see everything, you're so sensitive to what's going on around you, and then inside you're a firecracker. And there's something about your voice. It's so cosseting. I found I just wanted to listen to it. And for everybody else to shut up for a change.'

'For me it was that first night in hall,' I said. 'I just spotted you from the other side of the room, the back of your neck . . . I don't know why I noticed it. It's not as if it's a part of someone that usually attracts attention. I just wanted to get closer to you, I guess.'

'And now you are.'

'And now I am.'

We started kissing, and soon afterwards I said, 'I hope you won't think I'm a terrible slut . . . but I would rather like you to seduce me properly.'

'Are you sure? It's not too soon?'

'Please, Victor, don't be so scrupulous. I'm offering myself to you – the least you can do is take advantage.'

'Well, when you put it like that . . . I'd have to go out and get something first, though.'

'Just don't take too long . . .'

When he came back I was still naked and waiting. He stripped off and kneeled on the bed in front of me.

There was a brief moment of nervous anticipation as he unrolled the condom on to his cock, and a stab of pain as he lowered himself into me, and then we started to move together and I forgot to care that I'd bled on the sheet.

'Are you OK?' he asked.

'I think I could get used to this,' I said, and then neither of us spoke again till it was finished.

We were still in bed mid-morning when there was a hammering at the door.

'Yoo-hoo!' Clarissa's voice pealed out. 'Open up, lovebirds! Your considerate friends have taken steps to replenish your energy, and bought you breakfast.'

Victor and I looked at each other.

'Guess we better get it over with,' he said.

I yelled back, 'Give us five minutes,' and got out of bed – Victor reached out for me as I slid out from underneath the duvet, but I dodged his grip – and started to dress. By the time I opened the door to them we were both more or less our everyday selves again, though my hair was still wild and Victor looked as if he could have done with several more hours of sleep.

'We brought you croissants,' Clarissa said, shaking a brown paper bag.

'We want you to know that we think whatever you are up to is the best news ever, not that it is any of our business, and we are not going to pry,' Meg declared.

'Just so long as you don't expect us to take sides when you have arguments,' Keith said.

'So have you actually done it yet?' Clarissa wanted to

know, stepping forward towards the bedroom alcove as if hoping to spot a stray condom.

'Clarissa, boundaries, please,' Meg said. 'We just wanted you to know that we know, and actually all of college will probably know pretty soon.'

'We did try and call round earlier, but there were such odd noises coming out of the room, we decided we ought to creep away,' Keith commented.

'Banshee,' Clarissa said.

'All right, I think that's enough,' Barnaby said. 'Victor, I hope to see you back in our sitting room sometime.'

'Oh, they'll both be back,' Meg said. 'No one can stay in the love bubble forever.'

'Is it a bubble?' I asked.

Meg and Clarissa exchanged glances.

'Hopefully not,' Keith said. He was the first to back out.

In those first weeks, I soon found myself obsessed by sex – or rather, not sex in itself, but sex with Victor. The nights we spent together were a blur of intimacies, tangled limbs and new tricks, interspersed with talk – banter, teasing, confession: anything went – and deep sleeps during which we spooned and he folded himself around me, an arrangement that was practical as well as comforting, as we only had his single bed or mine to share.

During the day, when Victor wasn't around, I was occasionally visited by disconcerting flashbacks. Everything around me would be clear and tangible: wooden surfaces and worn upholstery, questions and answers, the essay or cutlery or pen or cup or whatever it was that was in my hands. But suddenly I'd be distracted by an unwarranted glimpse of erotic contact, the colour of skin and darkness. It was like being haunted. It was hard to believe that these fragmented images were my own memories, and one of the bodies framed in them was mine; and yet I knew it was so.

That spring, when Gareth and Mum and Tippy came for the mid-term visit, Victor was there to meet them.

I wasn't surprised that the get-together was a success – I had been reasonably confident that Victor would win them over – but I was taken aback by just how successful it was. He listened to Tippy's very decided opinions about various films and television programmes and actors, and turned out to have seen just about everything she mentioned, even though I would have expected them to have wildly different tastes. He listened to Gareth talking about stocks and shares and business, and contrived to impress him by talking about his plans for marketing his *Doctor Faustus*, and the tough rehearsal schedule he'd drawn up. And he somehow got Mum talking about her plans for the house and garden, and even what she'd been reading.

When we said goodbye to them Mum hugged me and said, 'I do hope you're being careful.'

'Oh, Mum, yes, of course I am.'

'You won't neglect your studies, will you?' she said. 'You've come so far.'

'I won't,' I promised. 'It's not like we're in each other's

pockets all the time. I promise you, I'm doing just as much work as I ever was.'

'Good,' she said, 'because it's so easy, at your stage in life, to make a mistake that wrecks your whole future.'

She withdrew and turned to smile at Victor and say how nice it had been to meet him, leaving me wondering if I had been the mistake she was referring to.

I met Victor's parents for the first time at Easter. I desperately wanted to make a good impression, so of course I was nervous, and my anxiety was compounded by doubt about how well I would cope with Victor's father, who had been diagnosed with dementia a couple of years earlier. Victor had given me to understand that when Eleanor, his previous girlfriend, had come to his home the meeting had not gone especially smoothly, though he had avoided going into details, which probably meant Eleanor had let herself down somehow or other, and he was trying to do the honourable thing by not revealing how she'd slipped up.

He met me outside Swiss Cottage tube and we set off together towards his parents' flat, which was in a block round the corner.

'Mum worries about Dad wandering out into the traffic,' Victor said as we headed down a side road. 'But I think he's safer here than he would be in a house. The concierge knows him, anyway. The problem is, you can never quite predict what he's going to do next. What if he remembers how to work the door release and nips out while the concierge's back is turned, or when someone's coming in, but then forgets how to cross the road? You just can never tell what he's capable of on any given day. The one thing he can still always do is play the piano. Mum says that as long as he can sit down and pick out the "Moonlight" Sonata, she'll know that despite whatever problems he has coming out with the right words at the right time, deep down he hasn't changed, and she hasn't really lost him.'

We carried on walking in silence.

'I don't want to let you down,' I said.

'You won't. I know you won't.'

He stopped and we turned to face each other. He put his hands on my shoulders and looked into my eyes, then took me into his arms and held me.

'I love you, Anna.'

'I love you, too.'

And there it was, the pledge, the act of faith, binding the two of us like a promise. We had finally said it.

'After that,' Victor commented, 'everything else is going to be plain sailing.'

He took my hand and led me to his front door. He let go of me to press the intercom, and his mother buzzed us in.

Upstairs in the flat, Denise Rose smiled and said, 'Anna, how lovely to meet you. I've heard so much about you. May I take your coat?'

Her voice still retained a trace of the US, where she'd been born and raised; she had met Victor's father after coming to London to study. Although her words were friendly, her gaze was assessing and wary, as if I might pose some kind of threat. I told myself that she'd relent once she saw how much I cared for her son, but it did also occur to me that love, with its capacity for upsetting the best-laid plans, might be exactly what she was worried about.

I passed her my jacket and she said, 'My, that's a pretty dress.'

'Thank you,' I said. It was new, bought for the occasion: not too short, black, but patterned with little sprigs of purple flowers.

I cast around for something to compliment her on in return, but her own clothes were plain and functional: beige cotton trousers and an ice-blue fleece. She wore no jewellery apart from her wedding rings, and no make-up. Her hair was greying and undyed, and her skin was sallow and lined. She looked more like a granny than a mother, and not a cuddly one.

There was piano music playing somewhere inside the flat: Victor's father? Or a recording? The melody was gentle, melancholy, unfinished; it looped round like a person who doesn't quite know what to think of next.

'That's beautiful music,' I said.

'It's Janáček. One of David's favourite CDs,' she said. 'He was a professional pianist for many years, and music still seems to calm him, so I'll leave it on for now, if you don't mind. Come and meet him; he's in the living room.'

She showed us through to a solidly comfortable room carpeted in green, with dark, polished furniture. I looked around for photographs of a younger Victor and saw, displayed on the sideboard, Denise as a hopeful young woman, cradling a sleeping baby whose head was covered in fine spikes of silky black hair; she was looking up flirtatiously at the camera, and her too-long chestnut-brown fringe was falling into her eyes.

Next to it was Denise with another baby, fairer this time, wrapped in a blue blanket; she was holding him towards her and it wasn't possible to make out his face. The son she had lost: Victor's dead brother. Her face looked pinched, as if she had been sucked dry; her shoulders sagged as if an immense but invisible force was pressing down on her, and her body was all there was to keep the weight of it from crushing the baby.

It was identifiably Victor who stood next to her, twisting as if he'd been told to move in closer so he could fit into the shot: poised and alert, caught in the act of switching his glance from his mother and brother to the taker of the photograph as if to say, 'Must this be my problem, too?'

The man behind the camera could only have been Victor's father. And there he was, sitting in an armchair opposite the telly, regarding me with polite interest. It was a shock to see how much Victor resembled him; I could have been looking at Victor forty years from now.

He had been carefully dressed. The creases in his trousers and sleeves were sharp and fresh, and everything about him, from his fawn slippers to the crisp collar of his checked shirt, looked as if Denise had just arranged it.

'Eleanor, how good to see you!' he said, and looked very pleased with himself.

'This isn't Eleanor, Dad, it's Anna,' Victor told him.

'It's Victor's new friend, David, not the old one,' Denise added.

David winced and screwed his face up as if physically pained. He said, 'Silly old me. Do forgive me.'

'Don't worry about it, Dad.'

'Eleanor. From college,' David said.

'Not Eleanor. Anna,' Victor insisted, and David looked dismayed again.

'Why don't we go on through and eat,' Denise said. 'Yes, straight through there, Anna. Victor, could I have a quick word?'

I found myself in a plain, biscuit-coloured kitchen, all immaculately clean. We were having sandwiches for lunch, by the look of it; they were already cellophaned and waiting on the worktop. I wondered if David would be eating with us. I considered trying to tell Denise and Victor that I didn't mind what he called me, but then I realized that would be a lie; despite his condition, I wanted to make an impression, even if only in passing – I wanted a sign. I wanted to know, however fleetingly, that he had recognized that I was important to his son.

Denise told Victor, 'You're going to have to cut him some slack. At the end of the day, what does it matter if he remembers her name or not?'

I couldn't make out Victor's reply, but I could tell that it was apologetic and soothing, and a moment later they came into the kitchen and we settled down at the table.

Denise served tea and we made small talk about college, and I began to think that all was going to be well. We were halfway through the sandwiches when David appeared in the doorway and said, 'Denise . . .

there's something I need to tell you,' and I realized the music had stopped.

Denise got up and took him by the hand. She said, 'Would you like to join us?'

David nodded, and she helped him to sit in the empty space at the head of the table.

He started to speak: 'It's . . .' And then he dried up, and his face conveyed only the disorientating shock of suddenly finding himself on stage with nothing to say, and no idea of what came next, or who was who or what was what.

Denise quickly intervened: 'Isn't it nice, us all sitting here in the kitchen together with Anna? This is Anna, David. She's Victor's friend from college. He's brought her to see us.'

'I remember!' David shouted. 'I'm not a bloody fool!'

'I know you're not,' Denise said.

'I'm sorry, my love, it's just . . .' He went blank again. Then, with a furious effort, he turned his gaze on me.

He smiled sweetly and said, 'I'm so pleased for you both. I'm a great believer in marriage; a married couple is always more than the sum of its parts. And there's nothing like a good wedding, is there? Everybody getting together to wish two people the very best? All that goodwill. All that hope. It's got to do something, don't you think? It's got to help. It can't hurt, at any rate.'

'Dad, Anna and I aren't married,' Victor said.

'Oh . . .' And again David looked lost, as if he was adrift on a cloud of unknowingness.

Then he said, 'Friendship is a great pleasure, isn't it? It

doesn't always last, but what does? You can only count on what's in here,' at which he pressed his hand to his heart. Next he tapped his head: 'Because, believe me, what's up here will get you into terrible trouble.' He leaned forward and added confidingly, 'The problem is, it doesn't always bloody work.'

The concentration required to say all this seemed to almost finish him off. He slumped back in his chair, and his eyelids drooped as if he was on the verge of nodding off.

'Let me change the music for you,' Denise said. She helped him up and steered him back into the living room.

Victor stared at the table. Then he looked up at me, and his expression was simultaneously defiant, mortified and remote.

'Maybe he has a point,' I said.

'Heart, head, there's no difference,' Victor said. 'It's just a question of degree. One day he won't know who Mum is either. But then, like he says, nothing lasts forever.'

There was another burst of music from the living room, but this time it was not a recording. The 'Moonlight' Sonata: hesitant in places, with one or two false notes, but still urgently beautiful.

David was playing the piano for all he was worth, as if that was the only hope he had of telling us all the other things he would never be able to remember to say.

Part Three

2012

The Valley

'You know why I'm here,' she said. 'Don't even bother saying you don't believe me. Do you think you're the kind of man a girl with no father dreams of laying claim to? Mum never told me. It was my auntie who thought I should know, and she'd be horrified if she knew I was here talking to you. But I thought I'd come down and see for myself.'

What kind of fool child was that? Who would, on learning that its father did what he did for a living, still want to look him up?

'And now you've seen. So what do you want from me?'

She shrugged. 'Certainly not tears and a big embrace. You don't look like the crying sort. How about "It's nice to meet you at last", and a handshake?'

From *The End of Mr D.*, by Benjamin Dock (1978)

10

'Reboot'

2012

I couldn't believe it. Not only had Meg decided to give me an old laptop she no longer wanted, she had sent Jason to set it up.

This was remarkable in many ways. First and foremost, I was going to have a computer of my own in the flat at last. I'd been too worried about eking out my redundancy money to splash out on a new one, and had got to know my nearest internet café very well when submitting job applications. There was also the incidental point that the founder and CEO of fineromance.com had temporarily become my personal IT guy. And also, it was surely a clear sign that Meg and Jason were now on good terms. Probably he could have sent someone round to set the computer up for him, but he'd come in person, and although I was very happy to see him, I didn't think I was the person he was really there for.

He'd brought quite a retinue with him, though no one else was actually in attendance to witness Jason down on his knees under my sitting-room table, exposing an inch of buttock cleft as he scrabbled round to plug in my new PC.

Minky, the part-time nanny, had taken one look at my small, cramped, toyless flat, and had opted to take the children out to the nearest park. She was a no-nonsense woman in late middle age, dressed in a sensible, easy-care uniform of tunic and trousers; I suspected Meg of having had some influence over the appointment. Meanwhile, Jason's driver was waiting in the car outside. So it was just me and Jason, and if I hadn't known otherwise, I could almost have kidded myself that he was just a regular bloke who made a living out of fixing people's computers, and saw his kids at weekends.

He got up from his knees and sat in front of the computer and tapped on the keyboard as the screen sprang to life.

'There, that's all working for you now,' he said. He stood and gestured towards the chair to indicate that I should take over: 'Want to give it a try?'

'OK,' I said, and settled into place in front of the computer. I put 'Victor Rose Winter's Tale' into the search box, and hit return.

'I'm going to the matinée this afternoon,' I told Jason. 'Victor gave me a free ticket.'

'Rather you than me. Meg was always trying to get me to go watch that stuff with her.'

The theatre blog came up in the search results. I clicked on it and started reading a post Victor had written.

> 'A sad tale's best for winter', and *The Winter's Tale* is sad – and surprising – and brutal (it includes the famous stage direction, 'Exit, pursued by a bear').
>
> Well, bears *do* eat people, on occasion, so that doesn't mess with reality – only with convention. But the conclusion of *The Winter's Tale*, surely one of the most poignant and memorable reconciliation scenes in all of literature, *does* mess with reality. How can a woman who has been irrevocably lost come back to life? And yet – sometimes, she can.

Jason said, 'You're getting on with Victor these days, then.'

'Yeah, we're in touch,' I said, closing the blog and opening up a plot summary of the play instead.

Jason patted the top of the computer. 'Now you've got this there'll be no stopping you. I promise you, it makes it a lot easier to keep up with people.'

'Thank you so much, Jason, I'm really grateful to you. It would have taken me forever to get it set up. It's so nice of Meg to give it to me.'

'Oh, don't sweat it, we've got plenty,' he said, turning away and getting his phone out to call Minky and tell her it was time to go. Then he looked around the flat, arms folded, taking it in.

'You haven't got anything from college days,' he commented. 'Meg insisted on having our graduation photos up, pictures of Oxford, the river at sunset, all sorts of stuff.'

'I didn't bother going back for graduation,' I told him. 'I got sent my degree certificate in the post. I don't even know where it is.'

'Fair enough, but there's nothing here to say you were ever there at all.'

'That's not strictly true,' I said, getting up and going over to the bookshelf. I tapped on one of the spines. 'There's the *Anglo-Saxon Treasury*. I wouldn't have that if I hadn't studied it.' I stooped and picked a green hardback off the end of the bottom shelf. 'And here's a memento of Keith. A book he gave me.'

The tops of the pages were filmed with dust. A movement caught my eye: a thin grey spider, scuttling on to the cover. I went over to the bay window, opened it, and shook the spider off, then blew the dust out into the air.

I withdrew, shut the window and turned back to Jason.

'I've never read it,' I said. 'I've always felt too guilty.'

I opened the book to the title page. *The End of Mr D.*, by Benjamin Dock. Underneath it, Keith had written, *To Anna, Happy Christmas, Love Keith X.*

'I never really knew him,' Jason said. 'I hope you won't mind me saying he seemed a bit odd. You were a tight little clique, weren't you? A bit incestuous. You can look back now and see that it was going to implode one way or another. I think Meg must be just about the only one who stayed close to everybody else. I know she lost touch with you, but you're back in the loop now, aren't you? You know, Barnaby was asking about you the other day.'

I shut *The End of Mr D.* and put it down on the table next to the computer.

'What did he want to know?'

'Just the usual stuff. What you're up to, where you are, if you've got any kids, whether you're seeing anybody.'

'Do you see much of him?' I could barely remember them ever having a conversation at St Bart's, but perhaps they had got to know each other somehow since.

'Yeah, we stay in touch. We were business partners for a bit, back in the nineties,' Jason explained. 'He invested in my first website. You probably heard of it. Travel.com. He had a legacy from an aunt and he ploughed it all into the company. Kept it going for the first six months when nobody else was interested. He's into property now. Travels a lot. He's mainly based in the States.'

'What happened to his parents' manor house?'

'He managed to get it turned into flats. Made him a fortune.' He checked his phone, then looked up and said, 'You'll be seeing Meg soon, I expect.'

I nodded. 'I'm going to be singing your praises.'

He hesitated – I could tell that he was already imagining himself outside my sitting room, in the car, taking the children to wherever they were going next, trying to answer emails on the way. He said, 'Can I ask you something?'

'Fire away.'

'Do you think, if you had a relationship that was

really good, but it got all screwed up, it might ever be possible to fix it and start over? To reboot?'

Clearly, he wasn't thinking of Victor and me – why should he be? Why should us attempting a reconciliation even be a remote possibility? No, he was referring to himself and Meg, and I told myself to answer accordingly.

'I think it might call for a grand gesture,' I said. 'A sign that things are going to be different from now on.'

He nodded and put his phone away. 'Maybe something could be arranged,' he said, more to himself than me, and then went down to the waiting car, which was glossily black and the size of a minibus. Minky was already there, ushering the girls into their seats. I waved goodbye to them from the bedroom window and went back to my new laptop to look up Barnaby Stour.

He wasn't as high-profile as Jason, but he wasn't exactly invisible either; he had profiles on various social networks, mentions in news stories about prestigious new property developments, a biography on his company website. The photos showed him dressed like a City gent in a dark suit and tie. Over the years he'd become corpulent; his face was heavy and jowly. His fair hair was cropped shorter now, and touched with silver.

I imagined the wealth pooled in various upmarket bank accounts under his name, the army of lawyers he would be able to hire, the private detectives and hackers he could set on anybody who threatened his good name. Suddenly my flat didn't feel like such a safe place after all, and the laptop Jason had just installed didn't seem quite such a boon. Yes, it might be a means for me to find out about anything or anyone in the world, but the traffic was two-way; it also allowed the world to get to me.

I closed down the computer and wondered if everything I was doing – getting back in touch with Meg, the reunion, having Jason round, and now Victor – was a recipe for disaster. But then, what could I do about it? It was too late. I'd spent years avoiding going back. Now the past I had tried so hard to flee had somehow also become the future I was moving towards, and the only choices were to press on or to stand still.

It was one of those clear, bright February days when you notice the first snowdrops coming up, but the sunshine didn't quite succeed in dispelling my unease as I made my way through the back streets near Waterloo to the Ploughshare theatre. I only forgot about Barnaby, and the questions he'd been asking about me, once the play was under way.

I hadn't seen one of Victor's productions for nearly twenty years – the last one had been back in Edinburgh in 1993. I'd avoided the flop film he'd directed during his stint in Hollywood, and I wasn't much of a theatre-goer. But this . . . This knocked me out. Victor had always been driven and full of ideas, but somewhere along the line – and I supposed that without ambition, this would never have happened – he had also become someone who could give a story a heart, and reach out to touch a crowd.

Had *The Changeling*, which had been Clarissa's breakthrough, been this good? All I'd really been able to see back then was the striking effect Clarissa had on the audience. Everyone had come away convinced that she was a brilliant actress, and if sexiness was acting, everyone was right. She certainly hadn't become someone else on stage; she had seemed herself, but magnified, costumed, and irresistible. At any rate, she had drawn the eye. Was that charisma, or talent, or something else? It had made her a star but, as she aged, it seemed uncertain whether it would be enough to keep her one.

Clarissa's old boyfriend, Desmond Cox, had been her co-star back then, though she had effortlessly upstaged him. He had a part in this too, as Autolycus, a pick-pocket rogue; he was surprisingly good, so much so that he ceased to be Desmond and became part of the machinery of a story: a sad tale with a happy ending.

After the bad but repentant old king had been re-united with Perdita, his long-lost daughter, the spotlight was turned on a statue of her mother, the king's dead queen; it was so life-like, nobody could quite believe it wasn't real – and then it was so real, nobody could believe any longer that it was a statue.

She breathed, moved, spoke, and was alive again, and her daughter was restored to her – the husband too, but that, it seemed to me, was more of an official after-thought, to show that he was properly sorry for having been so foul in the beginning, and had duly been for-given.

Was it really possible to be reunited with an absent parent after such a long separation and for that meeting to be neither hollow nor false, but to offer some kind of redemption and conclusion? Could it be possible for me? I sat through this magical encounter with tears running down my cheeks and the good citizens to each side delicately edging away from me. After the lights came up, I let them get out first and composed myself; and then I went out in a daze to find the ladies', and on into the foyer in case I could catch sight of Victor.

But he wasn't there. I went up to the theatre café, which was right at the top of the building, with a panoramic view of the rooftops of Waterloo and a glimpse of the distant circle of the London Eye. Desmond was there, signing a programme for a large, confident-looking old lady in an outsize silver-blue cardigan.

He had acquired a modest celebrity in recent years as the star of a BBC3 sitcom in which he poked fun at himself for being a failed actor. I'd never watched it, but it seemed the old lady had, because as I drew close and waited for my turn I heard her say, 'I just love *My Ex Is Famous*. You must carry on for a third series.'

'I will if they'll have me,' he said drily, and then it was my turn. As he scrawled his name I said, 'You might remember me. I'm Anna Jones. I used to be a friend of Clarissa's.'

He looked up, but didn't appear to recognize me. 'Where from?' he said. 'She has always had a lot of friends.'

'Oxford,' I told him.

'Really? Then you must know Victor too.'

'I do,' I said. 'Actually, I was hoping to catch him. Do you know where I might find him?'

'He's around here somewhere.' He studied my face

and frowned. 'Now you come to mention it, you do look familiar.'

But someone else approached him for an autograph before he could place me properly. I wished him well and retreated, and then I saw Victor.

He was sitting at a table round the other side of the café, gesticulating and talking into his phone. Opposite him was a dark-haired, sombre-looking little girl, sipping a lemonade.

I approached him as he finished his call. His expression seemed to say, *Please don't add to my stress – I can't cope with any more right now.*

'What's up?' I asked him.

'Nothing's up, I mean, nothing major,' he said, with a glance at Beatrice – for it was obvious that this was his daughter. She had already acquired his distant watchfulness; it was an oddly adult quality in such a young child, and gave her a curiously old-fashioned air, like a straight-backed infant in a Victorian painting.

Beatrice looked me up and down, without suspicion or hostility, but without any obvious desire to win approval, either.

'Mummy was meant to be here, and she isn't,' she said. 'So now Daddy's worried because he has a meeting to go to and children don't usually go to meetings. But it's going to be all right, because I'm seven years old now and I've just been telling Daddy that I can look after myself.'

'I'm sure you're more than capable of it,' Victor said, 'but technically, that would be illegal.'

'Who are you meant to be meeting?' I asked.

He pulled a face. 'Couple of the theatre trustees,' he said. 'They came to the show. They want to talk money.'

'All you have to do is get someone to watch me and then you can go,' Beatrice said. 'That's what Mummy would do.' She looked at me. 'Couldn't you do it?'

'Oh no, I'm sure Anna has other things to do,' Victor said. 'I'll go back to the office, see if I can find one of my colleagues.'

'But I want to stay here,' Beatrice said. She consulted her watch; it was white with a pattern of pink strawberries. 'Also, your meeting is now,' she added.

'I don't mind if Beatrice doesn't,' I said. 'I'm not in a rush to go anywhere. How long will you be, anyway?'

'Shouldn't be more than an hour,' Victor said, glancing round rather desperately, as if someone might be about to come and rescue him from his dilemma.

'Daddy, go!' Beatrice told him.

He gave me a look that was both resigned and commanding; I knew it meant, *I probably shouldn't be trusting you with this, but I am, so take good care of her or else*. Then he got up and bolted.

'He worries too much,' Beatrice said composedly, but I thought she looked a little less sure of herself the minute he was gone, and was not quite as self-contained as she might have liked to be.

I sat down in the chair Victor had left, and said, 'It was kind of you to tell him it was all right to go.'

'It was kind of you too,' she said. Then, 'So are you Daddy's new girlfriend?'

'Oh no. No, I'm not.'

'But he said you were a friend. And when grown-ups get old, they don't have friends of the opposite sex unless they're gay. Are you gay?'

I blinked. 'I don't know where you picked that up from, but it's not true.'

'I'm not prejudiced,' she assured me. 'I think everybody should be able to get married to the person they love.'

'Or not get married at all. Which is fine too.'

'I know,' she said. 'So you're not gay? It's just that I think Daddy really ought to have a girlfriend. It's only fair, because Mummy has had a boyfriend for ages and now he's given her his seed and she's going to have another baby, and they're probably going to get married one day, when the baby's old enough not to spoil it all by crying.'

'Really? So you're going to have a little brother or sister. Do you think that will be good? Or not so good?'

She shrugged. 'I expect it will be OK. It might be quite cute, when it's not crying. Are you a mummy?'

'No. I've never really wanted to be a mummy. Do you want to be one?'

'Yes. I'm going to have two children, a girl and a boy, after I've gone to university. And travelled the world. Do you have a boyfriend?'

'No.'

'I think you might like Daddy if you got to know him better. He's nice. Though he's a bit silly sometimes. Are you good at doing hair?'

'Only ponytails.'

This, it seemed, was a grave disappointment. She

shook her head, and said, 'You should be good. You have long hair. Can you draw?'

'I can try,' I said.

She produced a pad of paper and some pens from the pink rucksack at her feet. I glimpsed a sketch of a princess shrinking away from a wolf – I thought Victor must have done it, though I wouldn't have guessed he would have such a cartoony style. Beatrice turned to a blank page and pushed the pad across the table towards me.

'I'd like a wedding, please,' she said, passing me a pen. 'The bride needs to be in a very beautiful dress, and the groom should be handsome and not have a beard or a moustache. I would like six bridesmaids. But I'll tell you that bit when I get to it.'

'I'll do my best,' I said, and got to work.

Three-quarters of an hour later I looked up to see a tall, elegant, pregnant woman gliding across the café towards me.

Beatrice said, 'Mummy!' and her face lit up. Her mother leaned down to plant a kiss on her forehead and stroked her hair, then turned to me, still standing, her arm round Beatrice's shoulders, cradling Beatrice against her bump.

'I'm Caitlin,' she said. 'And you must be Anna. I've seen Victor's photos of you. You haven't changed all that much, considering it was twenty years ago.' She relinquished Beatrice and held out a hand for me to shake. 'Thank you for keeping my daughter entertained.'

'Oh, it was a pleasure.'

'Have you had fun, Bea?' Caitlin asked.

'It's been quite good,' Beatrice said judiciously. 'I think eight out of ten.'

I pushed the pad back across the table towards Beatrice and Caitlin glanced down at it, but didn't comment on my artwork, which was tactful of her, since it wasn't the best.

Instead she said, 'I've heard rather a lot about you, down the years.'

'Oh dear,' I said, 'not too awful, I hope.'

'No, not awful. I always used to think that out of all Vic's exes, you were the one I might have got on with. You were certainly less intimidating than Clarissa Hayes.'

At that point Victor came hurrying over towards the three of us. He took in our little tableau with undisguised dismay – the two exes going head-to-head, the daughter listening to every word – and said, 'Is everything all right here?'

'It is, I think,' Caitlin said. 'I suppose I ought to get mad at you for leaving our daughter in the care of a virtual stranger. But she seems all right, and I don't have the energy.'

Victor slumped into a chair. 'Thank goodness for that,' he said.

'We'll leave you to it,' Caitlin said. 'Time to say goodbye, Beatrice. Anna, it was nice to meet you at last.'

Beatrice kissed Victor goodbye and gave me a little smile and a wave, and then donned her pink rucksack and went off, holding her mother's hand.

'Are all seven-year-olds like that?' I asked Victor.

'Like what?'

'Self-possessed. Trying to figure out the world.'

'I don't know. You'd have to ask Caitlin. I don't spend much time around any other children. Beatrice has always asked a lot of questions. But I think all children do that.'

'I didn't,' I said. 'I think it's wonderful that she does.'

'I could really do with a stiff drink. Can I get you one?'

I hesitated, but only for a moment, and then I said, 'Yes. I think you could.'

Three stiff drinks later, I knew some of the ins and outs of putting on *The Winter's Tale*, Victor knew about the handful of dates I'd been on during the lean years before Pete, and I knew how he'd met Caitlin. She did PR for a big West End theatre; one of his productions had transferred there, and she had invited him out for dinner and bought him oysters.

'I knew it was over when I walked past the same restaurant one lunchtime,' he said, 'and she was in there eating oysters with someone else. A colleague, as it turned out. She said later she just wanted to feel glamorous again. Beatrice was a toddler then; we were both working, and we were both so tired all the time, all we seemed to do was argue. I knew I'd let her down but, at the same time, I really resented the fact that she'd found the energy to have an affair, but still kept on complaining about how exhausted she was. As if that was my fault.'

Then he filled me in about a few other women he'd

dated before Caitlin – a charity worker, a ticket agency boss, and a hypnotherapist, who had come along when he was at a particularly low ebb. 'It was after everybody hated my road movie. She was meant to be helping me to give up smoking, and it worked, but only because I went out with her for six months and she always gave me the cold shoulder if I'd been anywhere near a cigarette.'

At the end of the third drink I was finally relaxed enough to say, 'It was funny to find out that you'd called your daughter Beatrice. I don't suppose you remember, but it's my middle name.'

'Of course I remember,' he told me. 'I wasn't mad keen, to be honest. But Caitlin wanted it, and she said she couldn't see why you should make any difference. I love it now, though. I mean, I couldn't imagine it any other way.'

'Oh dear,' I said, 'I'm sorry if I put you off. Or nearly put you off.'

'That wasn't what I meant,' he said.

There was a pause. Our eyes met. My heart lurched. He looked away first, and glanced down at his empty glass.

'Let's go get something to eat,' he said. 'I'm plastered.'

'OK. Please, no oysters, though.'

'There's a great curry place just round the corner.'

And it was great. We ate poppadoms and raita, and decided not to drink, then caved in, and had half a lager each. He had rogan josh; I had korma. His leg brushed mine under the table, and we talked about before our break-up, and after, but not what had gone wrong.

He mentioned that Clarissa had broken up with him by fax from Table Mountain, where she'd been filming on location ('Or near it, anyway'). We did not speak about Keith, or Barnaby, and we did not refer to the part Clarissa had played in our downfall.

We spun it out for as long as possible, and then he gave me the chocolate that came with his coffee, and we split the bill and went outside, and I knew the same question was on both our minds: what next?

Outside in the dark street he pulled me to him and kissed me hard. Then he broke off and said, 'This is dangerous.'

'I don't know what it is,' I said, 'but I don't think it can be bad.'

'We fucked it up once. What's to keep us from fucking it up again?'

I touched my finger to his lips. 'We should go home,' I said. 'Separately.'

Parting was a wrench, but that was no surprise, and I schooled myself to smile and wave from my taxi before he slipped out of sight.

Surely you couldn't kiss like that and walk away. Sooner or later, it was inevitable that we would finish what we'd started . . .

But then, the next evening, I received an email from him.

Dear Anna,

I hope you don't mind me getting in touch this way – I got your address from Meg.

I just wanted to apologize for my stupid drunken behaviour and for spoiling what was a lovely evening. I promise that if we ever meet for a drink again it will be just that, and I hope I haven't spoilt our friendship, because having lost contact with you for so long I would really, really like to stay in touch.

I think perhaps we should leave it for a little while before we meet again.

I'm so sorry.

With very best wishes,

Victor

I cried. And then I looked out at the view of street-lights and stars from my sitting-room window, and told myself that it was all for the best; and that I was lucky to have even an occasional friendship, which was, after all, a great deal better than nothing, and much more than I once would have imagined possible.

A week later I met Meg for a drink in Dulwich. I thought going out would stop me brooding, and it certainly turned out to be an effective distraction.

It was obvious from the outset that something was going on, because I'd never seen her looking so hussyish. She was wearing a low-cut red silk shirt and big gold hoop earrings, and her hair had been coloured a shade or two lighter and was unusually tousled. Her habitually upright posture had slackened, and she exuded the surprised satisfaction of the middle-aged woman who has recently enjoyed lots of unexpected sex, and is looking forward to plenty more.

I greeted her and went off to the bar; when I glanced back she was checking her phone for messages, and smiling with the special softness that women reserve for lovers and children. When I sat down opposite her she tucked her phone back in her handbag – a little reluctantly, I thought – and then looked at me brightly and said, 'So, how are you?'

'Oh, fine, fine, nothing much going on,' I said.

This was far from true; I had been fretful ever since my trip to see *The Winter's Tale*. It wasn't just the near miss with Victor, and the fresh distance that had opened up between us; I kept thinking about Victor and his daughter. So tender and so close, in spite of everything . . . I couldn't help but wonder if my own father ever thought about me and Mum, or regretted his decision to turn his back on us and throw in his lot with someone else.

I was far from ready to explain any of this to Meg. However, she looked as if she might be too preoccupied by developments in her own life to notice that I was being tight-lipped.

'So how about you?' I asked.

Meg hesitated; then she gave me a slow cat-that-got-the-cream smile. 'Well,' she said, 'do you notice anything different about me?'

I looked her up and down. 'Yes,' I said. 'You never normally wear red. Or hoop earrings. And your hair looks like you've just been rubbing it up and down on a pillow. What's going on?'

By way of answer, she held out her hand. There was a large sapphire and diamond ring on her ring finger. I admired it, as you do; I imagined Jason, having put it there, doing the same thing. Then I let go and she examined it herself and wiggled her fingers as if testing that the hand and, by extension, the ring, and what it represented, were still a part of her. She laughed and ran her hand through her hair and put the magically transformed hand back in her lap.

'Congratulations,' I said.

'I know,' she said. 'After all these years, Jason's finally going to make a respectable married woman of me.'

'That's great news,' I told her. 'I'm so happy for you.'

'Thank goodness someone is. The Reverend Brian took me to one side and gave me quite the talking-to; he thought I'd been swept off my feet by the size of the ring. I ask you.'

Meg's little brother, Brian the vicar, was married with two children, and in charge of a parish just outside Oxford. Meg was plainly proud of him, but occasionally referred to herself rather forlornly as the black sheep of the family, and I got the impression that she would have preferred it if he hadn't been quite so consistently virtuous.

'I think I've just about won Bri over, anyway, and I've got him working on Dad,' Meg went on. 'Dad said he thought I was being irresponsible. Can you believe it? I have three kids with the man and suddenly marrying him is a rash decision. I mean, it's so clearly what we needed to do all along.'

'So when are you planning to get married?' I asked.

'We are not going to waste any time,' Meg said. 'It's already booked. Bri's got us into St Bartholomew's Church for the ceremony, then we've got the orangery in Shawcross Hall for the reception. But we've had to go for a Monday to squeeze it in. It's going to be the second of July. I thought I'd let you know as soon as poss, so you can save the date.'

Not a good portent as far as I was concerned: it was the anniversary of the night of the ball, just before I had left Oxford for good – or so I had thought at the time.

'My birthday,' I said.

'I hope you'll be OK to take the time off,' Meg said, as if she hadn't heard me. 'We've figured that the people we really want to come won't mind about it being a weekday, and we're not going to bother with all the awful old rellies. It's only going to be fifty or sixty people. Maybe a few more to the reception. Depends who can make it, really.'

'I'm so pleased for you,' I said. 'And I'm very touched to be invited. Who else is going to be there from St Bart's?'

'Victor,' she said, and raised her eyebrows as if inviting me to comment. I wondered if he would have told her about the kiss, and decided to assume he hadn't.

'We're on quite friendly terms at the moment,' I said, although I hadn't actually heard from him since his email, and had been unable to work out a way of replying to it.

'Good. That's great. I'm hoping Clarissa will be able to make it, and Michael, of course. I'm dying to hear all about how he's been getting on at college. He's got a girlfriend he's quite serious about apparently, so maybe she'll come too. If they're still together by then – you never can tell with student relationships, can you?'

'You certainly can't,' I agreed.

'We're going to invite Barnaby, too,' Meg said. 'I know it may be *slightly* awkward . . . with Victor there . . . given the way things turned out. They've barely seen each other since. But I'm sure everyone can manage to bury their differences for just one day.'

She glanced down at her ring, was briefly mesmerized by it, and then collected herself, and reached out to take my hand and squeeze it.

'I want us to have as many friends from Oxford around us as possible. Because not everyone from that time can be there.'

I withdrew my hand, shifted it on to my glass, managed another mouthful of wine.

'I'm grateful for the invitation,' I said, 'and I do very much want to be part of your big day, but I do have one condition.'

Meg frowned. 'Go on,' she said.

'Tell Barnaby to stay away from me. I don't want to talk to him. No social chitchat. No small talk. Nothing.'

Meg considered this for a moment.

'OK,' she said. 'I can take care of that for you.'

She peered at me assessingly, as if I was an experiment that had gone surprisingly wrong but was probably still salvageable, and I knew she was about to ask me what exactly my problem with Barnaby was.

I took a deep breath and thought back to the early days of Tippy's wedding planning. Once the venue was booked, there had been just one subject that had been capable of distracting Tippy from more or less anything.

'So,' I said. 'Have you thought about the dress?'

That night I got home to find I had another email from Victor.

> You've been very silent . . . I'm sure I deserve to be reproached, but wish you would tell me which particular aspect of my recent behaviour I should be most sorry about. Or maybe your lack of response indicates general disapproval? Or maybe you have just been too busy to reply . . . in which case I apologize for bothering you again!
>
> I suppose you've heard about Meg and Jason's wedding plans? We have four and a bit months to work out if we're actually talking to each other, and if so, how much . . .

He had signed off with a kiss. I read the message through again, and then made myself compose a reply then and there, without stopping to think.

> I've only been quiet because I don't know what to say and I don't want to lie. I miss you, and I want to see you again.
>
> But I do have some other things on my mind and I think I have to face up to them first. I need to talk to my mother. For good or ill, I want to find out about my dad, and if I can, I want to meet him. I am afraid of what I'll

find. But I also don't want to spend the rest of my life knowing that I was too scared to even ask. Hopefully when we next meet up I will be able to tell you how it all turns out.

I keep thinking back to your play, and to the moment when the statue moves and speaks.

Love,
Anna x

11

'What took you so long?'

So far, so good. The interview had gone well – better than I would have dared hope. Shauna Peters, the sleek-haired brunette director of the National Centre for Access to the Internet, had concentrated on asking me about my brief career as a teacher and the time I'd spent working in educational publishing, touching only lightly on the various temp jobs I'd done since. She'd been nodding along to my answers, had even smiled once or twice, and seemed shrewd and friendly. I had decided I liked her, though whether that was mutual, and would translate into a job offer, remained to be seen.

I'd been in for nearly an hour, and we'd got through to the part of the interview where I was invited to ask any questions of my own. Any minute now it would all be over, and I'd go home and try to forget that I was waiting to hear whether or not I was to become Shauna's assistant.

Which would be difficult, because over the course of the interview I had come to the conclusion that I really, really wanted the job. The salary was great, the work sounded interesting, and the offices had been a pleasant surprise, too. I'd expected them to be white and gleaming and minimalist and high-tech, like the insides of a spaceship, but the building we were in had once been a smart 1930s apartment block, and the art deco look of the lobby – all wood and brass and antique-rose carpeting – had been reproduced upstairs. The effect was plushy and reassuring, like a set for an old Hollywood romance with a chirpy heroine and a guaranteed happy ending.

We were in Shauna's office, which looked out over the street; we weren't far from King's Cross Station, and the flow of traffic below was constant, although the sound of it was muted. I was reassured to see that while Shauna might be an expert in new technology, she still made use of some of the older ways of finding things out and remembering them; there was a shelf of reference books behind her desk and a whiteboard covered with scribbles on the wall next to it. I couldn't make out what most of the notes said, but one, the largest, was a reminder: 'YOU HAVE TO WANT TO CHANGE'.

The only catch in all of this was Connor Dandry, the pale, red-haired man who was Shauna's communications manager. He took the lead on much of the work I would be contributing to if I got the job: the email newsletter, the website, the outreach visits to associations and clubs, the campaign materials aimed at persuading older people and others who, often for financial reasons, were not online, that it was worth their while to become citizens of the brave new digital world.

He was sitting next to Shauna directly opposite me at the small meeting table adjacent to Shauna's desk. But he had said almost nothing at all, had indeed barely moved, throughout the course of the interview. He had been listening intently and expressionlessly with his elbows on the table and his chin resting on his steepled fingers, ruminating as if in prayer.

At first I had thought his lack of obvious participation was odd, and not a good sign, and then I had got used to it. So I was surprised when Shauna said, 'I think that's pretty much all we have time for. Connor, did you have anything to add?' and Connor said:

'Yes, I do have a question for Anna, as a matter of fact.'

'Go on,' Shauna said.

Connor angled his head so he was looking directly at me; the rest of his posture remained unchanged. I could tell that he was about to put me on the spot.

'Anna, I understand your point that it's easy for you to empathize with people who don't have internet access or a computer at home because until recently you were in the same position yourself,' he said. 'You've explained how in the last couple of months you've been playing catch-up: you've started your books blog, you've got to grips with social networking, you've discovered the pleasure of making new connections online.' At this point he gave me a thin smile. 'Granted, you've done a great job of making up for lost time, but what I want to know is this, Anna: what took you so long?'

I hesitated. Shauna glanced at Connor, but he kept his gaze fixed on me. He raised his eyebrows and nodded encouragingly.

'That is a window on the world,' I said, pointing at Shauna's computer, and then gesturing towards the view out on to the street. 'There was a time when I didn't want to see what was out there. But I don't think that makes me a worse candidate for this job, I think it makes me a better one. You're looking for someone who can help you reach out to people who don't know what they're missing and persuade them to try something new. You don't need an expert. You need a convert.'

Shauna said, 'Anything else?'

'No, I think we're done,' Connor said.

'OK then, Anna, thank you for coming in,' Shauna said, getting to her feet and holding her hand out for me to shake. 'It was great to meet you. We'll be in touch. Connor, would you see Anna out?'

We went down in the lift. In the lobby Connor said, 'You've been on quite a voyage of discovery, haven't you? I hope you keep it up. Goodbye, then, and good luck,' and I passed through the revolving doors none the wiser about whether I'd managed to impress him or not.

As I made my way to King's Cross Station I mulled over what Connor had asked me and the answer I had given him.

A name would probably be enough.

I was due to go back to Deddington the following

weekend. If I approached Mum in the right way, at the right time, surely there was every chance I'd return with enough to go on.

Since Gareth had retired and sold his office-furniture business he'd taken Mum on a seemingly endless series of holidays. They had just come back from a six-week trip to Australia and New Zealand. Although Tippy and George, who lived just round the corner, usually saw them much more regularly than I did, this particular Sunday lunch was to be the first family get-together, with or without me, since Christmas.

Even though Mum had just been off on the other side of the world, and hopefully having the time of her life, as my taxi from the station pulled up in Topaz Close I felt the tug of the familiar guilt about confiding in her so little, and staying away from her so much. And now, instead of doing my best to give her a happy homecoming, I was planning to make a request that would almost certainly upset her.

Tippy and George's black BMW was already parked next to Gareth's silver Audi in the driveway. You'd have been hard pressed to say which car was more spotlessly clean and polished. Everything here was unmarked, pristine, weed-free; the borders were beautifully tended, full of daffodils now, and next time I came something else would be in bloom. Inside there would be no mess, nothing broken that was waiting to be fixed. They'd all be looking forward to a nice meal, a chat about the baby Tippy was expecting, maybe a walk. Did I really have to go and wreck it?

Mum came to the front door to let me in. We embraced, and then she held me at arm's length and looked me up and down.

'You look better,' she said, 'more rested. Did you finally go to the doctor like I said?'

'No, actually, I just seem to be managing to get a bit more sleep these days,' I said. 'How was your trip?'

'Very interesting but, to be honest, I'm quite glad to be back,' Mum said. 'I've decided to embargo any more long-haul flights for a bit. I think we need to stay close to home, what with Tippy's baby on the way. Anyway, we can tell you all about it later. I'm just at a crucial stage in the cooking – lunch'll be ready any minute.'

She ushered me into the living room where Tippy, who was now heavily pregnant, was reclining on a floral-patterned chaise longue while George leaned over her with a conscientious expression, massaging her bare feet.

'Excuse me if I don't get up,' Tippy said, 'I've got the most terrible water retention.'

I stooped to kiss her on the cheek. She said, 'My goodness, look at you! There is such a thing as too thin, you know. You need feeding up!'

'I think Mum's working on it,' I said.

George stood and we came together in a shy and fleeting embrace. He knelt down at Tippy's feet again and Gareth put his newspaper aside and got to his feet to give me a hug. It was as if we both wanted, in theory, to share a gesture of affectionate greeting, but when it came down to it, our bodies couldn't help but hold back a little.

'How's the job-hunting going?' he said, sitting down again.

'Oh, OK. I went for an interview a couple of days ago which seemed to go well, so I'm just waiting to hear.'

'Very difficult these days,' Gareth said, and shook his head. 'If I'd still been running my own business, maybe I could have helped you out, given you a way back in.'

'That's kind of you,' I said. 'I'm hoping I've got lucky this time, but we'll have to see.'

'I always thought it was a shame you jacked in teaching,' Gareth went on.

'I've sometimes thought that myself,' I admitted. 'I don't think I could go back to it now, though. So much of it is about crowd control. And the bureaucracy is insane.'

'I suppose even teaching's probably not so much of a sure thing nowadays, the way things are going,' Gareth said.

Tippy said, 'George, back rub?' and George came over to stand behind her and started massaging her shoulders.

'I honestly do not know how women do this on their own,' Tippy said. 'Personally, there's no way I'd want to venture down this route without having a major diamond on my ring finger first.'

She looked down at her engagement ring, and I thought of Meg in the pub, and how happy she was to be getting married to Jason at last, and of Mum in the kitchen, and how alone she must have felt before she started seeing Gareth.

'It must be tough,' I agreed.

'It's so important to have really good family support,' Tippy said. 'We're so happy that Mum's agreed to look after the baby when I go back to work. And Dad is just so excited to be having a grandson. I do hope you'll get involved too, Anna, as much as you can. Not straight away, of course, but by and by George and I will need to go out for a date once in a while, and we don't want to have to rely on Mum and Dad all the time. After all, don't they say that it takes a village to raise a child?'

'I'll try to help,' I said, 'though, as you know, I don't know all that much about babies.'

'We thought that it would be nice for you,' Tippy said, 'a way to have a connection with the younger generation.'

Because you're probably never going to have children of your own. But maybe Tippy's baby could bring us all closer, make us more of a family . . .

'So how's the love life?' Tippy asked. 'Have you met anybody new?'

'I'm not sure,' I said. 'I might have done, but I'm not sure if it's going to work out.'

'Really? Who is he?'

What harm could it do to tell her? And suddenly I wanted to tell, even though I wasn't quite sure what there was *to* tell, and everything was still so uncertain. But I wanted to be able to talk about Victor.

'An old friend from university, actually.'

Tippy looked sceptical. 'Old friend? Old boyfriend, you mean. There was only one, wasn't there? The theatre bloke. Oh no, you haven't hooked up with him again, have you?'

'If you have, it strikes me as a very bad idea indeed,' Gareth interposed. 'You were an absolute wreck after he'd finished with you. You were so quiet. You wouldn't talk to anyone, you wouldn't go out and do anything, you just sat in your room doing God knows what till the time came for you to move out and start your teaching course. Your mother was worried sick about you.'

'I know,' I said, 'but that wasn't Victor's fault.'

'Then whose was it?' Gareth said. 'I know there's a lot of this goes on these days, people going back into the past, looking up old flames on the internet, getting misty-eyed about things that happened when they were younger. I don't hold with it. You should be looking forward, not back. You're still young. Relatively young. You've got the best part of your life ahead of you.'

'Who is he, this chap?' George asked.

I looked round at them, at Tippy with her big belly and swollen legs, George fretting over her, and Gareth, the expectant grandfather who was apprehensive too. The energy of the family was already focused on the new arrival, which might just help to slacken the old tension around the question I needed to ask.

And as for Victor . . . if we were ever to become close again, close enough for him and my family to need to meet, for him to charm them all over again would be but a minor miracle, and one that would be relatively easy to accomplish.

'Really, he's just a friend,' I said. 'I'm not in a rush to get into anything. I've got plenty of other things to sort out first. So, no need to worry. I'm just going to see if Mum needs any help.'

I withdrew to the kitchen. Mum had the door shut and the radio on, and as soon as I went in I smelt the rosemary and roasting lamb. She had taken the meat out and was contemplating it with folded arms and a small smile of satisfaction, as if to say, *Another job well done.*

It occurred to me for the first time that all the effort Mum put into being a good wife and mother – cooking, and cleaning, and gardening, and entertaining – was also a way of carving out some space for herself, a private space within the life of the household that was under her control, and that only she could occupy. Which was what I had also done throughout the time we had shared a roof, though I'd found refuge in books rather than domesticity. Maybe that was what all women needed, however they did it, and however assiduously they worked at maintaining their relationships. And of course she had every right to her own sanctum.

I had never seen – had never wanted to see – that we might be alike; but perhaps her defensiveness and uncertainty had always been mine too, and when I was younger I had only pretended otherwise. But now I wanted to be sure of my place in the world for real.

I waited until we'd finished eating to present Mum with my question: at least that way I wouldn't ruin lunch.

We were alone together in the kitchen; she was washing and I was drying up. After a while I put my tea-towel aside and said, 'Mum, I've been meaning to ask you something.'

She was at the sink with her back to me, elbow-deep in soapy water, facing the garden. She finished with the gravy boat and put it on the drying rack, and said, 'What is it?'

'I've been thinking . . .'

The sentence died away as Mum scrubbed with unnecessary vehemence at the roasting tin.

'Have you,' she said. 'Good for you.' She kept her face averted, as if it was vitally important to keep on concentrating on the washing-up.

'It doesn't mean anything bad,' I said. 'It doesn't mean he's the least bit important. I know who my parents are, who my family is, and you're all here. It's just . . . he's just this slight niggle, that's all.'

'Don't,' Mum said. She turned round and pulled her yellow gloves off and threw them down on to the floor, where they landed with a wet slap. 'If that's all it is, why do you look so terrified about asking me? If it doesn't matter, why do you even need to ask?'

I launched into my prepared speech. 'If you had been separated from your child when that child was a baby, you would want to meet them, wouldn't you? It's the same thing. However much time has passed, there's a tie there that can't be undone.'

There was a slight, hesitant sound behind us: Gareth in the hallway, clearing his throat. He came in and said, 'Everything all right here?'

'She wants to know about Ben,' Mum said.

'Who's Ben?' I asked.

'Benjamin Dock,' Mum said. 'He's a writer. Or he was. It'll be easy enough for you to track him down. He even has a website. I like to keep tabs on him. I prefer to make sure he's at a safe distance.'

Gareth stooped to pick up the yellow gloves, and put them carefully back on the draining board. He stood next to Mum and put his arm round her.

'So now you know,' he said. 'If you're really determined to make contact with him, there's nothing we can do to stop you. You're a grown-up. It's your life. But be warned, he's a low-life. I wouldn't put it past him to come after you for money or something like that.'

'I haven't got any money,' I said.

'Well, he's not having any of mine,' Gareth told me.

'What's going on?' Tippy said, shuffling in with her arm arched behind her to support the crook of her back. 'It sounds like a soap opera in here.' She subsided heavily on to one of the stools by the breakfast bar and lifted her feet up so they were resting on the seat next to her.

'Anna's decided she wants to go and track down her biological father,' Gareth said, regarding me with a mixture of ire and disappointment, as if I'd just broken an unspoken rule. Mum was still avoiding my eyes as if she didn't quite trust herself to look at me, and her lower lip was trembling.

'What's brought this on?' Tippy said suspiciously. 'You're not up the duff, are you?'

'No, I'm not,' I said.

'There's definitely something different about you. You look younger, for some reason. Have you changed your hair?'

'No, I haven't changed anything.'

'I just can't quite put my finger on what it is,' Tippy said. 'Anyway, maybe it's me expecting that's got you thinking about all this.' She stroked her belly. 'I've found it's made me much more conscious of my heritage, who I am, what I'm passing on. Mum, Dad, this is Anna's choice, and you know what, if she wants to go looking for this person, it's high time she got on with it, and good luck to her. Have you told her who he is yet?'

'He's a writer,' I said, 'called Benjamin Dock.'

'Really? Never heard of him,' Tippy said.

'You wouldn't have done,' Gareth said. 'He wasn't very good.'

'Can we stop talking about him now?' Mum said.

George peered in and said, 'All OK in here?'

'George, I told you to stay out of it,' Tippy said, and then, relenting, 'but bless you anyway for checking up on me. And yes, we're all fine, aren't we?' She looked around as if to challenge us to say otherwise. 'Anna's just digging into ancient family history,' she explained.

'Oh, how interesting,' George said, looking confused. 'Are you going to do a tree?'

'I think she's at the very early stages,' Tippy said. 'Do you know what, I'm really not very comfortable. George, lend me a hand, will you?' She swung her legs down on to the floor and, with George's help, pulled herself up and made her way back out to the living room.

Gareth said, 'If everything's all right, then I'll leave you to it,' and followed them out.

Mum stooped to retrieve the washing-up gloves, and I picked up my tea-towel.

'I suppose we'd best finish up, then,' she said, and we carried on.

*

The rest of my visit was almost, but not quite, normal. There was a slight apprehensive tension in the air, as if further revelations might yet be sought out, or made. And yet nothing untoward happened. Tippy told us about her plans for the birth and the approach she had decided to take to sleep-training her baby; Gareth showed us the slideshow he'd put together of holiday photographs; we decided not, after all, to go out for a walk, and the political situation was, as usual, discussed and condemned.

After teatime I said I had better head off, and Mum said, 'Don't call a taxi, I'll give you a lift.'

'No, really, Mum, there's no need.'

'Anna,' Mum said in a tone that brooked no arguments, 'I will drive you.'

She drove a little faster than usual on the way to the station, and was almost in danger of breaking the speed limit. When we pulled up outside the entrance she turned to me and said, 'Do you know what, I actually feel better. I've been worrying about it for so long, without even really realizing it.'

'It wasn't so bad, in the end, was it?'

She grimaced. 'He is a rat, though. Gareth always hated him.'

'Gareth knew him?'

'They met a few times. We were dating when I was Gareth's secretary. Ben turned up at the office once or twice. Gareth thought he was a spiv. He tried to warn me and I wouldn't listen, and I told Ben and Ben said I should get another job, so that was exactly what I did. In my eyes Ben could do no wrong. I was such a little fool! But I was young, and in love, and I saw what I wanted to see.'

'How did you meet him?'

'It was when I worked at the hospital in Whitechapel. I was only seventeen. He used to drink in the local pub. I went in with a friend one evening and there he was.'

'What was he like?'

'He could talk the talk,' she said. 'Full of big ideas, seemed to know everybody. I didn't realize then that most of his cronies were pretty shady. Do you want to know why he dumped us? He'd found a better bet, or he thought he had. He'd been seeing a film producer's daughter. Thought she was his ticket to fame and fortune. Funny how things turn out. It was poetic justice, in a way. His new woman got wise to him, and he only ever wrote one more book. He still had the cheek to send me a copy, even though I was married myself by then. Gareth was furious, of course, and threw it out.'

The picture of Ben that was emerging was not attractive – this was someone ambitious, amoral, regretful when it was too late – but that was not surprising; I'd spent so long imagining him as an unsavoury character that these additional details just added clarity to the impression I'd already formed, as if he was coming into focus.

What surprised me was how detached I still felt. Ben was becoming clearer, but he still didn't seem quite real. Surely I would have felt much more involved in what Mum was telling me if I'd found out all of this when I was younger. But then, would I not also have been more disturbed, more bitter, more inclined to perceive myself as living in the shadow of the choice that Ben had made?

'Did Gareth warn him off?'

'No, Ben's wife did. Ben did come and see you a few times, before she found out and put a stop to it. He'll probably try and make capital out of that when he meets you, but the truth is he left us high and dry. I got the sack when my boss found out I was pregnant, and I had no family to help. I'd lost Dad when I was little, there had only ever been Mum, and then she'd gone not so long before. I went back to Gareth to ask if he had any work for me, and he couldn't take me on, but he helped me out anyway, sent me a bit of money from time to time. So you see, he really did provide for you right from the beginning.'

'And then you fell in love with him,' I said.

'Yes,' Mum agreed, 'then I fell in love.'

There was a pause. Then she said, 'You must have realized by now that the sort of love you feel when you are young doesn't always last, and sometimes it's a good thing that it doesn't. When you are older you appreciate different things.'

'I know,' I said. 'But sometimes . . . isn't it possible that both of you could change? So that you may be different, but the love between you can stay?'

'I guess it depends on what you both want.'

'Did you ever meet his family?'

'No. He didn't have anything to do with them. He didn't get on with his father and his mother was dead.'

'Did he have any siblings?'

'Yes, I think so. Some sisters. Some brothers. He never saw them.'

'So I might have cousins.'

'You might,' Mum said. 'Are you going to try and track them down too?'

'Probably not. It's just . . . I don't know . . . I always felt like it was just us. And it isn't.'

'To all intents and purposes it is,' she said. 'But for what it's worth . . . I think his mother was Jewish, and came from Russia or France or somewhere – not English, anyway. His father was a Presbyterian Scot who worked in the print trade.'

'That's quite a mix. I always thought of myself as totally English. But I guess I'm not.'

'Who is? We're all made up of people whose stories we don't know.'

'That's true,' I said. 'Thank you for telling me.'

'We were only ever trying to protect you, you know. He was a pretty awful, manipulative person, as it turned out. A drinker. He had a nasty temper on him, too. Gareth thought the best thing for you was just to start over. And you were such a sensitive child, so sweet-natured, so trusting. The last thing you needed was someone like Ben. But I'm sorry if you feel that we shouldn't have kept it from you.'

'You did what you thought was best at the time,' I said. 'What else could you have done?'

'Let me know how you get on,' she said. Then, in a voice that was so low I could barely hear it, 'You can tell him I'm well. Tell him I'm going to be a grandmother.'

'I will,' I promised.

I leaned over to kiss her goodbye, got out of the car and waved her off. As she turned and drove away a London-bound train pulled into the station, and I made a run for it. I couldn't wait to get home and google Benjamin Dock.

12

'Ghost pain'

Benjamin Dock
Born: 19 June 1944, London, UK
Occupation: crime writer
Nationality: British

Albert 'Benjamin' Dock (born 19 June 1944) is a British crime writer best known for his Aldgate series of novels set in London's East End.

Life and work

Dock was born in Spitalfields, London, the son of Arnold Dock, a printer, and Beatrice Dock, née Lafitte, a seamstress of French and Russian origin. He developed a love of reading as a result of childhood ill health and went on to attend St Olave's grammar school in Whitechapel, but left aged 15, after his mother's death, to take up an apprenticeship in the print trade. During his twenties, he was a barrister's clerk, a door-to-door

Bible salesman and a barman at the Brewery Tap pub in Whitechapel, known for being a favoured haunt of notorious East End gangsters of the day, including Terry 'Pliers' Pierce and the three Garrow brothers, Melvin 'The Gasman', Albert 'Bert' and Roy.[*citation needed*]

His first short story, 'Not the Teeth', was published in *Chase*, a popular crime magazine, in 1966. It was followed by the Aldgate novels, set in the East End criminal underworld: *The Fleet Ran Red* (1970), *Making a Killing* (1972) and *Death on Commercial Road* (1973).

A film adaptation of *Making a Killing*, starring John Neasden and Irma Miller, was released in 1974. Box-office receipts were disappointing following significant changes to the plot.[*citation needed*] A short story collection, *The End of Mr D.* (1978) systematically killed off the key recurring characters featured in the Aldgate novels: idealistic but ineffectual policeman Ted Boulter and his corrupt rival, Simon 'Rooster' Kaye; the gangster Jasper Scrote; and the enforcer Buster Dibbs.

Dock's 1973 marriage to Sharon Feldman, daughter of West Heath film studio magnate Jonathan 'Jonty' Feldman, ended in divorce in 1979. He has run the Propero's Nest writers' retreat in Blagdon Wells, Norfolk, with romantic novelist Carla Dunne, since 1995.

External links [edit]

- Prospero's Nest
- Carla Dunne

Categories: 1944 births | British crime fiction writers | British novelists | Living people | People from London's East End | Writers from London

My first reaction on reading this potted online biography of Benjamin Dock was relief. OK, so he'd known some dodgy people, and he'd done the dirty on my mother, and, by extension, on me too, but he didn't sound *that* bad. In fact, he sounded quite respectable. I'd expected some kind of pariah, but what I'd found was a person with a life in three acts: an early climb towards success, a long silence, and a comfortable retirement.

The second point that leaped out at me was a name. Beatrice: my middle name, and my father's mother's name. I suspected that if I asked Mum she'd deny that there was any connection. But what if she had felt differently at the time?

Maybe this had been a private way of acknowledging Ben, so that even though he was missing from my birth certificate, the words written on it alluded to the side of my heritage that came through him. It could have been a pure coincidence, but I doubted it. I wondered if Gareth knew.

A photo. I needed a photo. Surely there must be one somewhere. The online biography didn't have one.

I looked up Prospero's Nest. The website wasn't particularly impressive – a bit too much of it was purple, and whoever had designed it had favoured a peculiar pink cursive font that must have been chosen for the way it looked rather than readability, but didn't really deliver on either count. I suspected that the choice of design was down to Ben's partner in the venture, Carla Dunne.

The page dedicated to the life and work of Benjamin Dock pretty much repeated what I already knew. Carla's revealed that she was younger (born 1964, Norwich) and much better educated than her fellow 'creativity facilitator' (or so the website described them): she'd gone to St Paul's Girls' School in London, and on to Durham University. She'd written more than him, too. Sample titles: *A Mistress in Madrid, Passion in St Petersburg, The Favourite of the Sheikh*. And she was still going, more or less. The most recent item on the list was an omnibus collection (2010): *Innocent Virgins, Secretive Wives*.

I opened up the picture gallery. There was Prospero's Nest, a sprawling flint-and-brick bungalow set in a carefully landscaped garden, with a big, blue, mostly cloudless sky stretching overhead. I scrolled down and found photos of both of them.

Up until this point I'd been pursuing Benjamin Dock in the spirit of a long-delayed adventure, nervous about what I might find, and curious too, but in no danger of losing sight of my own reservations. I'd been much more preoccupied with my mother's reactions to him than my own. After all, he'd apparently been completely indifferent to my existence for the past forty years, so I felt justified in attempting to remain objective. Seeking knowledge was one thing, and looking for love, or even being open to the possibility of it, was quite another.

But the moment I saw the pictures of him and Carla something odd happened to my heart. It squeezed and pulsed, as if it was thinking about stopping, and then began to race.

Carla was one of those curiously youthful middle-aged women, pretty, big-blue-eyed, slender, with long straight ash-blonde hair and a fringe, and a winsome, hopeful expression. Ben's photo was blurrier and smaller. He wasn't smiling; he looked more sulky than anything, and also unkempt. He had straggly grey-brown hair, the colour of very weak tea, and it looked as if he'd refused to brush it.

Still, though, I could see it immediately, the way I'd seen Victor in his daughter – the other Beatrice – when I'd met her at the theatre. It had been the same when I'd spotted Clarissa and her son Michael walking along the beach together in that photo spread in Tippy's magazine. And when I'd walked into the café where Meg was waiting despondently with her pretty, wholesome, strong-willed daughters.

Even if you barely know someone, you can see them in the face of their child. If you've been really familiar with that person, even if it was long ago, the resemblance can be disorientating: bits of features, glimpses of expressions, the colour of eyes or hair are suddenly reformatted, spliced together with genetic material from who knows where. What you get is a blur of familiarity and strangeness, of history and now. How unique, after all, is anyone? We're all bits and pieces of other people, temporarily put together.

But when I looked at Ben, I saw myself.

I recognized the details of his face from a lifetime of seeing myself grow older in different mirrors and in photographs. The high forehead. The brown eyes. The jaw that was just fractionally out of proportion, as if designed for someone slightly bigger, so he appeared to be pouting slightly, even though he was probably trying to look dignified. Even the texture and thickness of the hair that must, once, have been exactly the same colour as mine.

He might not have been around when I was growing up, but he had certainly left his mark. Something else about him was familiar, too: the impression that he gave – though it would have been hard to say exactly why – of being lost.

There was a 'contact us' section on the website, which provided postal and email addresses.

Maybe, not so very far away – Prospero's Nest, Blagdon Wells, Norfolk, to be precise – Ben was also sitting in front of his very own computer screen. If he was, years of separation could be undone almost instantly. Even if he was not, it would surely not be long till he read whatever message I sent to him, and realized that he'd been found.

I set about composing an email. I'd been thinking about this for so long, I thought I knew what I wanted to say, but when it came down to it, it took forever. I kept deleting what I'd set down and starting over.

Taking a break for supper didn't help; it was just as difficult when I went back to it. By the time I'd finished evening had already drawn in, and the bay window in front of my sitting-room table was dark.

What if he never replied? Perhaps he just wouldn't care.

My hand hovered over the keyboard for a moment, apparently paralysed at the point of no return, before I forced it to press send.

To: info@prosperosnest.co.uk
Subject: message for Benjamin Dock

Hello,

I'm getting in touch with a request relating to some family information that I think you may be able to help me with.

My mother, Elizabeth Jones – formerly Elizabeth Sands – says she once knew you well. She believes you may be able to give me some idea of where my father is to be found, and whether he would be interested in making contact.

I look forward to hearing from you soon.

With very best wishes

Anna Jones

I made myself shut down the laptop – I didn't want to be checking my mail every half-hour like a girl in the grip of an infatuation, who struggles to carry on with life when her loved one is absent.

What now? I should try and find something to read . . .

I went over to scan the shelves for something that might distract me. And then the penny dropped.

The book Keith had given me on the way to Witcherley

Lock, the one I'd fished out and dusted down when Jason brought round the laptop, was by Benjamin Dock.

Keith had asked me once whether I had read it, and I'd told him I hadn't got round to it yet, and he hadn't asked again. I must have hurt his feelings with my lack of interest in a gift that he had obviously put some thought into.

And then *The End of Mr D.* had become a memento. Like any untold secret, it had been as invisible as everyday life. It had travelled from my third-year student house in Cowley back to my bedroom in Topaz Close, to Chester, to London, and then through a succession of houseshares to my current flat.

All this time, it had been hidden in plain sight, waiting mutely for me to open it and see what it might have to say.

I retrieved it from its place in the bookcase. Sure enough, my father's name was faded, but still clearly legible, on the spine, picked out in gold.

My twenty-first birthday card from Keith was still tucked inside the back cover, along with the one from Victor. Keith's had a picture of a dog with a bone. *Happy Bone-Day*, it said inside, and Keith had added, *Many Happy Returns*. His writing was loose and spiky and almost illegible, Victor's precise and angular and formal.

Victor's card did not say *love*, but it was signed with a kiss, and the card pictured a huge bunch of flowers, mostly, but not all, red.

I put the cards back in their place, turned to the front of the book and began to read.

The first story I read was one I had started years ago but never finished, the tale of Buster Dibbs, the morally bankrupt loan collector, and his long-lost daughter. As the words flowed past and I heard the echo of my father's voice in the story he had set down, I succumbed to a very strange feeling, a sense of suddenly altered consciousness, a buzz of recognition that started at the top of my head and ran right down to the base of my spine.

When I finished it I opened up the computer and checked my messages, readying myself for disappointment, and saw he had already replied.

To: Anna.Jones@freemailforall.co.uk
Subject: re: message for Benjamin Dock

Dear Anna,

Where are you? Who are you?

You must have many questions for me too, so ask away, and I'll do my best to answer.

It must have taken considerable courage to approach me . . . so thank you. I'm happier than I can say that you've got in touch. If Elizabeth's told you anything much about me, you'll probably be well aware that it's not a pleasure I deserve to have.

If you'd like to speak on the phone, you can reach me on the number on the website – evenings are good, I'm almost always here. The landline is best as mobile reception is patchy out here in the sticks.

Best wishes to you too. You've already granted one of mine.

Ben

The message had been sent scarcely ten minutes earlier, just after eight o'clock.

I didn't allow myself to think about it, or to work out what I would say; I just picked up the phone and called him.

A woman answered. Carla, I guessed. She said, 'Prospero's Nest?'

'Is Benjamin Dock available, please?'

There was a pause. 'Who shall I say is calling?'

'It's Anna,' I said. 'Anna Jones.'

This time the pause was smaller and tighter, as if she had just swallowed.

'I'll see if he's free,' she said.

There were footsteps, muffled voices, the distant friction of palms on plastic at the other end of the line as I was handed over.

He sounded like a smoker suffering from an acute attack of nerves: choked up, raspy, uncertain. We held on like that for a moment, just listening to each other's breathing, before I pulled myself together and said hello.

He said, 'Anna. Is it really you? I'm sorry. I can't quite believe it.'

'It is. It's really me.'

He let out a jagged breath. 'You sound like your mother. How are you?'

'I'm well. You?'

There was a throaty chuckle at the other end of the line. 'Could do with a drink. I dare say you could, too. Where are you calling from?'

'I'm at home. In my flat in Streatham. You're in Norfolk, right? In the bungalow, the Norfolk flint house? I saw it on your website. It looks nice.'

'It is,' he said. 'So you know what I'm up to these days. What about you? What's going on?'

'Oh . . . not so much. I'm kind of between things at the moment. I've done various things in the past. I was a teacher for a bit, then I worked in publishing.'

'Teacher? You got a degree, right?'

'Yeah. English.'

'Where'd you go to do that?'

I told him, and he said, 'Ha! You are a clever stick, then. Good for you. I bet Gareth sent you to a good school. Elizabeth said he would.'

'He did,' I agreed.

'So you're taking stock,' he said. 'It's a good thing to do, once in a while. Go back to the unfinished business, right?'

'Something like that.'

'Right now I just want us to keep on talking in case I mess this up and you disappear again.'

'It's not that easy to disappear,' I said. 'Anyway, you don't need to worry. This isn't just an idle whim. You could say I've been building up to it for quite a while.'

'It has been a long time coming,' he agreed.

I heard the rasp of a cigarette lighter, a sharp inhalation, and then a slower, more leisurely breathing out.

'You're smoking,' I said.

'Yeah. It's just about my only remaining vice.'

'I gave up.'

'I'm still trying. And failing, obviously.'

'I have one of your books,' I said. 'I have it right here. *The End of Mr D*. It's so weird that I had it for years and years before I had any idea who had written it.'

'Ah, that. My little literary act of self-destruction. My penitential gesture. Rather inadequate, of course, but I didn't have much else that I valued to give up. The idea was that the end of Mr D. would also be the end of Benjamin Dock. And it was, in a way. It was the end of me as a writer, though the book is still here to tell the tale, and so am I.'

'I read the first story just now.'

'Ha! You'll have spotted the relevant themes, then.'

'What, the child who tracks down her long-lost parent? Yeah, just a bit.'

'Well, I'm glad to know that my books haven't entirely disappeared from circulation. I still see 'em around from time to time. Car-boot sales, charity shops. I think they turn up when someone dies and the family get the house-clearance people in to turn out the attic. I don't suppose you've ever tried scribbling yourself, have you?'

'Me? No. I did when I was little. But when I was older, I just . . . I guess I didn't have it in me.'

'Me neither. Not now at any rate. You spoke to Carla. My other half. She's still at it. Endless hours at the keyboard. Never ceases to amaze me how long it bloody takes. Still, it's good for one of us to look productive. It reassures our paying guests. How's your mother?'

'She's well. She said to tell you she's going to be a grandmother. My sister's having a baby in the spring.'

'Just the one sister?'

'Yeah. Tippy.'

'Tippy? What the hell kind of name is that?'

'She's really called Olivia. When she was little she used to tip her toys out on to the floor all the time, and empty out all the cupboards and drawers, and the nickname stuck.'

'You get on with her OK?'

'She's all right, yeah.'

There was another silence. He exhaled thoughtfully.

'Come and stay with us,' he said. 'It's beautiful here. We're free Easter weekend. No one else'll be staying. We can put you up, go down to the beach, see the sights, whatever you want to do.'

'Let me think about it,' I said.

'OK. You think about it and let me know if you'd like to. Call me, email, whatever.'

'I will.'

'It would serve me right if you didn't.'

'I'd better go,' I said. 'I have work in the morning.'

'OK. It was nice talking to you, Anna.'

'You too.'

'Thank you for ringing. Take care of yourself. Stay in touch.'

'I will.'

He hesitated. 'Do you have a photo you could send?'

'Sure. Will do. Bye then.'

'Thank you. I appreciate it. Bye.'

The conversation was over. I put the phone back and

wondered if I could or should have wrung more out of it. Should I have told him more, asked more, shared more?

I had spoken to him. I had finally spoken to him. Why, then, did I feel a faint ache of dissatisfaction, as if some great illusion had just fallen away, and the power behind it had been revealed to be an ordinary and far from magical man, much less compelling than the spectacle he had created by hiding himself from view?

That night I slept badly, troubled by dreams of gangsters and stairs and a girl in a blood-red shirt, Oxford towers dissolving into the streets and pubs of London's East End, flying in an aeroplane with Victor with the Atlantic Ocean beneath us. It took a couple of strong black coffees the following morning before I was fit to set off for that week's temp assignment, which was on the reception desk at a health centre in Morden.

In the morning there was a chiropody clinic, and I was struck by the patient stoicism of the people – mainly elderly women – who hobbled in on their painful feet and waited uncomplainingly to be seen. The work was routine, and soothing in its way, and by lunchtime I felt I'd been there forever. But then I checked my mobile and saw that I'd missed a call.

It was from the National Centre for Access to the Internet.

I went out into the car park to ring back. After the muggy warmth and restive watchfulness of the waiting room, it was startling to find myself out in the cold fresh air, and alone.

Shauna picked up almost immediately. 'Anna! Nice to hear from you. Are you OK to talk?'

'Yes, this is fine.'

'I have some good news for you. I'm delighted to be able to offer you the job, subject to satisfactory references, and the completion of your probationary period.'

I just about managed to stop myself from shrieking like an over-excited teenager. 'Oh! That's great. I'm so pleased! When do you want me to start?'

'How does the second week of April sound?'

'It sounds great! I can't wait! Thank you so much . . .'

After she rang off I skipped back into the health centre building with an enormous grin on my face, startling a passing nurse and prompting one old lady to enquire if I'd just got engaged.

When I got home that night I had an email from Victor. 'Been thinking about you. How's it going? Did you make any headway with your family?'

I wrote back:

What a difference a day makes! 24 hours of wonder!

I have now spoken to my dad. He wants to meet and I do too but I'm still mulling it over. I guess it's just a question of how soon.

I want to tell you about him but I'm still digesting it all. I'm really happy that he has actually responded and is interested, but beyond that I just don't know where it's going, or where I want it to go. His name is Benjamin

Dock so you can look him up if you like and then you'll know about as much as I do.

And . . . I just got a job!!!!!!

Just before I went to bed I saw that he had replied: 'Congratulations. I'm so pleased for you. And I'm pleased for him too. Beatrice mentioned you the other day. She wanted to know if your hairdressing skills had improved. I said I would ask. How about lunch on Saturday to celebrate your new job?'

I wrote back: 'Lunch would be great. Please tell Beatrice that I have been quite neglectful, but am making renewed efforts now and hope to be rewarded with some progress soon.'

And then I wrote to Ben: 'OK, you're on!'

After that I went to bed, and slept a long, beautiful and entirely refreshing sleep.

That weekend I met Victor at a little Italian place on the Embankment, the sort that makes pizzas that remind you how delicious pizzas can be. We agreed first of all that we shouldn't drink, then ended up sharing a bottle of wine, and only just managed to resist the temptation to get another.

I told him about my interview and about what I'd learned about Ben and Carla. He told me that his ex had had her baby – a boy, called Aubrey – and Beatrice was mainly happy, but also a little sad that in a few years' time, her little brother was likely to cease to be cute and would become more obviously and tryingly masculine.

Then we set off across Hungerford Bridge, so he could return to the Ploughshare and I could catch my bus back to Nod Hill Road. It was overcast and the river was high and fast after days of rain. A train clattered past, and when it had gone I asked Victor to repeat himself.

'Meg said you're coming to her wedding.'

'I am.'

'But you don't want Barnaby anywhere near you.'

'No.'

'I don't understand it, Anna. It doesn't make any sense. Why are you so angry with him?'

'That's my business,' I said.

He was quiet for a moment. Then he said, 'Don't get me wrong, he's not my favourite person either.'

'Let's not talk about it. Please?'

'OK.'

Another pause. He said, 'At least we're friends again. Have you had any thoughts about how you're going to get to Meg's do? I was thinking of catching the train.'

'I'll probably do the same.'

'Want to travel together?'

'Sure.'

We came to the end of the bridge and went down the steps. When we reached level ground we stopped and faced each other and he reached out to touch my cheek, glancingly but tenderly, and said, 'Good luck with Ben. I hope you can get whatever it is that you need from him.'

He pulled me in for a tight, close hug. And then he released me and turned away and walked quickly off, as if he couldn't trust himself, or me, any further.

When I arrived at Caxton Station on Easter Saturday there was just one car parked outside. Since Ben had texted me earlier to say he'd see me there, it seemed safe to assume that he was in it.

I'd half expected seventies Dad, seatbeltless, in a big, dusty, bronze-coloured Rover, driven without much regard for the speed limit. But this car was more or less a dead ringer for Meg's dark-blue people carrier, though it wasn't quite as clean.

As I approached the passenger door swung open and I peered in and there he was. He was immediately recognizable from the photo on the website, but fatter and greyer-haired, an old man with a paunch and a heavy, weathered, saturnine face – the face of a movie Mafioso.

I said, 'Hi. I'm Anna.'

He said, 'You look better than in your photo. I'm guessing that's not what you're thinking about me. Come on then, jump in.'

We set off. There was a black lever to the right-hand side of the steering wheel, and I saw him pull and then release it, but it didn't occur to me to question what he was doing. We turned out of the car park and into queuing traffic on a narrow road, and he said, 'So how was your journey?'

'OK. Slow, but restful.'

'Might have been faster by car.'

'I can't drive. Took my test the day before I went to university, failed it, never took it again.'

'Don't get me wrong, I don't mind picking you up. I seem to spend half my life down that station, ferrying people back and forth.'

'Sounds like you have lots of visitors.'

'Yeah . . . can't complain. We're booked up pretty much all year round. It's Carla's birthday tomorrow, which is why there's no one this weekend. We always try not to work on our birthdays. If you make a living out of having people in your home, you have to keep some time in reserve.'

'Oh, I wish you'd told me earlier – I could have got her something.'

'No need. She won't mind. She's a very forgiving woman. Which is just as well.'

He pulled out into an almost non-existent gap in the traffic at a roundabout and moments later we had left Caxton behind us and were on a road that ran straight ahead to, as far as I could tell, absolutely nowhere. There were no other cars in sight, no houses, no sign of any habitation; just us, beetling along between two parallel planes, the flat stretch of land and the leaden expanse of sky, heading towards the compromise of the horizon. It looked cold and bleak and comfortless, and I imagined myself shivering at night, and wished I'd brought warmer pyjamas.

'I've never been to this part of the country before,' I said. 'You grew up in Aldgate, didn't you? It seems a far cry from central London.'

'It's where the royals go to the seaside,' he said.

'Sandringham's not far. So you could say I like it because I've got a chip on my shoulder.'

'The sky seems huge.'

'It's because it's so flat. It gets people thinking about God and eternity – that's why there are so many shrines dotted about. It's a place for religious fevers. Plus, the wind off the North Sea can be pretty icy, which encourages an ascetic frame of mind.'

'You don't strike me as particularly monkish.'

He laughed. It was a strained, gulping sound, as if he couldn't get quite enough air into his lungs.

'No,' he agreed. 'That's probably a fair character assessment. But I've ended up quite respectable in my old age.'

A small village came into view: low brick-and-flint cottages set back from the road and from each other. Landlocked and remote, it looked like the kind of place outsiders visit, but don't stay. A few turnings later we pulled up in front of Prospero's Nest.

A woman with long, fine, straight blonde hair – Carla – came flying out of the door towards us, but instead of coming to greet me she went round to the back of the car, opened it up, took out a wheelchair, unfolded it, pushed it round to Ben's side and helped him into it.

It was then that I realized the ramp leading up to the front door, which I had taken no particular note of, wasn't just there to make the place accessible to visitors.

I got out of the car. Carla was looming protectively behind Ben; he was looking up at me with an expression of pained, hapless resignation.

'You didn't know?' Carla asked me.

I shook my head.

'You should have told her,' she said to him. 'Why didn't you tell her?'

Ben ignored her. 'This is what can happen,' he said to me, 'if you have diabetes and stop looking after yourself.'

'He can still walk, it's just very hard for him,' Carla explained.

'Don't look so worried,' Ben said. 'I get by. I'm lucky to still be here. Your mother would probably think it was the least I deserved.'

I couldn't answer this. Carla pushed him up the ramp to the front door and I followed them into the house.

They showed me round Prospero's Nest. I saw that Ben was proud of the place, and also that he deferred to Carla; I concluded that I had been invited here because Carla had already decided to accept me.

The parts of the house that they shared with the paying guests had a public, bed-and-breakfast feel, like the dining room with its framed watercolours (painted by Carla) of Holkham Beach and Walsingham Abbey, and the side table with a display of tourist-information leaflets next to a small brass bell. I pictured Carla abandoning her tales about innocent virgins and experienced wives, or her painting, or her gardening, whenever the bell sounded, and dashing to meet whatever need she had been summoned for.

However harassed she might become, though, it was hard to imagine her being resentful. She seemed blissfully contented with her lot. Judging by the moony looks she kept giving Ben, this had something to do with being in love.

That evening we ate in the kitchen, which was in the part of the house that they kept to themselves. We talked mainly about books; Ben tried not to be too obvious about it, but I could tell he was pleased that in the weeks since we'd first spoken, I'd tracked down and read all of his. I didn't ask about what had happened between Ben and Mum, or about the lost years between the end of Ben's marriage and the beginning of his time here with Carla. I didn't want to press for potentially distressing details. Not yet, not while we were just getting to know each other.

After dinner I volunteered to help Carla clear away, and Ben retreated to the adjacent sitting room; I could just make out the faint patter of a TV news channel.

'I hope I haven't spoilt your birthday plans,' I said to Carla.

'Oh, no,' she said quickly. 'It's the best present I could have had. It means so much to Ben.'

I was tempted to say, *Then why did he never try to make contact?* But not that strongly. I could see she was being absolutely sincere, and, after all, what could she do but defend him?

'It's a lovely place you've got here,' I said instead. 'It must be hard work, though.'

'It is, but it's so rewarding,' she said.

'What kind of people come?'

'All sorts. Often they're going through some kind of change: they've broken up with a partner, or the kids have just left home, or they've hit a dead end at work and want something different.'

'Sounds like you've stayed pretty busy,' I said. 'It's surprising, in a way.'

'Is it?'

'Well, you know, given how tough things are financially for people at the moment.'

'Yes, but they still want to be reminded that there's more to them than others might think, and they hope that we can help them find out what it is,' Carla said.

She put the last plate in the rack. 'You go on through and sit with your dad. I can finish up here,' she said.

I was reminded vividly of Mum, who was always clearing up after other people, then felt a twinge of guilt, because it was almost certainly not an analogy she would have welcomed.

As Carla had suggested, I sat and watched TV with Ben, but we didn't talk, and I didn't take anything in. After an hour I wished them both a good night, and retreated to my bedroom on the guest side of the house.

I fell asleep much more quickly than I had expected, and dreamed that I awoke in Victor's old bedroom in college.

But where was he? I got up to look for him. The main quad was deserted, but as I passed the entrance to the hall I heard familiar voices, and when I peered in I saw Mum and Carla together at the end of one of the long tables, sticking candles in a huge chocolate cake.

I went over to join them.

Mum said, 'Your dad's not all that impressive, really, is he?'

'What I want to know is what you see in him,' I said to Carla.

Carla gave me a remote and rather superior smile, as if there was little chance that I would understand.

'What matters is what he sees in me,' she said. 'He makes me feel real. That's what we all want, isn't it? Isn't it what you want? It's what Victor could give you, if only you'd let him. You need to explain. You have to tell him what happened.'

'I can't. I'm too ashamed.'

'What chance have you got if you can't be honest with him?'

'No offence, but it's none of your business,' I said. 'Anyway, many happy returns.'

'No, no, the cake's for you,' she told me.

I got to my feet so I could lean across and light the candles, but lost my balance and crashed to the ground. The floor was dark and polished; I could see Mum's jeans and sturdy trainers, Carla's felt slippers and wafty linen trousers, rows of table and bench legs, the oak-panelled wall on the far side of the room. A child's eye view.

But I couldn't sprawl down here forever. I went to get up, but was knocked back down by a brutal surge of pain in my right foot; I clutched at it and saw that there was nothing there – below my knee, there was nothing but a smooth, scarred, puckered stump.

Mum and Carla knelt down beside me.

'It's a ghost pain,' Mum told me. 'Don't worry, it

happens, it's perfectly normal. The brain sometimes has trouble adjusting to what's not there.'

'But it is there,' I protested.

They looked at each other as if to say, *What on earth are we going to do with this one?* Carla shrugged and straightened up. There was the rasp of a match being struck, and the muscles in her legs flexed as she leaned across the table.

'Pretty,' she commented.

Mum hauled me up into my chair and I saw that all the candles were blazing.

'Thirty-nine,' Carla said. 'The question is, how are you going to celebrate?'

Mum frowned. 'She's got a wedding to go to,' she said. 'She's going to see Victor. She's going to see all of them. Keith will be there too. She can do it then.'

As they started singing 'Happy Birthday' I woke up.

The next morning Carla said she was expecting a couple of phone calls from family members and suggested that Ben and I should go out together.

'Take Anna to Cromer, and she can push you along the cliff path,' she said. 'She's got young strong arms; take advantage. That's if you don't mind, Anna.'

I did not; I was grateful to have another opportunity to be alone with Ben. This time it fell to me to be on hand to steady him as he got out of the car and into the wheelchair. I didn't have to do much; my hand slid quite naturally under the crook of his arm as he eased himself down, twisted and lowered himself, and then it was done. It didn't feel awkward or unnatural; it felt like something I might get used to, and one day do unthinkingly.

It was a better day than the previous one: still cloudy, but milder, and with a bit more movement in the air. Now we were close to the beach the breeze was gritty with sand and tasted of salt.

There were a few other people about. Women with pushchairs, older people with dogs; they all tended to overtake us. When we'd gone a little way Ben said, 'There's a bench there. Why don't we stop? We can take a breather, and look at the view.'

The town was behind us; the cliff path stretched on ahead, winding through flat, green headlands, scenery suggestive of scouring winds that had, over the years, worn away anything that offered resistance. In front of us was the edge. The earth went so far and then no further; it plunged down towards the beach and gave way to the sea, which was as grey and restless as the sky.

'I wonder if our paths ever crossed without us realizing,' I said. 'You came here in the late nineties, didn't you? That was when I moved to London.'

'Perhaps it's better for us to meet now you're older,' he said. 'That wasn't a good time for me, anyway.'

'No,' I agreed, 'me neither.'

'Come and see us again. You're always welcome. Don't be put off by the paying guests. You could even join them if you liked – have a go at a bit of free association, write an opening or two. You might even find you've got a book in you.'

'I don't know about that,' I said. 'I'd definitely like to visit, though. Maybe in the summer.'

He didn't say anything. There was a slightly uneasy pause. It was now or never: I could tell he was about to suggest that we head back for the car.

'It's been great to meet you and Carla,' I said, 'and this has been a really good experience and I don't want to put a spanner in the works. But, you know, it would have meant a lot to me to have seen you sometimes when I was growing up.'

'I tried,' he said. 'OK, maybe not hard enough. Your mother and Gareth told me it was upsetting you and I should stop.' He paused. 'My wife gave me absolute hell for it,' he added. 'But I did come and visit.'

'How many times?' I demanded.

There was another silence. I watched him and waited. He stared at the sea, then glanced at me and looked down. His face twitched, and I could barely hear his answer: 'Six times. You were three when I last saw you. Gareth had already told your mother he wanted to marry her; she was expecting, though you didn't know it. He wanted to make you all into a proper family. Or so she said.'

I could almost picture it: the nervous outsider, the small, doubtful girl, the mother standing by with arms folded. It wouldn't have been Topaz Close, but the first-floor maisonette Mum had rented before that, having taken over the lease when her mother died. I knew it only from photographs. There had been a gas fire, a shaggy brown rug with a yellow border, a bright red potty. Everything else was indistinct.

'You had this dodgy pudding-basin haircut. It was obvious Lizzie had done it herself,' Ben said. 'Your hair was fairer then. Not really blonde, but a bit more golden. I gave you a doll. A rag doll with plaits. I remember saying to you that its dress was the same colour as yours: you were wearing this kind of blue pinafore. You said you were going to call it Sandy Sands. You were still Anna Sands then.'

'I never had a doll called Sandy.'

'Then something must have happened to it. Perhaps it got lost. Or someone threw it away. I know it isn't much, Anna. For what it's worth, I'm sorry it wasn't more.'

I thought it over. Six visits. A doll. A name. An imagined presence in one story in one of his books, as the questioning daughter who finally catches up with the father she has never met.

'I don't know whether it's a coincidence, but I think my middle name is the same as your mother's,' I told him. 'It's Beatrice.'

'I know,' he said. 'It was nice of your mother to do that. Nicer than I deserved, no doubt. But then, I guess she didn't really do it for me. They never met – Mum died when I was quite young – but I used to talk about her sometimes.'

'I gather you have siblings,' I said.

He pulled a face. 'Horrible lot. I've had nothing to do with any of them since Mum died and my father kicked me out. I'd advise you to steer well clear, but if you want details I can send you what I know.'

'Yes please. I'm not in any rush to make contact . . . this is more than enough for now . . . but maybe one day.'

'Now can I ask you something?'

'You can ask. I can't promise that I'll answer.'

'You're very evasive,' he said. 'Let me just say what I want to say, and then we can leave it hanging. Who was it who told you to keep quiet?'

'What?'

'I can tell that someone did. You sound like your mother, but there's something else going on too. Your voice comes out in little bursts, as if it's being squeezed out under pressure.'

'Really? Nobody's ever said there's anything odd about the way I speak. I think I sound perfectly normal.'

'Yes – with an effort,' he said.

I squeezed my eyes shut: to my surprise I felt tears prickle behind them.

'Something did happen,' I said, 'a long time ago. Three things. Two of the people I loved the most betrayed me. I witnessed a crime. And someone died.'

I allowed myself to look again: the sea, the sky, the land were all as they had been, and he was still there, and waiting.

As if from a distance I heard Ben say, 'The older I get, the less I think I know. I don't believe in anything much these days. But there is one thing I've held on to. When you know the truth, the truth will set you free.'

'Not if nobody else believes you.'

'Even then. I promise.'

He put his arm around me and I leaned against him. After a while I said, 'Can we go home now? I'm getting a bit cold.'

'Sure,' he said. 'You want my jacket?'

'I'll warm up when we get going.'

'Then let's go home and do the birthday cake,' he said. 'We've been gone an hour. Carla must have stopped talking to her bloody relatives by now.'

As we headed back along the cliff-top path towards the car I pictured us saying our farewells. He would reverse neatly into a space at the Caxton Station car park, I would lean across to kiss him on the cheek, and then I would walk away and wait to board the train that would take me in the opposite direction, back where I belonged.

And there, as ever, waiting for me like the glimpse of a ghost that vanishes when you turn round, would be the neglected truth that I had never quite managed to bury and forget.

Part Four

1993–4

The Chasm

'It's easy to judge when you're an innocent,' he said. 'You don't lose that till someone hurts you, hurts you bad, and you realize there's nothing you can do about it. That hasn't happened to you yet. But one day it might.'

Suddenly he felt terribly tired, and a touch nauseous. His pint had gone. It was time for another.

'Let me get you a drink. Least I can do,' he said. But when he returned to his table he saw that the girl had gone.

Too late, he realized he had never asked her name.

From *The End of Mr D.*, by Benjamin Dock (1978)

Part Four

[illegible]

The Chasm

[illegible]

13

'Promise'

1993

'We're like an old married couple,' Keith told me one bright evening in the tiny back garden of our terraced student house. 'You make the tea, I put the rubbish out. We never fight. We like watching TV together. We even go out to the bingo.'

'Yeah, so where does Victor fit into this domestic fantasy?' I said.

Keith forked some more pasta into his mouth and pondered for a moment. It had been such a warm, fine summer, we'd taken to eating al fresco, and had moved the tiny dining table outside. It was so small that if we weren't careful our knees bumped underneath it.

'We may look like the picture of conventional domestic bliss, but actually, it's a very sophisticated, bohemian arrangement,' he said. 'You have a lover, and

I go for long walks at weekends so you can relax with your bit on the side.'

'You don't really feel you have to stay out of the way when Victor's here, do you?'

'Well, no, but there's only so much of being a third wheel that one can take. Anyway, I like walking, as you know. And also, seeing as how I'm a selfless sort of person, I want you two to have a bit of time to yourselves.'

'Yeah, while we still can,' I said. 'Before Victor disappears to the other side of the world.'

Victor, who had taken his final exams a year before the rest of our group of friends, had got a first, and had won a scholarship to spend a year studying theatre at a university in the US. The rest of us, including Barnaby whose Classics course was longer than the standard degree, would take our final exams the following summer.

'Oh no,' Keith said, waggling his finger at me. 'You do not get to complain about Lover Boy disappearing to California. Not when you're going to fly out there with him for a holiday first.'

Victor and I were going to stay with Clarissa at her father's house in Los Angeles for a week before Victor moved into his halls of residence in September. I'd never been to the US before, and I was hugely excited about it, although the prospect of saying goodbye to Victor at the end of the trip made me feel slightly sick.

'I'm not complaining,' I said, and tipped some more plonk into both our glasses. 'I know how lucky I am.'

'*Some* of us will not be getting the chance to go

traipsing around Venice Beach with the new young hot director and the celebrity's daughter,' Keith reminded me. '*Some* of us can't afford it. When you're out there being driven along Hollywood Boulevard in Clarissa's father's convertible, just make sure you spare a thought for poor Meg, nose to grindstone back in Norwich, toiling away to save up for her wedding dress. And think of me, cycling in all weathers to Shawcross Hall to tell tourists about the chinoiserie in the orangery, saving up my pennies so I can still afford to eat apples in the winter.'

'But you love being a tour guide, and the weather's been brilliant. Anyway, I've been working all summer too,' I reminded him. I'd been temping in the IT department at the hospital, which had somehow turned out all right even though I knew next to nothing about computers.

'Just remember to send me a postcard, that's all I ask,' Keith said. 'Add some variety to Barnaby's crumbling Peruvian ruins.'

Barnaby, having put in a couple of weeks' work experience with an investment bank to please his father, had gone off backpacking round South America with Sophie Adamson, his newish girlfriend. He'd sent us a number of very detailed postcards, carefully composed in minuscule handwriting and each summarizing the key historical and geographical information about wherever they were at the time. I hoped the time he'd taken over them hadn't irritated Sophie, who was a Classicist in our year, and known for expecting her boyfriends to pay her more or less undivided attention.

'I do wish you could have come with us to LA,' I told Keith.

'It is a shame. Especially now I have my new bike-riding muscles. I might even have ventured to wear shorts. Seriously, I think working at Shawcross Hall is beginning to turn me into a completely different person.'

He got up from the other side of the table and drew closer. 'Go on, prod it,' he said, gesturing towards his thigh, which was clothed, as usual, in tight-fitting black jeans.

I obliged. He said, 'See? Rock solid,' and sat down again.

'You are looking good, Keith,' I commented.

'Well, don't sound so surprised.'

His face was tanned instead of pale, he'd had his hair hacked into a quiffy short back and sides, and he was wearing the white shirt and skinny black tie he'd adopted as a uniform for work. He looked sleek and quirky, like a writer for a style mag, or a presenter on youth TV.

'Seriously, I shall have to watch you in Edinburgh,' I said. 'You'll have lots of drunken luvvies chasing after you.'

'I hope you're wrong. As you know, I like a peaceful life, and I don't much like having to run.'

'You might meet someone you like,' I pointed out.

'I very much doubt it. I'm doomed to monkishness, as you know,' Keith said.

Keith's love life had long been luckless to the point of non-existence. His infatuation with Magdalena Dale had predictably come to nothing. Then, during our second year, Leila Vetch, my tutorial partner, had taken a shine to him and contrived to entice him into some semblance of a relationship, which he had extracted himself from, in an agony of guilt over the hurt he was inflicting on Leila by rejecting her, after all of a fortnight. Since then the rest of us had come to regard the single life as a state with which Keith was rather more comfortable than intimacy.

'I'm not going for the girls, I'm going for the culture,' Keith went on. 'And for Victor. And for Clarissa, of course.'

'And Desmond,' I pointed out.

'Well, yes. Desmond too.'

We were due to take the coach to Edinburgh the following day, because, not content with his first and his postgraduate scholarship, Victor had decided to take a play up to the Festival Fringe between finishing at Oxford and moving to the States. The production had just opened for a week-long run, having already attracted some interest in advance, mainly because Clarissa was in it. Desmond was in it too, which was how Victor had finally got Clarissa. He'd given Desmond a leading role, and encouraged him to talk Clarissa into it.

He had held rehearsals in Clarissa's living room in her mother's house throughout the summer, starting almost as soon as he had finished his final exams and returned to London. Mandy, who was delighted that Clarissa had finally been coaxed on to the stage, had offered him the use of her home, as Victor's father was so confused, and so easily frightened, that Victor couldn't invite large numbers of new people into his own. The play Victor had chosen to put on was *The Changeling*, a Jacobean revenge tragedy with two parallel plots and a large cast, all of whom would be sharing a flat in Edinburgh for the duration of the run.

'Desmond's desperate for a leg-up because he's heading into his mid-twenties and still playing corpses in *The Bill*,' Keith said. 'Maybe he's having a quarter-life crisis. Apparently that happens, you know. People berate themselves for not having lived up to their early promise.'

'I hope that doesn't happen to us.'

'Of course it won't, because I shall be a cult writer, in defiance of my parents' expectations, and you can be my muse, or amanuensis, or whatever you like,' Keith said. 'And we'll all live together in a lavish pad in South Kensington and Meg will cook us Sunday lunch, and Barnaby will take us to his gentlemen's club and keep us in Château Lafite, and Clarissa will introduce us to exotic designer drugs and swan round looking glamorous. Meanwhile, Victor will be the newest *enfant terrible* of the London theatre, and we'll go to his premières en masse and get our pictures in the papers.'

'What if he doesn't come back from the States?'

'He'll have to, won't he? I believe they're not very indulgent towards students who overstay their visas.'

'He has dual nationality. His mother's American. If he wanted to stay out there I guess he probably could.'

'Ah. Well, who knows what the future holds? Just take it one year at a time.'

'At least it'll be really easy for us to write, now I have my email address.'

'Oh, Lord, now you're going to turn into a geek and end up hanging out in the computer room all hours with the likes of Jason Mortwell.'

'Who's Jason Mortwell?'

'That is exactly my point. I propose a toast.' Keith raised his glass and leaned forward. 'To fame and fortune for us all. Even Jason.'

We chinked glasses, and I said, 'You've been an excellent housemate. I'm going to be sorry to lose you.'

'I should think you will miss me,' Keith said, 'especially as I don't hog the bathroom in the morning, or insist on using up all the hot water. I think you might have issues with Clarissa on that front.'

I had hoped that, even though Victor had moved on, the rest of us would all spend this final year living together, but it was not to be. Keith had sub-let Meg's bedroom, which was the smallest and cheapest in the house, for the summer, but come the start of the autumn term he'd be living in the college's annexe for finalists in north Oxford. St Bart's North was less removed from the ever-watchful eye of the college authorities than our house in the east Oxford student haven of Cowley, and more institutional, but also less expensive than living out.

Barnaby wouldn't be around either, as he had won an obscure essay competition and was entitled to a particularly choice room in the central college buildings as his reward. Sophie, his demanding girlfriend, was going to be in St Bart's North, and it seemed likely that he'd be spending most of his spare time with her.

'I'm a bit worried it's going to feel rather small when

Clarissa, Meg and I are here all the time,' I told Keith.

As in a doll's house, everything in 52 Gladstone Road seemed to have been scaled down to fit. The squishy brown sofa in the living room was comfortable for one and distinctly cosy for two; it was possible to reach all the appliances in the little galley kitchen from the same central spot; and my single bed seemed particularly narrow, which was not a problem unless Victor was staying.

'Oh, it'll be fine,' Keith said. 'It'll be cosy. Especially when you all have your boyfriends round.'

'You know, I've loved this summer,' I told him.

'It has been good. And it isn't over yet,' Keith said. 'Shall we go in?'

I took the plates and the glasses, Keith carried in the table and went back for the chairs, and we settled on the small brown sofa to smoke a joint and play Cluedo. I was sad that our time alone in the house was over, but not enough to cast a shadow over what was left of the evening; and I was even more excited at the thought of seeing Victor.

When we finally got into Edinburgh coach station the following evening, after a long and tedious journey, the only person waiting for us was Desmond. He looked thoroughly fed up, and barely said hello before marching us to his car.

'So . . . where's Victor?' I asked as he started the engine.

'Whoring himself,' Desmond said and accelerated off.

I turned round to glance at Keith, who was in the back seat; he raised his eyebrows and said, 'Things are going well, then.'

'Depends on your point of view,' Desmond said, and proceeded to drive as fast and aggressively as possible all the way to the Victorian tenement flat where we were going to be staying.

The flat, which was at the top of a sweeping spiral staircase, turned out to be reassuringly big, bare, clean-looking, and quiet. Desmond showed us a generously proportioned double bedroom and said, 'Nice, isn't it? Victor bagsied this one. I'm afraid you're probably going to end up on the floor in the sitting room, Keith. I think someone else has laid claim to the sofa.'

He went off, and a moment later we heard a door slam somewhere down the corridor.

Keith and I exchanged glances. He dumped his sleeping-bag and rucksack next to my holdall, and we both sat down on the bed.

I bounced up and down a little. The mattress didn't squeak. Keith lay back and rested his head on the pillow and stared up at the ceiling.

'Aren't you and Victor going to be comfy,' he said.

'So what do you think is eating Desmond?' I asked.

'I suspect we'll find out sooner rather than later.'

He got up, and I followed him to the kitchen, where we found our answer: a newspaper on the table, left open at the review section.

'Here it is, look,' Keith said, 'four stars. Can't be all bad.'

> It is very much Hayes' show, to the extent that Desmond Cox's puny de Flores, a creature entirely lacking in the charisma of the heroine, seems little more than an agent in her downfall. Hayes portrays Beatrice's emotions with such clarity that you cannot help but pity her.
>
> This play is traditionally described as a revenge tragedy, but in Victor Rose's persuasive production, tragedy – the waste and destruction of goodness, love and innocence – is very much to the fore. Revenge – the enactment of justice on behalf of the fallen – only comes into play much later, as a melancholy grace note.

A key turned in the front door, and we heard Clarissa say, 'People are nosey. If you want to get anywhere in this business, you're going to have to get used to it!'

Victor came in looking less than happy – he was pale, and had big bags under his eyes, and the harassed air of someone who has been trying to manage other people's volatility and vulnerabilities for weeks on end. But as soon as he saw me his face broke into a smile of pure relief. He hurried over and wrapped his arms round me and said, 'I am so glad you're here.'

'My turn please,' Clarissa said, and embraced me. I was surprised to see that she was wearing jeans and a big old sweatshirt, and didn't have any make-up on; she could have been mistaken for someone much younger and less sure of herself than she really was. Even her hair was a bit limp.

I embraced Clarissa too, and Keith, who only did

hugs under duress, nodded a hello to them both and said, 'What have you been up to?'

'We've been nominated for an award, and the paper wanted to do an interview,' Victor told us.

'That's fantastic!' I said, but Clarissa cut across me: 'Where's Des?'

'I think he's resting,' I said.

Victor grimaced. Clarissa sighed heavily and went off, calling out his name as softly and plaintively as the owner of a lost cat: 'Des? Des, where are you? It's me, Clarissa . . .'

Desmond shouted back loudly enough to be heard from the other side of the flat: 'Just fuck off and leave me alone!'

Clarissa spoke just as carryingly, but much more coldly: 'Don't be such a baby. That was just a one-off.'

'Yeah, and if your mother hadn't starred in a crappy eighties sitcom, none of it would be happening!'

Next thing we knew Desmond had stormed out of the flat, with Clarissa following. They did not reappear. The evening wore on, and eventually Victor set off for the venue where the play was being staged, in a state of panic about what he would do if they both failed to show up for the nine o'clock performance.

By the time Victor got back I was in bed. As he climbed in next to me I said, 'How'd it go?'

'They were both in make-up when I arrived,' he said. 'She talked him into it.' He ran his hand down my midline from my neck to my abdomen and then added, 'She's a real pro.'

*

Keith and I spent most of the next day handing out flyers for the play on the Royal Mile. The flyers had the same image as the poster Victor had designed: a black-and-white, painted close-up of Clarissa, taken from a photograph. Desmond was a shadowy figure lurking in the background, waiting his chance.

Handing out those slips of paper with Clarissa's face on felt as if we were dealing out a new kind of currency, one that was just beginning to acquire value. That night we got to see for ourselves what all the fuss was about. It was just as well that Victor had reserved tickets for me and Keith in advance, because the performance was sold out.

The theatre was a former church that had been converted into an auditorium by a local drama society, and when we got there Keith pointed out the people loitering outside.

'Look,' he said, 'they've turned up on the off chance, in case there are some late returns. This is going to be big.'

And he was right. Victor hadn't let either of us, or anybody outside the cast and crew, sit in on any of the rehearsals, so we hadn't had a sneak preview. But as the action unfolded, I saw that I had never needed to worry about whether it would be a success. It was better than good; it was so good that I couldn't see how anyone could fail to admire it.

The knackered, sweatshirt-wearing Clarissa had disappeared, to be replaced by a sexy vamp in a wasp-waisted suit – Victor had gone for a film noir look – who was knowing, but not quite knowing enough; who tried to use what power she had to get her way, and lost. She drew us all in and made us listen to her, right to the bitter end; after which there was a small, quiet, almost religious silence, followed by the biggest storm of applause I had ever heard.

I was desperate to see the play again, but it proved so popular that I had to wait until the final night. There was only one return available, so Keith took himself off to see the Hungarian dance troupe that had become one of the surprise hits of the festival, and I went along on my own.

It was different this time. Right from the start, the atmosphere in the crowded church was restless, breathless, greedy, as if everybody was waiting for a miracle that was almost certainly, but not 100 per cent, guaranteed. The audience had read the reviews and counted themselves lucky to have tickets, and they didn't just want to lose themselves in Clarissa's performance; they wanted to witness it, to be the ones who were there when a newcomer proved herself.

When she finally died, no one stirred. They didn't want her gone; a little later, when she appeared to take her bow, they didn't want to stop clapping. Victor came on stage with a big bouquet of flowers for her and they both looked pleased but startled, as if the audience response still caught them by surprise. Even Desmond looked happy, though also, I thought, relieved that it was over.

After the last bows had finally been taken, the audience began to drift away. I remained in my place, and caught snatches of their conversation as they left: 'Really remarkable . . .' 'Yes, but really quite different from her mother – who'd have thought it . . .' 'Amazing hair . . .' 'I wonder what she'll do next . . .'

Eventually I slipped out and found the side door that led backstage, down a white corridor that smelt faintly of feet. After the dim glow of the lighting in the auditorium, it was bright and harsh. I was reminded of a school after hometime; a sense of tightly regulated crowd activity that had just relented.

I heard a murmur of voices from beyond a green door, pushed it open, and saw a dressing room with old-fashioned, bulb-ringed mirrors, and Victor sitting in front of one of them next to an open bottle of whisky and a near-empty tumbler.

Desmond was next to him; they both looked serious. I said, 'Why the long faces? That was a rip-roaring success. It was just fantastic! That audience will never forget what they just saw.'

Neither of them replied; they were both listening intently, and I realized that I'd spoken over a broadcast crackle. Someone was making an announcement.

'All right, lovely cast and crew, this is Clarissa here . . .' She cleared her throat. 'I just wanted to say this production has been an absolutely wonderful experience. It's been just fantastic to spend time with you all . . . Couldn't have been better. You're like family. And so I just wanted to share with you some very special news . . .'

She paused, then broke it in a skittering, breathless rush: 'Desmond and I are going to have a baby! We're very excited. This has been an amazing, life-changing time for us. So thank you all very much.'

There was another burst of static. Then the tannoy went dead.

I closed my mouth, collected myself, and went over to give Desmond a hug and offer my congratulations.

'Thanks,' he said. 'It's been rather challenging, as you can imagine.'

'Let's go find her,' Victor said, and we followed him out.

Clarissa was sitting at the desk that housed the loudspeaker system, regaling assorted cast members and stagehands with an anecdote about the number of pregnancy tests she'd taken. As we came in she broke off to say, 'Don't worry, I'm still coming to LA with you guys. I wouldn't miss it for anything,' and patted her belly. 'This is going to be one well-travelled, well-educated foetus,' she added.

'If you have any doubts about it at all, I'm sure Anna and I could make other arrangements,' Victor said.

'Oh, my dad'll put you up whatever happens,' Clarissa said.

Desmond hoisted himself up to sit on the desk next to Clarissa, opened his mouth to say something, then shut it again as Clarissa resumed her anecdote.

I said to Victor, 'You knew already, didn't you?'

'Yeah. Sorry I couldn't tell you. I really wanted to, but I was sworn to secrecy. Even Mandy didn't know.'

And then the door behind us was flung wide open, and Clarissa's mother swept in. She was wearing an embroidered silk jacket over white trousers, but whereas her clothes suggested celebration, her face was pale and tragic.

'Darling!' Mandy announced. She kissed Clarissa firmly on both cheeks, and pressed a huge bouquet into her arms. 'An absolutely stunning performance. My God, you nailed it. But the timing! To be just on the cusp and then . . .' She rounded on Desmond. 'This is disastrous,' she said. 'I hope you realize that. You've sabotaged her before she ever really had a chance to get started.'

'Oh come on, Mum. The play was only ever going to be a one-off, and I'm still going to finish my degree,' Clarissa said, laying Mandy's bouquet down on the desk, next to the one Victor had presented her with at the end of the play. Mandy's was conspicuously larger.

'You're due in the same month you're going to be sitting finals, Clarissa,' Mandy pointed out. 'How's that going to work?'

'The baby will be late though, won't it? And if it isn't, I'll just come back and do my exams a year later. I'll manage it somehow. Just imagine: I'll be a great big pregnant lump waddling into the Examination Schools. I expect everybody else will be in the grip of terrible anxiety and I'll be all blissed out with hormones and won't give a damn.'

'Even if you do manage to get your degree, how on earth do you expect to get started on any kind of career, let alone the career that is clearly your calling, given the way you powered through that performance tonight?' Mandy said.

'We'd better shoot off and leave you to it,' Victor said. 'It was good to see you again, Mandy.'

As we went out I heard Desmond say, 'I think it was a very strong ensemble piece, actually.'

Victor and I stayed overnight at Clarissa's before flying out to LA with her. Desmond was there too – he was going to drive us all to the airport before heading off to a small theatre in the West Country to play Malvolio in *Twelfth Night*. Mandy was clearly still not at all happy with him.

She prepared us all a full cooked breakfast and then told Clarissa, 'Darling, all you've had is a little slice of toast. You must tuck in. I insist.'

Clarissa glowered at her. 'Mum, that whole thing about eating for two is a myth. I don't want to end up fat as a barrel.'

'Well, no, but it's very important that you take care of yourself,' Mandy reminded her. 'As you know. You can't just run around doing what you like any more, and thinking it doesn't matter. Did you take your vitamins today?'

'I'm really looking forward to spending some time with Dad,' Clarissa said. 'At least he might still be capable of treating me like a normal human being.'

Mandy's face stiffened in distaste. 'Your father is not going to be the one who supports you through this,' she said. 'How can he be? He's on the other side of the world.'

'I think supporting Clarissa is my job,' Desmond piped up.

Mandy regarded him with evident disdain. 'I think you may find that you need some help with that. What are you getting for this Shakespeare you're doing? Equity minimum rate, I assume? It's going to be a stretch when you have other mouths to feed.'

'Oh, Mum, that is really none of your business,' Clarissa said.

'It is my business, because this is my grandchild we are talking about, and my daughter's education, and the ruin of my daughter's career,' Mandy said. 'And I am also concerned about you going off on a long-haul flight to see your father. Let's face it, Sean Hayes has never been the world's best when it comes to looking after other people.'

'Don't worry,' Victor said. 'We'll take care of her.'

'That's something,' she said. 'Promise?'

'I promise,' Victor said.

He glanced at me, and I said, 'Of course we will.'

'There, you see?' Clarissa told Mandy. 'Nothing to worry about.' She patted her belly. 'Me and the little one will be right as rain.'

And so peace was restored, although Desmond was very quiet as we packed our stuff into his ancient Honda, and I could tell that Clarissa felt much the same relief that I always experienced when I left home for somewhere else.

At Heathrow, Victor and I looked politely away as Desmond kissed Clarissa goodbye. It was a long and heartfelt embrace, and as he walked away she looked thoroughly dejected.

I gave Victor's hand a squeeze and shot him a plaintive look, as if to say, 'That's going to be us before long.'

But he raised his eyebrows at me and gave me his lopsided smile, and stooped to whisper in my ear: 'Just you watch.'

Sure enough, Clarissa seemed to perk up as soon as Desmond was out of sight. We joined the queue for the check-in desk and she started telling us how her dad had met her mum when he was booked to shoot an advert for washing powder, and Mandy, who was meant to be in it, ran out past him, crying because she'd been fired for refusing to wear a girdle under her dress. When we reached the head of the queue she stopped mid-flow and stepped up to speak to the attendant.

As we looked on, she appeared to unfold; it was like watching stop-motion footage of a bud opening up in the sunlight. Not only did she suddenly seem bigger – magnified, somehow, or maybe it was just that she was more immediately watchable – she was brighter, too, and everything about her was more Clarissa-ish: her hair was redder, her skin more pink and white, her expression more charmingly capricious, her stance more teasing.

I could see the woman behind the desk taking her in too, her mouth slightly open. Clarissa said something I couldn't hear; the woman smiled and replied, and there was a brief negotiation, with Clarissa looking concerned and mildly perplexed.

Clarissa turned to us and said, 'Bummer. They've offered me an upgrade, but they won't do all three of us.'

'Well done you,' Victor said. 'Obviously you must go ahead and accept. After all, you're the one with a baby on the way.'

I could almost feel the woman's relief when Clarissa beamed back at her and thanked her, and said that even though her friends couldn't join her, she would be delighted to fly business class.

During the eight hours of the flight Victor and I dozed, saw *Thelma and Louise* plunge to their deaths on the in-flight entertainment system, and watched the clouds pass by below us, so dense that they looked as if they would be sure to catch us, like a well-timed outstretched duvet, if we were to fall. The suppressed vibration of the engines combined with the stately vistas of the sky to give the flight an unreality, a sense of being deadlocked in time, neither here nor there.

As we came closer to landing we read our guide books, and talked about what we would like to do and see: the Hollywood sign, Venice Beach, Sunset Boulevard, Marilyn Monroe's tiny footprints. We did not discuss what we would do after we had seen these things: the return for the final year in Oxford for me, the Californian adventure for him. Nor did we touch on the more distant future.

Instead Victor stretched and said, 'I hope Clarissa is going to be all right. I think she's more nervous about telling her dad she's pregnant than she's letting on.'

I was taken aback by this; this was Clarissa – bold, impulsive, irreverent Clarissa, the disregarder of rules and conventions, who never seemed to be scared or daunted by anything.

'But she says she's never been happier. She doesn't seem to have any doubts about going ahead with it. I think she really wants the baby,' I said.

'You can want something and still be scared of it,' Victor pointed out. 'She's proud, and she doesn't want anyone feeling sorry for her. She's putting a brave face on things. She's not going to admit to feeling vulnerable.'

Up until this point, I had seen Clarissa's decision to keep the baby as a heroic adventure, a blind, pioneering leap forwards into an alien realm where none of the rest of us were yet ready to follow. I had always looked up to Clarissa, and I had complete faith in her ability to do whatever she wanted and get away with it. Why would I, or anybody else, feel sorry for her?

And yet Victor was right: Clarissa *was* vulnerable, whether she wanted us to see it or not.

'We'll look out for her,' I said.

Victor reached out and squeezed my hand, as if sealing a pact.

'We will,' he agreed.

When we next saw Clarissa she was waiting for us in a corridor at LAX, and it was still mid-afternoon – but a much warmer and sunnier mid-afternoon than the one we had left behind. She had shed her jacket and put on a pair of shades with heart-shaped lenses. She looked like a grown-up Lolita who'd never been anyone's victim. She also looked as if she'd just woken from a damn good sleep.

However, over the next half-hour she became increasingly jittery as our luggage failed to appear.

'I just can't believe it,' she said as another load of passengers who had touched down after us were summoned to a carousel to retrieve their suitcases. 'I could murder a cigarette. Not that I'm allowed to smoke any more. And you can't here, anyway.'

'I'm sure your dad won't mind you being held up,' Victor said, and Clarissa sighed loudly and did not reply.

We finally made it out to the arrivals hall, with Clarissa marching on ahead. Among the assorted people waiting on the other side of the railings to meet their friends and relations was a tall blonde carrying a brown cardboard sign with a message written on it in shocking-pink marker pen: *CLARESSA*.

Clarissa went over to her and looked her up and down. The woman smiled, exposing a mouthful of shiny white teeth. In her tiny denim hotpants and strappy vest, she was closer than I would have ever imagined possible to the physical ideal represented by the Barbie doll.

'You must be Clarissa. I've heard so much about you. I'm Trey,' she said.

She held out her hand for Clarissa to shake. Clarissa ignored it; Trey left it briefly hanging in mid-air, then moved it to clasp the cardboard sign, which now began to droop downwards like a defeated flag.

'Where's my dad?' Clarissa demanded.

'He had to work,' Trey said. 'He feels awful about it,' she added, nodding slowly for emphasis.

'But I have something important to tell him,' Clarissa said – it was almost a wail. 'I can't believe he's not here.'

'He's going to get back as soon as he can. He's been looking forward to seeing you all so much.'

She shook her head and puckered her mouth to indicate regret, and glanced at me and Victor to show that we, too, were included in the scope of Clarissa's dad's frustrated longing.

Clarissa jabbed a finger at the sign. 'That is not how you spell my name,' she said.

'Oh, I'm sorry,' Trey said. 'Spelling never was my strong point. Your dad always says it's just as well he wasn't looking for a girlfriend he could play Scrabble with.'

She smirked coquettishly at Victor, who said, 'Well, I wouldn't say that was an essential quality, either.'

'Let's get going, shall we?' Clarissa snapped.

Trey led the way to the car park; she didn't offer to help with our baggage, and made no further attempts at conversation. We stopped next to a huge old yellow sedan car.

'Ta-dah!' Trey said, gesturing expansively. 'We decided we wanted something fun, and here it is.'

'Must guzzle petrol like nobody's business,' Clarissa muttered.

'Your dad just loves this car,' Trey said. She smiled at me and Victor. 'Sit back and enjoy the ride!'

Once we were all in Trey hit a button on the tape deck and Guns N' Roses blared out.

'Oh, great,' Clarissa muttered.

Victor had ended up in the front. As Trey manoeuvred the car out into the flow of traffic Clarissa sank down into the upholstery next to me and closed her eyes.

'You OK?' I asked her.

'Yeah, just feeling a bit queasy,' she told me.

I reached out to squeeze her hand and she squeezed back. Hers was cold and clammy, even though it was hot in the car, and her face had lost its colour.

She wasn't usually somebody you felt sorry for, but I sure as hell felt sorry for her then.

Clarissa's dad and Trey lived not far from Venice Beach, in a little white bungalow with a picket fence at the front and a tiny yard at the back; it could have been the house that Dorothy was blown out of Kansas in.

Clarissa was to sleep in the spare room. It was empty apart from a clothes rail and a low bed, which I imagined Trey must have made up for her; it had been carefully covered with a Navajo throw patterned in red and black and white. There was a dreamcatcher tied to one of the bedposts, and I wondered if Trey had put that there too.

'I think I'll unpack,' Clarissa said. We left her to it, and she shut the door firmly behind us.

Victor and I were to sleep in a side room used as an office, on a blow-up mattress that was leaning against a wall. A large film poster pinned up above it showed a frightened young girl daubed in blood. I would have much rather slept under the dreamcatcher.

'We're just the other side,' Trey said, knocking on the

wall; it sounded thin and hollow, and I shot Victor a look of mild alarm that meant, *They're going to be able to hear everything.*

'I hope you'll be OK in here,' Trey went on, looking a little anxious. 'You will be careful of Sean's things, won't you?' She pointed to the Apple Macintosh computer standing on a pale wooden workbench, and added, 'I'm not allowed to touch that thing, not even to dust it. And don't even think about checking out the rest of his stuff.' She gestured towards the boxes on the shelving unit next to the window. 'They've got his old showreels in, and God knows what else – he doesn't let me go anywhere near them.'

After she had gone Victor sat down in front of the computer. He didn't touch it, but he gazed at it and flexed his hands as if he desperately wanted to.

'Maybe I could persuade Sean to take me to work with him,' he said.

'I didn't think you were interested in film-making,' I said.

'When in Hollywood,' Victor said.

I pulled the mattress down and sat on it; it squelched and bulged underneath me. He shifted over and sat next to me and put his arm round me.

'Anna,' he said, 'I can tell you're worrying about something. What is it?'

'Oh, I don't know. I'm being pathetic. It's just that a year seems like a long time.'

'It'll be gone before you know it,' he said. 'And the great thing about being apart is that we can have a wonderful reunion.'

'What if some beautiful starlet tries to seduce you?'

'What if some handsome student tries to seduce you?'

'I'll ask him politely to go away.'

'Just tell him to sod off. Otherwise your big, burly boyfriend will track him down and give him what for,' Victor said, and pulled me in for a kiss.

That afternoon we went to Venice Beach.

As we queued up to hire rollerblades Victor said to Clarissa, 'Are you sure this is a good idea?'

She glowered at him. 'Yes, why not?'

'Yes, why not?' Trey echoed. She owned her own pair, and already had them on. They were bright pink. I could tell she was itching to take off and show us what she could do.

Victor raised his eyebrows at Clarissa. 'I told your mother I'd look out for you.'

Clarissa's scowl softened.

'OK,' she said. 'I guess I'll sit this one out.'

And so she found a bench to perch on, and looked on gloomily as Trey skated off, and Victor and I slipped and slid and struggled to find our feet.

I fell over; he helped me up. But by the time we returned to where Clarissa was waiting, we were holding hands and skating along in perfect unison; and she looked the unhappiest I had ever seen her.

When Victor and I turned in that evening Sean still hadn't come home. Clarissa retreated to her room, presumably not wanting to sit up by herself with Trey. She looked exhausted but determined, and I suspected she was going to stay awake and wait for her dad for as long as she possibly could.

In the middle of the night I woke up and needed to pee. I eased myself off the mattress as gently as possible – Victor stirred as it sank and bounced under him, but didn't wake – and crept out to the corridor, clobbering my ankle on one of the legs of the workbench on the way.

There was a light on in the kitchen, and people talking.

Then I heard Trey say, 'She thinks I'm dumb. But being smart hasn't exactly got her very far, has it? She's just fallen into the oldest trap in the book. I don't see what gives her the right to sneer at me. Not in my own home.'

'She's not sneering at you because you dropped out of high school,' Sean said. His voice was crisply persuasive: even after all his years living in the US, he still sounded Scottish. 'She may have her faults, but she's not a snob. She's angry with you because she's angry with me, and you were there and I wasn't. And you know there was nothing I could have done about that. The schedule's all gone to shit and I'm just stuck with it until it's finished.'

It didn't seem like a good moment to advertise my presence. I crossed my legs.

'It'll all be fine,' Sean said. 'Have faith. Just you wait and see.'

I heard a chair scrape on the floor and shot back into the office. A moment later the light went on in the corridor and they made their way to the bedroom next to us; then everything went dark.

I left it as long as I could before venturing out towards

the bathroom again. The door to their room was slightly ajar and there was a faint glow coming from inside, as of candlelight. As I settled on to the toilet seat I was startled by a distinctly sexual moan, too high-pitched to be Sean.

At least I didn't have to worry that I'd wake them up by flushing the loo. It didn't sound as if either of them would be paying much attention to anyone else.

The next day Clarissa was up and dressed when Victor and I went into the kitchen. She looked up and smiled as we came in, and said, 'So what do you want to do today?'

'You've cheered up,' Victor said.

'I decided to stop sulking,' Clarissa said. 'Sometimes you've got to make the best of what you've got.'

'Where's Trey?' I asked.

'She's not going to come out with us. She has a script to read,' Clarissa said in a tone that cast some doubt on whether this was something Trey was fully capable of.

'I didn't know she wanted to be an actress,' Victor said.

'Yeah, well, this is the place to be if you want to be something you're not,' Clarissa said, not nearly quietly enough.

Clarissa's father made it back for suppertime that evening, soon after we'd returned from sightseeing in downtown LA.

He was compact and stocky, with a shaven head, neat features and a lithe, efficient way of moving; he made me think of a wily tom cat, the sort who rules his neighbourhood. When he came in he paid no attention to anyone else in the room, but went straight to Clarissa. She got to her feet, and they held each other, and for that moment at least, Clarissa had her dad to herself.

'You look absolutely fantastic,' he told her.

Clarissa spun round and looked daggers at Trey.

'You told him,' she hissed. 'Didn't you?'

Trey made vague, wheeling gestures with her hands. 'Well, I, uh . . . I . . .'

'Fucking couples!' Clarissa yelled. 'You can't be trusted. I hate all of you. You're all so bloody smug!'

She hurtled towards her room and slammed the door behind her, leaving us all not quite knowing where to look.

'Things not going so well with Desmond, then,' Sean said. 'Now there's a surprise. I expect Mandy's terrorizing him.' He shook his head. 'If she has her way, Clarissa will end up single for the rest of her life.'

'I can hear you!' Clarissa shouted from behind the shut bedroom door. 'Don't you dare insult my mother!'

Sean looked pleadingly from me to Victor. I said, 'I'll talk to her,' and knocked gently at her door.

When she let me in it was obvious that she'd been crying. I sat on the Navajo-patterned bedspread next to her and she said, 'Des just doesn't fancy me any more. He hasn't touched me since the pregnancy test showed up positive. It's driving me crazy.'

'I guess he's adjusting,' I said.

'Yeah, and how long is that going to take?' She shook her head. 'The worst of it is, I'm beginning to think Mum was right about him,' she said.

*

On our last full day in LA Sean took Victor into work with him. They were gone before the rest of us were up. Trey went off to her job at a wholefood store, and Clarissa and I sat down to write postcards.

For Keith, we chose one we'd bought at Disneyland the day before; it showed a girl standing at the bottom of the space ride. Even though she was dressed as Barbarella and was posing with a huge plastic water pistol, her expression was sombre and contemplative, as if she was gazing into an apocalyptic future.

'You write it,' Clarissa said. 'Just leave me a little bit of space to sign.'

I obediently picked up a pen and started writing.

Dear Keith,
Wish you were here . . .

LA is a future in which walking has gone out of fashion. I think you would be fascinated and repelled at the same time. Probably you would insist on striding about despite the heat and the fact that no one else does.

I look forward to seeing you again soon, back in the past!

Lots of love, Anna xxx

Clarissa said, 'Poor old Keith. You give him paper kisses, and save all the real ones for Victor.'

'Yeah, very funny,' I said. 'You know as well as I do that Keith doesn't fancy me and never has.'

'I know, but I do sometimes wonder if he isn't a little bit in love with you, in his own way.'

'Oh no, I don't think so,' I said.

Victor had made the same point, though he had been careful to emphasize that he wasn't threatened by it. I wasn't so sure, but I had an uneasy feeling that if I started to probe the mechanics of my friendship with Keith, I might lose it.

Without Keith, I might not be here at all, sitting next to Clarissa at her father's house in LA: why look a gift horse in the mouth?

'I just don't believe he can really be such a cold fish as he makes out,' Clarissa said. She took the pen from me, and wrote: *As for me, I'm just about coping as the hanger-on with the lovebirds . . . Clarissa x.*

I took the pen back, found Keith's entry in my address book and started copying it out.

'I'm so glad you managed to sort things out with Trey,' I said. 'It seemed to be touch and go between you two at the start.'

'Oh, that,' Clarissa said. 'I decided I could afford to be generous, since I'm almost certainly never going to see her again.'

'How do you figure that out?'

'Because there's no way they're going to last. By the time I next see him he'll be with someone else.'

'He seems to like her,' I said.

'He does like her. But this town is full of women like Trey. If he couldn't stick with my mother, why on earth would he settle for her?'

'That's a shame,' I said, adding Keith's postcode.

'I'm not so sure it is. He's very self-sufficient. He doesn't need someone to look after him. He and Mum are quite similar, really. It's not what I want, though. I think it's rather a lonely way to be, in the end. Now what about Meg? We mustn't forget about Meg. Do you have her address?'

I did. We picked out a postcard of Mickey and Minnie Mouse holding hands and Clarissa started to write it.

Sitting at Clarissa's side in that sparse, sunlit kitchen, waiting for my turn with the pen, I could almost forget that within twenty-four hours she'd be in London with Mandy and I'd be back in Deddenham with my family, and Victor would be elsewhere.

When Clarissa was hugging Sean goodbye at the airport Victor turned to me and said, 'It's time. We have to do it.'

'Let's make it quick,' I said. 'I don't think I can bear to draw it out.'

We embraced. We kissed. It was quick and urgent. He said, 'This is crazy. Why are we doing this again?'

I smiled at him. 'Because you wanted to,' I said. 'Because you got the chance, and it's the right time to do it, and I'll be waiting for you when you get back.'

Clarissa and Sean had pulled away from each other; Trey had moved a little distance away, and was already poised to head to the car park.

Victor said, 'You take care of yourself, you hear? Stay safe.'

'I will.'

He pointed at me as if warning, or accusing.

'Make sure you do,' he said.

And then he turned and walked away, and Sean and Trey moved off too. They looked back, and I waved at them, but Victor didn't turn round, and I knew it was because he was afraid that he would cry.

When we got to the check-in desk Clarissa's charm trick failed; there would be no upgrade this time.

'Oh well, I'm going to sleep all the way anyway,' she said.

It was night-time; from my position in the middle seat I watched the city lights recede beneath us. Then Clarissa, who was by the window, said, 'Do you mind if I pull down the blind?'

'No, go ahead,' I said.

The view, such as it was, disappeared. Clarissa snuggled down under her blanket and was almost instantly asleep. The stranger on my left-hand side, a huge woman with a reddish face and lanky hair, was soon dozing too, and snoring obliviously.

I took out Victor's annotated copy of *The Changeling.* I'd asked him to give it to me; I wanted to read the play with his comments to hand, so it would be as if he was telling me about it, line by line, even though he wasn't there.

Flicking through, I came to a passage he had circled in red:

O, thou shouldst have gone
A thousand leagues about to have avoided
This dangerous bridge of blood; here we are lost.

What was it Sean had said to Trey? *It'll all be fine. Have faith. Just you wait and see.*

The plane ploughed on relentlessly into the darkness of the future as I shut my eyes and tried to sleep.

14

'Dream girl'

Over the months that followed, as autumn gave way to winter, and winter gave up the ghost to spring, finals loomed ever larger. Nervousness broke out like a rash among my fellow third years as the Easter holidays approached. I'd seen Victor go through all this before me, and tried to bear his advice in mind, which was to keep going and to avoid being infected with angst by my peers as far as possible.

I was grateful to be living with Clarissa and Meg, as neither of them were particularly susceptible to panic. Clarissa, who had something much bigger to worry about than exams, had, it was true, become increasingly withdrawn and prickly as her baby bump expanded, and Meg and I worried about her, but she certainly wasn't stressing about Middle English vowel changes and the social and political context of *The Rape of the Lock*. We had noticed that as time went on, she mentioned Desmond less and less, and he rarely called.

There was still some uncertainty about where Victor was going to be the following year – he was applying for internships in the US as well as for assistant director jobs at theatres in the UK – but at least I knew what I would be doing: I'd been accepted on to a teacher training course at a college in Chester. Part of me would have liked to attempt something more glamorous – journalism, or advertising, or a career in the media – but these all seemed much more precarious and unobtainable, and I wanted to avoid crash-landing back at home if I possibly could. Gareth had made it clear that once I graduated, I could stay for a short time as long as I contributed to housekeeping expenses, but he would regard me as an independent adult, and I would not be welcome to return for anything longer than a stop-gap visit. And anyway, I liked the idea of teaching young children how to read, and encouraging them to take an interest in books.

Throughout this time, I kept reminding myself of the big night I had to look forward to once my exams were over. The second of July was to be a triple celebration: I would turn twenty-one, we would all go to the St Bart's Ball – a lavish event held once every three years on a different theme, this time *One Thousand and One Nights* – and Victor was coming back.

I hadn't seen him since the summer: neither of us had been able to afford the flights. If I ever began to feel overwhelmed by all the books I hadn't yet managed to read and absorb and now might never find the time to, as if English literature, instead of being a subject that I loved, was a great incomprehensible weight bearing down on me, I told myself that all I had to do was get through six days of exams, and I would have my reward: Victor in his dinner jacket and bow tie, ready to escort me to the ball.

It was Meg who suggested I should get a new dress for the big night. It was the last week before Easter, and we were side by side on the sofa, huddled under my duvet, watching *The Chart Show* on our little rented TV. The boiler was out of action again, and even when the central heating was working, it was never very effective. Only Clarissa seemed to be immune to the cold.

'I think we should go out and do something nice and girly for an hour or two, for a change,' Meg said. 'Have you thought about what you're going to wear to the ball yet? We could go to that hire place round the corner and see if they've got anything.'

'That wouldn't be much fun for you,' I said. 'I was going to wear my old black dress. I haven't really got the money for anything new.'

I'd already seen what Meg was planning to wear. It was her mother's evening gown from the sixties, sky-blue silk, sleek and glamorous. Even though Meg's waist was pretty tiny, she'd had it let out so she could breathe in it.

'Oh come on,' Meg said. 'This is your twenty-first, your farewell to Oxford, and your grand reunion with Victor. If there was ever a time to splash out, this is it. Anyway, we could do with a break from revising.'

'Well . . . I suppose it wouldn't hurt to go and look.'

As we went out to the hallway Clarissa emerged from

her bedroom and thumped down the stairs. She was wearing a big jumper and leggings, and looked tired and grouchy.

'Where are you two off to?' she asked.

'We thought we might go and have a quick look for a dress for Anna to wear to the ball,' Meg said.

Clarissa scowled. 'Am I not invited?'

'We thought you were still asleep,' Meg said.

'Please come,' I said. 'It would be an absolute pleasure to have two fairy godmothers sorting me out.'

'I think I better *had* come,' Clarissa said. 'God only knows what you'll end up with if I don't.'

She took her big green coat off the banister post and put it on. She got down to the third button before saying, 'Christ, I can't even do this up any more,' and giving up.

The dress-hire shop was called Coaches at Midnight. Its window display featured a male mannequin in a black dinner suit, gazing out at the street with his chin tilted at a superior angle, apparently indifferent to the females flanking him on either side.

As we approached I said, 'I quite like the dress on the right.'

'Really? The red one?' Meg looked unconvinced.

'I always think anything that catches your eye is worth trying,' Clarissa said.

As we went in a melancholy bell clanged to announce our arrival. The interior was dim and hushed, and smelt of dust and hope and clothes that are often handled but only occasionally venture out into the world.

'You're a ten, aren't you?' Clarissa said. 'God, to think I was once an eight!'

We started rifling through the endless dresses crammed on to rails around the walls. A solitary rack of men's evening clothes bisected the room; I went to look through the frocks on the other side, but was distracted by a tall wooden cabinet – white, with handpainted forget-me-nots – that housed feather boas, long gloves, rows of bow ties, and, on the top shelf, locked away behind glass, a feathered fan and a tiara that was probably paste, but glittered anyway.

A door on the far side of the room was wedged open, offering a glimpse of a shadowy corridor. Something stirred beyond it, and a raspy female voice said, 'Can I help you, ladies?'

Meg said, 'My friend would like to try on a couple of dresses, if that's all right.'

I squeezed round the line of dinner suits and saw a short, squat woman in an old fur coat and a turban, who was looking at us with a mixture of suspicion and anticipation, half ready to dismiss us as time-wasters, half eager for a sale.

A phone rang from somewhere down the corridor, and she said, 'There's a changing room upstairs. I'll be with you in a minute,' and withdrew.

Each carrying a dress, we trooped up to a small white room set in the eaves, with a big sash window looking down on to the street below, and a solitary cubicle created by a plum-coloured velvet curtain hanging from a curved rail. Meg drew it back to reveal a full-length standing mirror and a small stool covered in matching velvet. We hung up our finds on a row of hooks set in the wall and Clarissa settled gratefully on to the stool.

'Have you thought about what you're going to wear?' Meg asked her as I got out of my jeans and jumper.

'I'm just going to have to see how fat I am by then,' Clarissa said. 'When I get this baby out I'm going on the cabbage soup diet, I don't care what Mum says. I'm damned if I'm going to the ball with pudgy arms and everyone feeling sorry for me.'

I dropped the red gown over my head and said, 'Ta-dah!' but they both shook their heads in unison, and when I turned to the mirror I saw they were right. It was a no-hoper; bright, clingy and strappy, it made me look like a little girl playing dressing-up with a Vegas stripper's cast-offs.

The second, Meg's choice, was another disaster; black and fishtailed, it should have been sophisticated and vampy, but turned me into a drippy, washed-out Goth with a penchant for dungeons. The third was awful too: it was yellow – not quite sure what Clarissa had been thinking of there, but sad canary was probably not it.

'Maybe we should call it quits,' I said.

Clarissa appeared to have turned her back on the whole experiment, and was looking through a rail of ballgowns on the other side of the room. Suddenly she turned and said, 'How about this?'

The dress she held out was a dark, soft green, the colour of sea-glass, with a full skirt buoyed out by a layer of net, a close-fitting bodice, and a sweetheart neckline. I knew straight away that I wanted to wear it. I wanted to be the woman the dress conjured up: graceful, ladylike and serene, and possessed of an indomitable charm that any onlooker, whether friend, foe or potential suitor, would yield to.

Clarissa said, 'Just right for an English rose. It looks like the sort of thing an old-school romantic heroine would wear on the night she gets proposed to.'

'Yeah, right,' I said, taking it from her. 'Like that's going to happen.'

Once it was on I twirled, peered at myself, and twirled again. I actually couldn't quite believe my eyes. I never usually wore skirts or dresses; I'd spent my student years in jeans and jumpers. So it was strange – and intensely gratifying – to see myself transformed into a beauty: a slender, dreamy-faced young woman who would turn heads just by walking into a room, in a gown fit for a princess that could have been made for me.

Meg said, 'It's so pretty. Gorgeous! That's exactly the kind of look I'm after for my wedding dress. In white, though, of course. Well, ivory, I suppose. They say that you know the minute you try on the right one.'

'I feel like that about this,' I said, smoothing my hand over the green silk. 'But it probably costs too much.'

Clarissa moved in, tugged at something, and stepped away; I saw she was holding a paper tag in her hand.

'We'll have to ask,' she said.

She undid the hooks and eyes that fastened across the zip at the back, and I stepped out of the dress and was reduced to myself, a thin, dark-haired girl in once-white underwear that the launderette machines had turned grey.

I got back into my clothes and took the dress downstairs – the bodice was still warm from my skin – and the proprietor emerged from her office, inspected it, and announced her price, which Clarissa paid on her credit card ('Please don't fuss, Anna, I know you'll pay me back').

As we went out I felt exhilarated, but also slightly sick at the thought of having spent so much on something I will only wear once. But the melancholy bell clanged behind us and the glass door swung shut, and it was too late to go back.

All the way home I kept picturing myself in the green dress, and Victor taking me into his arms. Back in my room, I took it out of the bag and hung it up on the outside of the wardrobe, and was struck once more by how lovely it was: and the prospect of Victor seeing me in it filled me with a giddy happiness that was the perfect antidote to the familiar ache of missing him.

That evening Barnaby and Keith came round for dinner. Neither of them was in great shape, and Meg and I had decided to try and cheer them up.

Barnaby had recently broken up with Sophie Adamson, and had reportedly been found wandering round Main Quad late one night in a whisky haze without his trousers on. Keith, meanwhile, rarely ventured out of his room in St Bart's North. He had papered the walls with the most elaborate colour-coded revision plan I had ever seen, but had decided to ignore it and start working on a novel, and took offence if anyone suggested he should go back to worrying about his exams.

Clarissa and Barnaby got the table, since she was pregnant and he was the biggest; the rest of us ate on our laps. As we were tucking into Meg's spaghetti Bolognese Barnaby said, 'So what have you ladies been up to?'

'Shopping, of course,' Meg said, 'as ladies like to do. We went on the most amazingly successful mission this morning and persuaded Anna to splash out on a wildly expensive dress to wear to the ball.'

'Then you must model it for us,' Keith declared.

'Oh no, I might get it dirty or something. Anyway, shouldn't I keep it for the night?' I said.

'Don't be daft. That's for when you get married, and even then it's only your husband who shouldn't see,' Meg said. 'I'll put mine on too, if you like.'

I glanced across at Clarissa, worried that she would feel left out, but she said, 'Model away. Don't worry about me, I'm quite happy not being looked at. Especially now that I can't venture into college without being gawped at as if I'm some kind of living, breathing sex-education video. What are you going to wear, Keith?'

'Haven't really thought about it,' Keith said. He was as pale as I had ever seen him – the tanned glow of his Shawcross Hall days had long since faded – and dressed once more in black. 'Do you think they'd let me in if I just came as I am?'

'They might want you to at least wear a jacket,' Barnaby said. 'Personally I think it's only right to make a little bit of an effort.'

'I suppose you'll be wearing a waistcoat and a cravat,' Keith said.

'I shall be conforming to the dress code,' Barnaby said stiffly, 'and if you don't want to, I don't know why you're bothering to come.'

'Boys, boys!' Clarissa called out. 'No bickering. I'm sure you'll both look extremely handsome. Now, if everybody's finished, perhaps we could be treated to the fashion parade.'

As Meg and I gathered up the bowls the phone rang. Meg said, 'I'll get that,' and went into the entrance hall to answer it as I left the washing-up in the sink.

It was obviously Freddie; Meg wouldn't have sounded quite so pleased to be interrupted by anyone else, even her father or brother. Freddie was living in a flatshare in London now, having finished his degree and got a job with an engineering firm. Meg was planning to get a place with him after finals, when she started the job she'd got lined up, as a trainee manager at a crisp factory in Essex; it was the closest she'd been able to get to where Freddie was working.

She went upstairs, trailing the phone extension cord. I followed her up and went into my room to put the green dress on.

I didn't have a mirror, so I couldn't tell what it looked like, and I felt more than a little silly without Meg around for back-up. Also, I could just about get the zip up at the back, but I couldn't fasten it properly.

I went downstairs and stuck my head round the sitting-room door, and said, 'Clarissa, would you do me up?'

She came out to the hallway to oblige.

'It is a lovely dress,' she said. 'I'm glad you got it.'

'What did it say on that bit of paper you took off it?' I asked. 'I assume it was a price tag?'

'Oh, that,' Clarissa said. 'That was a ticket reserving it for someone else. It was meant to be for hire, not for sale. I just scrunched it up and threw it away. There, you're done.' I turned round and she said, 'Don't look so disapproving. I did it for you. I knew how much you wanted it. Go on, then, go show it off.'

Barnaby and Keith had started having some kind of vague, pointless argument about anarchism, and, as ever when they got on to politics, were disagreeing with each other more and more loudly. But as I stepped into the living room Keith trailed off mid-sentence and Barnaby said, 'Well. That certainly suits.'

'You look gorgeous,' Keith said. 'Like a dream girl. Victor isn't going to believe his luck.'

Clarissa came in behind me and said, 'Anna, I think something's wrong – can you hear that?'

I stopped to listen, and sure enough, there was a muffled wailing sound coming from Meg's bedroom.

'Come on,' I said to Clarissa, and we hurried back upstairs.

I knocked, but the crying carried on unabated. Clarissa pushed the door open and we peered in.

Meg was lying on her bed, face down on her pillow, and there beside her, placed as carefully as if on a cushion presented to a princess, was her diamond engagement ring.

We came in and sat down beside her, and Meg raised her head enough to say, 'Freddie's broken off the engagement. He's been fucking some girl at work,' and it was the first time I'd ever heard her swear.

Clarissa stroked her back and said, 'He's a bastard. All men are bastards. I hope you aren't going to send that diamond back to him. You should sell it and go on holiday on the proceeds. It's the least you deserve.'

Meg managed to sit up. She said, 'Of course I'm not going to do that. It wouldn't be right.'

'Meg, this is terrible. I can't believe Freddie's behaved so badly,' I said.

'I've tried to be as good as I possibly could all these years. I made a commitment, I've always been totally faithful even though I've had my chances, and still I've ended up feeling like this,' Meg sobbed.

'Oh, poor Meg,' Clarissa said, and drew Meg towards her and embraced her like a mother.

Meg said, 'There's something so comforting about your bump. You're even starting to smell of baby.'

'I know you probably feel like you'll never be happy again,' Clarissa said, 'but you will. Everything passes in the end. Even the bad stuff.'

Meg managed to smile at me. 'You put your dress on. You look nice.'

'Thank you,' I said.

She started to cry again. 'Of course Freddie won't be coming to the ball with me now.'

'I think we should ask the boys to leave,' Clarissa said.

'I'll tell them,' I said, and hurried off downstairs.

After I'd broken the news Barnaby said, 'Meg, jilted! What an appalling cad. You know, I never did like the look of that Freddie – kind of weaselly.'

He headed for the door readily enough, as if slightly

embarrassed to be so close to such an outpouring of feminine emotion, and cycled back off to college without delay. But Keith hesitated, and wondered if Meg would be all right and whether he could maybe ring the next day and if there was anything he could do to help.

'Keith, it's all right, go catch your bus back to Summertown. We've got it under control,' I told him.

'I think I'll walk. I could do with the air. Walking makes me feel like there's something I can do,' Keith said, and his expression as he left was one of pure despair, as if what Meg was going through – rejection, humiliation, loss – was entirely familiar to him, and he would have done anything to prevent any one of us from experiencing it too.

The next day Meg contacted the college authorities and secured permission to leave for home a week earlier than the official end of term.

I went into her room to say goodbye as she was packing up her things and was shocked by how different she looked. Normally she jingled when she came into a room; she always had on bracelets, brooches, a pretty pair of earrings or a decorated clip in her hair, as well as her ring and her cross. But today she had no jewellery on at all, and no make-up, and she was wearing a plain polo-neck jumper with her hair scraped back. Even though she was red around the eyes from crying and white from lack of sleep, she looked immaculate, and as hard and impervious as marble.

'You will come back, won't you?' I said.

'Of course I will. I'm going to get my 2.1, with or without claiming extenuating circumstances, and I'm going to move to London and start my new job. I'm not going to let that little shit wreck my life,' Meg said.

Clarissa hovered in the doorway, and said, 'Anna, you're going to have the house to yourself for a bit. I'm going to drive down to London. I'll be back for the revision seminar on Tuesday.'

'Is everything OK?' I asked her.

'Yeah. I just want to see Mum, and recharge the batteries a bit. I know I moan about her, but there really is no place like home.'

'I agree,' Meg said.

'I'll miss you both,' I told them.

Clarissa gave Meg a lift to the station, and after they had gone I stood in front of my wardrobe and looked at the green dress.

I admired the way the skirts gathered at the bodice; I rubbed the folds of the fabric between my finger and thumb; I buried my face in the bodice and sniffed it. It smelt very faintly of vanilla and sherbert, and I couldn't tell if that was my own scent or a residue of the atmosphere of the dress-hire shop, or even a trace of the girl who had tried it on before me, and had been looking forward to wearing it.

And then I sat down at my desk to spend two hours on Middle English, as per my revision schedule. I read the poem about the perfect pearl, the dead daughter who reappears to her father in a dream as a young maiden on the other side of a river he cannot cross. From time to time I glanced at my watch, not so much to keep track of how long it had been since I'd started work, but more to check how close it was now to four o'clock, when Victor would call from the States.

'I know it seems terrible, but I promise you it will be all right,' he told me. 'Meg and Freddie were childhood sweethearts, weren't they? Well, how many people do you know who are still together with the person they were in love with at school?'

'I was only eighteen when I met you,' I pointed out.

'Yes, but I was nineteen,' he said, 'and exceptionally mature for my age. Oh come on, Anna, this is about Meg and Freddie, not you and me. And as for Desmond and Clarissa, I'm sorry if they haven't been seeing each other much, but I'm not altogether surprised. He's got his strengths – or at least, he can be a stubborn bastard when he wants to be, which is a kind of strength – but I always did wonder if they were going to make it in the long term, once she got over being so determined to look up to him.'

'But what about the baby?'

'That baby is going to have so much love, he or she won't know what to do with it,' Victor said. 'There'll be Mummy, Daddy, a very committed and devoted granny, and I expect Sean will want to do his bit too, not to mention a whole host of adoring aunties and uncles. By which I mean the likes of you and me. What you have to do, my love, is have faith and let these changes happen around you without worrying that it all spells disaster. And keep on counting down the days till the second of July.'

'Do you know yet whether you'll be coming back for good?'

He sighed. 'I'm so sorry that it's dragging on. All I'm getting at the moment is rejections, and I'm just going to have to go with whatever I get – if I get anything at all.'

'You'll get something, sooner or later,' I said.

'I can't wait to see you. I think about you so much. You're still so completely clear to me, and yet it's like it's the idea of you that's clear, and the details are becoming more impressionistic. I want to reacquaint myself with the details.'

'Sounds good to me,' I said, and was surprised to learn that it was quite possible to feel lust and apprehension and sadness all at the same time.

I had the house to myself that night, and the next, and on Monday too.

On Tuesday morning I called Meg, and was relieved to hear that she sounded better and brighter already.

'Clarissa hasn't come back yet,' I told her. 'We've got a revision class. I'm wondering if she's going to make it in time. I'm surprised she hasn't showed up yet, unless she's planning to go straight there.'

'If you're worried, you could always call Mandy.'

But when I did, there was no answer.

I left a message, and tried to study, but I couldn't concentrate. I tried calling the payphone on Keith's block in St Bart's North – I figured that if I felt jittery, it was most likely because I'd been on my own for a couple of days – but no one picked up.

Clarissa's mother rang back just as I was putting my pad and pens into my bag and getting ready to cycle into college for the revision class.

'No need to panic, this is good news,' she told me. 'I just wanted to let you know that Clarissa has had a baby boy called Michael.' I let out a shriek of excitement, and Mandy permitted a small, sobering silence to elapse before going on.

'We had a bit of a panic first of all because she realized the baby had stopped moving, and we went into A & E for a check-up and they decided to whisk him out, so he was delivered by emergency caesarean,' she explained. 'He's fine, as it turns out, just rather early, so they're keeping a close eye on him. She's doing well too, though it's obviously all been a bit of a shock. I think you should leave it a while before you attempt a visit, though feel free to send flowers, of course. Would you let your friends know? I've notified Dr Custard, or whatever it is she's called – you know the one, the bony woman who wears the rather lurid silk coat?'

'Dr Kaspar.'

'Yes, Dr Kaspar. Feel free to call me for updates.' She rang off.

Poor Clarissa! It sounded awful and scary . . . But she was now a mum! As I locked up the house I was struck by how completely, disorientatingly different our lives had suddenly become. There she was, recovering in hospital, worrying about her newborn son. And this was me, running late, fretting about the gaps in my revision.

By the time I finally made it to college and got to the

seminar room – which was where we had been taught Anglo-Saxon in our first year, in the same block as Keith's old room – the class was already under way.

'I'm so sorry I'm late, Dr Kaspar,' I said. 'I've just had a call from Clarissa's mother. Clarissa's had her baby, a baby boy, delivered by caesarean.'

'Yes, Anna, we know, I've just made an announcement, thank you,' Dr Kaspar said as I sank into an empty seat. She cleared her throat and went on, 'Mark, would you care to kick off by explaining the thinking behind the traditional start and end dates that are used for the Enlightenment?'

Mark Flask, whose skin had exploded into furious acne in response to the pressure of imminent exams, said, 'It ends with the French Revolution, and . . . and . . . I can't remember when or why it starts.'

Dr Kaspar sighed. 'Leila? Anna?' She looked round at us in mild exasperation. 'Anybody?'

There was a silence, which Dr Kaspar permitted to lengthen until all of us were desperate for something, anything, to break it.

Finally she said, 'We are, of course, all delighted to hear Clarissa's news, and I hope very much that she will make a full recovery in time to take her final examinations along with the rest of us. Because let us not forget, the whole purpose of your being here is to come to the end. We do not have long. So let us attempt to marshal our knowledge. I can prompt you now to remember what you know, but I can only hope that it will not elude you when you are in the Examination Schools.'

And then she proceeded to tell us about the Enlightenment. Dates and names and theories and quotes and figures – on and on it went. Everybody around me was scribbling furiously, but I was barely listening. I was thinking about Clarissa, and how I must run over to the computer room after class and send Victor a message to let him know, and wondering whether Meg would be all right, and how long Keith would take to get out of the strange state he seemed to have got into lately: he seemed both withdrawn and overwrought, and had been so upset about Meg I should probably try to go easy on the details about what Clarissa had gone through. It was a shame that he and Barnaby had ended up being sharp with each other when we'd invited them over for dinner. It never would have happened with Victor there. Maybe we all needed Victor back, not just me . . .

And then, once more, I fell to imagining myself in my green dress, and Victor taking me by the hand and leading me into St Bart's as we had never seen it, the St Bart's of *One Thousand and One Nights*; and by the end of the class I was no better prepared for my exam than at the beginning.

15

'When can we talk?'

I had never been close to anyone who had a new baby before, and I didn't really know what to expect. I rang several times over the Easter holidays – I stayed in Cowley, alone, for most of it – and always ended up speaking to Clarissa's mother, never to Clarissa herself. Clarissa was fine, I was told, but she was out; she was tired; she was asleep. I conferred with Meg, who said she had managed to chat to Clarissa once or twice: 'I think she's OK. The thing is, though, she's not sure she's going to come back.'

In the end, we didn't go to see her until just before the beginning of the summer term, and when she threw open the door to her mother's house I was taken aback by how well she looked.

You'd never have guessed that she'd been in hospital just before the Easter break. Her figure was voluptuous rather than post-natal, her hair was wildly red and curly and glossy, her skin glowed as if she'd just come back from honeymoon with a particularly hot husband. Her nose-stud had gone, and she was casually dressed in a blue shirt, linen trousers and Birkenstocks; she had clearly left her pre-pregnancy student self behind. By way of contrast, Meg and I were greyish and grubby from too much swotting and too little fresh air, as if we'd literally turned into bookworms.

'Wow, you look fantastic!' Meg said, and stepped forward to embrace her. 'We were just debating whether or not we should ring the bell – we were afraid we might wake up the baby.'

'He's flat out,' Clarissa said. She turned from Meg to me, and we hugged each other.

I said, 'Congratulations! It's so good to see you. Motherhood must really suit you.'

'Yeah, I guess I'm lucky,' Clarissa said, holding her hands up as if to say, *I'm as surprised as you are,* and glancing down at her new physique. 'It's given me the most astonishing tits. Shame there's no one but Michael to appreciate them. Anyway – come and admire the new man of the house.'

We followed her down to her sitting room. The candles and ashtray had disappeared, and it had been painted blue and white, with a new sofa covered in matching striped ticking and a rocking chair. Michael was snoozing in a carrycot. His face was small, scrunched-up and red, and a slightly absurd little white hat was perched on top of his head; his body was cocooned by a fluffy white blanket. There was something startlingly animal about his obliviousness to us, and his helplessness, though it was disguised by a superimposed and very human desire to present a winning appearance.

'He's absolutely gorgeous,' Meg said, gazing at him adoringly.

'He's very sweet. What a cutie,' I offered.

Meg was still fixated on the baby. She settled on the end of the sofa nearest to him and I perched next to her.

'People moan about newborns, but honestly, apart from giving me a bit of a scare at the beginning, he's been no trouble at all,' Clarissa agreed, settling next to the carrycot on the floor and beaming at Michael proprietorially. 'And he *loves* breastfeeding, which is great because I'm planning to take him out to LA to stay with Dad for a couple of weeks, and it'll really help on the flight.'

'So . . . I guess you're not coming back to do your exams?' I asked.

Clarissa raised her eyebrows and looked at me with a slightly incredulous half-smile, as if what I'd suggested was absurd to the point of being a faux pas.

'No way,' she told us. 'Not this year, not next year, not ever. I have every intention of being out of the country while you lot are sitting finals.'

'God, I wish I could come with you,' I said. 'I'd much rather go rollerblading on Venice Beach than sit in the Examination Schools desperately scribbling about some obscure work of literature I can't even remember.'

Clarissa gave me a sceptical look.

'You don't need to feel sorry for me,' she said.

'I don't,' I protested.

'You do. I know you do. But you shouldn't,' Clarissa said. 'I've got it all figured out. I'm going to have a little break in LA, and when I come back I'm going to get a job.'

'Oh, what sort of thing are you looking for?' I asked.

'Acting,' she said. 'I know it probably all sounds a bit pie-in-the-sky, but *somebody* has to make it, and why shouldn't it be me? I need to find something I can actually do, and I seem to be better at that than anything else.'

'That's so exciting!' Meg squealed. 'I did wonder if you would reconsider, after *The Changeling* was such a success.'

'I bet your mum's pleased,' I said. 'She always did think that was what you ought to be doing.'

'Mum is actually a key part of the plan. She's going to help out with looking after Michael. So I think I can make it work. I mean, I *have* to make it work.'

Michael began to stir, and Clarissa took him out of his carrycot. She turned to Meg and said, 'Would you like a cuddle?'

'Oh, yes please,' Meg said.

Clarissa put a cushion on Meg's lap and carefully transferred Michael into her arms. Meg looked up at her reverently, as if Clarissa had just presented her with a miracle, and said, 'This is just the best feeling.'

'I have some good news, by the way,' Clarissa told Meg. 'Mum says you're very welcome to lodge in the spare room when you start your new job. She's suggested a nominal rent, forty quid a week, to cover bills and food really – how does that sound?'

'Oh my God!' Meg exclaimed. 'That is just incredible – so generous! Clarissa, I can't tell you what a difference this is going to make – I'll be able to save up for a deposit on my own flat!'

'It'll be great to have you around,' Clarissa said.

'I could babysit for you,' Meg offered.

'Perhaps you could,' Clarissa agreed. She picked a camera off a shelf and took a couple of snaps of Meg with the baby.

I said, 'So will you see Victor in LA?'

'I guess I'll try and meet up with him, yeah. I expect he'll be pretty busy, though, finishing his course and all that. You know what his plans are for next year yet?'

'No,' I said. 'All I know for sure is that he'll be back for the ball.'

'God, you two are going to be all over each other,' Clarissa commented.

She settled back on the floor at Meg's feet and threw me a look that caught me by surprise: resigned and faintly resentful, and – I wouldn't have believed this was possible – *envious*, as if I was a pampered usurper, and she had become an overlooked and excluded Cinderella.

'I mean, how long has it been? Since last August? You must be just about ready to explode,' Clarissa went on. 'I know I am. One of the worst things about being up the duff was that I was ravagingly horny all the time, and Desmond wasn't interested. And now I'm not up the duff any more, and he's still not interested.' Her face went blank and hard, but her tone remained light as she said, 'We've officially broken up, by the way, which I'm sure won't come as much of a surprise to either of you.'

I said, 'Oh, Clarissa, that's awful,' but she just shrugged.

'Is it? I don't know. I'm not even really angry with him any more. I was so furious with him all the time I was pregnant, I could have *killed* him, and now I'm just . . . *disappointed*.'

'Has he been round to see Michael?' Meg said. She was trying to focus on Clarissa, but her eyes kept wandering back to the sleeping baby.

'Yeah, and he looked like he couldn't wait to get away and have a stiff drink. He's probably already bending some girl's ear about what a nightmare it all is. Not that I want to know.' She wrinkled her nose in disgust, and I saw that the prospect of Desmond finding someone new was one that she had dwelt on with considerable bitterness. 'Let's face it, it's going to be a damn sight easier for him to move on than it is for me,' she concluded.

Meg said, 'Oh come on, they'll be beating a path to your door,' but Clarissa shook her head.

'It's not like I really care, because, frankly, I've got other priorities,' she said.

'You'll find someone, when you're ready,' I told her.

'Yeah, sure I will, but what kind of someone?' She reached out to touch Michael's tiny pink hand; it fastened round her finger as tightly as a claw on a branch. 'I come with baggage,' she went on, 'and men only go for women with baggage if they've got plenty of it themselves.' She turned towards me. 'How about you, Anna? Are you ready for your cuddle?'

'Yes, please,' I said, and Clarissa scooped Michael

up and got Meg to transfer the cushion to my lap, and then transferred the baby into my arms. But then his eyes flickered open and he pulled a face and wriggled, before emitting a plaintive, testing wail. He was still clutching her finger, and I was struck by how strong that instinct was, to hold on.

Was it unnatural of me to have made so little effort to reach out to the man who'd fathered me? The thought flitted across my mind like something half-seen in darkness, and then was banished as Michael squirmed and began to cry in earnest, and Clarissa said, 'Oh dear,' and took him back.

'There, there, my darling,' she cooed. She settled into the rocking chair with him in her arms, lifted her shirt and slipped his head under it. For a moment the squeak of the chair and the soft, squelchy sound of Michael suckling were perfectly synchronized, and were the only sounds in the room.

'You made that look easy,' Meg said.

'So how are the rest of my boys?' Clarissa asked.

'Barnaby's gunning for a first, Keith's slumping towards a third,' Meg said.

'Oh dear,' Clarissa said. 'Is Keith bearing up?'

'I think he's convinced he's going to do terribly, whatever happens,' I told her.

'Oh, he'll be all right, he just needs to get on with it,' Meg said. 'So come on, Clarissa, tell us about your acting plans.'

Clarissa began to talk about the lunch she'd had with Mandy's agent the previous day, and how she was toying with the idea of going for a part as a stripper in an edgy new play at a hip London theatre called the Ploughshare.

'If I take off my clothes first, I can always do the victims and the literary types and the ugly parts later,' she observed. 'Thank God, my caesarean scar is pretty neat and I don't have any stretch marks. If I soak up some sun and get some exercise, in a couple of months I'll be good as new.'

Clarissa was true to her word about getting out of the country while we were sitting our exams.

I rang a couple of weeks after our visit but didn't hear back, then tried again and got Mandy, who told me she was sleeping. When Clarissa and I finally spoke we were interrupted almost instantly by the baby crying. Clarissa just found time to say, 'See you when I get back. I'll give Victor your love,' before she hung up.

And I remembered that farewell, though I couldn't have said exactly why it made an impression at the time. I thought of it often later, and always with the same shocked incomprehension. It was as if her voice, always so deft and sure, had in that moment turned into a knife, and I, who had been oblivious to any danger up until the moment of impact, had barely time to register that I was its target before it cut me down.

The Sunday before my final exams started, I was expecting Victor to call at 4 p.m., as usual. But he didn't, and when the phone finally rang it was nearly eight.

'Are you OK?' I asked him, making my way upstairs to my room with the phone.

'Ah . . . Really really sorry. Yes. Absolutely fine.'

'I was kind of worried about you. I was beginning to think about calling your university office, if I could find a number. Or your mother.'

'Thank God you didn't,' he said. 'There's really no need to bother her, she's got enough on her plate. I just slept in . . . I haven't been feeling all that great.'

'Oh, no, what's up?'

'Bit of a stomach upset, I think. Yeah . . . must have eaten something that disagreed with me.'

'What were you up to last night?'

'Bit of a big one as it turned out . . . went out to a couple of bars with a couple of friends who are on the film course here . . . and Clarissa.'

And then I knew. I not only knew that something was wrong, I also knew what it was and who it had happened with. I didn't know exactly how it had happened, though I could almost see it: his face moving closer to hers, his hand on her neck, her long red hair, her smile, a darkness around them that was full of indifference and haste, the busy chaos of a world that was thousands of miles away. So very far from me, and suddenly so close to each other.

My heart started to thunder as if I'd just heard an intruder moving around in the house; everything around me came into vivid focus, as bright and inexplicable as a dream. My breathing stopped, and I had to remind myself to start it again.

I didn't want to know. I didn't want to see. But there it was. Not love – I didn't think it was love. It was *acquisition*. It was the moment when Clarissa had tugged at my green dress, and the tag – the label that said it had been put aside for someone else – had come away in her hand, and I hadn't even thought to ask what it was; and later she had thrown it away.

She did what she wanted, when it occurred to her to want it. I knew that much. Damn it, that was what I had *liked* about her. The difference was that this time she had taken something from me rather than for me.

But him . . . Victor. I would not have expected my Victor to be such a willing player in whatever game it was that she had introduced now.

'Clarissa,' I repeated. 'How is she?'

'She's OK,' he said, and I knew he was trying to sound casual, as if he didn't really care. 'She got a bit upset, actually. About Desmond.'

And then I understood; he had felt sorry for her, and that time she hadn't minded, not at all. Sympathy and lust and the lure of wanting what you ought not to want, and taking it, finding out what you ought not to know . . .

My legs weakened and gave way, and I came to rest on my bed. It was covered with scattered essays and notes and books, and a line of my own handwriting caught my eye. *His lost pearl is on the paradise side of the river and when he tries to cross, he wakes.*

The part of me that was detached, that was observing all of this, recalled just how much revision I still had left to do. *It's going to be hard to concentrate. But you'll have to, once this conversation is finished. You'll have to carry on, and it won't wait.*

'Are you still there?' Victor asked.

'Yes, of course, sorry. Just a bit distracted, thinking about tomorrow's exam. So how's Michael? I'm guessing he didn't come with you on your big night out?'

'Of course not. Sean's new girlfriend used to be a nanny, and she looked after him.'

I drew a deep breath. I could ask, could I? And if there was anything to worry about, he would tell me, wouldn't he?

'Victor . . . Did anything happen between you and Clarissa?'

'What do you mean?'

'Now that I had said it, it sounded ridiculous. He was my boyfriend, she was my friend: they wouldn't do that to me, would they? I was just being paranoid . . . insecure . . . It didn't help, of course, that I hadn't seen him for such a long time.

'I'm sorry. It's just a weird feeling I got, when you mentioned her,' I said.

'Anna, please, you have nothing to worry about,' Victor said – and this, too, was odd: he sounded pleading, and also unsurprised, as if for me to be paranoid, and him reassuring, was nothing strange. 'Just concentrate on getting through your finals, OK? One day at a time,' he went on. 'It's the medieval period tomorrow, right?'

'It is,' I said, and we talked briefly about exams and nerves and how my peers were bearing up, before exchanging 'I love yous' and saying goodbye.

It was only when I'd hung up that I realized I'd omitted the perennial question: 'Do you know when you're coming back?' and he hadn't mentioned it.

Perhaps he was planning on coming back . . . but not to me. And of course, he would want to let me down gently; he wouldn't want to dump me just before my exams, but afterwards, that would be different. Or perhaps, if something had happened, he genuinely didn't know what to do about it.

And neither did I. I curled up on my bed and began to cry. After a while Meg knocked on the door, and said, 'Is everything all right?'

I mumbled something, and she pushed the door open and came in and sat on the bed next to me, and I straightened up and she put her arms around me.

'You'll be fine, I promise,' she said. 'I know it's scary before the first one. But, you know, you just have to keep on going.'

'It's not the exams that I'm worried about,' I said. 'It's Victor. I think he might be . . . seeing someone else.'

I couldn't bring myself to say 'Victor and Clarissa'. I could barely believe it myself. And if I came out with it, wouldn't that just give it more of a foothold in reality?

'Look, I'm sure everything's fine,' Meg said. 'You just need to focus on the matter in hand, which is your exams.'

There was no arguing with this advice, but I couldn't help but hear, underneath it, another line: *Well, if he has got together with some girl or other, what can you do about it?* I shivered and pulled away slightly, and Meg said, 'Did you have a quarrel?'

'No, not exactly.'

'That's good,' Meg said. 'So you'll be OK, then?'

I caught sight of the green dress, which was still hanging from the outside of my wardrobe, holding out the promise of dancing, mingling, being admired; and I told myself that I could have been mistaken.

'Yeah, I'll be fine,' I said.

Meg sighed and got to her feet and said, 'I must get back to work,' and trudged out, leaving me to the reams of words on my bed, and the niggling feeling that what I really needed to know had been left unsaid.

The next morning I found myself lining up with my fellow English students to take a single white carnation from the box Dr Kaspar was holding, and fix it to my academic gown before we went into the Examination Schools to sit the first of our papers.

Dr Kaspar's face was sombre but encouraging, as if we were gladiators entering the arena and she was our sponsor. What awaited us, however, was neither weaponry nor wild beasts nor a display of gore, but rows of desks with papers on them, silence, and a ticking clock.

And so we wrote about medieval literature, and then stopped, and our papers were taken away and we filed out and went our separate ways.

I skirted the loud disagreement going on between Mark and Leila about how they'd tackled the question on *Le Morte D'Arthur*, and headed down the High Street into St Bart's. I was just about to go down into the computer room when I heard someone call my name.

It was Barnaby. He said, 'You just had your first exam, right? How did it go?'

'I think it was OK,' I said. 'Next one tomorrow. How's it going with you?'

'Few down, couple to go. Got a bit of a gap now, so I'm about to go and work on the old CV.' He brandished the folder he was carrying. 'How about you, what are you up to?'

'Just checking emails,' I said.

'Ah,' Barnaby said. 'Victor, I presume.'

'Yeah.'

He peered at me more closely. 'Are you all right? You look like you've just seen a ghost.'

'I'm OK,' I said. 'Just about.'

As we went down into the computer room together I said, 'Victor met up with Clarissa. She's gone out to LA with the baby to see her dad.'

'No doubt she'll show the lot of us,' Barnaby said.

'Show us what?'

'She's a very proud woman,' Barnaby commented, 'and wounded pride is a remarkably powerful force.'

'Why should her pride have been wounded?'

'Well, she's not here any more, is she? And you know how much she always wanted to prove she was intellectual.'

After months of emailing Victor the computer room had become a familiar haunt. Just then it was empty apart from Jason Mortwell, who was sitting in his usual place at the central bank of workstations, and gave us a slight nod of acknowledgement as we came in. Barnaby took the place next to Jason, and I went over to the machine opposite him.

Jason said, 'Have either of you seen Keith lately?'

'Not me,' Barnaby said. 'How about you, Anna?'

I put in my ID and password: SONNET116. My favourite Shakespeare poem.

Love is not love
Which alters when it alteration finds . . .

There was nothing waiting for me from Victor.

'Earth to Anna,' Jason said, waving at me over the top of our computers. 'Keith. He's still your friend, right?'

'Yeah, course,' I said. Though when had I last seen him? In the library a week or so ago maybe?

'He seems a bit down,' Jason said. 'Thinks his exams are going pretty badly. He keeps listening to very, very miserable music. Plus he kind of smells.'

'Doesn't sound all that different to normal,' Barnaby commented.

'No, it's definitely worse,' Jason told him.

'I'll give him a call sometime,' I said.

'Yeah, a bit of TLC wouldn't hurt,' Jason said.

'TLC won't write his exam papers for him though, will it? In the end, we're all in this alone,' Barnaby observed.

Jason grunted – a noncommittal little sound that could have meant objection, or agreement, or simply been an indication that he'd done his bit, as far as he was concerned, and the subject was now closed.

The room fell silent. I typed in Victor's email address. Hesitated. Kept on typing. 'Looking forward so much to seeing you. Not long now! Do you know when your flight is coming in? Shall I come and meet you at the airport?'

Then I logged off and tried calling Keith from the college payphone, but there was no answer, so I resigned myself to losing a couple of hours' revision time (equivalent to at least one Metaphysical poet) and cycled to St Bart's North to track him down.

He lived in the first block you came to when you passed the annexe gatehouse. I went round to the side and saw his blind was down, which was probably, but not definitely, a sign that he was there. I left my bike outside the entrance and went in.

His corridor smelt of bacon, overpowering the older, fainter smells of disinfectant and unwashed socks; as I walked past the tiny kitchenette I glimpsed Mark Flask with his back to me, bent over a frying pan. I carried on down to Keith's room, which was at the end. There were no notes written on the piece of A4 he'd tacked up on the door. At the bottom of it he'd written: *THE END.*

I knocked, and called out his name.

There was no immediate response, but a moment later the door was flung open and Keith said, 'What are you doing here?'

He was wearing some kind of dull grey tracksuit I'd never seen before, and there was no denying it, he looked pretty rough – even paler and more sombre than usual. The dark room behind him had a faint but unmistakable reek of animal fear.

'I just thought I'd come and say hi,' I said.

'It's a bit of a tip. But then, I wasn't expecting visitors,' he said. He stood back to let me in, and shut the door firmly behind him.

There were lots of files and notes scattered around, and that strange odour that made me think of penned cattle en route to the slaughterhouse, but apart from that, and the location, and the slightly dingier tone of the red-and-black zigzag duvet cover, nothing much had changed since his first year. He still had the same old grey trunk, the same sound system, the same broken-handled 'I ♥ Los Angeles' mug that served as an ashtray.

He pulled up the blind and pushed the window open. The room looked on to a stretch of lawn and the windows of the next block. I could see Violet Tranter at her desk, staring into space and eating a packet of crisps.

'It's a spectator sport, living here,' Keith commented.

I perched on the bed; he leaned against the desk, folded his arms and looked at me.

'So what's up?' he asked.

'Nothing, really. Just trying to get through finals, I guess.' I could hardly say, *Jason Mortwell told me you're losing the plot.* 'Things are a bit weird with Victor. But I honestly haven't come here to moan.'

'Weird how?'

I shrugged, but my heart had started to thump again, the way it had done when I'd been on the phone to Victor. Glancing down at my hands, I saw that they were twisting round each other as if trying to pull something out from under the skin.

'I don't know exactly,' I said. 'You know Clarissa's in

LA at the moment. They met up and had a big night out, and then he rang me hours later than he usually does, and he sounded kind of evasive . . .' I trailed off.

'You do realize how lame that is?' Keith said. 'Jesus Christ, woman, don't you have better things to worry about? Like your exams, for instance? Because I don't know about you, but I have rather a lot of work to do, and I would appreciate being left to get on with it. I am sick to the back teeth of you leaning on me because Victor's not around. I am not your substitute boyfriend.'

'I have never, ever thought of you that way,' I said. 'I'm sorry. I didn't mean to interrupt. I'll see you around. Good luck with your exams.'

But as I was mounting my bike I heard him calling out my name and turned to see him leaning out of his window.

'Victor does love you, you know,' he shouted.

I waved back and grinned, but as I cycled back to Cowley I was full of an apparently unjustifiable despair.

Meg was out when I got back, and she didn't come home at dinnertime. I assumed she'd bumped into somebody in college or the science library, and gone out for something to eat in town. I found out later that I was right, but there was more to it than that, because that was the evening Meg went on the rebound.

I was woken in the early hours by the sound of her giggling, and two pairs of feet making their way up the stairs. There was a thud and a shriek, followed by more laughter, then, after a brief interval, the creak of her bedsprings.

When I went downstairs the next morning she was sitting alone at the table, eating cereal.

'I didn't expect to see you up,' I said.

'Got loads of work to do,' Meg said. She was wearing her big fluffy pink dressing-gown over her Minnie Mouse nightie. I decided that it was a safe bet that her paramour had gone.

'So,' I said, sitting down at the chair opposite her. 'How are you this morning?'

'I was with Jason Mortwell last night. I presume that's what you want to know.'

'Jason. Wow. How did that happen?'

'I went into college to do some washing, bumped into him in the laundry room, got talking, went to the bar, one thing led to another.'

'Well, he seems like a nice guy. Will you see him again?'

'Anna, just don't, OK?' Meg said. 'I lost my fiancé and ended up shagging the geek from the computer room. That is not the beginning of a proper relationship. That is an embarrassing one-night stand.'

She took her cereal bowl out to the kitchen, and a moment later I heard the sound of furious scouring.

Later that day we wore pink carnations into the Examination Schools, and it was hot. A bird flew in through one of the open windows and panicked; it beat against the roof high above us until it knocked itself out. I thought: *I have to know for sure,* and then: *But I would rather not know at all. As long as I don't know, it isn't over.*

*

Over the next few days the exams ticked by one by one: history and theory of the language, Shakespeare, the Enlightenment. At night I found myself suddenly unable to sleep; when I managed to silence the part of my brain that was trying to remember quotes and dates and half-baked arguments, it became impossible to ignore my doubts about Victor and Clarissa. Fatigue and fear lent my surroundings – Cowley, the High Street, the grandeur of the Examination Schools – an unreal, hallucinatory quality, as if the light of day was blurring into a dream.

From time to time there were messages: a piecemeal exchange with Victor, relayed by email across the thousands of miles between us, and separated by days that felt like years.

I wrote: 'Now I am afraid that you haven't been in touch because you don't know what to say and don't want to lie. Can you honestly reassure me?'

He replied: 'Please don't worry about me. How are the exams going? Thinking of you.'

I mulled it over. I thought of Clarissa, reckless in the sunshine, ready to burn her bridges, to seize what she could of the day. *Somebody has to make it, and why shouldn't it be me?*

And I pictured Victor, wanting her and trying not to, torn between the woman standing in front of him in the country that might be his future and the girl on the other side of the ocean, already a year in the past.

Once the deed had been done, why not repeat it? What else would silence guilt and regret, at least for a time, and seem to vindicate the original lapse?

And so I sent him this: 'Please don't do this to me. I'm going out of my mind imagining what you may or may not have done, and I'd rather have been betrayed than be crazy. When can we talk?'

On the sixth and final day of our exams the carnations we pinned to our gowns were red. Red for blood; red for experience. I supposed the flowers were meant to signify that we had completed our initiation, but it felt more like a respite than a reprieve.

I sat at my desk in the Examination Schools for the last time, and regurgitated what I could remember about the Romantics. When I followed the throng of fellow finalists out on to to Merton Street I found a crowd had gathered to congratulate us English students on getting through to the end. Keith was there with proper champagne, ashen-faced but beaming; it cost me a pang to think of him splashing out on something so expensive.

'You did it,' he said, and caught me by surprise by reaching out to embrace me. As he held me he muttered, 'I'm sorry I was such an arse the other day.'

I said, 'I'm sorry I interrupted you when you were working,' and he withdrew and sighed and said:

'It's not like being interrupted is going to make any difference.'

Meg and Barnaby were there too, and there were plenty of others, people who studied other subjects, people I barely knew, and now never would: Maria the Greek-Cypriot musician, pretty Sophie who had once been Barnaby's girlfriend, Tim, who studied physics, sexy Inga who'd romped so noisily with the captain of the first eight, Violet, my first-term friend . . .

After a while the crowd began to dissipate and Barnaby said, 'I'm sorry to be a bore, but I have to go and work – exam tomorrow.' He touched his hand to his forehead in a melancholy little salute, shot Sophie a look of stony indifference which she didn't even notice – she was having a big heart-to-heart with Inga – and shambled off.

Meg said, 'What do you want to do now? We could go to the Wickham Arms and have a drink if you like. You should probably eat something. Line your stomach.'

'You should take it easy,' Keith said. 'You don't look too good.'

I was by now woozy and light-headed from the combination of Keith's champagne and lack of sleep, and these expressions of friendly concern caught me off guard. I felt tears come to my eyes, and willed myself not to let them out.

'I would really like that, but I ought to go check my emails first,' I said. 'I'm waiting for something from Victor. Things aren't great between us. I think . . .' I hesitated, drew breath, and then said in a sudden rush, 'I'm worried that something's happened between him and Clarissa.'

Meg and Keith exchanged looks, and I couldn't tell if they meant, *She's lost the plot*, or, *She may be right.*

'Victor wouldn't do that,' Keith said doubtfully. He stuck his lower lip out in a grimace that suggested he was struggling, and failing, to come up with other consolations. 'I'd offer you some weed, but I've smoked it all,' he said at last. 'I do have half a bottle of absinthe, though.'

'That's the last thing she needs,' Meg scolded him. 'Anna, you should come home with me, have a nice cup of tea and a hot bath, and go to bed. And when you wake up I'm going to make sure you eat something. Look at you, you're skin and bones.'

'I think you should listen to Meg,' Keith said. 'She is a sound sort of person who gives good advice, whereas I am quite obviously a deranged loser who would only drag you down into my own pit of futile misery. Have a good sleep, and I'll call you later.'

He patted me on the shoulder and turned to walk away, a thin, black-clad figure picking his way over the cobbles in the sunshine, his shoulders hunched as if was cold even though the sky above was blue and balmy.

Meg said she would wait for me while I checked whether Victor had got in touch. As I went into the computer room I met Jason coming out; it was the first time I'd seen him since his night with Meg.

'Afternoon,' he said. 'You finished your exams, then?'

'Yeah,' I said. 'Meg's just checking her pigeonhole, by the way, if you want to go and say hello.'

Victor had sent a message. It said only, 'I'll call you.'

I made my way out on to the main quad and saw Jason with Meg outside the porters' lodge. I don't know what line Jason had managed to come up with, but Meg was blushing. They had the look of two people who, if left to it, will sooner or later manage to come closer.

'I'm just heading home now,' I told her. 'I'll see you later.'

'Oh – are you sure you'll be OK?'

'Yeah, of course. I just need to unwind and get some sleep. I'll be fine.'

I gave them both a little wave, and went to get my bike.

The phone rang while I was still in the bath. I grabbed a towel and ran downstairs to answer it.

It was Victor.

'I don't know what to say to you,' he said.

'Did something happen?'

He swallowed. 'Yes.'

'Did you sleep with her?'

'Yes. I was drunk. We both were. She feels as bad about it as I do. She's gone now.'

'Are you in love with her?'

'No,' he said.

'Then why did you do it? Oh, don't answer that – I know. You just couldn't resist, could you? Oh, Victor . . . you've turned us into a *nothing*. Am I so completely forgettable?'

'You're not,' he said. 'Of course you're not.'

He started to cry, and I hung up on him.

I sat there for a while on the stairs with my hair dripping and the towel loosely draped around my wet skin. Then I went to my room, leaving the towel behind, and swept a slew of books and files off the bed and on to the floor, and threw whatever came to hand at the walls.

By the time I'd finished the place looked as if it had

been turned over by a very disappointed burglar. I found a pair of pyjamas I'd never worn with Victor and put them on. Then I lay down and stared at the green dress as if it was a looming apparition from another world, and cried myself to sleep.

Meg didn't come back that night; I guessed she had hooked up with Jason again.

I got up slowly, went to buy coffee and eggs, made breakfast, ate out in the garden. The sky was blue overhead; the leaves on the birch trees were a clear true green; it was quiet and calm.

The phone rang inside the house. I ignored it, and it stopped; then it started again.

I went to answer it, and Clarissa said, 'Hello, Anna.'

'What do you want?'

'I need to speak to Meg. Is she in? I need to know when to pick her up.'

'She's not here. Leave her a message at the porters' lodge and don't call here again.'

'It's my house too,' Clarissa said, 'I believe I'm still paying for my room. Look, Anna, I'm sure you're upset about Victor, and I know he feels bad right now, but I've always had feelings for him. If I hadn't been so busy being loyal to Desmond, I'd have got together with him before you did.'

'That's a pretty desperate attempt at self-justification, isn't it?' I said.

'Oh come on, he was ready to move on – I just helped him on his way. Though, to be fair, the first time caught us both a bit by surprise, having been friends for so long. I think we'd both forgotten what it's like at the very beginning of a relationship, when everything's new and exciting, before it has the chance to turn stale. By the way, I don't know if you knew, he's definitely moving back to London. We're planning on spending a lot more time together. In fact, I guess you could say we're a bit of an item. He might be too scared to tell you, but that's just how things are. You should face facts, Anna. You two are over.'

'We can't be,' I said stupidly. 'We're right for each other. I know we are.'

Clarissa laughed. 'I used to think that about Desmond,' she said. 'I suppose we'll see you at the ball, if you still want to come. Are you going to wear that green thing I picked out for you?' I didn't answer, and she went on: 'It's a nice dress, don't get me wrong, though it does make you look rather . . . *virginal*.'

She hung up, and so did I.

I went upstairs and got the dress, and crept into Clarissa's old room and held it up against myself and looked at my reflection in her full-length mirror.

'It isn't virginal,' I said out loud.

I couldn't really digest what she had just said; it didn't seem quite real – although none of the old times when she'd been sweet or kind seemed quite real now either.

Perhaps it had all just been so much role-playing. Or maybe everything had been fine until she realized I had something that she wanted, and decided to take it from me . . . And maybe she really did believe that Victor had been hers first of all. Her schoolfriend. Her find. Her addition to her little handpicked coterie.

'If you want Victor you're going to have to fight for him,' I told my reflection.

Was a prize that was compromised by betrayal still worth winning? It was going to be easy to hate Clarissa; I could feel it starting already. But Victor? What he had done was even worse; he was the one who had said he loved me, and then turned me into a sack of spare parts.

As I turned away from Clarissa's mirror and went to hang the green dress back up in my room I remembered what Victor's father had told me. *You can only count on what's in here,* and he had pressed his hand to his heart, and then he had tapped his head: *Because, believe me, what's up here will get you into terrible trouble.*

But what if all you could feel was hurt?

16

'Over the precipice'

'It has *not* been a good few weeks,' Keith said, 'but I think the happy pills must be kicking in, because right now I feel on top of the world. There is something to be said for heading for a ball with a goddess on your arm. Especially a birthday goddess.'

We were in the garden of the house in Gladstone Road once again, sitting on either side of the tiny table and drinking wine on an early summer evening; but this was also a night unlike any other night, the night of my twenty-first birthday, the night of the ball. The last few nights had been torrentially rainy, but now the sky was clear and the air was mild enough for me to sit out with bare shoulders and feel no inclination to fetch my wrap.

I was wearing the green dress, along with the necklace Mum and Gareth had given me for my birthday, a chain with a single pearl. Keith, who had come up from his parents' place in Kent, had arrived early, while

I was still in my dressing-gown and before I'd done my make-up. He'd sat in the bathroom and drank wine and chatted to me as my reflection in the little spotted mirror over the basin changed; my lashes lengthened, my lips turned red, my eyes grew larger and darker, and I had twisted the length and weight of my hair up and away from my face.

By and by I'd gone into my room and got into the green dress and he had done up the hooks and eyes for me, and then he had said, 'I think you'll do.'

He had dressed up too – he had a bow tie on, and a white shirt, and he'd got a black dinner suit from somewhere, though the trousers were fractionally too short and the jacket was too big. When he had arrived, my first thought had been how very uncomfortable he looked, though he had relaxed somewhat since, and was now more loquacious than he'd been since well before finals.

He had told me he was now taking anti-depressants – the 'happy pills' – and I had asked him if it was all right for him to drink, whereupon he had glared at me, and said, 'It most definitely is, and it would be unhealthy not to.'

'It's really good to see you,' I said. 'It's been pretty quiet round here since Meg went.'

It had also been pretty quiet *before* Meg left, because we'd barely been speaking. She'd told me I should accept Clarissa and Victor's relationship so we could all stay friends, and then we'd fallen out over my attempt to remind her how she had felt after her own break-up with Freddie; in Meg's view the end of an engagement was much more serious than my own situation, and not a fair comparison.

I had made sure I was out of the house when Clarissa showed up to collect Meg and her luggage and drive her back to London. When I came back I found Meg had left a little note with her key saying, 'I do hope we can still be friends.' She'd taken the corkscrew with her, which I supposed made sense, since I vaguely recalled that it had originally been Clarissa's.

Keith sighed. 'It's lovely to be here.'

'Maybe you could get a job in Oxford and move back,' I suggested, but he shook his head.

'It wouldn't be the same,' he said. 'Not with everybody gone. Too much has changed.'

Keith had been so despondent about what had happened that I'd been reluctant to lean on him. In a way, Meg's sturdy refusal to be partisan had been comparatively bracing; I preferred feeling angry to being dejected.

I held up the wine bottle; he nodded, and I topped us both up. I said, 'Remember that big thing you had for Magdalena Dale in the first year?'

'Oh, that,' Keith said. 'Well, obviously it was not to be.'

'Nobody else ever seemed to catch your eye in quite the same way.'

'Well . . . no.' Keith took a big swig of wine, and went on, 'I've thought about this a lot, as it happens, and I've come to the conclusion that unrequited love is really just a way of having an absolutely terrible relationship with yourself. I have an enormous but extremely frail ego, and I'm very disappointed with my own physicality, so my prospects for romance are doomed really. I mean, who would want someone who would settle for me? Nobody. So there's nothing for it but to become a lone eccentric with bad hair.' He reached into his jacket, fished out his cigarette papers and started skinning up.

'I don't believe that's true for one minute,' I said. 'You're eminently lovable. You just haven't given yourself a chance.'

'If it was easy for me the way it is for you, believe me, I would do it. I know you probably think it's not easy at all, especially at the moment, but you don't see what I see.'

'Which is?'

He didn't answer straight away, and I wondered if he'd heard me. Then he said, 'I've come to the conclusion that it's all about numbers and timing. If you and Victor were twenty-five, you'd have moved in together. If you were thirty, he'd probably have married you. Or got you pregnant or something. But you're not. You're twenty-one and he's twenty-two. It's too *early*.'

He stuck the joint in his mouth, took a deep drag, exhaled a thin plume of smoke. 'Victor and Clarissa will never work out,' he went on. 'He'll get bored of her and she'll dump him to get it in first, or he'll underperform professionally and she'll decide he's not up to her exacting standards and give him the boot.'

'You're very cynical about her.'

'I admire her, actually, but one thing I know for sure about her is that she has a very low boredom threshold. Also, she needs an awful lot of adoration.'

'She might be different now that she has a baby.'

'I think all the signs are that she's just going to become even more focused on getting exactly what she wants. It's going to make her tougher, and she's already as tough as old boots. Which I would imagine makes her quite intimidating as a love rival.'

'So, Mr Wisdom, what's your advice?'

Our eyes met, and his were mute and pleading, as if he was attempting to talk to me through a glass wall that muffled everything he said; but his voice was quite clear and steady as he went on.

'I think you just have to hang on,' he told me. 'In fact – I'm *begging* you to hang on. You and Victor are good together. You *ought* to be together. I've always thought that, ever since . . . well, ever since I got over the idea that you *were* together. Just don't do anything really awful tonight, like, I don't know, chucking your drink in her face or something. Actually, maybe *do* do that, though be prepared to unleash Clarissa's inner animal.'

'I don't think I'll do that,' I said.

'Has he been in touch at all?'

'He called once. I tried to be all cool and crisp, I really did, but then . . .' I shrugged, remembering myself snivelling down the phone, and Victor saying, 'Oh, Anna. Please, please don't. I'm sorry . . . I guess I'd better not call again.'

I smoothed the skirt of the green dress and reminded myself that tonight I was not Anna who had just been dumped. I was somebody else: a woman you might turn your head to look at, perfumed and gowned in silk, and ready for the ball.

'Victor did send me a card for my birthday,' I told Keith.

'That's good. What did he say?'

'Just wrote his name and a kiss. Not "love". It had flowers on the front.'

'Flowers, the language of love,' Keith reflected. 'It sounds nicer than mine, which I must apologize for.'

Keith's card, which he had handed over to me on arrival along with an enormous custom-made chocolate cake, was now standing on the mantelpiece next to Victor's. It had a spaniel on the front, looking up pleadingly with woebegone eyes.

'Yours is cute.'

'Mine is tacky and inappropriate, but I guess that's all right since I'm your slightly useless friend rather than the man of your dreams. I have to confess, I got it from the garage shop round the corner. It cost me some blushes to go in there, given that the manager fired me a couple of weeks ago.'

'Why, what happened?'

'I was awful and they let me go. Kept doing things wrong with the till. I couldn't really concentrate. I think my medication hadn't quite settled down.' He shuddered. 'The worst part was when Simon Blatt came in. He said, "Haven't seen you around for a while, I thought you went to university." I said, "Yes I did." He said, "So you're back now, are you?" I said, "Yes I am," and he paid for a tankful of petrol and roared off in his sports car, which looked exactly like the sort of car I would like to drive if I could drive. Though of course I can't.'

'Who's Simon Blatt?'

'Ohhh . . .' Keith grimaced, and looked around the garden as if something or someone might come to his aid. 'He was just someone I knew at school.'

He offered me the joint; I took it, and said, 'So what about your novel?'

'What novel? Oh, you mean that thing I started on as an excuse for not revising my maths? It was terrible, Anna. I looked at it in the cold light of day and saw I'd written five thousand words on the semiotics of toilet paper, so I threw it away.'

'I used to secretly think I wanted to be a writer,' I said. 'I had a film review in *Cherwell* in the first term. That was as far as I got, though. I mean, maybe I could have done more, if I'd pushed for it, but in the end I just didn't really think I was very good.'

'Really? That's a shame. I don't think I could have known you very well then, because I don't remember it. I do have quite a vivid picture of you when I first saw you, though. It was in the bar, and you looked so shy and intimidated and hopeful, and that was exactly how I felt myself. Of course Clarissa had already adopted me because she'd discovered I'd come up with a stash of weed.'

He took back the joint, and went on, 'This teaching lark . . . is it really what you want?'

'I want it more than anything else I think I might be realistically able to do,' I said. 'Maybe you should think about it too. Or you could do TEFL, and go overseas.'

'To be honest . . . I don't really feel that I'm consistently capable of doing anything. I mean, I feel fine right now, better than I have done for a while, in fact. But it hasn't been good.'

'In what way not good?'

'Mostly, things just haven't seemed real. It's very odd to have your surroundings shuttling past you as if they're absolutely nothing to do with you, and you can't actually reach out and touch them. Don't look so worried! Like I said, here and now, it's all right.'

He glanced at his watch and said, 'We should go.'

'I suppose we should,' I agreed.

'Let's be decadent and cab it,' he said, and I went off and phoned for a taxi.

When I came back out I said, 'So tell me a bit more about this Simon Blatt from school, the one who drives a sports car. He sounds really annoying. Was he always your nemesis?'

'Actually, I hero-worshipped him,' Keith said, discarding the end of the joint. 'He was the sexy, cool, rock'n'roll boy in the year above. You know the sort, dishevelled and a bit dirty and most likely not wearing any pants. He let me suck his cock once. Oh God, now you look shocked.'

'I'm not shocked, not at all,' I said. I was, though, not so much because Keith – fastidious, chaste, steadfastly single Keith – had done such a thing, but because he had acknowledged it.

'Well, OK, I'm a teensy bit surprised,' I admitted.

'So was I at the time,' Keith told me, raising his eyebrows and giving me a tight, challenging little smile that suggested the surprise had been pleasurable rather than otherwise.

'So you liked it,' I said.

'He did have a remarkable penis, very long and slightly curved.'

'Was it better than losing your virginity to your baby-sitter?'

'What an excellent memory you have. It would be un-chivalrous to compare, don't you think?'

'Don't you think . . .' I dried up, and tried again. 'This may be presumptuous of me, but are you telling me you think you might be gay?'

But Keith stared at me with sudden coldness, and I realized I'd overstepped the mark.

'You don't have the right to categorize me unless I choose to categorize myself, and I don't choose,' he said.

He got up and gathered up the wine bottle and the glasses and went into the house. I sat alone in the garden for a moment longer, and even though it was still bright and mild, I felt chilled. *It's all about timing,* he had said; and I had jumped the gun.

How could I have been so Meg-like – so black-and-white – as if I could only accept what Keith had told me if it came with a publicly acknowledgeable definition? I would have done better to just carry on being blindly unquestioning.

I followed him indoors and found him slumped on the sofa, staring into space, and I knew then that I'd broken something, some part of the mechanism of our friendship, and I had never before appreciated how delicate it was, or how precious.

'Keith, please . . . don't be mad at me. I'm sorry I was

so insensitive. I didn't mean to go wading in with my big feet. Please, just forget I ever said it?'

There was a ring at the door, and Keith said, 'That'll be our taxi. About time, too.'

I said, 'Keith, are you sure you're OK?'

He looked me up and down as if I were a stranger. 'You want to go, don't you?' he said. 'This is the big moment, the big goodbye to all of this. So let's go.'

We left the house and climbed into the taxi and were slowly driven down Cowley Road, over Magdalen roundabout and along the High Street. Passers-by were strolling along hand in hand in shorts and sandals, enjoying the evening sun, making their way to pub gardens and curry houses and cinemas, idling on the riverside, waiting for buses, taking photographs, cycling home. The taxi driver kept up a litany of complaints about students who'd thrown up in his cab, which covered our silence.

He pulled up outside St Bart's and Keith paid him and refused to take my tenner. The taxi did a U-turn and drove off, leaving us standing together on the pavement just outside the gates, but neither of us moved. Keith looked at me and said, 'I can't come in with you.'

'What?'

'I thought I could, but I can't.'

'Why not? Is it because of what I said just now?'

'No,' Keith said. 'It's because I'm not ready to see Victor again. I thought I would be, and it wouldn't matter. But it still does.'

'Victor? What's Victor got to do with it?'

'You should have worked out by now that you weren't the only one who liked him,' Keith said. 'You remember that first time we talked, that night in my room, and you were going on about Victor and I said about Magdalena, and we agreed we were in the same boat? Well, we were. I wasn't really talking about Magdalena at all. Then you got him, and I tried to tell myself it was the next best thing . . . though you were so *blind*, and so stupidly, smugly happy, sometimes I used to wish that you would lose him as well. And now you have, and it doesn't make me happy at all. If anything, I hate myself more now than I ever hated you. Because there were times when I did hate you, Anna. Jealousy hurts, and it turns you into someone you don't want to be. But I think you know that now.'

I couldn't begin to take this in. I knew it would force me to refocus everything I remembered about our friendship over the past three years. Everything was changing, everything . . . even what I thought I'd had was no longer what it had been . . .

So many looks, exchanges, shared moments that Keith must have witnessed with a peculiarly lonely and painful kind of happiness; so close to Victor, and to me, disguised, resigned, cut off from all of us, and shielded, too, by our assumptions and our ignorance. We had been so close. All that time, I had never really known him at all; and perhaps he had not really known himself.

That summer we'd spent living together in the tiny house in Gladstone Road. A doll's house of a place, and two friends who were as comfortable with each other as family . . . *We're like an old married couple* . . .

That hadn't been a pretence or a game, surely; that had been true. But also, the long walks Keith had gone off on whenever Victor was around . . . the sex he must have overheard from time to time when he was in . . . *There's only so much of being a third wheel that one can take.*

And now Victor was Clarissa's, and both Keith and I had lost him.

'OK. You don't want to come to the ball,' I said. 'It doesn't matter. It's probably going to be awful anyway. Let's just go to the pub instead.'

'I'm going home.'

'Then I'll come with you. We'll go back to Cowley and I'll take my glad rags off and we'll just have an ordinary evening. It'll be nice. Or I can keep the dress on, if you want company in your dinner jacket.'

'I'm not going back with you. Don't be such a coward, Anna. You don't need me to see you through this. You can handle it.'

'So can you,' I said. 'We'll be in it together . . . in the same boat. Like we were at the beginning.'

But Keith shook his head. He said, 'That's not where we are. I want you to go, Anna. I want you to be happy. It's a beautiful night, after all.'

He raised his hands and gazed around as if the High Street, the gates, the blue summer evening sky overhead were a blessing he was bestowing on me; then he held out his arm so I could link mine with it, and said, 'I'll see you to the gate.'

We proceeded right up to the entrance. Then he let me go and said, 'Good luck. You'll be fine.'

'But, Keith, I can't just let you go like this. What about you? What are you going to do?'

'Just try and enjoy yourself. Isn't that what you're meant to do, at a ball?' He turned round, glanced in the direction of the bus stop on the other side of the road, and said, 'I think that's my cue to leave.'

The London coach had just pulled up. I said, 'Are you sure—?' but Keith had already plunged across the road towards it.

And then another bus went past, and I lost sight of him. As I stepped on to the road to follow him a taxi swerved to avoid me and the driver hit his horn. A couple of bikes sailed by. Then the road cleared and I dashed across.

As I came round the end of the coach I saw the last passenger disappear inside, and as I approached the doors they slid shut. I knocked on them but the driver glanced at me with an expression that said, *Tough luck – too late*, before looking away over his other shoulder to check the traffic. I stepped back as the coach pulled out into the road and watched it go. I couldn't see Keith, and had no way of telling if he'd spotted me.

And I was relieved – and ashamed of myself for feeling that way. After all, if I had been in time, what would I have done? Ridden with Keith all the way to London and tried to talk about it? Made a scene on the bus? Clarissa might have pulled that off. But I was not Clarissa, and Clarissa was not here, because she was inside St Bart's with Victor.

I caught my breath and composed myself; then I crossed over, got my ticket out of my bag and went in to the ball.

The college was already packed, and had been transformed. A huge red silken tent had been erected in the main quad to keep off the drizzle, with crimson cushions and ottomans and low tables inside, a raised dais for the bands, and a central space for dancing. As I came in, a phalanx of belly dancers in lime green and purple and yellow were working their way across the floor.

I spotted various familiar figures among the spectators – Leila was swaying in time to the music like a very tall tree in danger of taking a tumble, and Mark Flask, who'd developed a small pot belly from finals comfort eating, was shimmying gently – but no Clarissa, no Meg, no Barnaby and no Victor.

I wandered around, taking it all in, feeling both dazzled and disconnected, and not a little drunk. It was a carnival mixed with a festival with a dash of a very posh summer drinks party and a seasoning of fancy-dress student debauch, framed by the pale stone of the medieval college buildings.

A huge Ferris wheel had been erected on the library lawn, and towered over everything else. There was a bouncy castle, dodgems, a barbecue, a pavilion for green tea and Turkish coffee and cakes, and another for would-be hookah smokers; a caterer offered falafel and stuffed peppers next to a long free bar laden with samples of flavoured vodka. The air smelt of cigarette smoke and sweat and rain and spice.

There were crowds of us everywhere, students and soon-to-be-ex-students from St Bart's and other colleges, people I knew or recognized and others I thought I might know but probably didn't, and now never would. We were ambling and stumbling and drinking and dancing and gossiping and smooching together in corners, girls in strapless or backless or halternecked gowns, boys in dinner suits and white bow ties, more or less dishevelled. Among us were the entertainers and the workers, security guards in yellow jackets stationed by trees and low rooftops on the lookout for gatecrashers, jugglers and stilt-walkers and barmen and masseurs. There were cigarette girls with long, honey-coloured limbs and dewy skin, a harpist, a flautist, a tambourine player, and a storyteller perched on a pouffe beneath a tall brass lantern, with a girl in a purple cocktail frock snoozing at her feet. Somewhere, underneath it all, there was a faint drumbeat that I could never quite trace to its source.

Sophie Adamson, Barnaby's ex, came over to wish me a happy birthday and we chatted about our dresses, and I tried the lemon vodka and the pear, and began to feel better. Sophie hadn't asked me where Keith was – why should she? Was I responsible for him? It was almost possible now, with a shot glass that smelt of mandarin in my hand and the bright distractions of the ball all around me, to forget what Keith had said before we parted, or, indeed, that we had parted at all. Soon, perhaps, it would also be possible to forget that Clarissa and Victor were somewhere nearby, or at least to be less agitated at the prospect of bumping into them.

Sophie and her boyfriend, a medical student from another college, went off to try the dodgems, and I followed them and got into a car with Tim Rosewell, the physicist, who turned out to be an expert and surprisingly violent driver. Then I felt giddy and had to get out and as I moved away I tripped and righted myself and realized I was on my way to being well and truly plastered, and didn't care.

I fell in with Damon Adkin and his rowing cronies and smoked a cigarette and knocked back a bottle of beer, and it occurred to me that, despite Keith bailing on me, I could handle this; I was rootless without my close friends around me, but I was also free. And so I drifted on, meandering from one shoal of friends or acquaintances or strangers to the next, joining them only in passing before either they or I ebbed away.

As the light began to fade the fireworks went off and the Ferris wheel was illuminated. The tiny lamps that had been strung up around the college walls and along the tent frames and stands came on, so that the darkness was full of scattered points of light, like brightness refracted by black water.

There was a fortune teller just off Main Quad, and every time I went past there were at least four or five people waiting for her. But then there was a general movement towards the main marquee, and the queues for other attractions dwindled. I realized the music was about to change.

The Pigtoes, a relatively obscure indie band who were popular only with a small segment of the college community – Keith was a fan – went off. A swing band started playing. I saw my chance, and went straight into the fortune teller.

She was in exactly the same room where Victor and Barnaby had carried out their duties on the welcoming committee, though it had been turned into a dim, fabric-covered den, lit up by dozens of tea-lights. She was sitting on a chair swathed with purple velvet; a pack of cards and a dish full of money stood on the small brass table in front of her. I peered in and she gestured to me to come over and take the seat opposite her.

She was veiled and robed in crimson gauze and it was impossible to make out her shape, or much of her face, but her eyes were familiar. Almost certainly she was a fellow student, and I'd met her or passed her somewhere, perhaps in a pub or in the supermarket or on the street, or at one of the few lectures I'd attended, or even in the queue to go into the Examination Schools.

'First you must cross my palm with silver,' she said, and I dropped a few coins into her upturned hand. She put them in the dish on the table, took my hand and studied it, and turned over a line of cards.

'Your card is the hanged fool,' she said. 'Look, here you are, stepping over the precipice. You will be lost and you will have to find your way back, but one day you will cross the water again. You will have to ask the question you have forgotten and when you have the answer you will climb the winding stair. You will speak out, and the others will listen but they may or may not hear.'

'I was wondering how things might turn out with my

boyfriend. Ex-boyfriend. He just dumped me for one of our mutual friends.'

She stared at the cards and ran her fingertips over my palm. 'I can't say,' she said. 'It's too cloudy. I think it is all in the balance.'

'I have this other friend who was meant to come tonight but changed his mind at the last minute. He seems kind of lost . . . very down, and unsure about the future. Can you tell me anything about what might happen to him?'

'I cannot answer for people who are not here,' she said.

'Is that it, then?'

'Yes,' she said, 'that's all. Please send in the next person, and tell them to make sure they've got some cash. I only give predictions to people who pay.'

I went out and a giggling, lurching blonde took my place; the friend who was waiting for her called out, 'Go for a tall dark handsome stranger!' I brushed past her and made my way into the main tent, hoping to find a spot on a divan and watch the dancing.

That was when I saw them: Victor and Clarissa. A small, respectful space had cleared around them. He curled one arm round the small of her back as she arched and flexed and leaned away from him and presented him with the smooth white curve of her throat, and her long red hair swung down behind her and swayed in time with her red dress.

'They're quite a spectacle,' said someone behind me, 'aren't they?'

I turned round and saw Barnaby. His bow tie was

undone, and he was red and sweating. He wiped his forehead and took a swig from his bottle of beer.

'Personally, I think Victor's a fool,' he went on. 'I'd take you over her any day. He still goes on about you when she's not in earshot.'

'Let's not talk about it,' I said. 'I'm trying to celebrate. It's my birthday.'

'Of course it is. Then we must find you a drink. Come on, let's leave the lovebirds to it.'

As he took me by the arm and steered me out of the tent I caught sight of Meg on one of the couches with Jason embracing her; they looked as if they'd be in need of a room sooner rather than later. I said, 'Where are they all staying, anyway? Nobody mentioned anything about coming to Gladstone Road for the night.'

'They assumed they wouldn't be welcome. Correctly, I imagine. I'm still in my room in college. But Clarissa's booked a couple of suites in a hotel.'

'How lavish of her.'

'Don't be bitter, it doesn't suit you.'

We came to the vodka bar and Barnaby picked out a couple of shots and passed one to me.

'Down the hatch,' he said, linking his arm through mine, and down the hatch it went. I couldn't identify the flavour this time: barely even noticed it.

'I think at this point in the evening, with so many casualties around, we can stop worrying about pacing ourselves,' Barnaby said. 'You been on the Ferris wheel yet?'

I said I hadn't, and we went over to wait for a carriage, strapped ourselves in, and began to slowly ascend.

'It's rough on you, the Victor and Clarissa thing,' Barnaby said. 'A bit shoddy, really. I don't approve.'

This wasn't a view I'd heard him express before. Just about the only conversation we'd had on the subject had taken place in the lunch queue shortly before the end of term, when he had shifted uneasily from one foot to the other and murmured something about plenty more fish in the sea, looking round as if seeking an escape route in case I burst into tears. Still, if he was willing to condemn Victor and Clarissa, I was more than happy to hear it.

'That's not what Meg says,' I told him. 'She's been very emphatic that she can't take sides.'

'Well, she has, effectively, hasn't she? Of course she has, she knows what side her bread's buttered, what with the peppercorn rent for the nice room in the north London house, and the celebrity landlady who likes nothing better than to cook for her daughter's friends. She hasn't exactly thrown her lot in with you, as far as I can see.'

'I suppose she hasn't,' I agreed.

College retreated beneath us, and the view opened up. Oxford at night, darkness and ghostly white lamplit stone, libraries and spires and towers, and, falling away from the shrieks and drumbeats of the ball, the meadows and the woods and the river and the roads that led to everywhere else. To Mandy Martin's house and baby Michael sleeping in his cot, Gareth and Mum and Tippy in Deddenham, and Keith, wherever he had got to; and on and on, over the seas to the distant beach where Victor and I had last been happy and together.

The Ferris wheel juddered to a halt, someone screamed, and Barnaby said, 'Oops, looks like we're stuck here.' He fished a hip flask from inside his jacket pocket and passed it to me. 'Luckily, I came prepared.'

'The whole ball is awash with booze, and you brought your own?'

'You never know when you might run out. How about a quick game of twenty questions?'

And so we played – his first answer was Cerberus, the three-headed dog that guards the gates of the underworld, and mine was a unicorn – and we drank, and waited, and eventually the wheel turned and returned us to earth, where I trotted obediently along with him to the main tent and found that it was possible to dance quite freely and not mind in the least if Victor saw. I would have a good time, I would not care if my lover loved someone else, I was free to flirt with whomever I chose, and if Barnaby was willing to play with me, well, then Barnaby would do just fine. At one point Victor approached me, he grabbed my arm and said something angry, but someone said, 'Oh come on, Victor, just leave her alone,' and then he was gone. But Barnaby was still there, big, steady, durable Barnaby, who proved adept at catching me when I stumbled, a constant in the whirl of people and impressions and colours all around me, as if I was dreaming and then resurfacing, and he was beside me whether I was awake or asleep.

And then a great wave of nausea overtook me and I said, 'Oh God, I think I'm going to be sick,' and he guided me away into the cobbled lane that led to the parking spaces and over the lawn to Rhys House, which was quiet and dark.

A couple overtook us: the girl said, 'I say, did you remember the condoms?' but they were going at such a pace that the boy's reply was too faint for me to make out. They hurried on towards Hanover Buildings and disappeared.

'Love is all around,' Barnaby said, punching in the key code to Rhys House. 'There's a bathroom in here.'

I went into the small, white-painted room, breathed deeply, watched it spin. The nausea receded and after a while I came out again.

'I thought you'd have gone,' I said.

'No, no, I wouldn't abandon you like that.'

'I think maybe I should go home.'

'Oh no, don't be silly, there's hours to go yet. You don't want to miss the survivors' photo, or the breakfast! Come up to my room and have a lie-down, and revive yourself.'

He took me by the hand; we seemed to have been holding hands a lot lately, though I couldn't remember that we'd ever done so before.

'I'm right up the top of the stairs, though,' he warned me.

We climbed up, and he unlocked the door and I went in.

'Oh dear, it's going round and round,' I said.

The room was circling as if I was trapped in a slowly wobbling gyroscope. I closed my eyes and opened them again to see if it would make any difference, but everything was just moving even faster. Barnaby shut the door and stood behind me and put his arms around me. I turned round and he kissed me and I pulled back and laughed and said, 'Oh, Barnaby, we can't get into all of that.'

'All of what?' he said, frowning.

'I just . . . I mean, it's been lovely to have your company and I'm very grateful to you . . .'

'A kiss is just a kiss,' Barnaby said, making a dismissive gesture with one hand.

I sat down on the bed and he sat down next to me and said, 'Have you hurt your foot?'

I looked down and saw that my shoes, which were new, had rubbed me raw; one of my heels was bleeding.

'I suppose I have. I didn't even feel it.'

'I probably have some plasters somewhere,' he said, 'or maybe I left them in the bathroom. Back in a sec.'

He dimmed the light on his way out. Now the room was not so much turning as swaying. I managed to ease my shoes off and find a tissue in my bag and dabbed at the blood on my heel. My tights were shredded. It took an enormous, impossible effort to get them off and stuff them in my bag.

A huge wave of exhaustion bore down on me and I allowed myself to sink on to the bed. My head sagged; I could feel my eyes rolling back in my head. I laid my head down on the pillow and was subsumed by a darkness that seemed deeper and darker than any I had ever known.

17

'The benefit of the doubt'

The girl on the bed was asleep in her green dress. It was partly open at the back and partly not, and the wide straps had fallen down around her upper arms and the skirts were rucked up around her bare white thighs. Some of her long dark hair was pinned up but most of it had come loose and was covering her face and back, and she was so still, and so pale, she could have been dead.

The boy next to her was awake and naked. It was hot in the room, and the covers were tangled around their legs. He kicked them away and reached for her breasts and dragged at the shoulders of the dress. There was a metallic popping sound and a few stitches burst and the silk gave way. He rummaged under her skirts, tugged and pulled. There was the dry rasp of synthetic lace tearing, a quick discarding gesture, and then he stroked her hair aside and pressed himself against her back, started moving against her, rearranged her limbs, and pushed himself into her.

She began to surface. She squirmed and writhed like a bug with a damaged leg. Her head jerked forward and backward and her free arm, the one that wasn't pinned against her side, underneath him, thrashed against the bedding. She made a strange noise. Not a good noise. It was not quite possible to make out what she was saying.

He stopped. He grabbed a handful of her hair and yanked it so hard her head snapped back. He said, 'You have to be quiet.'

She screamed. He grabbed the pillow next to her and put it over her head and held it there and shifted until all his weight was bearing down on her. He moved very quickly and groaned and rolled away and she was free to move and push the pillow away and come up for air.

She lay very still for a moment, just breathing. Her first thought was, *I'm still alive*. Then, *I have to get out of here*. Then, *Where am I?*

And then she realized that she was me, and he was Barnaby, and I was in his room in college.

He wasn't holding me or even touching me any longer. I could see the door. Not far away, a couple of paces. Everything shifted and swayed and surged back into focus. I could see my evening bag on the floor, my black suede shoes, one heel scabby with blood. I could hear traffic outside. The room was still dim – the blind must be down – but it was morning.

I straightened up. My head throbbed and the room swayed ominously. Something was wrong with my dress. One of the shoulder straps was torn. I stooped and pulled my shoes towards me and put them on, reached for my bag, checked for my keys. Still there.

His dinner suit was hanging up on the outside of the wardrobe, the bow tie dangling round the neck of the hanger. How could he have been so capable, so deliberate?

He sat up and said, 'You were making a hell of a racket.' He looked as if he didn't know whether to be scared or angry.

'I have to go,' I told him.

'What are you looking at me like that for? It was what you wanted, wasn't it? You don't get to change the story now. Oh come on, Anna, half of college saw us together last night. You were all over me. You wouldn't leave me alone!'

He called my name as I reached for the door, but whatever he said next was cut off as it closed behind me.

I hurried down the stairs. My tread sounded empty and echoey; most of this part of college was empty now. I emerged on to the cobbled lane that led out to the High Street and made my escape.

Outside the air was cool, even though the sky was blue and the sun was already climbing. By midday it would be stifling.

I made my way across the High Street and started limping towards Cowley. Past the café, past the delicatessen where we had shopped for sun-dried tomatoes and Brie in French bread one idle summer afternoon, when Clarissa had instructed Barnaby to take us punting. Past the off-licence where we had bought sparkling white wine for our Gladstone Road housewarming party, because if it fizzed and was intoxicating, who would care, who would even notice that it wasn't champagne? Somewhere just over the other side of the roundabout was the shop where I'd got the green dress.

Around me other people were going about their business. A female student in a Breton top and jeans clip-clopped past in high-heeled sandals; a young man in a grocer's apron arranged a display of fruit outside his shop; a bookseller examined his shelves in a dim interior. Everything was calm, orderly, promising: Oxford on a beautiful midsummer morning. And yet it was as if I was not really there. How could I be, how could I possibly be part of such a scene? It hurt to walk and I was conscious of the tears in my dress, my nakedness underneath it, and Barnaby's semen trickling down my thighs; and the pavement was shifting, undulating almost, and shimmering, so that I was afraid that I would fall.

I glimpsed a taxi and hailed it, and it carried on past but then pulled up and turned and came back for me. I settled gratefully into the back and closed my eyes and whispered a thank you to Keith for refusing my tenner, which would now pay for me to get home. Then I concentrated on not being sick as the car rattled and bounced along all the way back to Gladstone Road.

With the sunlight pouring in, the small, grubby sitting room, with its dusty beige carpet and coffee table and corduroy sofa and tiny table, looked perfectly familiar and friendly, and yet also remote, as if it belonged to another life.

There was the birthday cake that Keith had bought me in its striped pink-and-white box, the wine glasses we had used, one marked with my lipstick, the empty bottle, the ashtray. And there, on the mantelpiece, were the cards I'd been sent from my family, and from Victor and Keith, and a picture of a National Trust garden from Meg.

The only thing I could think of to do was to strip off and immerse myself in water. It wasn't so much a seeking of comfort as a necessary ritual. This body I was in was still mine, and this was what I could do for it. And then we would see about the rest of the day, and whatever else needed to be done. But first: this.

I went upstairs in my bare feet and turned on the bath-taps and wriggled and pulled at the hooks and eyes at the back of the green dress until I was able to get myself out of it. It was then that I realized my necklace, the one my parents had given me for my birthday, had gone. The chain must have broken. Probably it was in Barnaby's bed.

I caught sight of my reflection in the mirror that I'd used to get ready for the ball the night before. Was that really me? White face, dark hair, obscured by steam, as if lost in a mist.

The bath was near overflowing. I eased myself into it and lay for a long time, then shampooed my hair, soaped every bit of my skin, rinsed myself clean, emptied the bath and filled it again. I thought of Keith, taking a knife to himself, the red blood swirling, the white of the bath. *It hurt like hell, which is why I only did one of them.* And then, *That's not where we are.*

At first I didn't hear the doorbell. I'd submerged myself so that only my face was above water, and the sound was a faint vibration at the edge of my consciousness, like a ripple. Then I sat up and heard it quite clearly.

I waited to see if it would go away, but after a few minutes it rang again. I got out and wrapped a towel round my head and pulled on my dressing-gown and went to peer out of Clarissa's bedroom window, which was at the front, to see who it was.

There was a police car outside the house and a uniformed policewoman standing back with arms folded, and Dr Kaspar in her bright silk jacket, saying something. Her expression was keenly, acutely anxious. Not angry. Not disappointed. Not dismayed. But disturbed, and dutiful, and afraid.

I padded downstairs and opened the door.

The policewoman said, 'Good morning, sorry to intrude, Miss . . .'

'Jones,' Dr Kaspar murmured.

'Jones,' the policewoman repeated. She was a sturdy-looking, impassive woman of perhaps thirty or thirty-five, with her brunette hair pulled back into a ponytail and modest gold studs in her ears. 'I'm PC Arlington, and I'm afraid I have some bad news for you, concerning a friend of yours. May we come in?'

But I could barely move; I seemed to have frozen, while everything around me had become unsteady, as if it could cave in at any moment. I leaned against the doorframe and said, 'Is it Barnaby?'

PC Arlington looked blank. 'No, I don't think I know anything about a Barnaby.'

'Anna,' Dr Kaspar said, 'I do think it would be a good idea if you were to sit down.'

I stood aside to let them in, and we went into the living room. I settled on the sofa. Dr Kaspar sat at the table, at a slight remove from the proceedings, as if this was a viva voce examination and she was moderating.

PC Arlington remained standing, and I said, 'Please sit, if you would like,' and she took the place next to me.

'I'm sorry to say that your friend Keith Greaves has been found dead in the water by Witcherley Lock,' she said, 'in the early hours of this morning. One of your teacher's colleagues identified the body for us. His parents have been notified and I'm here to talk to you because we're trying to get a clearer picture of the events that led up to his passing.'

'Keith? I'm sorry, I think there must be some mistake. I saw him just last night and he got the coach back to London at around eight o'clock. There's no way he would have been anywhere near Witcherley Lock.' I turned to Dr Kaspar. 'Who identified him?'

'It was Keith's tutor,' Dr Kaspar said.

'I'm afraid there is no mistake,' PC Arlington said, 'and he did not get that coach back to London.'

I stared at her and her face began to blur and melt and I realized it was because I was crying. Dr Kaspar stood and approached me and offered me a tissue. I wiped my nose and dried my eyes and said, 'I'm sorry, I just can't believe it. It seems impossible. What happened?'

'We're still trying to establish that,' PC Arlington

said, 'but we have no reason at this present moment to believe anybody else was involved. We've already spoken to the publican at the Witcherley Arms. Keith called in there at about ten o'clock and that's the last sighting we have of him when he was still alive. We were rather hoping you might be able to fill us in on what happened in the earlier part of the evening.'

'Keith came here about six o'clock,' I said. PC Arlington started scribbling in her notebook. 'We ate some pasta, drank a bottle of wine, sat out in the garden. Then at about quarter to eight we got a taxi to college. We were meant to be going to the St Bart's Ball together, but Keith changed his mind at the last minute and said he was going to go home instead.'

'Any idea why?' PC Arlington said.

I glanced at Dr Kaspar, but her expression was blank and unyielding. I said, 'I think he decided he didn't really want to see his old friends after all.'

'I see,' PC Arlington said. 'I'm sorry to ask a personal question, Miss Jones, but what was the nature of the relationship between you and Mr Greaves?'

I looked her in the eye and held my head up straight. I said, 'He was my friend.'

'Not a boyfriend?'

'No. I have a boyfriend. Had. It wasn't that kind of relationship.'

'I see,' said PC Arlington. 'Were you aware of him using any particular drugs or medication?'

This time I wasn't even tempted to look at Dr Kaspar. I said, 'He mentioned anti-depressants. Also, he smoked a little bit of pot sometimes.'

'Including last night?'

'Yes.'

'Here, with you?'

I hesitated. 'Yes.'

I waited for her to ask me if I'd smoked it too – perhaps she would want to caution me, or take me down to the police station, or do whatever they did. But instead she said, 'I'm very sorry to have troubled you, Miss Jones, and to have brought you such bad news. I do just have one more question, which is if you are aware of any note he might have left behind, or passed to you for safekeeping?'

'No, nothing. Just a card. A birthday card. That one. The dog with the bone.'

'I see,' said PC Arlington. 'Well, I think that will be all for now, if I could just take some details where we can get in touch with you over the next month or so.'

I gave her the Topaz Close address and phone number, and said, 'Will there be an inquest? Will you need me to give evidence?'

'There will certainly be an inquest,' PC Arlington said, 'but as to whether you'll be needed, I can't really say. To be honest, I think it's probably unlikely. Coroners tend to like to give the families the benefit of the doubt in these cases.'

'What cases? You mean . . . suicides? But I don't think Keith would have intended . . . He said he was feeling better . . .'

'I meant situations where a healthy young person dies unexpectedly,' PC Arlington said smoothly, 'which are obviously tragic whatever the cause. I don't suppose you know if Mr Greaves was able to swim?'

'Oh – no. He hated swimming. He said they used to make him do it at school . . . They threw him in the deep end . . .' My eyes filled with tears again. 'And he never did learn.'

'I see,' PC Arlington said. She made a final note and stood. 'Well, I'm very sorry for your loss. I won't trouble you any longer. Dr Kaspar, thank you for your assistance. Would you like a lift?'

'I'll make my own way, thank you,' Dr Kaspar said. She was still standing by me, her arms folded.

'I'll let myself out,' PC Arlington said, and withdrew.

Dr Kaspar came round and sat down next to me.

'I won't stay long, Anna,' she said. 'I just wanted to say one thing to you. I know this has been a terrible shock and it's a tragedy for Keith's family and a loss for all of us. But don't let it be the thing that you think of when you remember your time here. Don't let it be an end for you, too.'

She drew a pen and a piece of paper out of her handbag and scribbled on it.

'My number. You can call me any time,' she said, and then I showed her out.

Keith gone. Keith gone! It wasn't possible. I could still hear his voice . . . picture him on the sofa, at the table, slightly hunched, quizzical, uneasy. How was it possible for him to be unmoving on a mortuary slab somewhere?

I gathered up the cards from the mantelpiece and went to drop them into a cardboard box full of books.

There, on the top, was the green hardback Keith had given me years ago, that first Christmas. I opened up the back of the book and slid Keith's card in, and then, on impulse, put Victor's in with it, and shoved it back into the box.

What to do with the birthday cake he had given me? The smell of it – so chocolatey, so sweet – induced a wave of nausea so intense that I thought I might be about to faint, but it passed, and I managed to get the cake into the bin and seal up the bag of rubbish and take it out to the front yard. Then I went back out with the green dress and left that on top. Let it bleach in the sunlight or rot in the rain; let anyone who wanted it help themselves, or the binmen could take it away to the tip. It should probably never have been mine in the first place, and now no one would wear it again.

Somehow I managed to dress, dry my hair and brush my teeth, tidy and pack away the last remaining things, and carry my boxes of books and bags and bedding down to the hallway.

By the time Gareth pulled up outside I was ready for him.

He came in and said, 'Well, you look like you've got everything shipshape and organized.'

'I think so. I just need to load up the car and drop off my keys, and then we can go.'

And so I locked up the house for the last time and went out past my discarded balldress and hurried as quickly as I could to the letting agent's office round the corner while Gareth waited in the car. It still hurt to walk, but I reminded myself it wasn't far. Then I climbed gratefully into the passenger seat and Gareth drove slowly through the traffic, back the way that I had come that morning: past Magdalen roundabout, the deli, the off-licence, the grocery, the antiquarian bookseller's with its rows upon rows of old red spines.

'So,' Gareth said, 'you had a good birthday?'

'Yeah, good, thanks.'

'And now you're twenty-one.'

'Uh-huh.'

'You remember what we discussed a long time ago? About all that old family business, and you said you wanted to know more about it?'

'Yeah. I remember.'

We edged past St Bart's. I glimpsed the cobbled lane, the wooden gates shut across the entrance to Main Quad. And then I saw them: Victor and Clarissa, arm in arm, strolling down the High Street, as inviolably happy as if they had their own separate golden sun.

'Well, fire away with the questions,' Gareth said. 'I'm game for it. I promised, and I never go back on a promise.'

'Do you know what, Gareth, I don't think I really want to know any more,' I said. 'Right now I couldn't care less.'

'Fair enough,' Gareth said. 'If that's how you feel. Don't say I didn't offer.'

We turned off the High Street and the university buildings began to thin out, and were replaced by rows of Victorian houses, interspersed with pubs, B & Bs, here and there stretches of open ground – tennis courts, allotments, pasture grazed by a couple of horses – and then we were on the dual carriageway and Gareth put his foot down and the city was behind us.

I leaned back against the headrest and closed my eyes, and felt everything flowing away from me and shrinking and closing up, like a flower that folds into itself when the light fades, in readiness for a long cold night. Before long I was asleep, and I didn't wake till I was back in Topaz Close, and my mother was walking down the driveway to welcome me home.

I saw my friends three weeks later, at the crematorium in Kent.

In the anteroom, waiting to go in for the service, were the two who had tried to get in touch with me: Meg, Victor; and the two who hadn't: Barnaby and Clarissa. Victor had his arm round Clarissa; she didn't have the baby with her. Meg looked teary, and Barnaby was standing stoically by with his hands deep in the pockets of his black suit.

Dr Villiers, the tutor who had despaired over Keith's lack of devotion to mathematics and had identified his body in the mortuary, was there, talking to Keith's parents. I had seen them once or twice before, when they had come to visit Keith at St Bart's. They were both fair, tall and sturdy-looking, one of those couples that resemble each other so strongly they could have been related by blood rather than marriage.

Keith's little sister Kelly was standing next to them; she, too, was blue-eyed and freckly and well built, and her long straight hair, which she'd dyed jet black, had honey-blonde roots. Physically, they all had much more in common with each other than with Keith – I wondered whether he had been aware of this whenever they went out together, and had imagined onlookers speculating about the nature of his relationship to the family into which he had been adopted. Keith had been so self-conscious that it seemed quite possible.

And yet there was something Keith-like about each one of them, too. It was easy to imagine Mr and Mrs Greaves going out together for long country walks, and Kelly's slouchy, cagey demeanour reminded me quite vividly of her brother. She also struck me as looking very young, even though she was only a couple of years younger than I was.

I approached them and gave my condolences, and Mrs Greaves nodded and held out her hand for me to shake. Keith had told me she liked gardening, and even though she was stiff and white with grief I could imagine her tending her roses in happier times, thorny stems in one gloved hand and secateurs in the other, a hat on to protect her from the sun.

'I'm sorry, dear, I didn't catch your name,' she said.

'I'm Anna, Keith's friend from college.'

She didn't smile. Instead she regarded me with a glimmer of suspicion. 'You're not the one who was with him the evening it happened, are you?' she said.

'Janet, please,' her husband said.

'I just want to get this straight,' she said. 'Well, are you?'

'I am,' I said.

She looked me up and down. 'The one he took drugs with.'

'He did smoke a little. Yes.'

'That stuff rotted his brain,' she told me. 'It was the ruination of him. And then when he was on his pills and everything, drinking, drugging, no wonder the balance of his mind was disturbed. Did you have the least idea what state he was in? Well, did you?'

'I knew he was . . . worried about things. He said he was going home. I even saw him get on to the bus, or at least I thought I did . . .'

'What kind of a friend *are* you?' Janet said, her fists suddenly clenching.

'Mum,' Kelly said, 'don't get yourself all upset. We'll be going in soon, and there are other people here who want to speak with us.'

Mrs Greaves made a visible effort to calm herself. 'Well, I've said just about all I want to say to you,' she told me. 'You keep your distance from me, young lady. You pay your respects by all means and reflect on what you could have done differently that day, but I don't want to see your face again, not around at the reception, not anywhere.'

'I'm so sorry,' I said, and backed away.

Someone came up behind me and said, 'That was a bit harsh,' and I found myself looking at a stranger – tall, dark, good-looking, dressed in a battered leather jacket and jeans. He had a slightly worn face, as if he'd spent too much time in smoky pubs.

'It's no more than I deserve,' I said. 'I wasn't a particularly good friend to him.'

'I'm not sure I was either,' he said, 'and Mrs Greaves doesn't like me any more than she likes you. Do you need a lift anywhere after the service? I could drop you back at the station.'

'Yes, thank you so much, I would really appreciate that,' I said, and then, on impulse, 'You're not Simon, are you? Simon Blatt?'

He frowned. 'Yeah. How do you know that?'

'You went to school with Keith, right? You drive a sports car,' I said. 'He told me a little bit about you.'

Simon looked surprised. 'Right. Yeah.'

'He said you came into the garage where he was working,' I explained, and tried to put the thought of what else Keith had told me about Simon out of mind.

As we joined the queue filing into the chapel Clarissa called out, 'Anna, wait a moment,' and I stopped and all four of them drew closer.

'We just all want you to know how sorry we are,' Clarissa said.

I felt beads of sweat prickling my forehead and underarms. 'I appreciate that, Clarissa, but I would much prefer it if all of you would just leave me well enough alone.'

'I know you're angry with me and Vic, and that's fair enough, but we're all grieving too, and Meg hasn't done anything, nor has Barnaby – and look, Victor and Barnaby are still getting along just fine after you two had your little fling at the ball—'

'Clarissa,' I said, 'just shut up, will you?'

I looked from her face to Victor's to Barnaby's to Meg's.

'The truth of the matter is,' I said, 'Keith was the only one out of all of you who was a friend worth having.'

I walked on into the chapel and took up a position at the far end of one of the rows of seats, and the vacant spaces next to me were soon filled by a row of strangers. I could see them all, a couple of rows ahead; when we stood to sing I noticed that Meg's shoulders were shaking, though I could barely make out the sound of her crying above the music.

The official gave a little speech about Keith from which I barely recognized the person I had known. We stood to sing again, and red curtains began to jerk across the stage, moved not by hand but by a slow and rigid mechanism, and the coffin began to disappear from view.

I closed my eyes and thought of Keith in the orangery at Shawcross Hall, telling tourists about the provenance of the porcelain. I opened my eyes and the music stopped, and the coffin had gone.

I did go back to St Bart's once more, for the memorial service in the college chapel, which took place in the autumn term. I arrived just before it started and took one of the last available seats, and as the first hymn got underway I took stock of who was there and realized, with some relief, that neither Keith's parents nor any of my former friends had come. Perhaps Victor and Clarissa had gone back to the States, and Meg would have started work, and might not have been able to get away; as for Barnaby, who knew?

The chapel was hot and airless and packed; it was lit with dozens of candles that wavered and guttered in their holders but did not go out, and although I felt dizzy and strange I followed the order of service and sat and stood and sang and prayed along with everybody else. Afterwards, we spilt out into the main quad, formed clusters, exchanged greetings and news; and, as if in accordance with some tribal instinct, in twos and threes and fours, the rest of the congregation began to make its way towards the steps that led down to the bar.

I didn't go, though. I stood there till the last possible minute, smiling, nodding, exchanging courtesies, taking it all in; not just the rapidly thinning gathering of the people I knew, but other passers-by who had never known me or Keith, the freshers, the new faces. The Virginia creeper had turned flame-red and the roses that edged the lawns were dropping their petals, the air was cold and smelt of autumn, but the faces were as shiny and untouched as the first shoots of spring: and yet they were so endlessly familiar . . .

Shy girls, pretty girls, geeks, rowers, former head girls and boys; thesps, caners, arty types, hearty types, eccentrics, innocents, hopeful and nervous and swaggering and unsure; I felt that I already knew them all. And, yes, lovers too; I saw a couple wandering round with their hands tucked into each other's pockets and indistinguishably blissful expressions, as if passion had obliterated their capacity for independent thought. But it was just the beginning of fifth week; who knew if they would make it through . . .

Time to leave it all to them.

As I stepped out through the gates I felt myself break through the skin of something, transparent and fragile as the surface of a bubble.

I made my way across the steady stream of city traffic and drifted out into the throng of tourists and students passing along Cornmarket Street. I had the strange illusion that I was floating overhead, watching myself, one small figure amongst many: all of us busy, distracted, oblivious, weighed down by what we had already done and what we still had left to do, having long since forgotten that we were really as free and all-seeing as the air.

Part Five
2012

The View from the Top

Much, much later, long after last orders, he made his way back to his flat.
His key was already in the lock when he realized he wasn't alone. Someone was waiting for him.

He closed his eyes and leaned his forehead against the door and thought of the girl he had met that day – his daughter – whose name he would now never know, and he wondered if there was anything, anything at all, that could confer protection upon her once she had lost that terrible innocence.

There was a footstep, very light, and something cold and hard prodded the back of his neck.

And then he exploded outwards into total quietness. He knew himself to be composed of blood and light; he was recognized and received like the end note of a song. And then he fell, and was folded back into a self that was gone and lost as if it had never been, beyond nowhere; an exhalation, a drift of ash.

If, somewhere, his daughter breathed in sharply, stunned into wakefulness, and put her hand to the back of her head as if feeling for the pulse of blood and was surprised to find that she was whole, it was not for him to know.

From *The End of Mr D.*, by Benjamin Dock (1978)

18

'You and me'

2012

Victor and I spoke very little on the train. He kept trying to get the conversation going, and I kept on missing the point, or giving him half-hearted or evasive replies. I was too agitated at the prospect of being shut in a room with Barnaby again to be able to give my full attention to what he was saying.

He wished me a happy birthday; I thanked him. He asked if I'd heard from Ben; I said I had, and was going to Prospero's Nest to attempt a writing course in a couple of weeks. He asked if the rest of the family was still speaking to me; I reassured him that they were. He asked if the driving lessons I'd just started were going OK; I said yes, so far so good. He asked about work; I said it was going fine.

By this stage he looked rather hurt by my apparent terseness, so I rallied and asked about his daughter; he told me that his ex was dropping her off at nine o'clock sharp the following morning.

'I think she doesn't want to give me the satisfaction of a post-wedding lie-in,' he sighed.

I didn't smile, and he mistook this for disapproval.

'Not that I was planning to take advantage of being off parental duties by getting wasted,' he added quickly. 'Nobody really gets drunk at weddings any more at our age, do they? Apart from your ex-boyfriend, of course.'

It took me a moment to figure out who he was talking about.

'I haven't thought about Pete for ages,' I said. 'It's funny how some people can be part of your life for a time and then go and you realize that they never really made much of a difference to you.'

'Maybe sometimes that's what you need. People who are around your life, but not really in it.'

'But people who aren't quite right can be very tiring. Much better to get a cat and settle into blissful spinsterhood.'

Victor looked as if he was about to say something, but changed his mind at the last minute and fell to reading the newspaper he had bought for the journey, which was lying on the table between us.

The view of London suburbs through the train window next to us gave way to green fields. In less than an hour we were in Oxford, and in a cab on our way to Shawcross; and then we were pulling up outside the tiny church, and it was all just as I remembered it.

The church was still obscured by yew trees, and as we

got out of the taxi one of the neighbouring goats came up to the farmyard fence and regarded us assessingly, as if we might be bringing food. The sky overhead was cloudless and everything was still and drowsy in the heat, though lush and green from recent rain.

I went through the gate past the yew trees and was enveloped in silence; I didn't even hear the taxi turn and drive away.

Victor followed me, and we walked past the crumbling gravestones towards the little hidden church, and went in.

It was packed; despite having opted for a weekday wedding, Meg had a full house. The church was filled with hats: red, pink, yellow, blue, wide-brimmed, pillbox, feathered and netted and trimmed with bows; they turned towards us as we entered, like flowers seeking the sun, and then faced the altar once more.

One burgundy fascinator, in a pew towards the back, higher than all the rest, stayed facing in our direction. It was Leila Vetch, my old tutorial partner, and she was smiling and gesturing at us to join her.

We slid into place next to her, and she introduced us to her husband, a small, polite man with round glasses, and their daughter, a sombre child of perhaps eight or nine in a dress that looked as if it might be made of hemp. I smiled and nodded and scanned the congregation to try and work out where Barnaby was sitting.

There was a slight stir, a refocusing of the attention in the church in our direction, and I saw that the vicar was approaching us. He was young but prematurely balding, and had an oddly familiar expression of determined goodness. But of course – this was the Reverend Brian, Meg's little brother, who had ended up with this church in his parish, and had made it available for Meg and Jason's wedding at relatively short notice, having overcome his reservations about them getting married so soon after their temporary separation.

He leaned into our pew and said in a loud whisper, 'Excuse me, are you Victor Rose?'

Victor nodded, and he said, 'We have a problem, and it's just possible that you might be able to help us out, if you are willing.'

Victor held up his ringless hands. 'I don't have a spare, I'm afraid,' he said.

The Rev. Brian didn't smile. 'The difficulty is this. Meg had asked Clarissa to give one of the readings, but she and Michael have been held up, and unfortunately it looks highly likely that they won't be here in time, so she wondered, is it possible that you could step in? She's very keen that it should be one of her old friends from her Oxford days, and she knows you're well used to public speaking, given your theatrical career.'

'I'm not as used to it as you might think, but I'd be very happy to help out. What's the reading?' Victor asked.

The Rev. Brian thrust a piece of paper into his hands, and said, 'Good luck. You're on second,' and hurried off back to the vestry.

Victor scanned the text he'd been given. 'It's short, anyway,' he muttered.

Jason came in, and stood at the altar with his back

to us, the tails of his morning coat trembling slightly. Finally the organist struck up the Wedding March and we all got to our feet. The bride had arrived.

Meg wasn't wearing white – not quite. She was in cream silk, long, elegant, empire-line, and she was carrying roses. Her hair had been put up and decorated with diamanté pins in the shapes of stars and flowers, though their glitter was obscured by her veil. She looked demure and modest and every inch the daughter of one vicar and the sister of another, but all the same, I was pretty sure that there'd be a frilly blue garter tucked away under her sweeping skirts.

She looked to left and right and beamed at all of us. Next to her, her father smiled too. Dressed in an impeccable morning suit, slighter and frailer than I remembered him, he was the picture of paternal pride.

The Rev. Brian cleared his throat and welcomed us all, and the organ launched into the introduction to a hymn:

> Ransomed, healed, restored, forgiven,
> Who like me his praise should sing?

What would Keith have made of it all? I tried to picture him in the little space left next to me in the corner of the pew: dressed, perhaps, like an Edwardian gent, or a middle-aged goth, or the hip cult writer he had once attempted to become, his hair long again, or cropped short the way he had it when he worked at Shawcross Hall. Maybe he would have come with a boyfriend or partner. Surely he would have been more settled in himself than the Keith of twenty years ago, whether he was alone or not.

I remembered Keith the way I'd seen him first, wearing his black leather jacket, standing in the college bar next to Victor. How mixed up it had all been, and intensified by living in such proximity! It was all too easy now to see how Keith might have been attracted to Victor, and fond of me, and ambivalent about us both.

Did Victor have any idea? If he knew, would he feel guilty? I had a very strong feeling that Keith would have preferred me not to tell, and it seemed only fair to respect that. Surely it was the least I could do; a final act of friendship to someone I might have been able to save, and had instead failed, and let go and lost.

The verdict at the inquest into his death had been one of misadventure; he couldn't swim, the river had been particularly high, and he'd had a mixture of alcohol and anti-depressants and marijuana in his system. But I had always – reluctantly – believed that he had intended to die. Not because he had been at his lowest ebb, but because he had begun, that day, to feel better; he had recovered just enough self-will to destroy himself.

Over the years, I'd tried to read up about suicide. I'd studied accounts by people who had survived their attempts to end their own lives, and by others who, like me, had never tried it but had been affected by those who had. I knew that it required both a violent impulse and the opportunity for harm, and that the impulse could draw strength from depression and an overwhelming sense of failure. But most of all, I had always wished that he could have just fought off whatever urge had seized him, and made his way back to safety.

I longed to turn back the clock, to stay with him. I wished that he could have known the exam results he'd never found out, which had, despite all his worries, been perfectly good – as if that might have helped to persuade him that he did not deserve his own condemnation. Yet what had happened to both of us that night was irrevocable, and only I was still here to reflect on it.

That was when I heard him, as subtle and undeniable as a tap on the shoulder, or an echo, or a memory: *I want you to be happy.*

The next minute he was gone, as if he'd been drawn back into the splendid quiet of the yew trees, or faded like the imprint of warm breath on a mirror.

I shifted on my feet. Victor whispered, 'Are you all right?' and I smiled and nodded, but he didn't look convinced.

Meg and Jason's baby began to cry, and was taken out by Minky, the nanny. The service began in earnest, and rolled on, gathering momentum, the familiar refrains and invocations unfolding, the questions, the vows.

I will. I will. What more could anybody offer than that? To face the future with resolve, to chart a course, to make a promise . . . that took courage as well as optimism.

Meg's father made his way to the lectern. His voice trembled a little as he gave his reading:

> 'When I was a child, I spoke like a child, I thought like a child, reasoned like a child; when I became an adult, I put an end to childish things. For now we see in a mirror, dimly; but then we will see face to face.'

Then it was Victor's turn. As he made his way down the aisle, Barnaby, sitting in the pew at the front, turned and caught my eye.

His expression was remote and calculating, as if I was a dog he had placed a bet on, but also, I thought he seemed apprehensive.

I looked away. Victor was at the lectern now, and he smiled down at me so warmly, so privately, that I knew whatever he was about to say was meant for me. And then he cleared his throat and began.

> 'Set me as a seal on your heart,
> A seal on your arm;
> For love is as strong as death,
> Passion fierce as the grave.
> Its flashes are flashes of fire,
> A raging flame.
> Many waters cannot quench love,
> Neither can floods drown it.
> If one offered for love all the wealth of one's
>   house,
> It would be utterly scorned.'

Towards the end of the reading I was aware of a slight movement in the air, even though everyone was still, and listening intently. It wasn't until Victor rejoined me, and the congregation collectively exhaled and permitted itself to fidget and scratch and whisper to its neighbour, that I realized what had caused the sudden draught.

It had been Clarissa and Michael, slipping in as discreetly as a Hollywood star and her son could be expected to manage, and sitting down in the pew at the back.

After the exchange of rings we all filtered out into the greenish shadow of the churchyard. Lined up on either side of the uneven and meandering path that led back to the gate, we waited to disturb the perfect stillness of the air by pelting the newly-weds with pink confetti.

Meg was glowing as if she'd just won a race; Jason looked pale and overwhelmed, as if he'd just witnessed a birth. I just about got the chance to congratulate them before the photographer steered them away.

Victor was talking to Violet Tranter. I couldn't see where Barnaby was. Clarissa and Michael were standing by the wall of the wishing well. She caught sight of me and gave me a little wave, and I headed over to join them.

The dress Clarissa was wearing wasn't overtly sexy, but she still looked mildly provocative, like a 1950s pin-up trying to appear respectable for church back home. Her hair, which had been blonde for the gaudy, was red again, and as vigorously curly as ever, with a neat little hat perched on top of it, in the same summery blue as her dress; her make-up was an artful, perfect mask.

'This is Michael, my son,' Clarissa said, and Michael and I shook hands.

'You have met before, but you wouldn't remember, Michael,' Clarissa said. 'You were in nappies at the time.'

Michael rolled his eyes.

'Why do you have to say stuff like that?' he protested.

'Because it's true,' Clarissa said calmly.

He'd changed since I'd spotted him in the pages of Tippy's magazine, the morning after the hen night dinner. He'd filled out, got the better of his curly hair, and looked as if he'd taken up sport, rowing maybe, and probably sex. It was quite a transformation: from awkward boy to young man.

'You're at St Bart's, aren't you? I hope you've had a good first year,' I said.

'He hasn't done a shred of work,' Clarissa said. 'And it's costing me a fortune.'

The wedding photographer came over to ask Clarissa and Michael to join in some of the group shots; he looked both embarrassed and delighted to have a bona fide celebrity to line up with the others.

I opened my handbag and rummaged for a coin in my purse, then moved so that I was standing at the top of the flight of steps that led down to the wishing well and let the copper fall from my fingers down into the darkness.

Just let me get through this.

'Making a wish?'

I realized I had squeezed my eyes shut; I opened them and saw Victor standing beside me.

'Do you remember when we did this before?' I asked him.

'Of course I do.'

'And did your wish come true?'

'It did. For a while,' he said, and gave me a regretful smile. Then he rummaged in his pocket and sent another coin down to join mine.

'You never know,' he said. 'Maybe it'll be a case of better luck second time round.'

We were summoned to join in a group photograph. I was aware of Barnaby standing on the outside of the group, keeping his distance.

Victor said, 'Are you going to get the minibus to Shawcross Hall?'

'I'm going to walk,' I told him. 'You can join me if you like.'

'It's quite a hike, isn't it? Still, it is a beautiful day . . .'

We headed towards the gate in between the yew trees, emerged from the churchyard, and began to climb towards the house on the hill.

Shawcross Hall's orangery was, as its name suggested, painted orange. It was a long gallery with the artworks Keith had once told tourists about on one side and a sheltered verandah on the other. The miniature citrus trees that the room had been designed to shelter were placed at intervals along the tall French windows, interspersed by white classical busts on fluted columns. It was warm inside and the air was still, even though all the windows were open.

Meg had put me next to Victor, on the same table as

Jenny Holloway, whom she'd studied chemistry with, and Leila, and their families. Barnaby was with Michael and Clarissa and some others I didn't know on the far side of the room.

As the meal got under way I was aware of Barnaby turning towards me from time to time, as if he wanted me to notice him, wanted something from me. Reassurance, perhaps; a social smile that would say: *Don't worry, it was just one of those things, I'm not going to make a scene, I expect I asked for it, one way or another, or you thought I did . . .*

I ignored him. The starter and then the main came and went; I drank and ate a little, but without really tasting anything. Conversation – babies, schools, parents, property prices, glass ceilings – ebbed and flowed.

Jenny Holloway said something that made my ears prick up: 'Barnaby's putting a brave face on it, isn't he?'

'On what?' Victor said. 'He looks pretty much like his usual self to me.'

'You didn't hear? The administrators have been called into his property business. He'd sunk a load of money into commercial lettings, and the whole thing's just gone pop.' Jenny shrugged. 'That's the way it is with speculators, I guess. Easy come, easy go.'

'I imagine he's got plenty to fall back on,' Victor said.

'I don't know. It's a pretty spectacular fail. Losses in the millions, I believe. You gamble big, sometimes you lose big.'

Meg's dad stood to give his speech, and ran haltingly through the usual thanks to relatives who had travelled from far-flung corners of the globe to be there. His voice steadied as he paid tribute to Meg's children: 'It has been no surprise at all to me to see Meg become such a wonderful mother, because her own mother was wonderful too: steadfast, and patient, and infinitely loving.' When he sat down, the audience applause had the special warmth reserved for those who speak with difficulty, and from the heart.

Jason's speech was very short and involved two jokes I didn't get, and then it was Meg's turn. The microphone squeaked and gurgled as she adjusted it, and then she glanced round commandingly and was off.

'As everybody here knows,' she said, 'Jason and I have taken our time getting to the altar. But when the time is right, it's right. Life can seem very slow when your kids get you up in the middle of the night, or you're stuck in the Monday-morning traffic and running late for an important meeting, or you're in the meeting and it's dragging on forever and you're desperate for your lunch. Life can seem slow, but that's deceptive – it's actually very fast, and as I and my family know as well as anyone, there's often no warning when the end's in sight.'

At that point Barnaby walked past, heading towards the washrooms beyond the double doors at the end of the orangery. He didn't look at me, but my throat tightened, and suddenly I wanted nothing more than to get out and breathe fresh air.

Everybody at my table was listening intently to Meg, who was saying, 'If the chance of happiness comes your way, grab it with both hands, and hold on to it for all you're worth . . .' Only Victor noticed as I gathered up my handbag and got to my feet. I fanned my face with my hand to indicate that I was just too hot, and went out through the nearest French window into the still, sunlit quiet.

I went over to lean on the balustrade at the edge of the verandah. The stone was warm to the touch, radiating the long heat of the day. I could hear running water; below me, a flight of steps led down to a lawn with a central fountain.

The green slopes of the Hall's landscaped gardens stretched out to either side, and the sky overhead was flawlessly blue. Close to the horizon, on the far side of the valley, I could just make out the tips of the white towers and spires of Oxford, gleaming in the early evening sun like the dream of a city, or its ghost. Somewhere beyond that, out of sight, was the distant outline of the ancient chalk horse, galloping throughout history, etched into the swell of the land.

I went down to the lawn and settled on the lowest step. The meal would be over any minute, and everybody would start milling around, and my absence would be less conspicuous. By and by I'd be able to nip back into the house and make my excuses to Victor, who would probably want to stay a bit longer, and say my goodbyes to Jason and Clarissa and Meg.

And if Barnaby was lurking, so what? What could he do to me now? I was very much awake, and I was not alone. He could say something, but if I kept my distance he wouldn't even be able to do that. So, let him lurk . . .

And yet I didn't move. My heartbeat began to slow, my breathing eased until I was no longer aware of it. A fat bumblebee buzzed past me and settled on a dandelion that had rooted itself in the verandah wall. Back in the orangery, a string quartet started to play. Mozart: transition music. Soon there would be an influx of fresh guests, the ones who had been invited to the evening do but not the ceremony itself or the sit-down meal, and the disco would begin.

The music stopped, and after a while Frank Sinatra started singing 'I've Got You Under My Skin'. That must be the song Meg had chosen for her first dance with Jason. Then it was time for Abba. I imagined Jason retreating to the bar, and Meg being joined on the dance floor by her older daughters, and probably Clarissa too.

I was so lulled by the sun and the champagne and the scent of grass and lavender and roses, and the gentle thud of elderly pop hits issuing from the grand house behind me, that I didn't even jump when I heard footsteps and realized that someone was about to find me.

It was Victor.

He said, 'Mind if I join you?'

'Be my guest,' I said, shuffling along, and he settled on the step next to me.

We sat in a companionable silence and gazed at the view.

I said, 'Oxford looks like something out of a fairy-tale.'

'From a distance, it always does,' he said. 'Anna . . . I've been thinking about saying this for a while, and I haven't really known how to put it. I owe you an apology. For not trying harder to stay in touch. After everything that happened with Keith. And as for me and Clarissa . . . well, I think it's fairly obvious from this perspective that that was a mistake.'

Somewhere in the distance a dog barked. A breeze stirred the grass. I felt myself coming into focus, like a long-neglected piece of evidence that is suddenly identified as a clue.

'I suppose you could have persisted,' I said, 'but I don't think you would have got anywhere. I was pretty adamant about being left alone.'

'That was what Meg said. And then I was back in California anyway, and I thought it was all over between us and that was an end of it. But it wasn't.' He drew a deep breath. 'I know I had no right to mind about you getting together with Barnaby at the ball,' he went on. 'I know it didn't even come to anything, in the end. But I have to admit, it did hurt a little bit.'

'You were already seeing Clarissa,' I said. 'So that was rather hypocritical of you, don't you think?'

'It was. I knew that even at the time. It just seemed so final. You know: as if we'd both moved on.'

'I did go off with Barnaby, but not in the way you think,' I said. 'I went back to his room because I felt sick and he said I could lie down. That sounds stupid to me now. It was stupid. I crashed out and I came to the next morning with him inside me.'

I was already pulling away; every muscle in my body had tensed in readiness to get up and go. Victor reached out and put a hand on my knee and said, 'Wait. I want to understand. But I'm not sure if you mean what I think you mean.'

'I'm telling you that what happened between me and

him happened because I was passed out drunk, and should never have happened at all,' I said. 'You might say that I brought it on myself, or that I asked for it. You could say I was giving off mixed messages, or that I didn't fight him off hard enough, or that I should have gone straight to the police. But you can't say that I was conscious when it started, and you can't say that I didn't try to tell him to stop.'

'What happened afterwards?'

'I left. I went back to Gladstone Road. Then a police officer turned up. She was with Dr Kaspar. She told me about Keith and asked some questions, and they both left. Then Gareth came and picked me up and drove me back to Deddenham. The next day I went to our family GP and said I needed the morning-after pill, and he asked me if I'd forgotten to take the condom out of the packet.'

'Did you talk to anybody about it?'

'No. What proof did I have? It would have been my word against his. Plenty of people had seen us together that evening.'

He was looking at me intently; I turned and met his eyes, and that was when I knew for sure that he believed me.

He said, 'What you just described is a rape.'

'Can you call it that without a conviction?' I said. 'Because there wouldn't have been one.'

'It's not too late, you know. You could still do something about it. If you wanted to.'

'It is too late, Victor, and you know it.'

'What if he's done the same thing to someone else?'

'I know,' I said. 'That troubles me, too. I just try not to think about it.'

'Well, it makes sense,' he said. 'I wish it didn't. But it does. Of how wary you are. Watchful. As if you're waiting for the worst.'

'I don't want you to think of this every time you think of me,' I said. 'It's something that was done to me. One thing. It's not who I am.'

'I know,' he said.

We sat there together for a moment longer. I shivered and said, 'I think I'm ready to go home.'

'I'll come with you,' he said.

'There's no need, really there isn't. I can get myself back. I'll be fine.'

'I have Beatrice being dropped off on my doorstep at nine o'clock tomorrow morning, remember.'

'Well. All right then. So long as I'm not dragging you away.'

'You're not.'

He stood and offered me his hand; I took it and he pulled me up. We went up the steps to the verandah, and there was Meg, sitting on a bench next to Jason, who was smoking a cigar.

Jason looked slightly chastised, as if Meg had just been scolding him, but also gave off the profound relief of the husband who has overcome long-established stage fright to get through the public performance of the marriage rites, and who is now looking forward very much to catching a plane somewhere else for the honeymoon.

'Where did you two disappear to?' Meg said. 'We've

decided to have a breather. Or rather Jason's decided to indulge himself, as you can see, and I'm having a little time out. My feet are killing me.'

'We wanted to congratulate you on a wonderful day, and wish you well for the rest of it,' Victor said. 'We're going to head back to London now.'

'Oh no, you can't do that,' Meg said. 'The night is still young. Jason and I are child-free – the nanny's going to sort out the girls. I say, bring it on! Let's make the most of it. Party like the old days.'

She looked from me to Victor and back to me again, and then a theory presented itself to her and she nodded in slow recognition.

'A-ha, I see what's going on here,' she said. 'I know what you two are sneaking off so early for.'

'Which is what?' Clarissa said, stepping out from the orangery. She looked as if she'd been dancing; her hair had gone a little wild and her face was flushed.

She was followed by Barnaby, who was scarlet and perspiring. Clarissa approached us, and he came to a halt a few paces behind her.

'Not you two as well,' Meg said, looking Clarissa and Barnaby up and down.

'We've been dancing like mad things,' Clarissa said. 'That's what you're meant to do at a wedding, isn't it?'

'Victor and Anna are leaving,' Meg said to Clarissa. 'Together.'

Clarissa was just reaching into her handbag for her cigarettes. She stopped and collected herself before turning to smile at me. I could see that it was costing her an effort to be so pleased.

'I'm glad that you and Victor have finally made up,' she said, and stepped forward to embrace me.

'Thank you,' I told her as we released each other. 'It was a pleasure to meet Michael.'

She rolled her eyes. 'Oh, he's back in the thick of it, flirting like mad. And he has a girlfriend. But that's eighteen-year-olds for you.'

I was just about to say goodbye to Meg when Barnaby descended on me.

Too late, I realized that he was aiming to kiss me on the cheek – of course, he wanted everything to appear normal, no bad blood – but I had already instinctively veered away from him. He froze; I looked at him aghast.

'Shall we try that again?' he said, and stepped forward and put his hand on my waist.

'Don't touch her, you fucking creep,' Victor said, and the next thing I knew Barnaby was staggering backwards clutching his nose and leaking blood, and Victor was moving in to thump him again, and then the two of them were rolling around on the verandah, with Barnaby thrashing around and Victor laying into him with a viciousness that I would never have thought him capable of. For a moment I thought Victor really was going to kill him. And then I screamed at him and managed to get hold of him and he let Barnaby go and stepped back.

Barnaby got to his feet. His face was streaked with red, his shirtfront was stained, and his suit was torn and dirty.

'You'd better stay away from me,' Victor told him. 'Because if I ever see you again, you're dead.'

'I don't know what she's told you,' Barnaby said, 'but I very much doubt it's the truth. She's just trying to manipulate you.'

'You're a liar,' I told him.

Clarissa had gone over to stand by Barnaby. She rested her hand on his sleeve and said, 'What are you talking about?'

In the hush that followed I realized they were all waiting for me to answer. Barnaby with his bloody face; Victor still looking a little wild; Meg, the bride, pale with shock but not far from anger, on her feet now but keeping her distance; Jason, lurking behind her, still clutching his cigar; Clarissa, poised and icy, wanting the truth.

I opened my mouth to speak, but Barnaby cut across me.

'If this is all about our little indiscretion on the night of the St Bart's Ball – that ancient history – then I have to say I think your memory may be playing tricks on you. If, that is, you can remember it at all,' he said. He gestured towards Meg. 'You were there. You know the state Anna was in. She was so drunk by the end she could barely speak.'

'I remember waking up,' I said. 'You and I both know what you did.'

There was another silence. Then Meg said, 'I don't want to know, and I think now is neither the time or the place.'

But Clarissa lifted her hand from Barnaby's arm and held it up to indicate that Meg should be quiet.

She said, 'Barnaby, what did you do?'

'It's called human nature,' Barnaby said. 'You cannot expect to rewrite the rules of engagement that have applied for millennia.'

Clarissa turned on him. 'You really are disgusting, aren't you?' she said. 'You thought you'd got away with it.'

Barnaby stared at her. His mouth dropped open, but nothing came out.

I saw he wanted to protest; he wanted to convince her that he was charming, reasonable, hard done by. But he had no idea how to do it. He didn't know how to win; and if he couldn't win, he couldn't be anything at all.

It was as if he was dwindling in front of my eyes, becoming someone who was no longer Barnaby Stour – the player, the privileged, knowledgeable, successful eccentric who'd never had much time for self-doubt – but was, instead, a deluded has-been, someone who, in his more lucid moments, was bitterly ashamed.

He said, 'I never expected to meet with this kind of treatment here.' Then he turned on his heel and walked quickly away.

Clarissa said, 'Good riddance,' and got her cigarettes out and lit up.

Meg settled back on to the bench with a rustling of creamy silk and surveyed her dress as if checking for signs of damage. Jason sat down next to her and started twisting his gold wedding ring round on his finger. I imagined he was doing his best to think of other, more manageable things – the next strategic plan for his website, perhaps – and waiting for Meg to get up and go inside so he could follow her.

Meg looked at me and shook her head. 'Why didn't you say anything before? What chance is there of any of this being resolved now?'

'I'm sorry that this had to happen here,' I told her. 'I only have good wishes for you and Jason, and if this messes things up between us I will be sad, but I can't undo any of it. Victor, I think it's time for us to go.'

'Do you want a lift to the station? My driver's parked up round the front,' Clarissa said. 'He could get you there in no time.'

Victor and I exchanged glances and agreed, and said our final goodbyes to Meg and Jason. We left them sitting there on the bench in the fading light of early evening, Meg looking both aggrieved and bewildered, and Jason keeping his counsel.

We followed the path that led around the side of the Hall to the gravelled area at the front. There was no sign of Barnaby. I wondered how far he had got, whether we would pass him as he stumbled towards the village, and what was on his mind. Fury, probably, and a sense of being hard done by. Would it have made any difference – would I feel any differently – if he had expressed regret? But he hadn't. He had chosen to maintain that he had been entitled to act as he had, that it had been a lapse, perhaps, but nothing worse than that.

And yet part of him must know that he had done something wrong, and surely that unacknowledged guilt would eat away at him down the years, turning him into the small and shabby shadow of himself he had seemed to me to be when he was standing there on the verandah, confronted with the truth.

Clarissa's driver was asleep in the front seat, his newspaper folded next to him. Clarissa knocked on the window and he came to and she told him where to take us. We climbed into the back and Victor put his arm around me, and the car turned and moved smoothly away.

My last glimpse of Shawcross Hall was of Clarissa in her cornflower-blue dress, turning and walking back towards the main entrance through the gloom.

The next morning I awoke in a large, white, unfamiliar bed, and the empty space next to me was still warm.

On the bedside table next to me there was a cup of coffee, and that was warm, too. And next to it was a note in Victor's handwriting: *You might want to get dressed before you come down.*

Next to the cup was an old-fashioned round metal alarm clock. I recognized that clock. He'd had it for years.

A quarter past nine.

I got out of bed and put the dress I'd worn to the wedding back on: white and printed with splashy poppies. It was very quiet: no traffic, no noise from outside, just the soft sound of fine summer rain, and the faint chuntering of a radio somewhere downstairs.

The coffee was good. I pulled the curtains and found myself looking down on to treetops. So Victor's house was next to a patch of woodland. It was a grey, still morning, with only a little breeze stirring the wet leaves.

I made my way downstairs and into the kitchen.

Beatrice was sitting at the table, and Victor was standing at the stove, frying eggs and bacon. He turned and smiled and said, 'Good morning. Did you sleep well?'

'Very well,' I said, and sat down next to Beatrice.

'Then you're lucky,' Beatrice said. 'I was kept up all night by the new baby. It was screaming all the time.'

'Ah,' I said. 'Well, they do that. But they grow out of it eventually.'

Victor turned the gas off and put the food on to plates and brought it to the table.

'It seems you've learned some new skills down the years,' I told him. Suddenly I was ravenous – how come I hadn't realized that until breakfast was right in front of me?

He grinned, and said, 'Please, tuck in. Be my guest.'

'Daddy can only do brunch, you know,' Beatrice commented, squirting a neat pool of ketchup on to her plate.

'That's all right. Brunch strikes me as a very good place to start,' I said, and began to eat.

THE END

Read an extract from Alison Mercer's sharp, amusing and brilliantly observed novel,

Stop The Clock

Three friends, beginning the risky business of being grown-up.

Lucy knows exactly what she wants: her marriage to be a success, her children to be perfect, and to be the ultimate home-maker. Tina knows what she wants too: her journalism career to take off and to see her name as a byline in a national newspaper . . . and the illicit affair she's started leaves her free enough to follow her dreams. Natalie just wants to be happy – happy with the boyfriend she's dated since college, happy with the job she's drifted into, happy with a life she *thinks* is enough – but is it really?

Ten years later, all three women have the lives they *thought* they wanted. But somehow, reality isn't quite as neat and clean-cut as their dreams . . .

Prologue

New Year's Eve, 1999

The closer they came to the house, the harder it was to see the way ahead. It was past midnight, and the lane was unlit, and was also obscured by ghostly drifts of fog that clung to the branches of the trees to either side and hung in heavy swirls in front of them. Lucy was beginning to wonder if they'd somehow missed the entrance when Adam said, 'Hang on, isn't that it?' and hit the brakes.

They came to a rest just beyond a pair of big wrought-iron gates. It was just possible to make out the copper-plate lettering on the sign mounted on the wall by the gatepost: *The Old Schoolhouse*.

'Yup, that's it,' Lucy said.

Beyond the gates was a stretch of lawn and a big red-brick, three-storey Victorian Gothic building, complete with parapets, a round tower, an array of steeply pitched roofs and mullioned windows, all of which were dark.

'I thought they were going to wait up,' Adam said.

'I can't see Tina's car,' Lucy said. 'And why would they have locked the gates?'

She rummaged in her handbag – God, there was so much kiddie crud in there! – and fished out her mobile.

'Damn! No signal. Back of bloody beyond. What are we going to do now?'

Adam hit the horn. Lucy nearly jumped out of her skin.

'What are you doing? You'll wake the baby!'

She swung round to check, but Lottie was thankfully still sound asleep.

'Sorry, shouldn't have snapped,' she said. 'I just don't get it. Tina knows we're coming – I even rang her before we left. What if they've had an accident or something? Oh God, they could be lying in a ditch somewhere . . .'

'I bet you anything you like they're down the pub,' Adam said, 'and there's a lock-in and they're in there gossiping and they've lost track of time.'

Lucy thought it over.

'So what do we do?'

'We wait,' Adam said.

In the Black Swan, Tina had told Natalie everything – well, almost everything, and Natalie was doing her very best not to pester for the one crucial detail that Tina had withheld.

Natalie was drunk, and, in spite of her best efforts to take Tina's news in her stride, more than a little shocked. Tina, who was driving, was stone-cold sober, which was a measure of how badly she'd needed to confide in someone; she'd spilt the beans pretty much as soon as they were settled in a snug corner, before she'd finished her first roll-up.

Now Natalie's glass was empty, the bar was finally shut, and the other patrons were heading off, letting in cold blasts of wintry air as they slipped out through the side door.

'I'm not sure it would be a good idea to tell Lucy about this, you know,' Tina said.

'Why not?'

'I think she might disapprove.'

Natalie opened her mouth to disagree, but then realized that Tina was probably right.

'And she wouldn't mince her words,' Tina went on. 'No, I think we should keep this just between you and me.'

'If that's what you want,' Natalie said.

'We should go,' Tina said. 'They'll be here soon.'

As Tina drove them away from the village down the winding lane Natalie reflected that maybe it was a blessing in disguise that her boyfriend was in Singapore, working on a potentially career-making case for his law firm, and would not be joining them to see in the new millennium.

If Natalie's Richard had been there, Tina wouldn't have said anything, Natalie was sure of that – and she was equally sure that Tina had *needed* to come out with it, and felt better for getting it off her chest.

And thank goodness Tina's other friends had different parties to go to, or had bailed out at the last minute. She and Tina would never have had such a heart-to-heart if Tina had been playing hostess to a full house.

How amazing to be bold and reckless and foolhardy enough to lay claim to what you wanted, as Tina had, even if it was so obviously doomed to lead to heartache and a dead end! How good it must have felt for Tina to tell someone the truth, if not quite the whole truth – and how shocked Tina would have been if Natalie had trumped her revelation with one of her own!

But Natalie had kept her own counsel, and probably always would, because what was there to say? Doubts and dreams were not enough to make a secret, and if she didn't act on them, there was nothing for her to tell.

They turned a bend, and there was Adam and Lucy's sensible family estate car, parked and waiting for them outside the gates of Tina's parents' holiday home.

Tina pulled up behind it, and for a moment they both stared at the BABY ON BOARD sticker displayed on the rear windscreen. Then Tina exhaled, slumped forward and pressed her forehead against the steering wheel.

'Oh crap, crap, crap!' she moaned. 'How could they have got here so quickly? Adam must have broken the speed limit most of the way – and he's got a baby in the back!'

She hurried over to apologize. Natalie knew she ought to follow, but as she reached for the door handle she found herself lingering and watching Tina.

Somehow Tina always had the right clothes for any situation. In the city she wore suits and heels and looked groomed, or went out at night in little shiny dresses that got her past the velvet ropes and into wherever she wanted to go; in the country she appeared in old jeans and a padded jacket and was equally in her element.

Tina was stooping to talk to Lucy through the car window, and her long blond hair had swung forward so that Natalie couldn't make out her expression. Then she straightened up, and Natalie saw that she looked as self-possessed as ever.

How did Tina do it?

Natalie knew she'd never be capable of the sort of adventure Tina had told her about in the pub. She wouldn't be able to handle it. She'd feel much too guilty, and she wouldn't be able to hide it.

Once she was outside, the cold air was instantly sobering.

The next day was New Year's Eve. Lucy had forgiven them for not being there when she arrived, and the slight awkwardness of the previous night was forgotten. Tina had always found that staying at the Old Schoolhouse had a pacifying effect; she'd always got on much better with her parents there, on holiday in Cornwall, than back home in London.

At one time, the Old Schoolhouse had accommodated twenty daughters of the Cornish gentry, who learned needlework and a little Latin under the guidance of a maiden great-aunt of Tina's father's. The furnishings and decor were still simple to the point of austerity, and it wasn't exactly homely, but it didn't seem institutional either. It felt sequestered and accepting, as if it was far enough removed from society to take on whatever those passing through chose to bring to it. At a time when she was both excited and unnerved by what she'd just got herself into, it was exactly what she needed.

Tina had invited Natalie and Lucy to stay once before, at the end of their postgraduate year in Cardiff. The three of them had gone on to live in London together and start their first jobs in journalism. But then Lucy had moved out to set up home with Adam, and speed through to marriage and motherhood by the age of twenty-five.

Barmy, Tina thought – not to say anything against Adam, who was obviously gorgeous and the perfect gentleman and made Lucy blissfully happy, but what was the rush? Inevitably she and Natalie had seen less of Lucy since Lottie was born. This little trip was a chance to catch up – though, as she had said to Natalie, Tina had decided that it wouldn't do to tell Lucy absolutely everything.

Luckily Adam seemed to be willing to do his bit with Lottie, who was rising two now, and struck Tina as being jolly hard work. They went to the Black Swan for lunch, and Adam entertained Lottie while the three women got on to cosy do-you-remembers about their journalism course, and the party house they had shared afterwards.

It was inevitable that, having revisited the past, they would start to talk about where their lives were heading.

Tina started telling them how she'd been so nervous on her first day in her new job that she'd spilt her boss's coffee in his lap. Then she realized Natalie wasn't listening, and was looking at Lottie with a sort of muted, hungry longing.

Oh no! Natalie was *broody*. How was that possible?

It was bad enough that Lucy had jumped the gun and reproduced already, but why would Natalie want to join in with the nappies and dummies and vomit and poo and endless crying, and getting fat and not being free? Given the choice between a baby and her brand-new secret, Tina knew what she'd go for, no contest.

Natalie inclined her head towards Lottie and said into a sudden silence, 'So how do I get Richard to give me one of those?'

Lucy and Adam exchanged glances.

'Don't ask me. I think Lucy employed witchcraft,' Adam said. Lucy elbowed him in the ribs.

He gave her a sleepy, disarming smile, and then turned to Natalie and said, 'If it's what you want, I'm sure he'll come round.'

'What I want is what you and Lucy have,' Natalie said. 'I want to marry Richard and have his babies. But he doesn't even seem that sure about the idea of us getting a place together.'

'Getting married and having children isn't everything, you know!' Tina said. 'What about your job?'

Natalie shrugged. 'I'm kind of bored of it.'

'Then get a new one,' Tina said. 'Get back on track. You used to want to do news stories with a social conscience. What about that?'

'Just not sure I want it enough to put the work in,' Natalie said.

'You can't give up so easily, not after we've come so far,' Tina said.

'You should do whatever makes you happy,' Lucy said.

'OK, well, here's what's going to make *me* happy,' Tina told them. 'I've got a foot in the door at the *Post*, and I'm going to make the most of it. This time ten years from now I want to have my own newspaper column, with a nice big picture byline.'

'A job can't love you back,' Lucy said.

'Maybe not, but you can love your job, and that's worth something,' Tina said, feeling impelled to defend, not just her ambition, but the other, secret choice she had made. 'Marriage and babies isn't the only thing worth having. It can't be. It's not the only kind of love. And anyway, you can't seriously tell me you don't ever miss *Beautiful Interiors*. You used to be so into that magazine!'

Lucy reached across to take Adam's hand.

'I'd much rather make a beautiful home of my own than tell other people what to put in theirs,' she said. 'That's my ten-year plan. I honestly can't think of any better way to spend the next decade. If we can get this house we've found, I'll have everything I've ever wanted.'

'Yeah, but you are going to go back to work eventually, aren't you?' Adam said. 'To help with the mortgage.'

'Of course, darling.'

And then Lucy started telling them all about the house she and Adam were trying to buy.

'We call it the Forever House, because that's what you call the place you want to live in for the rest of your lives.'

'It sounds like something out of a fairy-tale,' Natalie said.

'For ever is a long time,' Tina said. 'If you ask me, ten years seems quite far enough to look ahead.'

After lunch they went for a stroll on the beach, and Adam got the three women to line up for a photo.

'Just for the record,' he said as he looked through the viewfinder and fiddled with the focus. 'Tina, Natalie and Lucy, on the cusp of the new millennium.'

After a while Lottie fell over and refused to toddle any further, and Adam hoisted her on to his shoulders and volunteered to take her back to the house.

'Let's all go,' Tina said. 'We should stick together. Anyway, it's starting to get dark.'

The light was beginning to fade. The horizon was a deep band of shadow rather than a fine line between the ocean and the clouds, and as they made their way across the sand a chill breeze blew in from the waves. The final night of a thousand years was already rolling in, and the dark, pressing sky, grey sea and icy breeze seemed to harbour the power of transformation, and to be reminding them that change was imminent, inevitable – and already upon them.

Connect with Alison via her blog at
www.alisonmercer.wordpress.com or on Facebook
at www.facebook.com/AlisonMercerwriter